Books By Eve Marx

101 Things You Didn't Know About Sex

Flirtspeak: The Sexy Language of Flirtation

Read My Hips: The Sexy Language of Flirting

The Goddess Orgasm

What's Your Sexual IQ?

Passion

10 Nights of Passion

View From The Porch: Tales of the Anti-Hamptons

Beddington Place

Watch Your Back, Cover Your Tracks

A Novel by Eve Marx

Cover to Cover Publishing
PO Box 128
Katonah, NY 10536
ISBN-13: 978-0-9711626-2-4
Copyright © 2012

"We are all travelers in the wilderness of this world, and the best we can find in our travels is an honest friend."

— *Robert Louis Stevenson*

Cast of Characters

Principals

Paige Turner — celebrity blogger; gossip columnist
Tamsin Delacorte — former pageant queen; Beddington Place real estate agent
Diandra Fox — beautiful and brilliant British-born Beddington Place horse trainer
Janey Epstein — a Beddington horsewife and friend to Diandra;
married to Billy, a Forbes-ranked gazillionaire
Chessie Jones — another friend of Diandra's; married to Phil,
who's "just a landscaper"
Alex Manos — brutish, bedazzling Beddington horse trainer

Supporting Players

Michael Swett — roué, playboy, entertainment director
Sal — Tamsin's shifty step-brother
Ric Martin — Paige's L.A. boyfriend; jazz musician, screenwriter
Pat Floss — Paige's editor and boss
Roy Ralsten — a local artist
Doug — Paige's new pal from Teddy's Lounge

The Celebs

Princess TaTas — a rising pop star
Marla Tudor — Beddington Place's numero uno celebrity
Martin Romanoff — celebrity guru; married to the actress Michelle Morreau
Rafe Laurence, Choo-Choo Palmetto, Chester Chasen, George Further, Stanley
Pucci, Jacques Ellen-Stern, and his wife Mariella —
some of Beddington Place's most revered and gossiped about glitterati
Tickled Pink — an X-rated sensation
Kai Mason — vampire film ingenue

Bit Players

Estrella — Tamsin's maid

Leeza Luciano — ex-con, poet preacher

Lucas Babcock & Penny Lane — engaged couple, friends of Alex's

Darby – ethereal waif and Breatharian; obsessed with Alex Manos

Peg and Herbert Dickler — friends of the Old Homestead

Lurch & Rollo — gatekeepers at Shangri La

Miranda Van Oonk — countess and equestrian trainer

The Real Housewives of Toronto: Toby Fish, Lucky Lagerfeld and Greer Horagin

Biddy Maxwell — a grand old Beddington Place matron

Suzette – Beddington Place domme and role play therapist

Monty McCallum & Edmund Darrow — retired fox hunters

Gary Goldfinger — Master of the Hunt

Silver Surfer & Pudding — Beddington Place realtors

Locket – Bengali film star and client of Alex's

George – Michael Swett's driver

Orestes Milikides — Swett's money man

Esteban — Diandra's mucker

Sally, Gwen, Licia and Kimberley — Diandra's riding clients

Tom & Gaye — Diandra's neighbors

Stuart — coffee bar bum

Ralph — a rolfer

Ben & Brad — Tamsin's video team

Alice — Tamsin's mother; recently released from prison

Nalda & Alvaro — employees of Chessie

The Animals

Galahad, Lord Kensington, Butterscotch, Marcus Aurellius and Vladimir —
horses in the care of Alex Manos

Cassius — Michael Swett's valuable hunter jumper

Twinkie, Ollie & Hush — Tamsin's dogs

Lupa — Alex's wolfhound mix

Space Cadet, Rascal, Roman, Rolex, Blackstone & Frisco —
horses in Diandra's care

Cuddle — Chessie and Phil's pet pig

Congo — Paige's loaner ride for the pace

'I Will Not Wear A Helmet, I Will Not'

"*I* will not wear a helmet, I will not," Princess TaTas said, all up in arms. "The paparazzi would have a field day. I don't think so. Forget that."

"Honey, there are no paparazzi here," the Realtor soothed, her sweet Alabama accent dripping honey. "I promise no one's lurking in the bushes to jump out. This is Beddington. We don't have paparazzi. We've got coyotes and deer and Lyme ticks up the wazoo, but in those tall boots, I got you covered. So what d'ya say? To get the full effect of this spectacular property, you must see it on horseback. But you gotta wear a helmet. It's the law," Tamsin lied.

The Princess pouted. She rolled her large, limpid brown eyes. Reluctantly she accepted the helmet from her assistant's hands and clamped it on her head. Striding over to the mounting block, she tapped her foot impatiently, waiting for her horse to be brought up, a handsome dapple grey. The Hispanic groom boosted her shapely ass into the saddle, and TaTa took up the reins. "Don't worry, I know what I'm doing," she said. "When the Prince and me got hitched, he insisted I have equestrian training.""That's wonderful," Tamsin said. "But nevertheless, I still insist you wear that helmet. Horses are unpredictable creatures and you're too valuable a commodity to let anything ugly happen. Besides, you're so pretty; you don't want a big ole bump on your head at the Pink Pop Festival, do you? I heard you were headlining. What an honor. You must be so thrilled."

I admired Tamsin's smooth handling of Princess TaTas, a rising if not terribly talented pop star. Working with celebrities and their outsize egos is never easy, and to top it off, this one was a bonafide princess, even if she was a high school drop out. A former teen scream queen with a few tiny roles under her belt, she'd met her prince in a Las Vegas casino; he was royalty from Dubai. After the nuptials, performed in record time, the prince immediately purchased for his bride a new pair of boobs (hence her new name "TaTas") and bankrolled a career for her that gained him celebrity, too. Today I was on assignment for Hello! magazine, to cover the royal couple's purported move to Beddington Place, home to WASPy old money and hedge funders and what was becoming a steady stream of boldfaced celebrities.

Tamsin Delacorte was the lucky realtor to draw the job of squiring TaTas around. Tall, slender, attractive, and bosomy herself, while not exactly model material, Tamsin worked her natural assets and made good use of her exceptionally mobile mouth. She wore her honey blond streaked hair pulled back in a neat, Republican chignon. Stacks of diamond rings and bracelets adorned her hands and arms. A former pageant queen, she'd mastered the art of being both professional and perky. She wasted no time letting me know she'd been in touch with my editor and agent, and TaTas' publicist, and that she knew the drill; she was experienced working with celebrities and adhering to the magazine's and the celebrity's exhaustive list of rules.

She was right on time fetching me at the train station in Beddington Hills, tooting on the horn of her silver Range Rover. How long did I plan to be with the Princess, she asked (my idea was one jam- packed day), while at the same time bringing me up to speed on her own agenda. Her plan was to show TaTas four properties, followed by lunch at the country restaurant owned by reality star turned Buddhist guru, Martin Rogonoff. An avid equestrian herself, Tamsin had conceived and arranged for this guided mounted tour of the regal grounds once belonging to Margarthe Mangelsdorf, famed breeder of Hanoverians, and a documented member of Eulenspiegel Society, the New York branch. The old lady's storied estate, Schloss Monbijou, had recently come on the market; while not exactly in shambles, after nearly a decade of neglect, the old house was a wreck. Nothing in the way of plumbing or wiring had been updated in decades, and the mansion had seriously deteriorated after its mistress had taken to her bed. It was widely rumored through some leak among her staff that the old lady had lain in a semi-comatose state for months, her arthritic old hands clutching a riding crop. The grounds, while overgrown, remained magnificent. In addition to the crumbling house and a half dozen outbuildings and barns, the property included 60 acres of fenced paddocks and rolling fields, replete with stone walls, and an orchard. So far no buyer had taken a serious interest, largely due to the roar of the interstate highway that ran right through it and which could be heard everywhere. Right now Tamsin was working hard selling TaTas on the notion that this was the place to create a world class breeding and show jumping facility. Why the horse fever, Hello! readers would want to know? Because Madonna had competed in the Hampton's Classic, and now TaTas' prince had set his cap for her to do so as well.

Tamsin tucked her bun up under her helmet and readied to mount. "Are you sure you won't join us?" she said. "I know the magazine didn't approve this part for insurance purposes, but you did say you ride. And it's such a stunning property. It would be a pity to miss it."

I hesitated. After all, I was wearing boots and jeans. It only took about 30 seconds for me to consider. "Okay," I said. "Tell them to bring me a horse."

Moments later we were riding through a lushly overgrown meadow while Tamsin ran her spiel. She was in the middle of pointing out the property's most salient details; the rolling acreage, the privacy, proximity to airports, when TaTas let out a yell.

"Omigod, what is that?" she screeched. Spooked, her horse began behaving like an idiot, spinning and whirling. I spun my own head around to see what had freaked it out just in time to see a magnificent stag with a rack of antlers, bounding through the woods. It was riveting to see the animal's lean, muscular body nimbly leaping through bosky brush. It was a large, handsome young buck, a magnificent creature. It was amazing to see it so close up.

"Wow," I breathed, mesmerized by the sheer beauty of the beast. "That was awesome."

Meanwhile TaTas' horse was still doing airs above the ground.

"Jose, help her, help her," Tamsin briskly ordered the groom, who was trotting on foot alongside us. TaTas continued shrieking, which only further upset the animal. Jose lunged at the animal to grab its bridle, but it skittishly shied away. Thinking fast, I brought my horse up next to it and bravely seized its reins.

"Shhhhhhhhhhhh," I breathed to the horse, whose eyes were white and rolling. "Focus," I told it, stroking its sweaty neck. Telegraphing peace and calm to the animal, I willed it to calm down.

"Omigod, thank you so much," Tamsin gushed when the emergency was over and TaTas was merely gasping in shocked relief. "I so appreciate what you did." Tamsin's own breath was running a little ragged and who could blame her? No good ever came from concussing a celebrity.

"Let's call an end to our ride and head back to the house," she suggested in a "slop sugar on it" voice. "I really want you to see the lower level, TaTas. I know that as soon as you see it, you'll agree it's the perfect recording studio, and right in your own home."

"I've got plenty of places to record my work," the Princess said, sullenly. While I kept a fast hold on her reins, she niftily dismounted. "I think I'd prefer to walk, if you don't mind," she sniffed. "And forget about this house."

We all dismounted. Tamsin hauled out her iPhone and a squadron of grooms appeared. They whisked away the horses and moments later we were climbing into Tamsin's Range Rover, off to the next listing. But before she could even pull into the driveway, the Princess nixed it; plans for house showing derailed, a few minutes later we were being shown to our table at Romanoff's. Tamsin, aware of her client's schedule, had pre-ordered our food. Naturally as soon as I parked my ass in a chair, my phone started ringing.

"Hello," I said to my caller, signaling the waiter it was okay to put down the plate. He held up the pepper grinder. "Yes, I'm here with Princess TaTas right now," I said to Pat, my editor/agent. "We're just sitting down to lunch. Of course I'll be sure to namedrop the restaurant. Yes, it's beautiful. No, I'm not having wine. You know I don't drink on the job! Of course I'll ask for an expense receipt. Oh, you know what? This nice real estate agent is signaling me lunch is on her. No worries. I'll have the story to you this afternoon."

No sooner did I end the call than my cell rang again. This time it was the photo editor.

Meanwhile, at the sight of Princess TaTas, the lunch crowd was all a-buzz.

"God, you'd think they'd never seen a celebrity," TaTas said snarkily, grinning from ear to ear. Off the horse and surrounded by potential fans, her mood improved considerably. I didn't think the house hunting was much of a success. She'd made it clear she didn't care for any of the stellar homes Tamsin had shown. She was unimpressed with the 12,000-square-foot stone mansion and matching stables set on nine pristinely groomed Guardian Hill acres replete with tennis court, pool house, a yoga studio and six bedrooms. She'd turned up her nose at the 1870 antique horse farm in Salem with hand-hewn beams and period millwork. The center hall colonial in nearby Catoonah on 11 acres bored her. The only thing that seemed to excite her interest was the famed homemaking and decorating doyenne Marla Tudor's place on Oak Road which Tamsin pointed out as we drove down the wooded boulevard. "Now that's a property," TaTas said, drooling, as I eyeballed a lone female rider trotting her horse up the bucolic dirt road. The two of them looked so relaxed and bonded; they were a lovely pair. "So tell me, is Marla selling? Make an offer. That house I can't resist."

"I don't believe Marla's place is for sale," Tamsin said diplomatically. "Although everyone has their price."

"Princess? Princess TaTas? Could I trouble you for your autograph?" said the most beautiful young person I'd ever seen. The face and the physique were arresting, but I was confused. Was it a he or a she?

"Of course," TaTas said, playfully batting her Shu Uemura lashes. The kid preened and tossed its head.

"Why thank you," the teen simpered, thrusting a slim, leather bound book towards TaTas' hand. The voice itself was a sweet soprano; the accent posh British. "This is my autograph book. I collect autographs," the teen said, producing a Meisterstuck Montblanc Diamond pen. A luxe accessory in the hands of such a youngster only added to the intrigue. And the get up! She or he was costumed in haute equestrian drag; polished black knee high field boots, a pink broadcloth shirt, checked Emporio Armani lambswool waistcoat, and fawn Pikeur breeches that clung to well developed thighs.

"You sexy thing, I love your outfit," TaTa gushed.

"I love yours, too," the kid said. Flanking it were two adult women, one a petite, whippet thin, quivering, Botoxed blond; the other a tall, big boned, handsome brunette with a Cleopatra hair cut and the kind of leathery skin that screamed too much Florida. The tiny one was bedecked in intimidating jewels, indicating she was the wife of Croesus. Obviously a fan of TaTas, she was itching to shake the star's hand. The Amazon, demur in khaki Calvin Klein, stood indifferently to one side. She either had no idea who the Princess was, or couldn't be bothered. "Write anything," the kid said airily. "Whatever you feel like writing. Even just your name."

"And what's your name?" the Princess said playfully. "I like to know my fans."

"Oh, I know you live for your fans," the kid said. "I saw an interview with you where you said your fans are the most important thing."

TaTas smiled. "Sweet. Now tell me who you are. And please introduce your friends."

"I'm Diandra," the kid said, putting the issue of gender to rest. "And this is Chessie," she said, indicating the leathery one, "And this is Janey. Tamsin and I are old friends. We're all old friends. We always lunch here."

"Really?" TaTas said, archly. "You don't look old enough to have old friends."

"Aren't you and I nearly the same age?" Diandra said, smirking. "Look how much you've achieved. I consider you a role model. Thank you for being so fabulous!"

"Cheeky, aren't you?" TaTas teased.

"Okay, Diandra, that's wonderful but that's enough," Tamsin said, her tone indicating she was a bit put out. "Great running into you! Hey Chessie! Hey Janey! Another time, let's do lunch!"

Diandra laughed meanly and led her train away.

My phone rang again. This time it was my boyfriend, Ric, back in Los Angeles.

"Sorry, I'll take this outside," I said, standing up.

"What's going on, I can't talk right now," I told Ric in my most "you're annoying me at work" voice. "I'm with Princess TaTas."

"This is totally important," Ric said. "This is a newsflash regarding my career. I'm giving up screenwriting. I'm taking my show on the road, putting it out there what I can do with the trumpet. You know how I've been taking lessons from that guy who plays on Jay Leno? He says I'm really good. And if I spend four hours a day for the next two years I could be one of the best. So, what do you think?"

"I think you're crazy," I said.

Ric groaned. "Don't you realize this my dream? I'm trying to tell you something important, Paige. I want to quit screenwriting. I'm sick of being a rewrite hack on a studio payroll. It's turning me into a zombie! I'm only alive when I'm playing the trumpet. Don't you like my sound? And by the way, I scored two tickets to the Maynard Ferguson Tribute Concert. It's in two weeks in Santa Monica. All the greats will be there. You'll love it. Okay, you might not love it, but you'll appreciate it."

"I'd appreciate it if you'd stop calling me with these juvenile fantasies," I said. "Just get back to doing what you're paid to do, please. Do you realize how many writers would kill to be on a payroll?"

"It's not a fantasy," Ric protested. "I'm insulted that you would demean my dream. Lots of women find it very hot."

"Marry them," I said. "Listen, I have to go. I love you. I'm hanging up."

"Paige, it would mean a lot to me if you'll be here for the concert. I love you and I miss you."

"Over and out."

"Hope everything is okay," Tamsin whispered as I slid back into my chair. I gave her the thumbs up, and stared at my plate, incredulous someone had filched my food in my brief absence. What did it matter, anyway? I wasn't hungry. I took a couple of sips of water to moisten my throat and pulled out my notebook.

"So, Princess, what would you like Hello! readers to know about your house hunt?" I said, adopting a professional tone. Come hell or high water, I had to get this story.

"I don't know," TaTas dithered. "I didn't see anything that immediately grabbed me and screamed, 'Princess TaTas Does Beddington' but I'm not ready to throw in the towel."

"So does that mean you'll be back for further explorations?" I said, scribbling furiously. "I don't want to put words in your mouth, but do you see yourself living in Beddington Place?"

"Well, it's hard to say," TaTas said. "I need something big, but not too big. I need a pool, but not a tennis court. Although tennis courts are nice," she said, nodding at Tamsin, who had pulled out her iPad and was typing. "The prince needs privacy, big gates, maybe something with a moat or a drawbridge, possibly something with a rooftop helicopter pad. I've got to say it seems kind of sleepy, way out here in the woods. Where's the action? What do you do for fun here?"

"I may have a listing that has a helicopter pad," Tamsin broke in. "In fact, I'm sure I do."

"Great. Work on that," TaTas said. "Paige, as far as your story goes, you'll have to speak with my publicist. What's that expression? My people will talk to your people? I so love that I can say that! Meanwhile, sorry, but I've got to run. So sorry to have missed Martin — I'm such a fan! But I have a meeting in the city, so I'm out of here. Hey. It's been real. Bye now."

"Wait a minute," I said, running after her out the door. A limo was waiting. "Can I use any of the part where you were on the horse? Can I say how you almost fell off? I'll be good about it. I don't have to make any reference to that guy who played Superman. He was a Beddington resident, too, even after the accident."

"Wha?" TaTas said, sliding into the town car. At that moment a large blond woman sprang out from behind an Escalade, brandishing a camera. It was Marla Tudor.

"Princess TaTas!" she shouted. "Over here!"

"Damn, I knew there would be paparazzi," TaTas squealed. Her driver stepped hard on the gas, and she was history.

Why the Clampetts won't be buying in Muskrat Dam

*W*hen I returned to the table, Tamsin was texting, her fingers flying across the keyboard.

"Hey, just give me a minute," she said, not looking up, but still able to flash a glorious mega-watt pageant queen smile. To amuse myself while she was working, I let my eyes roam around the room. Romanoff's was jumping. Every table was filled, and up by the hostess station, a line was forming out the doors. The charm of the restaurant was that it looked like a shed, but French country style. The floors were tiled in blue and white hexagons, and an enormous white brick fireplace took up an entire wall. A row of old French doors opened on to a sheltered pavilion, shielded from the road by a hedge of thick, old, boxwood. The restaurant was clatteringly noisy. In fact, there was a frightful din. A stairway set to one side of the fireplace suggested additional seating — Siberia, obviously — upstairs. The main room was the room to see and be seen. At one o'clock, it was lively with people laughing, people talking, but at the same time, everything very controlled and tame, tame as in no one was getting loaded.

Tamsin stopped texting.

"The real story you should be writing," she said, looking up, "is about who already lives in Beddington Place. You know that outside of Los Angeles and New York City, this is the biggest residential concentration of American celebrities you'll find anywhere."

"But I'm here to write about Princess TaTas."

"Peeps like Princess TaTas come and go," Tamsin said airily. "I show her type properties all the time. My personal opinion is certain people, especially if they're in the entertainment industry, should rent first and not buy. Most don't have the right temperament for this quiet country life. But then others feel right at home! Young married celebrity couples with kids do the best. Take Chinois and Willy? Wonderful Beddington residents, but then the whole family had to return to L.A. for his career. Then there's Ford and Zaynee. Wonderful people. Marla Tudor has been a terrific fit. Look at all she did for the town next door, Catoonah, helping to preserve its name!"

"Didn't Marla Tudor try to steal the name of the town of Catoonah so she could own it and use it to sell curtain rings?" I said, having boned up on Marla and her local escapades. When I got an assignment, I definitely did my homework.

"I don't know anything about that," Tamsin shrugged. "You might be right. But my point is, while there are celebrities living here with major public profiles, movie stars, pop singers — you know Dobbs Roberts lives in Beddington, and the rapper BMZ — quite a few of them don't stick around because they don't really crave a low profile and want a lot of attention."

"Didn't the Clampett's try to buy a house in Beddington," I said, referring to Mike and Milly, a famous high ranking political couple.

"Yes, they did," Tamsin said. "And Mike is such a flirt! One of my associates showed them a few properties, Mike and Milly together, and then another day just her and their daughter, Kelsey. I don't know why they didn't ask me! Maybe Milly didn't want me around her man! But the Clampett's won't buy that house in Beddington that was featured in a national magazine," she confided, leaning towards me, her voice dropping to whisper. "Anyway, it's just as well they don't buy it. It would be terrible for the WRA. They'd have to close the trails all around it because it'd be too much of a security risk. And that would ruin the ride to Muskrat Dam."

"Muskrat Dam," I said. "What a great name. Can I quote you on why the Clampett's won't be buying in Beddington?" If I couldn't get a story on Princess TaTas, there always were the Clampett's. Either name was solid gold on the gossip blogs. "What's the WRA? What do those initials stand for? Tell me more about that."

"No, you can't use that thing about the Clampett's. I would deny I said it," Tamsin said prissily "Don't you dare. The WRA is another story. I'd love to give you some quotes about that. There's a horseback riding trail system that is quite remarkable, actually. It's miles and miles of connected, groomed trails, maintained and managed by the Westchester Riding Authority, also known as the WRA. Every bit of the system is on private property or town land throughout Westchester, and conserved land owned by the county designated to remain open space. The WRA holds a huge event every year at the end of the summer. Oh look who's here! It's Martin Roganoff! He's a WRA member. He'll be so sorry to have missed TaTas!"

Sure enough, here was Martin Rogonoff, much taller than I'd imagined, still sexy, and accompanied by his beautiful, much younger wife, the former French singing sensation Michelle Morreau, and their offspring, an adopted Asian girl called Peaches. With them, were a trio of Bhikkhu monks. As they passed by Diandra's table, Martin stopped to hug Diandra and kiss her cheeks.

"Who is that kid?" I said to Tamsin who was back at her texting.

"You mean Diandra? Just warning you, she hates to be called a kid."

"Well, she is a kid, isn't she? She looks about 17."

Tamsin laughed. "Well, she is 20, but lately she's been telling people she's older. Like almost 30."

"30? Is she serious?"

"Well," Tamsin considered. "I think she's telling people she's older because she wants to be taken seriously. She's had her own business since she was a kid. That's quite an achievement."

"What kind of business?" I said. I'd profiled and interviewed teen prodigies who had their own corporations — Justin Bieber, Miley Cyrus, the Backstreet Boys, just to name a few — but they all had managers and handlers, and for the most part, over-involved parents. Or parent figures. Maybe that was Chessie and Janey's role.

"Equestrian," Tamsin said blithely. "It's an important industry here. Beddington boasts literally dozens of horse farms, that is if you include all the rinky dink backyard barns, although some of them are adorable! There are facilities for show jumpers, hunters, pony clubbers, trail riding, retirement horses, lay-up. The only thing we don't do here is polo, but it's a breeze to get to Greenwich. Do you play?"

"Are these all private stables or are there places where the average joe can rent a horse and ride the trails?" I asked.

Tamsin looked aghast. "Oh, no, everything in Beddington Place about horses is private. There are a few places where the public can take lessons, but nothing about the Beddington horse world is truly open. It's exclusive because you have to have a horse. If you don't own one, your trainer will find one and sell it to you. Or you ride with your horse owning friends. I know it sounds snobby, but this isn't a place where you can hop any old horse like you're at a dude ranch on vacation. That's not what we're about. Diandra's got dozens of horses in her care, plus she's a trainer and consultant. She helps me with my horses. Diandra's amazing. She can ride anything and charm anyone. Look at that. She's charming the robes off those monks."

Suddenly there was a cackling laugh from behind.

"Michael Swett!" Tamsin exclaimed. "Darling, how are you?"

"All is bliss," Swett said. He was an attractive man with a full head of russet hair that curled rather devilishly across his large forehead.

"How do you do, Ms. Delacorte ? And who do you have with you here?" he leered, staring down my bosom.

"How are you, Michael," Tamsin said, offering her cheek. "Amazing running into you. This is Paige Turner. She's a celebrity journalist on assignment from Hello! here to do a story on Princess TaTas relo to our beautiful neighborhood."

"Delightful," Swett said, eyebrows waggling. "Can I assume Ms. Delacorte is showing you around? Giving you the grand tour, I hope, including the women's prison."

"There's a prison in Beddington? " I exclaimed. That surprised me. "What kind of prison?"

"Oh, maximum security," Swett said airily. "Major lock down. Cavity searches, solitary confinement, the whole ball of wax. It's the place where they stash away the state's female murderers, plus those poor women from teensy tiny states that don't even have a maximum security women's prison, like Rhode Island. Oh, they've got plenty of celebrity prisoners locked away. Remember the society dame woman who murdered her lover, the lipo doc? She was there. And the glamour girl bank robbers, too, Trudy King and

Nancy Long."

"They're all out now, aren't they?" I said.

"Not Trudy," Swett replied. "Not a snowball's chance in hell they'll let her out, poor dear." He caught me sneaking a peek at Martin Romanoff, who was still chatting up Diandra. "Sweet how Martin and Diandra get on so well, as though they were made for one another," Swett snickered. "No surprise there. They're both so original."

"Who's original?" I said. "Romanoff or the girl?"

"Ha ha. You're delicious. If you're really a trained journalist, surely you must know Romanoff's history. As for the girl, and I see you can't take your eyes off her, if you're thinking of having sex with her, just warning you, she's a virgin."

"She'd be great if I were bi," I deadpanned. "Which I'm not. It's a moot point, anyway, because I'm in a relationship."

"Ms. Delacorte, who is this woman?" Swett said. "Not only is she ravishingly beautiful, but so witty and clever. I love the way she talks. We must keep her around, just for our own amusement."

"So what do you know about Princess TaTas," I said to Tamsin, trolling for more info. Pat would be mad. The story was going badly. It wasn't good Princess wouldn't be back in Beddington for days. Hello! was definitely not going to like this.

"All I know is I'll be showing her more properties," Tamsin said. Just then my cell rang again. It was my editor, Pat. "Hey," she said. "I need that Princess TaTas piece right away."

This was just what I did not need to hear. "Uh," I said, stalling. "Listen, there's been a little complication. Princess had to rush back to the city. She won't be back in Beddington for days."

"Whaaaa?" Pat wailed into my ear. "What are you saying?"

"I'm saying I'm working up a new angle for the story," I said, making it up as I went along. That's half the challenge of freelancing; you have to be able to wing it. "Um, I'm thinking I'll grab the next train back to the city and interview her there. I'll ask her if the equestrian thing isn't just a passing fancy and doesn't she really want a killer loft. Brooklyn's hip. All the boroughs are happening. That's new and fresh. Perfect for Hello! doncha think?"

"You don't get paid to think; you get paid to get stories," Pat growled. "I think you're fucking with me, girlfriend. You're really disappointing." I heard her sigh. "Can't you write something based on what you've got? You spent three hours with the woman, good Jesus, and toured some fancy grounds."

"Well, nothing much happened, "I said. "Unless I write about her nearly falling off a horse."

"She got dumped?" Pat was thrilled. No news like the lurid to get the juices flowing. "That's terrific. Write about that."

"Almost dumped," I corrected. "It would make great copy, but I don't think it's a good idea. Sure, TMZ and everyone else will eat it up, but her publicity team will go ballistic. If I write that, I'll never get permission to get that much access to her again. She didn't fall. It's not real news. So let's not rock that boat, cos you've got to admit I've got amazing access."

"Well, fuck me, Paige, you're a writer, aren't you?" Pat said irritably. "Hello! is waiting. They need copy. Just make something up."

"Who is that?" Swett said, interrupting loudly. "Whom are you talking to?"

"Who is that idiot talking?" Pat said. "Tell him to mind his own fucking business."

"It's my editor," I told Swett.

"Well," he said. "What's her name?"

"Pat Floss."

"Pat Floss? Oh. My. God. Can it be? The one and only Pat Floss. We partied in Ibiza together. Give me that phone right now." I handed it over and he and Pat began yakking. I could hear Pat making soft cooing noises on the other end. That floored me. Pat? Cooing?

"Darling, you've got to let this girl stay in Beddington for as long as she needs," Swett said. I was pretty sure nobody in twenty years had told Pat she had to "do" anything. "She needs to stay in Beddington. She has to get the story. Besides, we're not letting her go. Consider her kidnapped."

I could hear Pat giggling. That was a new concept. Pat. Giggling. I ordered Swett to give me back my phone.

"Hello, Pat? Okay, Just get me a little time on the TaTas story. I'll get you something soon. You have my word."

Just then a waiter came over to the table.

"Miss," he said. "You'll have to get off the phone. Mr. Romanoff doesn't permit the use of cell phones in his restaurant."

I was tempted to tell him a thing or two, but then I saw the monks staring.

"Pat," I said. "I've really got to get off." I hung up and Tamsin and Swett trained their eyeballs on me.

"Forget about Princess TaTas," Swett said, regally. "We'll get you a story much bigger than that silly strumpet."

Nature Calls

*I*t was a woodpecker that woke me up. The bird was making an amazing racket, a din of staccato drilling sounds, persistent, loud, and repetitive. Reluctantly, I opened my eyes and was greeted by an infusion of gorgeous spring sunlight streaming in through mullioned window panes.

I had no idea what time it was, only that I had zero desire to leave the bed. It was an amazing bed, soft, deep, luxurious, made up with the most wonderful sheets. It was also a rather large, imposing piece of furniture that easily could dominate any room. I was grateful to have slept in it, thankfully accepting Tamsin's hospitality and offer to stay the night in her guest cottage, instead of crawling back to the city. My reservation at the Howard Johnson Express Inn on West 49th was booked for a single night based on my assumption that after spending a couple of hours with TaTas, I'd be catching the next flight out. It was a long time since I'd spent a night in the country, and I'd forgotten the sounds of a rural dawn.

I wasn't ready to open my eyes. Closing them again, I focused on the next rally of the woodpecker's hammering, marveling at the bird's persistence and musicality. It was an astonishing sound, a cross between a power tool and an electric drum machine, a perfect rat-a-tat-tat of rhythm. Ric, I thought, would appreciate it. But what kind of woodpecker was it? Without leaving the bed, I reached for my MacBook, which I'd left on the night table, and quickly typed the phrase "woodpecker sounds," into the search engine. In less than 30 seconds I was listening to the distinctive trills and hammerings of seven different species of woodpeckers, but felt no closer to making a determination. To my raw, untrained ear, it sounded like my woodpecker might be one of the Lesser Spotted species, but a deeper Google search informed me that couldn't be right, as Lesser Spotted woodpeckers are found almost exclusively in the U.K.

Getting out of bed, I padded to the window to get a better look. I couldn't spot the bird, but was surprised to see a small herd of deer grazing on Tamsin's lawn. I lightly rapped my knuckles against the windowpane, but

22

they didn't run away. They were a trio of mature does and their commingled offspring, spotted fawns no bigger than billy goats. A little further away, watching over them, was the buck, a magnificent, virile creature, his noble head crowned by an enormous rack. A shockingly visceral electric current of excitement coursed through me as our eyes locked and met.

Someone was knocking on the cottage door. It was Tamsin, carrying a loaded silver tray. Dangling from one arm was a pile of clothing.

"Good morning!" she said brightly. It wasn't even 7 a.m. but she was already spectacular, kitted out in a pair of tight fitting Tailored Sportsman breeches, tall boots and a canary vest. Today her blond-streaked hair was swept off her face and secured by a velvet headband. An eentsy smudge of dirt adorned one of her cheeks and I noticed the boots were a bit muddy. "I hope you got your beauty sleep," she said. "I didn't want to wake you. Did you sleep okay? I hope the bed wasn't too uncomfortable."

"What, are you kidding? This is the most amazing bed." It was a Vera Wang bed. I knew it was a Vera Wang bed because Tamsin had made sure to tell me so just before she tucked me into it.

It had been one helluva day, action packed. When we were done at Romanoff's, while Tamsin dashed off to assist other clients, her buddy Michael Swett took me under his wing to squire me to show me the charms of Beddington. First we went to Claramore Park, a luxurious Mediterranean style villa, former home of Wendell and Lucretia Posen, Lucretia a social register blue blood who had turned the Beddington Place family home into an internationally renowned summer music festival not unlike Chicago's Ravinia. After that, we nipped over to the Catoonah Art House, a small but prestigious premiere gallery with a monthly jazz series and an internationally recognized sculpture garden. After that, Swett escorted me over to Historic Hall, an impressive white clapboard antique erected in 1816 as an Episcopal church. We broke for a short breather with take out lattes which we drank sitting on a bench on the Beddington Place Green, a charming pastoral parcel of land set smack in the center of the cozy village. An antique sign noted this was once the place where the town's cows and sheep once grazed. I snapped a picture of the sign. It was definitely going to play a role in my story about TaTas, which of course, I still had to write. Tamsin ramped up the excitement by pulling together a late night dinner soiree with her brother Sal and some of his business associates. We trundled a few miles north to a town called Salem where she'd made reservations at a casually swanky roadside joint known as The Hide Out. The kitchen produced plate after plate of delicious finger food: chicken wings and crispy calamari, and Korean style pork sliders served with house pickles and hoisin sauce. A deceptively innocuous drink Sal ordered for me called a Redheaded Slut made with peach schnapps and Jagermeister went down easy, and the last thing I remembered before they literally poured me into his BMW was the realization I was snockered.

Pouring out a cup of hot chocolate ("I love starting the day with chocolate, don't you?" Tamsin trilled. "It's so cosmopolitan!"), she proceeded to say she had a special surprise in store for me, "for your article." If I wasn't so hung over I would have laughed, she was that transparent. I knew Tamsin had set me up in her guest cottage to hold me hostage until I agreed to plug her business as a Beddington Place real estate agent. She'd already told me she was seeking national promotion. Did I feel sour about this? Not really. As long as she kept producing celebrity clients, Pat would go for it.

"Today I am taking you to see the Old Homestead," Tamsin announced as I took a cautious sip. I could have killed for a cup of coffee, but she was right; not only was the chocolate delicious but it was thoroughly decadent. "The Old Homestead is an enormous state park that was the country home and working farm of one of the first governors of New York," she gabbled. "I've asked a friend to trailer over some horses so we can take ride around. So much of the quintessential Beddington Place experience can only be appreciated on horseback, as you've probably realized." She gave me an appraising look. "Of course, not everyone knows how to ride. But you do."

"Well, I haven't had many opportunities lately," I said, groaning a little and rubbing my eyes. The time change was rough. My body clock was still in L.A.; even here it was barely morning. Not to mention, after yesterday's adventures, I was feeling pretty stiff. "Can't say I've done much horseback riding, living in Venice Beach."

"Is that where you live?" Tamsin said, perching one tiny, taut, yoga-trained butt cheek on a desk carved of burled oak. On it sat a vase of fresh wildflowers, no doubt picked from her own garden. "I just adore California."

"Yup," I said. "Superba Avenue, just off Lincoln Boulevard and around the corner from the Great Western Steak & Hoagie Company, which makes the best damn cheese steak you ever ate." Hoping to impress Tamsin a little bit, I launched into my own real estate vernacular. "We're in a Mediterranean style stucco single family house, two bedrooms, one bath, a studio out back for my boyfriend to fool around on his trumpet. Minutes from the beach. Not that I ever get to the beach. I'm always too busy, working."

"Own or rent?" Tamsin said.

"Rent."

She frowned.

"What kind woodpeckers do you have here?" I said, changing the subject. "I'd love to know what bird it was that woke me up. Do you have a native bird book around I could reference?"

"Hmm, I think that must be a redheaded woodpecker," Tamsin said authoritatively. My mind immediately jumped to that drink. "They have four distinctive notes, the drum, the pik, the distress, and the whinny."

"Whinny?" I said. "I thought that was a sound horses make."

"Oh, no, some birds whinny. It's a sound they make during mating season."

It was mating season? Well, that was news to me.

"I always thought it would be cool to ride on the beach in California," I said, my mind turning straight to horses, which as a girl were my first love. "There are places along the coast where you can ride on the beach, but not Venice. You wouldn't want to anyway. Even if it were legal, you'd have to jump over the homeless. Lots of homeless people living on Venice beach, and Santa Monica, too. It's because the restaurants feed them."

"Homeless people? Ewwww, that's not a problem we have in Beddington," Tamsin said, her nose crinkling. "There are no homeless people in

Beddington Place, I promise you that."

"Really? No one ever has to sleep on a park bench? Everybody rich enough to live under their own roof?" I said. "But you're only 40 miles from the city. There must be some poor people who find their way up here."

"Well, of course there are poor people," Tamsin said prissily. "But they're all hard-working honest people, mostly from Mexico. They clean houses and mow the lawns. Actually, lots of Mexican men are employed at the stables. But they all live in Peekskill or Mount Kisco."

"So they're the people who do all the dirty work," I said. "Your de-facto slave class?"

Tamsin chose not to answer. Instead she wondered out loud if I'd lived in California my whole life. Poverty and illegal immigration, she added, were not things she hoped would find their way into my Beddington story. "You seem so Californian," she mused.

I wasn't surprised. I got that all the time. Maybe it was my nonchalant manner, or my perpetually messy, bed head hair. Or the fact that when asked, I've always been an advocate of medical marijuana. "No," I said. "I grew up on the Jersey shore. As a kid, I did ride horses on the beach. You could only do it in the winter, though, when the sand was hard packed. Half-hour rides on Western ponies up and down the shoreline. We galloped them at wave's edge. It was pretty cool, come to think of it. Hey, are there any beaches around here? Where's the nearest body of water? Westport? Greenwich?"

"Well, there's the reservoirs for the New York City watershed, and an itsy bitsy stretch of hard packed sand along the Muskrat Dam, but I mean tiny," Tamsin said. "I wouldn't dream of describing it as a 'beach.' People do ride horses on the beach in the winter, though, just over the border in Connecticut. It's an easy trailer ride getting there. But I want to hear more about the Jersey Shore. Is it really like that awful TV show? Please tell me you weren't like Snookie."

"We lived in Atlantic City," I said. "My father was a lawyer for the mob. I never met anybody named Snookie or The Situation, but I'm not saying they didn't exist. I don't know. You grow up some place, you get used to it. It seemed pretty natural to me."

Tamsin blinked.

"Too funny," she said, after a moment. "Now I know for sure you're pulling my leg. What do you say we get this show on the road? While you've been a sleepy head, I've been out hunting. Marrrrvelous daybreak fox run up on Claxton Road. Up where we all met last night for dinner, in Salem."

"You killed a fox?" I said, shuddering.

"No, I don't think so," Tamsin said blithely. "Ran it to ground, but there wasn't any blooding. Blooding is a social ritual, you know. It's a very old ceremony where the master of the hunt smears the blood of the fox on to the cheeks of a newly initiated hunt follower, often a young person. The young woman you met at Roganoff's yesterday? That beautiful girl, Diandra? She was recently anointed."

"I'm not sure I want to hear about this right now," I said. "It's kind of early in day to talk about pagan rituals."

"Sorry," Tamsin laughed. "Whenever I talk about hunting, I just get so excited! I forget not everybody is into it. But only the best people do it! Listen. I know it must be unbearable to think about wearing yesterday's clothes, so I've brought you some things from my closet. I hope everything fits. We are about the same size, aren't we?"

I looked at the pile she dropped on the bed. There was a celery green baby soft cashmere sweater, and a pale pink short sleeved polo shirt, and a narrow silvery belt and a pair of brand new, never worn, cream colored, Pikeur breeches, the price tag still dangling from a belt loop.

"These are riding clothes," I said, stating the obvious.

"Yes, remember I told you we were riding? The boots you wore yesterday will be fine with these pants. They are riding boots, aren't they? So lucky you wore them, so sensible for the country."

"Well, they're Frye boots," I said. "Paige Tall Riding Boots, they call them. That's why I bought them. The name. You know. Paige. I don't think most of the people who buy them ever get anywhere near a horse, though," I added.

"They worked fine for you yesterday with TaTas," Tamsin said. "Paige is a great name, by the way. I love it."

"Annoying choice with 'Turner,' which is my last name," I said, polishing off what was left of the hot chocolate. It was so good, I wished there was more in the pot.

"Why do you say that?" asked Tamsin. "I think it's cute."

"My mother had a strange sense of humor, I guess. Or she hoped I'd grow up to be a novelist. Guess I missed my mark."

"Don't say that!" Tamsin said, sagely. "You never know what life will bring you if you just stay open. That's my mantra. Now hurry up and get dressed. Bring your soiled things to the house and Estrella will launder them. And don't worry about the riding clothes. They're yours to keep. I've got scads. Tee hee, Sal says I must be single handedly keeping the tack shop in business, I buy so much. Meet me at the house in half an hour."

It's Just Pheramones

*I*s it just too disgusting, too embarrassing, too humiliating, really, to admit that the first time I laid eyes on Alex Manos, my heart skipped a beat? At first sight, he was dazzling, a vision torn straight from the pages of a romance novel, a book genre, I might add, I abhor. But here I was standing in a grassy field, staring up at him, salivating.

"Morning," the vision said, telegraphing he was a man of few words. He was dark complexioned, tall, muscular, but slimly built, wearing a some-what ridiculous, romantic, turn of the century styled ruffled shirt. On closer inspection I noticed that his chocolate brown eyes were set a little closely together in his head, but his ruby red lips, were as shapely as a girl's. He had thick, wavy black hair he wore sexily disheveled; ages must have passed since it had seen a brush or scissors. To top it all off, the first time we met he was riding a large, steel gray horse whose mane and tail were the exact shade of gun metal. A lazy, ironic grin played across his handsome face. He deliber-ately avoided my eye contact, training his eyes instead on Tamsin's tits.

It didn't pass Tamsin's notice that I was instantly smitten. "Don't give those palpitations you're having a second thought," she said in a half whisper. "Every woman — and quite a few men for that matter — have the same reaction. Alex is a total hunk on a horse, and he's not bad to look at on the ground, either."

"I don't know what you're talking about," I said tightly, not wanting Tamsin to get the wrong idea.

"Hey, Alex," Tamsin said, leading me over to the vision. "This here is Paige Turner. She's from Hello! magazine. She's writing a story concerning Beddington Place. Paige, meet Alex Manos. He's a famous horse trainer. You might have seen him on "Extreme Mustang Makeover."

"'Lo," Alex said. "The horses are on their way over. They should be here in a minute. I don't know your level of riding ability so I brought you what we call a babysitter," he said to me. "His name is Butterscotch."

"I know how to ride," I said, tightly.

"Tamsin, I brought you Galahad," Alex continued. "I know you like him."

"Oh, Galahad! He's such a lover boy," Tamsin exclaimed. "And who is this you have here? I don't think I've seen this magnificent beast."

"This is Lord Kensington," Alex said. "He's at my farm for training. Belongs to an actor out in Hollywood. Sorry, can't divulge his name. Had to sign a confidentiality agreement. You know these Hollywood types, heh heh," he said, winking at me as though we were conspirators. "And I guess you do, since you suck a living off of 'em." I froze. Was that last comment an out-and-out attack?

A few minutes later, Alex's trailer arrived. Soon we were touring the grounds on horseback. Just as Tamsin had promised, the Old Homestead was gorgeous, its bucolic gardens and sloping lawns reminiscent of 19th- century landscape paintings I'd seen in museums. "You get this whole sensibility of what it must of felt like driving up to the house in a carriage between the beech trees," Tamsin, the perfect tour guide, prattled on. "It's so picturesque. I've always thought of this place as one of the prides of Beddington Place."

As we tack walked along, she sang the praises of the gardens and the various garden clubs that tended them. "There's the Beddington Garden Club, the Hopp Ground Garden Club, the Rusticus Garden Club, and the New York Unit of the National Herb Society," Tamsin said. "And here we have the Herb Garden."

"The Beech Allee is my favorite," Alex commented. Butterscotch, the Haflinger he assigned me, was a pipsqueak compared to Lord Kensington; riding side by side, the pony barely cleared the Warmblood's muscular haunches. As Tamsin trotted along in front on Galahad, her butt cheeks bouncing in perfect harmony to the big bay's gait, Alex confided, "The gardens are beautiful all year round, but especially in the springtime, when the lilacs are in bloom and the grounds explode in shades of white and lavender." Hmmm, I thought. That was nicely put. Who knew this twin of Fabio possessed the soul of a poet?

"Some amazing events have happened here," Tamsin gabbled from up ahead. "Incredible garden parties, the Farmerettes lecture, and Paige, you're going to love learning all about the Farmerettes. They were a group of women who banded together during the first World War. They were part of the Women's Land Army. There was a book written about them you could reference. It was called, 'The Fruits of Victory.'"

"'Fruits?'" Alex said. "Is that because they were lesbians?"

I laughed.

Tamsin ignored this. Instead she nattered on about the Farmerettes. "I've always found them to be so inspiring. Paige, I do hope you'll stick around to attend the Country Fair, which is held right on these grounds. They have pig races, and a barn dance, then there's the Curator's Series. Beddington is really a cultured place. Do you think you'll be able to use any of what I'm showing you in your TaTas story? Or am I giving you too much?"

"It's fine," I told her. Just then Alex caught my eye and winked and I had to suppress a fit of laughter.

We rode the horses over to the front steps of the house. As promised, Butterscotch was a sweetheart. He was a cute pony, caramel colored, with an ivory tail and mane. I dismounted and gave him a pat and a kiss. "Good boy," I said, wishing I had something better than an Altoid to offer him.

Tamsin and Alex dismounted and the Mexican who drove the trailer over approached to lead away the horses. "Bye, little guy," I said.

"Now it's time to show you what's inside," Tamsin said. She steered me up the front stairs and through the old front door. "You may or may not already know this," she said a little breathlessly, "but in 1801 all 750 acres of this land was acquired, either by inheritance or purchase. During the governor of New York's second term, renovations were done to the farmhouse in preparation for his retirement from public life. Unfortunately his wife died before they got to move in, but he moved in anyway as a widower. It was so sad. A man alone with four children, can you believe that? But of course in those days they had piles of servants! The poor man never remarried but enjoyed a quiet life as a country farmer. He was a very pious Episcopalian and one of the founders of the St. Matthew's Church here in Beddington."

"Speaking of servants, didn't he keep slaves?" I asked.

"Yes, he kept slaves, but he really was against the practice," Tamsin said, lowering her eyes reverentially. "His son, you know, went on to become an important abolitionist."

"Do you think as a realtor she has to memorize all this stuff?" I whispered to Alex, who was making the site staff anxious. He kept touching things even though there were signs all over the place saying no touching. "Listening to her go on like this is like sitting in history class."

"I never listen to a single thing she says," he said, running his fingers over a patch of wallpaper. "But I'd sure love to tap that ass."

"What was that?" Tamsin said. "Are you asking did the governor keep asses? Well, I don't know for sure, but it's a pretty safe bet he did. Probably to pull carts."

"What's the difference between a mule and a donkey, and what exactly is an ass?" I said, not sure if I really cared to know the difference.

"A mule is the offspring of a male donkey and a female horse," Alex said. "A donkey's an ass. You'd know one if you saw one."

"I think that's enough talk about asses," Tamsin said, smiling tightly. "So what's next, kids? Shall we grab some lunch?"

"I'm not hungry," Alex said. "At least not for food." He came over and stood very close. I could feel his breath fogging my forehead. "So are you going to take me out for dinner tonight or am I not good enough?"

"Me? Take you out to dinner?" I squeaked.

"Yeah. You're the big writer from California," he said. "How much are you making on this story? You've got an expense account?"

"Well, I do have a per diem."

"Good. Let's start spending it."

"Wait a minute!" Tamsin said, pulling me aside.

"You shouldn't go off with him," she hissed. "He's dirty! He's dangerous!"

"What do you mean?" I said. "I thought you two were friends."

"I wouldn't trust any woman with him," she said. "Or any man either."

"You should listen to her," Alex sniggered. "She's right. I'm getting the car now. Meet you out front."

Getting to Know You, Getting to Know All About You

*A*lex was waiting in the car, the engine running. I stepped off the front porch of the Old Homestead and traipsed over to him, Tamsin's galled eyes burning a hole in my backside. He leaned over to unlatch the passenger side door, and I hoisted myself into the cab of a dented, crud- encrusted Ford pick up truck that strongly reeked of horse sweat. The first thing that caught my attention were the rumbling transmission and gear box, the stick shift vibrating spasmodically. Gingerly, I arranged myself on the ripped upholstery. Something hard was poking me in the butt. Swirling on the floor around my feet was a miasma of debris: dirty socks, empty paper coffee cups, scraps of newspaper, and a tattered volume of poetry by Federico Garcia Lorca.

"What's this for?" I asked, as a baseball bat rolled out from under the seat.

"I play in a Sunday game," Alex said. "You may have heard of it. It's locally famous. The Ball Game is what it's called."

"I think I've heard of it. A funk singer, a famous crooner, sometimes plays in it, right? Is it Jon Secada?"

"You've heard of it?" he asked, surprised. "Yeah," I said. "The guy who started it created a famous video game which launched a major website, and after he made a ton of money, he began lecturing at major colleges and universities as an expert on game theory. That's why he's so into softball."

"Huh," Alex said. "Just thought he was another rich dude who loves the game."

He headed out the long driveway and made a sharp left. A stench emanating from the behind the seat made me swivel around to see what was behind. It was a pile of moldering clothes. There was a jumble of shirts and pants and several boots and shoes, including a pair of very high spiked high heels.

"Nice ride," I said, allowing just the tiniest sliver of sarcasm.

"Want to buy it?" Alex said, swerving to avoid a squirrel. I fell against him when the car lurched, clinging to the grab bar. "Like everything else I own, it's for sale."

"Watch it," I warned.

"Live dangerously," Alex said, eyes pinned on the road. I tried buckling the seatbelt, but it didn't work. He stepped on the accelerator and hit a bump that sent the truck airborne. I let out a holler.

Alex laughed, a dirty rotten sound that came out like, "heh heh heh." Then he checked out my breasts. "You're so jiggly, you aren't wearing a bra, are you?" he said. I felt violated.

We drove on in silence for several minutes. Everything was so green and lush. After the bone dryness of LA, I felt like I was in Ireland. On either side of the road were amazing houses, rather nicely spaced, the majority of them older, stately, white clapboards set among a smattering of cedar contemporaries with multiple rooflines and complicated decks. There were also some substantial new colonials, and a few brick mansions barely visible from the road. All the driveways were adorned with wrought iron gates and statues of eagles and lions. At one point, we passed a large meadow with jumps.

"Is that a private jumping field?" I asked.

"It's part of the WRA trail system," Alex said. "This whole side of the road belongs to a rich old queen who was married to a Mellon. He's an old deviate."

"Why do you say that?" I said. "Did he make a pass at you?"

"His old lady was big into horses," Alex said. "He's an important sheet music collector with an inventory of rare works. I heard it's been valued in the millions. The guy must be about 100 but he's still a horny bastard."

"I've heard of him, too," I said, recalling a few details. "I read he's having the collection archived, and at some point it all goes to a musical hall of fame."

"A friend of mine works for him. She helps keep it organized. She told me there's a framed of copy 'Take Me Home,' in the barn by John Hewitt. It was one of the most famous songs sung by the armies of the American Confederacy. Not that the horses appreciate it."

We drove around some more until we came to a residential street that looked like time had forgot. The houses were tiny and ramshackle with chain link fenced yards. Alex steered the pick up into a weed-clogged gravel driveway and past a peeling, sad-looking cottage. At the rear of the property was a garage. Just behind, I could see train tracks. As soon as he stopped, the mountain of clothing on the back seat began to stir and an enormous dog emerged, its tail wagging.

"Who's this?" I said, surprised. I couldn't believe a dog had been with us all along.

"This is Lupa," Alex said. "She's one quarter wolf. She's my true companion. People are a disappointment, but you'll never be betrayed by your dog."

Lupa was barking and carrying on, begging to get out. Alex opened his door and she took off behind the garage like a shot.

"This is where I live," Alex said. "Come on in."

Going around to a side door, we entered the garage. It was raw and unfinished space, cluttered with old dressers, a metal worktable, and a sagging easy chair. Pushed into one corner was an ornate double bed. The, bed was seductively dressed with a billowing comforter and what looked like expensive linens, but it was unmade, and the sheets were filthy, covered with dog hair and stains of every description.

Alex walked over to the worktable and held something up. It was a necklace made of leather and a large, dark red stone, the leather crudely tied around it.

"In my spare time I like to make jewelry," he said. "A woman I know is trying to hook me up with one of the jewelry stores in town. She says I'm good. She compared my stuff to things they sell in Barney's."

"Hmm," I said, noncommittally. The necklace looked like something I'd made in summer camp. I looked around the work table, hoping to fix on something I liked. I picked up a tiny metal sculpture of twisted wires hanging from a simple black cotton cord.

"What's this?" I said. "This is different."

"I'm glad you noticed that," Alex said. "It's a tortured man. He's bent. He's been broken. It's a statement about the male role in modern society. Men were meant to be warriors and heroes, but instead we're slaves and eunuchs. The modern world has stripped men of our masculinity, and instead of protesting, we're supposed to say thanks. That's bullshit."

"Really," I said, squinting at the thing. If I closed one eye and twisted my head, I could just make out the silhouette of a head and shoulders. Or a torso. Or not. I kept looking but it still looked like a, hodgepodge of metal wires, but to be fair, no editor ever assigned me to be a jewelry critic.

"Time to split," Alex said, abruptly. "There's one more place I'd like to show you. It's on the way back to Tamsin's." He called the dog, who came running, and we got back into the truck. Driving on, we left the sad little neighborhood to turn on to yet another road that led to a small white church. Alex parked in the lot.

"Where are we going now?" I said, eyeing the thick woods just behind the church.

"Something really special," Alex said. "They call this place, 'The Fen.'"

There was a trail and plenty of signage, but it was an arduous walk. There were steep hills and the ground was slippery with wet leaves. There were loose stones and pointed rocks. We passed a thicket of shrubs and trees to enter a long narrow passageway bordered by a ravine. The foliage was so thick, it shut out the sun. I heard the sound of moving water ahead somewhere, and a red-tailed hawk flew between the trees, shrieking.

"What was that?" I said, freaked by the sight of a dozen wild turkeys scrambling across the path. The underbrush rustled wildly, and a dog, or what looked like a dog, emerged in hot pursuit. Lupa tore off after it, and only returned, shamefaced, when Alex shouted.

"Can't have you chasing after coyotes, silly girl," he said nuzzling, his face in her fur and stroking her as she panted from excitement and exertion.

"Was that a coyote?" I said, seriously scared. The thing looked nothing like coyotes I'd seen in L.A. mangy, feral creatures, built low to the ground, and timid. This animal was an enormous, muscular beast.

"A few weeks ago I came across a mother coyote and her kits," Alex said. "Those kits must be half grown now, which means it's a good sized pack. These are Eastern coyotes; they've been mating with Canadian wolves, which explains why they're so much bolder and more aggressive. They're nothing like those scrawny specimens out west."

"You've been out west?" I said."

"I'm originally from Nevada," Alex said. "Grew up just outside Elko. I've been around horses all my life. My first job was as a cowboy. I broke wild mustangs."

"Hmmm," I said. "I can't imagine that background has much relevance in Beddington's world of show jumping and fox hunting."

He snorted.

"Ever see horses in the wild? They're vicious. They kick and bite and tear the living flesh off each other. They think nothing of breaking another horse's leg, or killing it. Horses in Beddington Place are molly coddled. You've got to show a horse right away you mean business. The first thing I do when I meet a horse is punch it in the nose. No room for mistakes about who's the boss."

"I guess you're not a fan of Monty Roberts," I said, naming the famous horse whisperer. "Or that guy they made the movie about. You know. Buck. Those guys don't break horses. They gentle them. I'm guessing you don't think much of those techniques."

Alex didn't answer. Instead he led the way to a rustic bridge that crossed a deep and noisy stream. "I love this river," he said. "Most of the I stones I use for my jewelry are harvested right from this riverbed. That woman I mentioned who was supposed to get my work shown at a fine arts show at Historic Hall last spring? She effed me. I was so mad, I threw my best piece in the river here. It's still down there, somewhere."

Before I could say anything, he turned on his heel to leave. Calling the dog, he marched back across the bridge, setting off up the trail at such a rapid pace I had to scramble to keep up.

"Hey, wait up," I said, breathing hard. I wasn't in as great as shape as I'd imagined. In L.A. I hit the gym every day but this was like climbing mountains. "That sounds bad. Tell me what happened."

"I entered it in the fine art show they hold every year," Alex said, still giving me his back. "That woman said I was a shoo-in. She knows everybody on the judging committee — it's a juried show — and she said they'd love my work. Turned out some other woman who used to keep a horse with me blackballed me. Said my work lacked sophistication. I didn't, realize you had to have an advanced degree to be a jewelry maker," he said, sarcastically.

"Then what happened?" I said, feeling sorry for the guy, his ambitions dashed and shattered.

"Ehhh, nothing, really. The woman who said I was a shoe-in did some smooth talking to the rest of the committee, and then they did some backsliding and told me I could show my work at a table on the sidewalk. Said it would be the first thing people would see when they arrived."

"Well, that sounds all right," I said. "People would still get to see your work."

"But not take it seriously," Alex said angrily. "That's bullshit. So I brought it to The Fen. It's fine. It makes sense having it in the water. Proves my man isn't just tortured, they're trying to drown him."

"Okay," I said, feeling uneasy. This guy had a temper and was more than a little weird. But maybe he had every right to be mad. The woman had promised him something, when she wasn't in a position to make promises. I suddenly remembered the high heels on the truck floor and wondered who they belonged to. "So who was that woman? Somebody special to you, like a girlfriend?"

"I don't have a girlfriend," Alex said sullenly. "Women just latch on. Everybody wants a piece."

What an ego, I thought as we made our way back to the car.

Lupa got there first and leaped into my lap the moment I sat down. She proceeded to lick my chin with her rough tongue and I laughed because even if she was a quarter wolf, she was sweet, and the most genuine thing to respond to me since I'd set foot in Beddington.

"Well, don't worry, I don't want a piece of you. For starters, I've got a boyfriend."

"You don't act like you've got a boyfriend," Alex said, giving me the eye. He very deliberately looked me up and down, his eyes boring into me like an auger. It was uncomfortable. Not in the least pleasant. His gaze was uncompromising and so appraising, that my face began to burn. Never in my life had I felt so judged. At the same time there was something coolly impersonal about it, as though he were assessing an animal.

The moment passed.

"I've got some things to do at the barn," Alex said. "Chores. You can tag along and help me bring in and feed my horses, or I can take you back to Tamsin's and pick you up. You're taking me to dinner tonight, remember?"

"Um, I think I'd like to freshen up," I said, breathing in the fumes of the dog and the smelly clothes in the truck and wondering what on the trail I might have stepped in. And I still had to pound out my piece on TaTas. "Where are we going for dinner, anyway? Give me a clue what to wear." "Go in your birthday suit," Alex said, shrugging. "Seriously, whatever you've got will be fine. It's not Manhattan."

We drove on for in silence, me enjoying the scenery. We came to a long hilly road Alex said was Tamsin's. The view was awesome but the road was terrible, paved and not paved in some parts. Where it wasn't paved, the dust was choking.

"What's the name of this road?" I said, coughing and covering my mouth.

"They call this Guardian Hill," Alex said. "It's old. It's historic. A Revolutionary battle was fought where it crests at East Patent. There's a farm there now; the whole area's been farmland for decades."

"So who lives here now?" I asked, curious. "They're farmers?" Tamsin didn't exactly strike me as a farmer, although she was awfully fond of those Farmerettes.

"Gentlemen farmers," Alex said. "Originally The Hill was all old money Republicans, the same people who preserved The Fen. But the old guard's dying out. The second and third generations never worked, they just ran through their trust funds. The Hill's filling up now with hedge funders, and Wall Streeters, people working in the entertainment industry. Basically it's for anyone with money and the need to have the cache of an elite address to make them feel important."

"Gotcha," I said. This was information I might be able to use in, my TaTas story. Alex was useful. The guy had a glacier sized chip on his shoulder, and he didn't know the difference between "cache" and "cachet," but his social observations were viable.

He put on the blinker just before Tamsin's mailbox and I was struck anew with the sheer grandeur of the place. Tamsin really did live in a palace. A long cobblestone drive led past a scenic pond and an allee of flowering trees. At the end of the allee, the drive became a sea of white gravel; a towering fountain created a round about where at 12 o'clock stood the main entranceway to the house, a 10,000 square foot L-shaped stone manor designed to evoke a centuries-old European castle, set imposingly on a rise. It seemed less a dwelling for human beings than something in a movie. If a liveried footman sprang out to throw open the double front doors, it wouldn't surprise me.

Getting out of the car, I was unsure what to do next. Was I supposed to let Tamsin know I'd returned, or could I slip quietly out back to the guest house?

"Yoo hoo," a voice trilled from behind just as I entered the cottage. It was Tamsin, all smiles and cheerful chatter.

"Be careful of Alex," she said, after grilling me about my afternoon. "You shouldn't go out with him. You should go out with me. I'm hosting a networking event for women in real estate and I know everyone would love to meet you." That sounded deadly.

"Shucks, that sounds awesome," I lied. "But I think I'll stick to the plan. Don't wait up."

It's Called The Big Kahuna. It's The Hot New Thing.

*W*hat is this place, I asked Alex as we slid into our seats. Clearly it was a restaurant but nobody was eating. A few people had glasses of wine sitting in front of them, but more were clutching bottled water. All the tables and chairs were positioned to face a podium set up in front of a bank of windows. A microphone on a stand was positioned next to the podium, and there was an air of expectation.

"It's a live poetry reading," Alex said, sipping from the container of take out coffee he'd picked up at Dunkin Donuts. For our night out, he was wearing a beautifully cut jacket with leather patches at the elbow, but had left on the Ariat men's lace up paddock boots he had on earlier. An aromatic stink of horse rose up from his feet.

"I'll have a Chardonnay, please," I called out to a passing server who cast me a withering look. "What's up with that?" I said. "Isn't this a restaurant? I know you said we're here for a poetry reading, but can't we get some service?"

"This place is called The Blind Walrus. It's supposed to be a wine bar. The staff hates the poetry nights because the poets never order and just take up all the tables," Alex said. "But the management is trying to build, community. That's the big thing now," he said sarcastically. "Community building. I've been coming these poetry nights for about a year. They get some pretty good poets."

"Yeah, and a cheap night out for you, especially when you bring your own beverage," I said, looking pointedly at his paper cup. "Next time I'll bring my own bottle. That server is still giving me cold shoulder."

The room was filling up as poets and fans of the genre took their seats. They were an eclectic group, these poets and poetry lovers, more the type I'd expect to find in a coffee house in Silverlake than the 'burbs of northern Westchester. One guy was actually wearing a beret and there were a number of Slim-Lipo-ed cougars flaunting their boob jobs in low-cut blouses, sporting extravagant eyeliner.

A flyer scattered on the tables announced the featured poet, a lady who had done time. Time as in she'd been imprisoned, a few miles away, at a correctional facility not far from Beddington.

"My name is Leeza Luciano and my crime was not violent," the featured poet said, stalking to the front of the room, a wireless microphone in hand. She coughed into it a few times. It sounded like a smoker's cough. It was rough. "Just FYI, all I did was rob a couple of banks," she said, grinning. She was a tall, blond, rangy woman of indeterminate age, wearing head to toe denim. Her was cut in a long shag, Charlie's Angels-style, to frame her still-pretty face. She was older, but grizzled. Her voice was compelling, soft and feminine, with just a hint of the twang of Staten Island.

"You may recall my name from when it ran in all the newspapers," she said importantly, although I didn't. Whatever she did, it must have been local and not heinous enough to make national headlines.

"My point is," she said, "I am my name and not a number, which is something they try to do to you in prison."

The audience let out a small cheer.

"That's the focus of the poems I'm about to share with you tonight. They're about humanity and being a woman and a heterosexual woman who found herself with a lot of dykes. And who tried being a dyke," Leeza added. "Cos that's what women do when they're forced to cohabitate in that kind of situation."

"Excuse me, aren't you Paige Turner?" the guy sitting at the next table whispered in my ear.

"We met in L.A. at a small dinner party and you were in fine form. You were hysterically funny. But not very nice, if I recall."

If we had met, I didn't remember. "Where was the party?" I parried, in hopes something might jog my mind. "Who was giving it, do you remember? I go to a lot of parties."

"It wasn't a huge party," he said. "It was an intimate gathering. You were seated to my left. Across the table was your boyfriend."

"I go to a lot of small dinner parties, too," I said, starting to feel boxed in. I sensed Alex grinning at my discomfiture. "Why don't you just tell me your name and we'll start again?" I said, pleasantly. "We can begin right now making friends."

"I don't know if I care to be a friend of someone who could sit next to me for two hours and not remember a thing," the guy said, turning sour and belligerent. "Could it be because you were drunk and running your mouth and hogging all the attention? Although it was funny, the things you were saying. Really great gossip, and so indiscreet."

Horrified who might be hearing this, I immediately tuned this jerk out and turned my full attention to the ex-con poet who was pounding the podium with her fist, declaiming lyric poetry based on her personal saga of childhood abuse, rampant drugs, biker lore, and a stab at homosexuality, culminating in a burst of religiosity and love for her fellow "woe-man."

"She's pretty good, doncha think?" I said to Alex who appeared to, be listening closely. Was it my imagination or had his leg slid closer to mine? His hot, heavy thigh pressed up against my flesh, a fact I found disturbingly thrilling.

"Nah, she sucks," he drawled. "But she's got great tits."

Fifteen minutes later, the poet left center stage. A tiny birdlike woman took her place to announce the commencement of the open mike portion of the program. "I do hope everyone who would like to read tonight has entered his or her name on the reading roster," she chirped. "That was the piece of paper my excellent assistant passed around when you came in. We ask only that you limit yourself to one or two poems, and not go on for more than five minutes. Now let's all give ourselves a big round of applause for the success of this program, because incredibly, tonight, we have twenty three poets who have signed up to read! " She consulted a piece of paper and called out the first name. "If Rosalind Rosenberger would like to come up to the podium, we're ready to begin."

"Are you going to read?" I asked Alex, who was fidgeting and messing about with a many times folded, graying piece of paper, a scrap of loose leaf that looked torn from a kid's composition book.

"No," he said gruffly. "I wrote this today but it's not ready to share yet."

"Let me see it," I said, making a grab. "I'm a professional writer. Maybe I can assist."He closed his fist around the scrap. "I said I'm not ready to share," he said slowly. Did I detect a hint of menace? He gave off the same vibe as a junkyard dog whose bone I was about to take away.

"Okay, have it your way," I said, retracting my hand and moving my leg. I slid my chair over a few inches. "Listen, I disagree with you about that poet. I'm surprised how good she was, and I really did think she was great. Raw stuff, but well strung together. She had a real cadence going, artful language. But if we're going to sit and listen to all these people, I'm really going to need a drink. Where's that waiter?"

"We can go now," Alex said, standing up. "I only came to hear the featured poet." He pushed past the crammed tables and headed for the exit. I looked around and saw there must have been at least two dozen people waiting their turn to read.

On the sidewalk Alex lavishly exhaled as though he'd been containing something noxious. For the first time, I noticed he was wearing glasses, classic, fragile looking things with old fashioned gold wire rims. He took them off and carefully slid them into his breast pocket. In the fading spring night light his dark eyes looked fatigued. "Let's get some dinner," he said. "You don't have to buy. We're meeting a friend of mine, and his girlfriend. He's a rich man from New York City who keeps a horse with me. He owns Galahad. He's a client, but he's also a personal friend. You don't find too many of those in this business. By the way, don't mention you, went on a ride with his horse. He doesn't know I let other people ride it, understand?"

"What's the name of where we're going?" I said, pulling out my notebook. I figured I might as well take notes. Being on the job as a journalist would allow me to participate in whatever was happening, but provide a scrim of distance. It would also prevent me from engaging in any verboten lustful thoughts I might be harboring toward Alex, who despite the siren call of pheromones, I was finding quite odious. He was rude, abrupt, and a disgusting chauvinist. Or maybe that was the attraction.

"It's called The Big Kahuna," Alex said. "You'll like it. It's the hot new thing."

Minutes later we pulled into the parking lot of what looked like an ordinary suburban strip mall. Coming from California, I was used to the phenomena of terrific restaurants in mall settings, but I knew in other parts of the country, this wasn't the case. In this neck of the woods, a restaurant that couldn't command its own four walls usually rated a value on par with KFC.

Tucked between a bank, a nail salon and a dry cleaner, The Big Kahuna looked unassuming enough out front, but inside was surprisingly city-glam. The décor was urban rustica; the interior walls covered over with weathered barn siding and scads of chrome and white leather.

The place was packed to the gills. The atmosphere at the bar was, frantic. A stunning black girl was bartending. So far she was the first person of color I'd seen in Beddington Place. I put the age of the crowd between their late 20's and 50. Despite the breadth of the range, everyone seemed to be getting along, but that could have been due to the strength of the caipirinhas.

A tall, attractive guy was beckoning to us from a table at the rear.

"There's Lucas," Alex said, striding ahead. I followed his lead and then waited while the men did the man hug dance before the introductions.

"Nice to meet you, Paige," Lucas said, as I spread my napkin across my lap. Next to him was his date, Penny, a pretty, copper-haired woman whose hair curled across her jutting collarbones. Penny was that enviable combination of extremely bony but bosomy, but unlike so many women with that figure in L.A. Penny's boobs looked for real. That was intimidating.

"So, have you known Alex long?" Penny said, slyly.

"We just met today," I said. "I'm a journalist for Hello! magazine, doing a story on Princess TaTas. Allegedly she's moving to Beddington Place, but we shall see. The thing is I turned in my story this afternoon, so I'm on my way back to Los Angeles, tomorrow, actually."

"Oh, that's too bad, you should stick around," Penny said. "This is one of the most exciting times of year. There's so many parties and galas and grand events, I'm sure you could convince your editor you have a good, reason to stay. You are aware this town is lousy with celebrities, aren't you?"

"So I've heard," I said, scanning the wine list. "What are you drinking?" I said, looking at her glass.

"Water. I only drink water," Penny said. "Anything else makes me nauseous. So did you spend the entire day with Alex? That must have been so interesting."

"Um, sort of," I said. A server appeared at my elbow and I ordered my standard Pinot.

"Anything for the gentleman?" the server asked.

"What kind of beer do you have on tap?" Alex said. The server reeled off a list of 15 and Alex made his selection, a beer crafted in Alaska. "You know the water's got to be purer," he said to the table. He flicked his eyes towards the bar where a wispy woman with waist length black hair was staring moodily in our direction.

"So, Paige, tell us a little about yourself," Lucas said genially. Right off the bat I had him pegged as one of those friendly sorts, a happy-go- lucky glad hander. Lucas was attractive in that standard rich guy sort of way. He had a great haircut and his teeth were unnaturally gleaming. "So, you work for a magazine. Does that mean you're a writer or an editor?"

"Writer," I said. "My specialty is celebrities. What they eat, where they shop, where they live, their houses, who they marry, who they adopt. The occasional scandal story aside, like a high profile divorce or a drug bust, basically what I do is promotional because the public just wants to have the same things famous people have. For example, If I write that Katy Perry swears by a particular brand of lipstick, hordes of young women rush out to buy it. Actually that information was reported in Glamour magazine. Don't quote me on it. I didn't write it."

"Does a mention like that really boost sales?" Penny said. "Does that mean the product manufacturer pays you to plug their products?"

"I wish," I said. "Unfortunately, it doesn't work that way. Although I do receive the occasional bag of swag if something major develops. But most people don't read by-lines and hardly anyone remembers a writer's name. It's the celebs who really benefit. You should see the piles of stuff they receive just for wearing a designer's outfit, or being seen dancing or dining at a new club or restaurant! And now that everyone's a paparazzi, thanks to advancements in cell phones, pretty much if a celebrity buys a tampon, someone is documenting it."

"I've heard about a celebrity who never pays for any meal," Alex said. "There's a restaurant in Salem claims she regularly stiffs them."

"Not surprising," I said. "Celebrities have been known to do that. But there's always the chance they'll mention the place on Twitter, the place gets a ton of attention, and then, voila, all is forgiven."

"Excuse me, I must use the ladies," Penny said. I studied her back-side (it was annoying small and high and hard) as she moved across the, room, but she didn't go to the lavatory. Instead she went directly to the bar, where she sidled up to the black-haired wraith and began whispering.

"I've got a bone to pick with you, Alex," Lucas said in a buddy-buddy tone after the waiter took our order. I asked for a Cobb salad; both men ordered steak. "That guy you introduced me to who sold me the Sully portrait? Well, it turned out the thing was a fake. I only got tipped off after a friend of mine at Sotheby's took a gander. Of course I immediately got rid of the thing to a dumb schmuck collector from Minnesota who found me on eBay, but it was risky. Hopefully he'll never come to New York and track me down to kill me. Lost a little sleep after that one, buddy. How d'ya know that guy?"

"He gave me his card," Alex said, buttering a sesame wheat roll and cramming the whole thing in his mouth. "I don't know him, but he seemed legit."

"Well, the thing is out of my hair now but it was nerve wracking. I've got my reputation to consider, you know."

"So who's the Sotheby's character who told you it was worthless?" Alex said, buttering more bread. He signaled to the server and called out, "Hey, could we get another basket? And some olive oil while you're at it."

"A woman who works in decorative arts. She lives in the apartment below mine in the city. Nice woman. Very smart.

"You must be banging her," Alex said.

Moments later, Penny, returned to the table, looking peeved. "Did you order anything for me, sweetheart?" she asked Lucas, her lips pursed in a pout.

"Darling, I didn't know what you wanted, I forget if your favorite thing here is the crispy shrimp or the chopped salad." His hand shot up as he waved for the waiter who was approaching with more bread. "My good man, could you take this lady's order? It appears she's been overlooked."

"What did you get?" Penny said to me. "Waiter, whatever she's having, I'll take the same."

"I just got a salad," I said. "You might think it's not enough."

"What, are you kidding?" Penny said. "I order, but I never eat."

The conversation, unsurprisingly, turned to horses. I'd already noticed from driving around with Tamsin, Michael Swett, and Alex, that the logo for almost every business in Beddington Place somehow incorporated a horse. The entire town was fixated on the image, because horses instantly telegraph wealth and nobility. Lucas expressed his interest in buying another mount, but was concerned what would become of Galahad.

"There's always Alpo Camp," Alex said.

"Alpo Camp?" I said. "What's that?"

"It's when you can't get what you paid for the horse because it's older or broken down, or you can't be bothered trying to find a good home for it," Penny said. "So you send it to a kill broker, who in turn sells it to a, feed lot."

"After that it's dog food," Alex said. "Happens all the time. You can't get worked up about it."

The waiter brought our food but suddenly I'd lost my appetite.

"You're not serious," I said. "A beloved animal's destiny to be dog food? That's sick."

"Who said it's beloved?" Alex joked. Or not.

"Where are you staying?" Penny said, seeing how distressed I was and wanting to divert topics. She shot a warning look at Alex and began prattling on about accommodations. "Beddington Place is amazing but so inconvenient. There's no hotel, and no bed and breakfast. The only place you can stay that's close by is the Holiday Inn and let's face it, it's not that fabulous."

"Hey, I like the Holiday Inn," Alex said. "I've had some of my most incredible tete a tetes there."

"You mean threesomes," Penny said. "I heard how some guy hired you to screw his wife." She smiled so sweetly I didn't think she could be serious.

Alex frowned.

"I'm staying with Tamsin," I told Penny. "I'm in her guest cottage. Which is bigger and nicer, by the way, than any place I've lived. Do you know Tamsin? She's a realtor. She seems pretty connected.""Actually, we haven't met," Penny said. "But I have heard of her. You do know one of her family members was under criminal investigation?" Before I could respond, she got up and went back to the bar for another pow wow with the black-haired staring one who was still firing If Looks Could Kill daggers in my direction.

"Do you know that woman?" I said to the men.

"Never saw her in my life," Lucas lied. I could tell he was lying.

"We went out a few times, " Alex said. "It's nothing special."

"She's just like all his other women," Lucas said. "Madly in love. I'm jealous."

"Jealous?" I said. "But isn't Penny your girlfriend?"

"Not sure about that, actually," Lucas said. "I think she's more interested in that woman over there who can't take her eyes off you and Alex."

"If you know that woman, why don't we just invite her to join us?"

"Sure," Alex said. "Ruin a perfectly good evening."

Penny returned to the table, smiling slyly.

"Did I miss anything?" she said sweetly.

"Only your entire dinner," Alex said. "Sorry, I ate it."

"Darby wants to know if you're coming tonight," Penny said. "She wants to know, should she leave the door open and the lights on?"

A black cloud passed over Alex's face.

"Hey," he said to Lucas. "We're heading out. Thanks for the dinner, my friend. Will I see you at the barn tomorrow or are you heading back to the city?"

"City," Lucas said, shrugging. "Somebody's got to work."

I barely had time to say goodbye to Lucas and Penny, let alone thank Lucas for my dinner as Alex bolted the restaurant. I felt like a fool running after him, but unless I planned on walking miles in the dark on unlit dirt roads, did I have a choice? Of course I could have called for a cab or asked Lucas and Penny for a lift, but that seemed weird and out of the question. Besides, I was curious what was going to happen next, and why Alex didn't even speak to the raven haired wraith at the bar whose eyes smoldered with pure hatred. I could be wrong, but I sensed her hostility was focused on me. Not that it was particularly surprising. As a journalist, it happened to me every day. I considered it part of the territory.

"So was that black haired woman sitting at the bar your girlfriend?" I said once I was back in the truck, maneuvering Lupa. I wondered if the dog lived in the car and if she'd had any supper.

"I told you, no girlfriends," Alex said, grinding gears. "She's just a woman I see from time to time. Claims she's some kind of witch and put a spell on me. Like I said, everyone wants a piece."

"She seems quite attached to you," I said. "Did she know you were going to be at the restaurant, or did she just happen to be hanging at the bar? Is she a barfly? There must not be a lot to do in this town at night other than drink."

"She doesn't drink alcohol," Alex said shortly. "She and Penny have that in common. One only drinks water and the other sticks to tea."

"Is that because she's in AA?" I asked. In L.A. half the people I knew were in the program.

"No, it's because she comes from a family of drunks," Alex said, scornfully. "Her father's a drunk, her mother's a drunk, her sister's a drunk. It's a typical story in Beddington."

"What's Penny's story?" I said. "She said she never touches alcohol either."

"Penny claims she's a Breatharian. It's against her religion to drink. Don't pay attention to anything Penny says. I've known her for years and she's a liar. Everything she says, she makes up. So listen, I have to do night check. You can wait in the car while I check on the horses and then I'll take you back to Tamsin's."

He drove for a little while in the dark and I marveled at the blackness of the sky and the moonlight. It was a beautiful evening. The stars were white lights. In L.A. you never got to see the stars because even at night it was smoggy. Also in L.A. it never got dark enough. All those houses, those restaurants and movie theaters and street lights lit the place up like Vegas.

We turned in to a driveway flanked between massive brick pillars. The tires of the truck crunched over gravel. A large, gabled house stood shrouded in darkness. Under a canopy of trees, we came to a stop in front of a small barn set to one side of a grass paddock. Alex cut the engine. From inside I could hear the low whickering of horses.

I scrambled out of the pick up truck to follow him inside. The barn was a wreck; cobwebby, littered with tack; blankets and grooming supplies flung willy nilly. Chicken shit and piles of twine and hay lay everywhere. The radio was tuned to a classical guitar station. Alex strode over to a fresh bale of hay stowed under the loft ladder and began peeling off flakes. "Give one to Butterscotch," he said. "Tristan takes two; he's the Trakehner in the last stall. Galahad, Lord Kensington, Marcus Aurelius, and Vladimir, they all get three. Don't worry if you get mixed up, their names are on their doors." Like a wind-up toy, I hustled back and forth, ferrying the hay to each horse, surprised by how much pleasure I got from the sights and sounds of them digging in.

"They sure love their hay," I said, admiringly. It was entirely satisfactory, watching them eat.

"They'd eat me out of house and home if they could," Alex said grimly. "Horses live to eat. And destroy things. Give a horse half a chance and he'll destroy your barn."

"Oh, no," I protested. "They're lovely." I couldn't take my eyes off the one he called Marcus Aurelius, a big bay with soulful eyes.

"This guy's really special," I said. "Who owns him?"

"He's mine," Alex said. "My one and only possession, besides the truck and Lupa."

"Can I pet him?" I said. "I know some horses bite."

"Go ahead, he's a lover," Alex said. "He's got a sweet disposition. Nothing like mine."

I reached out my hand to stroke the animal's nose and was rewarded by the confident shoving of his muzzle against my open hand. At first I touched him gingerly, but as he seemed to enjoy it, stroked him more firmly, focusing on his poll and then down the long length of his beautiful intelligent face, and then back up to his soft, silky, ears, warm as bunnies. I caressed his cheeks and then his neck and then rubbed his bony withers. He pressed himself up against the wood door of his stall, getting closer and closer. I laid my cheek against his. He let out an enormous sigh of pleasure, and groaned, and then breathed a vaporous cloud of hot steam over me. It was enchanting. It was like being bathed in a sauna.

"Marcus Aurelius likes you," Alex said, watching. He leaned against the open door to the tack room, arms folded over his chest, bracing one foot up behind. He was smiling and looked so sexy and warm and appealing that I forgot he was a cocky asshole.

Suddenly feeling self conscious, I tore my eyes away and looked around the barn. It was undeniably dirty and run down and in need of a serious scrubbing, but utterly charming, in an Anthropologie catalogue sort of way. Through the open door to the tack room I could see piles of moldering blankets and a tangle of bridle leather; it appeared this was also where he kept the horse's feed, stored in big metal containers, their scuffed and dented lids tied off with bungee cord to deter and keep out vermin. Something small and fast and dark moved across the floor, and Alex's gaze followed mine and he took in my involuntary shudder.

"That was the rat," he said. "You just saw it, right?"

"Rats? Why don't you clean the place up, or at least get a couple of barn cats?" I said, suddenly wanting to leave.

"I hate cats," Alex said. "Despicable, selfish creatures. Actually the real reason I hate cats is they remind me of myself."

"Is there anything else we need to do here?" I said. Besides being grossed out by the rodent, I was starting to feel chilled. The day had been warm enough, but the night air was damp and cool. My blood was California-thin. I realized I was shivering in my bare legs and sleeveless dress.

"You're cold, aren't you?" Alex said. He went inside the tack room and drew out a beautiful camel hair coat, soft as cashmere. "Put this over your shoulders," he said, draping me in the garment.

"Where'd you get this?" I said. "It's gorgeous."

"A consignment shop," he said curtly. "Where I do all my shopping."

"Well, whoever had it first had amazing taste," I said, cuddling in. "And you have great taste, too, picking it out."

"I do have a few things I have to do here," Alex said, ignoring the compliment. "I like to refresh their water and pick out the stalls. Saves on shavings if I can get the manure out before they stomp or roll on it. Why don't you bring over that wheelbarrow and grab a couple of those pitch-forks? If you give me a hand, it won't take more than a minute."

And that is how I found myself mucking stalls in the moonlight. It turned out I didn't mind the work at all, not even dressed in Tamsin's BCBG evergreen print jersey cowl necked halter dress and Miu Miu pumps.

A few minutes later we were standing outside, the horses moving quietly around in their stalls, gently nickering.

"Thanks, that was fun," I said, surprised I really meant it.

"You mean the poetry reading or the restaurant or the mucking?"

he teased.

"What's that?" I said, pointing across the street. On the other side of the paddock I could see the main road, which was crowded with Escalades and other vehicular mammoths. "Somebody's having a big bash. Isn't that your neighbor? How come you weren't invited?" I teased back.

"The person who lives there is a major celebrity," Alex said. "People like that don't have friends," he said. "They have sycophants. If you want to be their friend it means you kiss their ass, and I think you know by now I'm no ass kisser."

"I dunno," I said. "You got your client to buy our dinner. You must have to do some ass kissing to keep a guy like that. He looks like he could afford to keep Galahad in any barn. No offense, but your place is a dump."

"I give him personal service," Alex said stiffly. "And he admires my training techniques. It's time I get you back to Tamsin. She's probably pissing her pants."

"And what about you?" I said as we climbed into the pick up. Lupa immediately began snuggling, sniffing me all over, captivated by horse stink. I didn't blame her; it was kind of kind of an intoxicant. "Heading over to Darby's? She's probably waiting up."

"Darby is none of your concern," Alex said. "But anytime you feel like mucking, you've got my number."

TaTas Unsure About of Equestrian Future
By Paige Turner

Will she or won't she? Whispers and rumors abound in bucolic Beddington Place, a quaint equestrian oriented, celebrity-driven community just 40 miles north of Manhattan, whether or not their newest neighbor might be Princess TaTas. The singing, dancing diva recently spent a morning touring possible estates where she might hang her hat, er, hats. Like her primo predecessor Madonna herself, TaTas has, for the moment, revealed an interest in Beddington to take up show jumping. (For the record, Madonna didn't buy.) So far, the house hunting has been extremely hush-hush as no estate agent dares jinx what could be a multi million dollar deal. Property in Beddington ranks among the priciest in the nation. So far TaTas is playing it close to the vest, refusing to go any further than to say she's "just looking." If the Princess ultimately chooses to make this her trendy zip, the lady will be in good company as other notable Beddington Place residents include the film stars and media tycoons and public relations royalty Rafe Laurence, Marla Tudor, Choo-Choo Palmetto, Chester Chasen, George Further, and Martin Rogonoff. Princess TaTas recently dined at Martin Rogonoff's restaurant following a morning of house hunting and deemed it, "Yummy." Stay tuned for what happens next. And just how many closets does Princess TaTas need?

On location reporting by Paige Turner, Hello! correspondent.

Toast of the Town or Just Toast?

*O*nce my Hello! Princess TaTas story broke, I was the toast of the town. My Blackberry exploded with voicemails, phone calls, and texts. On Facebook I had too many friend requests; the company warned I'd reached my limit. It was super exciting, but nerve wracking too, considering how much content I was suddenly being asked to produce, and not just for Hello! either.

Thanks to a perfect storm of confluent events, there was a media stampede on Beddington. The first stampede happened when the story broke the rich old international philanthropist Jacques Ellen-Stern, one of the wealthiest men in the world, announced he was about to buy a house. ET blew into town with their video cameras to set up on the Village Green. On the slender lip of sidewalk outside the charming, old school tack shop, ET interviewed passersby how they felt about their new neighbor. Moments after the slot ran on TV, the locals, many of them amateur bloggers and pseudo-journalists themselves, began FB-ing and Tweeting about their celebrated neighbors. It was a media throw-down and Pat, acting as my agent, was all over it.

"You're not going anywhere," she chortled into the phone. "I don't know how you did it, but you've landed in the hot zone. Get me an, exclusive with Jacques Ellen-Stern! Who else important can you dig up? Did you text me about the Gossip Girl and her boyfriend who just bought a house on Guardian Hill? Good, interview him. Don't forget about back stories, has-beens, forgotten celebrities and definitely defectees. Yeah, Beddington defectees. That means everybody who was ever anybody who ever lived in town, whenever. Here, hold on a sec, my assistant just passed me a note. She says some Grammy guy, the guy who produced Billy Joel, is a Beddington bailer. Hunt him down and find out why he ditched. Tommy Schmomolla's another one. And Maria."

I quickly realized that by simply hanging out for an hour in the company of Tamsin and her crowd, I could suss out stories that were immediately saleable to Page Six. Once a week I fed The Post an item about who was lunching at Roganoff's. I dished up tidbits. As long as I did not reveal Tamsin as my source, she was more than happy to feed me info about any celebrities passing through town, or who had made inquiries about living there. To amuse myself, I began focusing in earnest on celeb has-beens and also-rans. Just by dint of their living in Beddington, I made them news again. For Hello! Pat devoured every scrap and sound byte of Beddington-centric celebrity news I sent her way, but she was also working other media outlets, too, and I was shooting off short pieces to TMZ, PopSugar, Perez Hilton, Hollywood. com, AccessHollywood, US, and even People, who suddenly were in love with me and whatever news I could dig up.

Meanwhile, my social life was heating up.

"Darling!" Michael Swett shouted into the phone a half dozen times a day. He was awfully persistent. I'd been in Beddington Place less than two weeks and already had attended 14 events. Tonight Swett wanted me to be his arm candy at a dinner dance being held at the country club. "It's a fabulous to-do to benefit the Lupine Conservancy," he howled. "Is your hair done? If not, have Janey text her stylist and get you squeezed in. Nothing to wear? Just raid Tamsin's closet!"

"Sorry, but I'm already booked," I said. I had already agreed to attend a Revolutionary War re-enactment commemorating the 230th anniversary of the burning of Beddington, all proceeds going to line the coffers of the historic society. Someone from their office had faxed me a press release which read in part: "Imagine the entire village of Beddington burned to the ground, its villagers terrorized, all but one home destroyed, almost 100 years of history erased in a few hours." Who could resist?

Janey was driving. She picked me and Tamsin up in her Range Rover. It took Tamsin over an hour to get dressed. She invited me to go through her closet (just as Michael Swett predicted, she was tremendously generous) and seemed just the tiniest bit miffed when I opted to wear my own clothes. For the re-enactment, she'd turned herself out in a flowery summer frock topped off with an enormous wide brimmed hat that tied, under her chin. On her feet were a pair of high-heeled strappy sandals which I knew would be a mistake, as I had learned you often had to walk miles to any event from wherever they let you park your car, and the terrain could be treacherous.

Janey honked her horn in Tamsin's ridiculously huge driveway and I saw right away I was underdressed. Janey also was wearing a fizzy summer outfit, and on the seat beside her also sat a hat. As soon as we were all in the car, Janey shot out, her satellite radio station blasting Rihanna.

"Let's party down!" Janey screamed over the din.

We bumped over a couple of miles of dirt road until we came to a stone pillared driveway. I was beginning to get a little sick of the stone pillars, to be honest. Where was the imagination? Did no one build in brick? An off-duty Beddington Place police officer was directing traffic.

"Just park along either side of the drive, ladies," he advised as Range Rover after Range Rover formed a line. "Then follow everyone walking up the hill to the top. You'll see a big tent and that's where you'll find the sign in. The bar is to your left." Janey rolled the wheels of her monster truck over a small hillock, barely avoiding steering the front end into a ditch.

"I'll just leave the keys here," she said, breathlessly. "Maybe by the time this thing is over they'll have rustled up some valets."

The three of us climbed uphill for what seemed like miles until, we reached the crest. There was no house to be seen on this property; just acres and acres of rolling green hills and clover meadows and bosky thicket. My instinct was to make a beeline directly towards the refreshments, but Janey and Tamsin had to stop and air kiss at least 50 of their friends. From the flurry of events I'd been to, I recognized the town judge, the town supervisor, various members of the town board, the town historian, a couple of assembly-men, an assortment of historical society committee matrons, and thanks to Tamsin, many real estate agents, the most intriguing a pair who were always seen together, him a movie star handsome fellow with a thick head of silver hair, her a leather-complexioned battle ax everyone called Pudding whose fashion sense, no matter the occasion, was to go whole hog equestrian. This re-enactment was a big deal, apparently, attracting 250 people all jostling for recognition and sipping from plastic cups of Pimms.

I elbowed my way through the crowd gathering under the tent until I found the bartender.

"I'll take a sparkling wine, please," I said to a cute guy wearing a madras bowtie.

"It's Pimm's only," he said. Was I wrong, but was he leering? "Hey, haven't I seen you somewhere? Aren't you a Victoria's Secret model or something?"

"I'm sure you're mistaken," I said, turning away.

"Paige, over here, there's someone I want you to meet," Tamsin trilled. The lower part of her face was stretched out in a wide, beauty queen grin. It was uncanny at times how much she resembled Farrah Fawcett. She was standing next to a portly man and his anorectic wife, a woman so bony and wizened, she resembled a skeleton. This fat man/skinny woman combo, I noticed, was a common sight in Beddington. This fellow had a moon shaped, florid face, and his thinning dark hair was combed in strands back over his high, sweaty forehead. It was going on six o'clock, but still over 70 degrees. Most of the men were milling around in boat shoes and khaki cargoes, but this guy was decked out in a three-piece, pinstriped worsted wool suit and pricey Italian loafers. His concession to the heat was to loosen his silk, polka-dot tie. His wife was a pallid, bug eyed thing whose fine blond hair was pulled back in a Psyche's knot. She was wearing a Chloe sundress; a cascade of diamonds dripped from both ears. Prada peep toe pumps revealed coral toenails that needed attending, soiled as they were from trekking around the dew-bedecked, dusk-dampened, sprawling, late spring lawn.

"How do you do, nice to meet you, I'm Paige Turner," I said, reaching for the guy's hand. He pumped it vigorously, his eye balls glued to my cleavage. What was it with these Beddington Place men who letched at you right in front of their spouses?

"I've been hearing a lot about you from Tamsin. All of it good," he chortled.

"How nice of you to say," I responded. "And you are?"

"We're the Dicklers," he said, still pumping as I attempted to extricate my hand. "We're big supporters of the historic society, in fact everything historic in Westchester."

"Yes, we've been members of the historic society for quite some time," squeaked the wife. "We always support their events."

"I'm a member of the Rotary as well, and Peg here runs the Republican women's booster club," the husband said. "There's a lot of work to be done and they're always looking to increase the membership, get some publicity. Think that's something you might be interested in?"

Saved by the bell, er, rather the phone, I excused myself to make it stop ringing.

"Hello," I said not checking to see who was calling, so eager I was to get away from any talk about me joining a group of lady Republicans.

"Honey, how come you haven't been returning my calls?" Ric said, his voice sounding sweet, but aggrieved. "I've been trying to reach you for days but you never pick up. What's shakin', baby? Tell Daddy what's happening."

"I sent you a text," I lied. "In fact, I sent a couple."

"You did?" Ric said, surprised. "Honestly, I never got them. That's weird. But never mind. Why don't you tell Daddy what's going on and when, you're gonna get that sweet ass of yours back home."

"No time soon," I said, forcing myself to sound disappointed. To tell the truth, I was in no rush to get back to California. With all the work and money flowing in, I was having a great time. "Ever since my TaTas story broke and then this thing happened with Jacques Ellen-Stern, Pat doesn't want me to leave. She wants me to stay on and keep working the celeb angle, which it turns out, is huge. I'm getting a lot of play from other outsourcers, too. Right now, I'm at a Beddington burning. Hahaha, literally. You'll never believe where I am. It's a re-enactment ceremony. It's pretty cool, actually. In a minute they're starting a bonfire."

"Oh brother," Ric said, disappointed. "That bites. A bonfire? Sounds like kid stuff. You must be bored out of your gourd, huh? Listen, I've got big news to tell you, baby. I got a gig."

"A gig? What kind of gig? How can you do that? Aren't you supposed to be working on a screenplay?"

"Oh yeah, that old thing. It's still percolating. The studio keeps sending it back with changes. You should get a load of some of their notes. Anyway, this is real, baby. As a jazz musician I'm really cookin'."

"What?"

"I'm doing the AVN awards."

"What?" I said."

"Adult Video Awards, sweetie. You know that band I've been, rehearsing with? We're called Brass for Ass. We're playing the Friday night opening cocktail party. We know all Herb Alpert's tunes now. You know, 'A Taste of Honey,' 'The Look of Love.' You get it?"

"No, I don't get it. I thought we discussed this."

"They love me, Paige. The adult actress Tickled Pink asked for me personally. She's even talking about having me score her next gang bang flick. This is really good news, Paige. This could be huge."

"Yuck," I said. "Gang bang?"

"She likes it. She loves group sex. She's an animal, Paige. You gotta appreciate her talent."

"Yeah, yeah, yeah," I said. "I've got to go."

"But you'd actually like Tickled Pink. I thought maybe you could fly back Friday and hear me play. I can get you a flight for $99 if you don't mind leaving at midnight from Newark into Burbank."

"You're breaking up. I'll talk to you later."

"But wait, I love you. How are you doing? What's going on there?"

I hung up.

Suddenly a band of riders cantered up the hill. It was the regiment, dressed in full Revolutionary drag and riding fat, out of shape horses. A loud amplified voice blared across the hilltop, horrible feedback from the amp that pierced my eardrums. "Attention ladies and gentlemen!" the voice said. "You are about to witness an important historic moment. Under, the command of patriot Lt. Col. Samuel Birch, you are about to see the colonist soldiers preparing for battle with the British troops. When this actually happened, 230 years ago, a British lookout posted on Guardian Hill fired his pistol three times, but there was a miscommunication! The lookout on Yeager Hill, where Historic Hall now sits, mistook them for friendly forces. After realizing his mistake, that Yeager Hill lookout rode hard to warn the patriots of the approaching menace. But there was no defense," the voice intoned, growing ever more dramatic. "That was because the night before, Washington had ordered his men to the Connecticut coast where the British were mounting an offensive. With no one to stop them, the British troops rode into Beddington Place and plundered the houses and the farms, setting fire to the meeting house and then burning practically every home in the village. Only one house, owned by a widow reputed to have Tory sympathies, escaped unscathed. By noon the next day, the British had finished their ugly assignment, and the soldiers rode out, leaving behind only wrack and ruin."

Three shots rang out at the end of this exhausting speech. One of the horses reared and nearly bolted. Soon after, another flurry of mounted soldiers arrived. There were more musket shots and then complete pandemonium took over as another horse, terrified by the boom and ensuing smoke, madly took off, headed towards the tent area. While everyone watched in dismay and horror, a single bold rider daringly, separated off from the rest of the crew to race after the panicked horse and effect a rescue.

Behind me, Tamsin let out a little scream.

"That's Diandra," she gasped. "Look at her ride! She is incredible! Have you ever seen anything like it?"

Everyone watched agog as Diandra tore up the hill behind the runaway horse whose rider was still hanging on, just barely. In a move straight out of an action movie, Diandra daringly pushed her mount on up right next to the runaway and acrobatically leaned out of the saddle, managing to grab its reins. The frightened animal stopped but reared, and Diandra shouted, "Hang on!" to the rider who struggled to stay mounted. The two animals collided, nearly unseating Diandra, who was now gripping two sets of reins. All around me, people were holding their breath. It was terrifying because anything could happen, and someone could be seriously hurt. I looked around for an ambulance but there was none; no provisions had been made for a possible accident. And then, just as quickly as the danger had developed, the crisis was over. You could hear a collective sigh of relief as both horses set their feet back on the ground, and the riders were able to sit up and gather their reins. With a grand flourish, Diandra removed her re-enactor's authentic French Fusilier Tricorn hat and shook out her hair. She smiled and waved. A roar of applause broke out and Diandra bowed her head.

"Ladies and gentlemen! I give you the Second Connecticut Regiment!" the announcer shouted on his microphone over the clamorous din. "The Second Connecticut Regiment is a unit member of the Living History Association, the Connecticut Colony Military Association, and the Continental Line, Northern Department. Let's give them a big hand and thank them for coming to help us celebrate this important historic anniversary and commemorate the burning of Beddington Place! And brava to that wonderful rider! What an exhibition of riding excellence!"

"Can you believe that brave girl?" Mrs. Dickler said, offering her husband a cotton hankie which he used to mop his head.

"Whew," he said. "That was close."

"Where did she learn to ride like that?" Mrs. Dickler asked.

"That's Diandra. She's incredible. She's British. She's related to royalty, actually. Her mother is a cousin of the Windsors. She's ridden all her life," Tamsin said. "She's very well regarded as a hunt trainer. I can give you her number if you like."

"Oh, no, no, no we're not riders," Mrs. Dickler protested. "Although I do adore the outfits. Herbert, wouldn't you love to see me wearing a nice tight pair of breeches and a fitted coat? That would suit me, don't you think so, darling?" she tittered.

"Hmmm, don't forget the crop," Herbert said. "You know I love a saucy wench with a riding crop," he sniggered.

Herbert? There really were people living here who were called Herbert? Saucy wenches? Were these people for real? I shuddered.

Someone was tapping at my shoulder. It was Michael Swett. "I've been looking all over for you, darling," he drawled.

"I thought you were supposed to be at the lupine thing," I said.

"Such a bore," Michael said. "Some concert pianist banging on the piano while a wolverine, or maybe it was just a weasel, howled in the background."

I laughed.

He grabbed my elbow. "Let's bag this ordeal and go some place fun."

"What about Tamsin and Janey?" I said. "What will I tell them?"

"Tell them you're coming with me," Swett said, grinning evilly. "Besides, they're coming too. Follow me."

Outed

"God, please tell me how amazing was that?" Janey said. Somehow it had gotten surprisingly late. It took ages to escape the re- enactment, given how mobbed Diandra was by everyone exclaiming about her heroism. Now we were crammed all together into Michael Swett's car, a Titanium Silver Metallic BMW 328i xDrive sedan, its interior kitted out in Gray Dakota leather with illuminated door sills and a complete navigation system. Which hadn't been switched on, for some reason.

"Turn right, no turn left," he directed Tamsin, who was driving. I was in the backseat, hemmed in by Diandra and Janey. Even in the car, they were still talking about Diandra's miraculous save at the re-enactment.

"Di, you were amazing, but seriously, have you ever meet such a tiresome bunch?" Janey concluded, lighting a cigarette. "You don't mind me smoking, do you?" she said to me. "I know all you L.A.-types deplore it. I just do it because I'm orally fixated. If I didn't smoke, I'd constantly be putting things in my mouth."

"What kind of things?" Diandra said, slyly.

"I don't care if you smoke," I said. "In fact, I might take one myself. I'm not against smoking per se and for the record, I'm not really from L.A."

"Really? Do tell," Diandra said, slouching further down in her seat.

"We're almost there, kids," Swett said. "Tamsin, bear left and then follow that road to the end, and then it's all uphill, and then we're there."

"Why don't you just use the navigation system?" I asked. "Isn't that what it's for?"

"This place is so secret you can't type in the address," Tamsin said. "As they say, it's off the map."

"What did the straw say to the man?" Diandra said suddenly. "You suck." She screamed with laughter at her own joke before succumbing to a fit of hiccups. "My life is so boring. I've seen and done everything," she said, a few moments later.

"I can think of something you've never done," Janey said.

"She's never gone down on a midget," Michael chimed in. Janey and Tamsin broke out in a fit of laughter.

"That's awful, that's awful," Diandra squealed. "Michael, I'm going to get you."

"Why did the midget need a loan?" Michael said. "Because he's always a little short. Hey, you back there, Paige, dig around under the seat. There's a bottle."

I reached underneath and extracted a bottle of Johnny Walker Black. It was nearly empty.

"Here," I said, handing it up front.

"No, no, put that away," Tamsin said sternly. "Not in the car and not while I'm driving. I don't want to end up like Julie. I don't want to be in the police blotter."

"Who is Julie?" I said.

"A drunken fool," Janey said. "Even if she is our BFF. Did you hear she was trailing a police officer? When he turned on his lights and siren, she tried to pass him. Stupid cow."

Guzzling from the bottle, Michael Swett said, "Why didn't she threaten to have her husband get him fired? She's got the juice."

"Michael, pleeeeeeze," Tamsin said. "You're giving Paige the wrong impression." She steered the car into an opening in the woods and then we drove into pitch darkness. The road was so steep as to be nearly vertical and suddenly everything went quiet.

"Where the hell are we?" I said as Tamsin edged the car into a tight parking spot beneath a canopy of trees. A few hundred feet away across a gravel driveway was a grand old turreted stone house

"They call this Shangri La, darling," Swett said, opening his door and stepping out. As he gathered up his belongings of pen, phone and man-purse, Janey and Diandra were already scrambling ahead, their high heels slipping on the gravel. Tamsin remained in her seat, cell phone in hand.

Swett took my arm and steered me towards the house. "Now don't, say any a word," he advised. "This is sort of a private club. Well, not really a club, because there aren't any dues or official membership. It's more like an old fashioned speak easy. Not that there's a password, nothing hokey like that, but you have to know someone. The thing is, we're the crowd everyone wants to know, so there isn't any problem. This is my go-to place at least twice a week and the owner's a good friend. We go way back. We attended the same prep school, and our fathers knew each other in college when they were on the same rowing team."

"But what is this place?" I insisted. "Is it a restaurant, a bar, a dance club? And where are we anyway? Is this still even Beddington?"

"No, darling, it's not," Janey tittered as we joined them at the door. "As Michael just told you, it's Shangri La. Now just hush."

Standing before a thickly recessed oak door, Michael lifted a heavy hand carved knocker carved to emulate the wizened face of an old monkey. He let it drop once; the resultant sound was like a tree felled in the forest. A tall, pale, sepulcher of a man responded to the knock, opening the door only inches. I immediately thought of Lurch, but Lurch was better looking. A cracked, twisted smile played across his lips as he acknowledged recognition. "Welcome friends," he said, throwing the door open. He and Swett solemnly shook hands as Janey and Diandra and I stepped inside the entry, a cavernous, low ceilinged room with doorways opening off either side. A dead deer's head, pearls around its neck, adorned one wall, and the, stone floor was partly covered by a tattered oriental carpet. An enormous dog lay on the rug, watching warily. "Enjoy yourselves," the man said as Michael paused to stroke the beast's head.

"You know this breed?" he said to me. "This is a Kuvasz. Originally they were bred to guard livestock." He spun on his heel and took a hard right into a Deco-influenced parlor where two men sat in chairs drinking. "Hmm, it's still too early," he said, not bothering to stop. He led us on, continuing into a second room, which contained a bar where a lone man in a checked cap was sitting. Swett forged ahead, passing through to a dimly lit narrow hallway. From there we climbed a short set of back stairs, which led to a mezzanine level. On the landing were four closed doors. Michael rapped smartly three times on the first door to the left. There was the sound of locks turning and then a huge, red faced older man threw the door open. He greeted Swett warmly and kissed him on both cheeks, clapping him merrily on the back before offering him a stogie. "This is Rollo," Swett said. "He runs the joint."

"Ladies, welcome," Rollo said, bowing slightly.

"This is the smoking chamber," Swett said. "Although I suppose that's obvious." We assembled ourselves on a pair of old, slightly musty burgundy velvet sofas flanked by matching armchairs.

I looked around and saw the windows had been blacked out with layers of Venetian blinds covered with dark damask drapes. Portions of, the stained dark wood floor were covered with old needlepoint. It felt deliciously licentious to be able to smoke indoors. It had been years since I'd had a cig, but suddenly I wanted one.

"Wow," I said. "I thought this was illegal. I mean, smoking in a public place."

"Au contraire, darling," Swett said. "This is the opposite of public. You have no idea. Now, for some drinks." He snapped his fingers and a server magically appeared at his elbow, a peach fuzz faced boy wearing a dinner jacket. "We'll start with a bowl of olives and round of G&T's," Swett said. "Put it on my tab." Any protest that I never drank gin fell on deaf ears. Swett jabbed his finger into Diandra's sinewy upper arm and said to her, "Bet you could have that boy."

"If I wanted him," Diandra replied. "What's taking Tamsin so long? And did she call Chessie? Janey and I want to see her."

"Of course you do," Swett said. "The four of you are inseparable. You're like the Musketeers." His attention had shifted to the opposite side of the room where a tall, hatchet-faced but not unattractive blond dressed in dirty riding clothes was holding court before a half dozen people.

"Ugh, that's Miranda Van Oonk," Swett said, his lip curling. "The countess. I can't abide her."

"I don't really know her," Janey said. "I just see her at the hunt."

"Yes, well, she's a dangerous character," Swett said. "Filthy rich and, looks like butter wouldn't melt in her mouth but I don't trust her. Let's snub her if she comes over here. Are we all agreed?"

"I don't know, I might like her," Diandra said. "You know I adore anyone with a title." She pulled out her phone and began dialing. "Tamsin," she purred into the phone. "Get in here."

A few minutes later Tamsin arrived, accompanied by her brother.

"Sal, Sal," Janey chanted, rising up to give him a kiss. He playfully grabbed her ass and said, "You need to eat." Janey laughed and plopped back down on the sofa, kicking off her heels. "Okay, party's started, let's have another round."

I sat up to greet Tamsin's brother. "Hey, remember me, I'm Paige," I said. "I'm staying in the guest cottage."

"Sure do, honey. Be our guest as long as you like," Sal said, genially. "We love company, as long as you don't write about us," he guffawed.

"Why would I write about you?" I said. "I'm here to write about celebrities."

"Hey, I plan on being famous," Janey said, taking a large swig of her drink. "I just haven't decided on exactly what I'm going to be famous for."

"Hey. I'm feeling restless, like I need to move around," Tamsin said. "Anybody up for a game of darts?"

Darts? Diandra and Janey had their heads together, whispering. Sal, was slipping something into Michael's hand. Smooth jazz filtered through the sound system and a reek of cigarettes filled the air.

The gin was making me tipsy. I had to hit the loo. I got to my feet and walked towards the door, having to pass muster for a minute with Mr. Jowls. I asked where I might find a bathroom and he pointed down the hall. "Second door on the right."

"Come in," someone said as I tried the door. It was a bathroom but it was occupied. A man and two women stood in a semi circle in front of the sink to ogle the spectacle of the woman Swett called a countess on her knees, carpet munching. The recipient, an athletic looking older babe with attractively bobbed silver hair, had her panties pulled down, but not off. The countess's head was wedged between the older woman's thighs, which were trembling. Deep, grunting groans of pleasure, punctuated by primitive, animalistic gasps emanated from the older woman. The countess possessed an exceptionally talented tongue, judging from the amount of noise the other woman was making. The one being serviced fiercely clamped the other one's head between her thighs, her French-tip manicured hands tugging at the countess's hair, dragging her closer, deeper, into her hotly squirming core.

"Jesus, will you look at that," the man said as the woman bucked and grunted.

"Sorry, wrong room," I said, backing out.

A moment later I'd located the stairs and wandered through the second front parlor and through some other rooms, which were comfortably furnished with old leather and rapidly filling up. The attending crowd was, for the most part, the Beddington Place country set, with the random couple in evening clothes, including one woman in a satin evening gown. The crowd wasn't young, but, then again, it wasn't old. All in all, aside from what was going on in the bathroom, everything looked quite sane. Poking around, I found another bathroom and used it without incident.

Outside the door to the loo a man was waiting. It was the ghoul who opened the door at our arrival.

"I'm very sorry, but I've just learned you are a journalist," the man said. "I must ask you to leave."

"But I'm not working," I protested, taken aback. "And I came with Michael Swett. I'm his friend. He told me you and he go way back."

"Yes, and that's why I'm surprised he brought you here," the man said. "Shame on Michael. He knows better."

He accompanied me back through the parlors and the hallway and then up the stairs. He rapped at the door of the smoking chamber and Jowly let him in. As soon as we entered the room, he went directly over to Swett and began whispering in his ear. Michael's eyes went wide and then narrow and then back to wide again.

"Why, Paige," he said, smirking. "Were you snooping?"

"Yes, she was in the back room just now with Miranda," a new person said, butting in. I recognized her as one of the women in the bathroom. "Check her phone now and see if she tweeted."

"That was an accident!" I cried out. "I just had to pee!" I turned back to Swett and said, "Tell this guy I'm off duty and that I came here as your guest."

"Come on, honey. Are journalists ever off duty?" Swett said. "Did you get what you need?"

"But I am not working now. See? I don't have my camera or my notebook. Besides, I don't even know the name of this place. I doubt it's really called Shangri La. Or is it?"

"I think you should leave," the club owner said. I looked at Swett who looked at Sal who looked at Tamsin who looked at her feet. Just then Diandra cried out, "We can't leave now. Look who's just arrived! It's Chessie and Phil! Hey, guys, get on over here. We've been waiting for you all night!"

"Hello, beautiful," a short, barrel chested, extremely hirsute man grunted to Diandra, giving her a squeeze. The man wasn't just hairy; he was an ape, albeit a very well dressed ape. He was wearing a custom made Brioni suit, and his feet were clad in butter soft calf skin loafers worn with no socks. Thick tufts of coarse black hair sprouted out from every millimeter of his exposed skin. His thick fingers and hairy wrists were covered in gold, plus in one ear he wore a grotesquely large gold and diamond earring.

"Philly! How are you, fella?" Michael said jovially. Tamsin and Janey rushed in for their hugs. Throughout this display, his wife, Chessie, who towered over him, stood decorously to one side, her expression, as always, inscrutable. The bitch who had outted me for being in the bathroom hovered nearby, angling for an invitation. "Hey, Phil, remember me?" she said, moving closer.

The owner of the place coughed. He looked torn, unsure whether to let things slide or not.

"Please, all I ask is that you and your guests be discreet," he finally said to Michael. "And keep an eye on your consumption. I don't need to be linked to another of your DUI's." Looking directly at me, he said, "You don't know where you are. You were never here. You don't ask any questions. You are leaving." Not a single person I had arrived with said a word to help me out. Instead, Tamsin shot me a weak smile and a "What can you expect?" sort of shrug and Michael mouthed, "I'll call you later."

"Hey, Phil, whadja bring me?" Janey said, all excited.

I was unsure what to do next. What exactly should I do, and how was I going to get home, er, at least back to Tamsin's guest house. Diandra, Janey, and Sal had disappeared. Michael and Tamsin were at the bar, giving me their backs. Chessie discovered someone she suddenly had to talk to. Phil sat quietly on a sofa, observing.

"Need a ride? I can call you a car service," he said, lighting up a stogie. It was an Arturo Fuente Hemingway Short Story cigar. The guy had excellent taste.

Smiling weakly, I shook my head and made my way out of the smoky room and down the long hall and down the stairs and through the twin parlors until I got to the parking area, which was dark and a little creepy. I had no idea where I was or if there was cell service, or how far it was to the road. I pulled out my phone and trolled through my contact list, dialing the only number of a person I knew in Beddington Place who hadn't thrown me under a bus. Not that I really cast any blame. And it wasn't as though as a journalist I hadn't ever been asked to leave. But under normal circumstances, I had my own wheels, it wasn't late at night, I wasn't in the woods, or at anyone's mercy. It was excruciating, feeling this vulnerable.

The phone rang five times before he picked up.

"Lo," Alex said, sleepily.

"I'm sorry. It's Paige. Did I wake you? The thing is, I could use a little help. This is really awkward but I'm at some place called Shangri La and I could use rescuing."

"I know where it is," Alex said. "Hang on. I'll be there in 10 minutes."

Everybody Knows Every Rotten Thing About Everybody Else

"Not exactly your scene, huh?" Alex said, expertly steering the fish-tailing pick up down the steep slope of Shangri La's hidden driveway.

"Well, if you mean I don't need to witness lesbians on exhibition, no, it wasn't," I said, accepting a giant lick on the chin from Lupa who whimpered in joy, crowding me.

"Diandra?" Alex said with interest. "Giving or getting?"

"Huh? Diandra's gay?" I said. "No, it wasn't her putting on the show. It was some countess."

"Oh, yeah, Miranda Van Oonk. Voracious sexual appetite, that woman. Too much for me."

"You had sex with her?"

"I don't tell tales. Or kiss and tell," Alex said, smirking. "Let's just say she's not a confirmed lesbian."

"So you had her," I said.

"Hey, she's somebody you could write about. She's a big deal in the horse world."

"Whatever," I said, not caring. A feeling of ennui or sadness suddenly washed over me, and for the first time in weeks, I felt homesick.

But the work was happening here. To distract myself, I stared out into the darkness, looking for a sign where there was none. Somewhere around the Beddington Cross, we turned on to an unfamiliar road. "Hey. Where are we going?" I said. "This isn't the way back to Tamsin's."

"I thought we might go swimming," Alex said.

"Swimming? It's too cold."

"Don't be chicken."

Lupa became wildly excited as we turned on to an unpaved junction that bounced the pick up to and fro. We carried on that way for several excruciating miles. Lupa's head was hanging out the window and even through my pant leg, her claws were digging into my thighs. "Ouch," I cried, complaining.

Alex steered the car up a hidden driveway which went on for a quarter of a mile. In front of us loomed an enormous house, 12,000 square feet of white stucco punctuated by dozens of windows. He killed the engine and opened his door. Scrambling on top of me, the dog shot out.

"Where are we?" I said. "And whose house is this? Are we supposed to be here?

"Don't worry," Alex said, getting out. "This place belongs to one of my boarders but he's in Italy right now. There's a private lake on the property beyond some woods. It's not far. It's just a few minutes walk."

"You need to trim Lupa's nails," I sputtered, rubbing my tortured, thighs. "They're like razors. God, I think she drew blood."

Alex grunted noncommittally and led the way down a short, uneven path cutting through woods so dark, I could barely see three feet in front of me. Suddenly, an enormous rock the size of a crater jutted out of the ground and beyond it all I could see was water. Driving around Beddington with Tamsin and her friends, I'd seen stunning lake-like vistas stashed away here and there, many of them accessible only by breeching woods or dirt roads, each and every one of them clearly marked with signs that said, "Do Not Enter."

"We're not trespassing, are we?" I said. "Are you sure you have permission to be here?"

"Stop asking so many questions and take your pants off," Alex said. "I want to see how much damage Lupa's done. And we are going swimming so you have to get undressed."

I could hear Lupa already splashing around in the shallows, whining for us to join in.

"Okay," I said, unbuttoning my shirt. "But I'm not getting naked."

"Suit yourself," Alex said, stripping off. He shed his clothes and made a run for the water before I got a chance to get a good look.

Draping my shirt and pants over the enormous rock, I crept along in my skivvies to the water's edge. Alex was already out about a hundred yards, performing a languorous backstroke, Lupa at his side, doing the dog, paddle.

Over the cacophony of frogs, I could hear him laughing and talking to her, his tone praising and encouraging.

A tiny wavelet washed over my feet. The water was deliciously beckoning.

"What are you waiting for?" Alex called from afar. He had switched to the Australian crawl, swimming in broad strokes perpendicular to the shoreline.

Sucking in my stomach, I stepped in. The bottom was rocky, not muddy or murky or slurry as I'd feared. It dropped out after only a few feet and then I was treading water. I closed my eyes and put my head under, the water closing over me. I was instantly numb from the cold.

Popping up for air, I saw Alex and Lupa swimming further out. I couldn't see them as much as I could hear. I struck out in their direction, or what I thought it was. The lake was large. In the distance there were humps that looked like islands, but the water was surrounded on all four sides by thick woods. I swam around for what seemed like ages before I realized I'd lost my bearings and had no idea where I was. I stopped and treaded water and turned back to look around.

"I'm right here," Alex said just as I was beginning to feel a bit panicked. His wild black hair was tangled and plastered down his neck. Droplets of water shimmered like diamonds on his spectacularly muscular shoulders, which I suddenly yearned to seize. He treaded water slowly and, deliberately as the dog paddled in circles around us. "Are you all right?" he said. "You seem nervous."

"I'm okay," I said, my teeth chattering. "Just a little cold." I had a déjà vu flashback of a dream I'd had where I was drowning. In truth, I was a good enough swimmer, thanks to my Jersey shore summers filled with beaches and boating, but the dark night and the cold stillness of the water and the remote location was bewildering. Plus I was swimming in a thong and a lace demi bra, both of which were clinging. For the moment, Alex's eyes remained decorously glued to my face, but I was quaking from self consciousness about my up thrust, heavily cantilevered and underwired breasts, ridiculously exposed nearly to my frozen nipples.

"Hey, Lupa's getting tired. I'll race you back," he said after a moment while I calmed myself listening to the lovesick call of a quacking duck in the nearby marsh. There was a loud splash as Alex executed a flawless somersault underwater and began heading to shore. Lupa yipped once and took off after him, her tail sticking out straight behind her, legs churning.

Breathless, I reached the shoreline as he vigorously toweled off, using his shirt which he'd tossed along with his shoes and pants in some bushes by the rock. Lupa shook herself.

"You want this?" Alex said, holding out the shirt.

"No thanks," I said, shivering, hurrying back into my clothes. "It's, really late. I think we should go."

"Not before I stop at the barn first," Alex said. "I've got to check on the horses."

He plugged in a CD of John Prine as we drove to his farm. Inside, the horses were softly nickering.

"Here, throw them some hay," Alex said, opening up a fresh bale.

"Is this a new horse?" I said, eyeballing a large bay with a white blaze on his forehead.

"Yeah, that's Cassius," he said, topping off water buckets. "He just came in tonight. See the way he's pacing back and forth in his stall? He's having a hard time adjusting."

"Really? How come?" I said, stroking the animal's nose. He seemed friendly enough, for a horse.

"Eh, he came from a fancy barn. He's offended by the accommodations. He's used to having his own squadron of grooms and about six inches more bedding."

"So why don't you give him more bedding?" I said. "Maybe he wants to lie down."

"Shavings don't grow on trees," Alex said, annoyed. "Well, they do, because they're wood shavings and wood comes from trees, but that's not what I'm saying. Horses prefer it when the bedding is thick so when they piss it doesn't splash their legs. But he'll get used to it. He better, or his ass, is grass. I'm not into spoiling horses. He's got to learn."

"Why don't you just tell his owner you need to charge him more for extra bedding and let him make his own decision?" I said. "What's the big deal? If he had the horse at a fancy barn, he won't mind making up the difference."

"Nah," Alex said. "He doesn't need to concern himself with things like that. He won't know anyway; I doubt he'll even come around check on the horse for weeks. He's a busy guy. Doesn't ride that much anyway and when he does, he just likes to go fast and see a lot of action. What happened is he brought Cassius here for training because he wasn't happy with what they told him at his other barn."

"What kind of training?" I said.

"Field jumping. The owner loves to jump. He bought the horse on impulse and paid a fortune for it, but then his trainer told him the horse is not a jumper. He's a dressage animal. Which is not what this guy wanted to hear. So I told him his trainer is wrong. I said give me a few months and he'll see a different horse. As a matter of fact, I wish you'd quit petting him. He's been spoiled and he's been molly coddled and it's my job to toughen him."

"Who's the owner?" I said, curious. Such a magnificent animal surely had an important exchecquer.

"A guy called Michael Swett," Alex said.

"You know him?"

I started to say it was Swett who had brought me to Shangri La, but decided to hold my tongue. "Where'd he keep the horse before?" I said, feigning know-nothingness.

"He was boarding him with Miranda," Alex said.

"Van Oonk — ?"

"Yeah," he added, sarcastically. "Thing is, Miranda doesn't know where he's gone and Swett isn't telling. I expect she'll throw a fit when she finds out I've got him." He laughed that low, dirty har har har sound. It was kind of sickening.

"Does everybody in the Beddington horse world just like to give everyone else the shiv?" I exclaimed. "I've never seen such a dog eat dog world, pardon the expression."

"It's pretty simple," Alex said, turning off the barn lights. We got back in the car and he revved the engine. "Get in here, Lupa," he said, sounding mad. "Goddamn dog, always taking advantage of my good nature. Get over here, you bloody hound," he said as she crawled towards him on her belly. He slapped her hard as she shimmied into the back seat.

"Was that really necessary?" I said.

Alex said nothing but stepped on the gas. I closed my eyes and listened for awhile to John Prine bawling. "What do you mean, 'it's pretty simple,'" I said, referring to his last comment. I had spent enough time with Alex to know he was almost pathological in his ability to hold on, even cling, to, the tiniest fragments. I imagined he could carry on a grudge until hell froze over, unlike Tamsin and her crew who loved and hated and adored everyone and everything on a whim.

"It's simple about horse people," Alex said, staring at the road. "They all hate each other's guts. Most of them don't even like horses. It's all about status and competition and fucking each other over. The trainers all steal each other's clients. The clients have no sense of loyalty. At the same time, if there's a major problem that attracts outside interest, everyone in the horse world is invested in closing ranks and looking the other way, or worse, out and out denying the thing ever happened. Even if it turns out somebody is a complete crook or a horse killer. At the end of the day, the horse people hate each other, but they've got each other's backs. There's a guy in this town who burned down his own barn for the insurance money. Another guy electrocuted a bunch of horses for the same reason — and with the consent of some of the owners', and yet they still get invited to the smart dinner parties. You want to make a horse disappear? There's someone to take care of it. Everybody knows everything rotten thing about everybody else, but nobody does anything about it. The horse world is a club. It's a conspiracy."

This was certainly the longest speech I'd heard him utter.

"Well," I said, feeling around for my words carefully. "You seem angry about all of this. And yet you seem to relish your role as an outsider. You know, Tamsin keeps warning me about you."

"Oh yeah, what's she say?" he said, jocularly. "I know she's mad cos I've never tried to fuck her." His phone rang. Reading the screen, I saw the call was from Darby.

"Yo," Alex said, picking up. There was a rush of indecipherable jabber. "I'll call you later," he said after several minutes. "I'm with someone." He stopped the car at the mouth of Tamsin's driveway. "I'm not turning in. I don't want to set off all her security cameras. Hope you had fun swimming. Hope Lupa didn't wreck your legs. By the way, you look pretty good nearly naked. If you want to ride tomorrow, give me a call. You know how to reach me."

Tamsin was waiting for me by the guest cottage.

"You're crazy hanging out with him," she said, her face flushed, eyes glittering. I wondered how much she'd had to drink.

"What did you expect me to do?" I said. "You didn't leave me a lot of options after I got kicked out of that joint."

"Oh yeah. Well. Sorry about that. Michael didn't mean for that to happen. He didn't anticipate any problems. But then some guy downstairs recognized you and he mentioned it the owner and then it turned out you saw that business with Miranda. Can you believe that woman? What a scene. Anyway, we didn't bring you to humiliate you. Michael thought he could slip you in, incognito. Well, hell, chalk it up to an adventure. Maybe you'll write, about it. What was that Michael said? A journalist is never off duty?"

I brushed past her and ducked into the guest house. My phone was ringing. It was Ric.

"It's like two in the morning here," I said. "This better be important."

"Hey, I just took a chance you'd be up. It's only 11 here. I want to brag a bit. You know my gig at the AVN awards show? That gig of mine you so don't want to hear about? Well, listen to this. Brass for Ass made a video and I put it on YouTube and we got over 200,000 hits. We're a sensation! Brass for Ass is it! Tickled Pink did a bit for the vid where she did this thing with whipped cream while I played 'A Taste of Honey.' Paige, it was awesome."

"Congrats," I said, unimpressed.

"But that's not why I'm calling. This is what I wanted to say. It turns out the big surprise winner at the awards is a guy who walks around with a high def camera in his underwear all over the San Fernando Valley. He's all over the internet. He's a huge hit. I think you could do the same thing in Beddington Place."

"In my underwear?" I said. I was starting to get mad.

"No, not in your underwear," Ric said. "Although that would be very cute. But look where you are, Paige. I've been reading your Hello! bits and your ET Twitters and your Perez Hilton blog posts and you're in the, belly of the beast. You're in the center of cyclone, babe. You're in the eye of the hurricane. It's hot stuff."

"Enough," I said. "Enough."

"My point is I'm going to send you a flash camcorder and I want you to use it. I know some guys in the Silicon Valley who are going to hook me up with a VPN for one of the big studios."

"Is this porn?" I said, horrified.

"No, no, absolutely not. Although if you haven't noticed, every leading edge technology got its start in the porn industry."

"Well, that may be well and good but chipmunks don't watch videos. It's nothing but squirrels here. And cows. And goats. And lamas."

"Listen to me. I want you to make a documentary. You're going to take the camcorder, and wherever you go, you'll record it."

"I will not," I said. "They get bent out of shape if you even talk on your cell at Martin Rogonoff's."

"All I can say is I've got investors. Figure it out. Hey, I've got to go."

"Where are you going? It's 11 o'clock!"

"That's like 9 a.m. to Tickled Pink," Ric laughed evilly. "Love you.

Talk soon." He hung up.

"What was that about?" Tamsin said. She was hovering just outside the door, blatantly eavesdropping.

"Nothing. My boyfriend was just checking in."

"And a good thing, too," Tamsin said, nodding sagely. "Your reputation will be soiled if you keep hanging out with Alex Manos. But why did you just say 'is this porn?'"

"Forget it, Tamsin," I said, wearily.

All I wanted to do was go to sleep. But not before I checked my Facebook messages and tweeted and clocked in with TMZ. And screw it, I was going to drop a veiled note about Shangri La.

"Okay, the last thing I want to do is bother you," Tamsin said, backing off. "I'm just trying to give you a friendly heads up. So, what are you doing Friday? I've got tix to a big horse event being held at Historic Hall. It'll be fun, it's for a good cause. You'll love it."

"What should I wear?" I said, giving in. I wondered how fast Ric would be able to get me that camcorder. "I guess this means I'll have to go shopping in your closet."

Hysteria at Historic Hall

"*T*hese are the wrong flowers," Diandra said, scowling.

"I'm sorry, Diandra, I really am," Janey said apologetically, fiddling with her hair. "These are what the florist suggested."

"The florist? You're listening to the florist? Don't you realize he just wants to pawn off on you whatever he didn't sell?" Diandra said through clenched teeth. "Why must you be so thick? I specified waxy substantial flowers because they won't wilt. This place is a bloody hothouse! You weren't supposed to think. All you had to do was follow directions. I said orchids, tiger lilies, and birds-of-paradise. So where are they? And why does it have to be so bloody hot? Damn these antique buildings. This is America! Why can't they install air-conditioning?"

"But these calla lilies are beautiful, Diandra," Janey said cajolingly. "The blooms are just gorgeous. They make such a statement. And I just adore the fragrance."

"Fragrance. That's another issue," Diandra huffed. "The fragrance is vile! It's hideous! It's so common! It's sending the wrong message! Turn on some fans! This place smells like a bloody brothel!"

While Tamsin set about getting the ceiling fans to spin faster, Janey sighed, pulled out her cell, and began punching numbers. "I've got it all, under control," she said, assuming the mantel of Diandra's secretary. "I'll direct the florist to pick these up and bring us others. Of course we'll have to pay for both."

"Oh, no, we're not going to pay," Diandra declared, stalking the room's perimeter. "Insist it's their mistake. Can't you do anything correctly, Janey? Give me the phone if you can't. Would someone please tell me why I have to do every bloody thing?"

I stood fanning myself in the heat, waiting with my pen and notebook. In less than half an hour Historic Hall would be filling up with the friends of The Society of Retired Fox Hunters, convening for their annual fundraiser. I'd already pre-sold my coverage of it to TMZ based on a tip that two of The Real Housewives of Toronto, Toby Fish and Lucky Lagerfeld, were coming. The Post's Page Six had noted the two had recently feuded at another charity event; personally I was hoping tonight for a high profile public drama. Diandra was beside herself to get the party right; she was wound up like I'd never seen her, bolstered by Janey, Chessie, and to some degree, Tamsin; Diandra's very own personal mod squad, who functioned as consorts, confidantes, and her private army. In the past few weeks, Diandra was flying high. Recently anointed as a premiere member of the hunt, not only had she achieved the much coveted red jacket, but she also was kept busy plotting her way up Beddington's social ladder. Using Tamsin's and Janey's and even Michael Swett's social connections to pull in favors, Diandra had got herself elected co-chair of this fundraiser, the hunt's most important event. Ostensibly as co-chair, her primary role was to play handmaiden and assistant to a Beddington Place biddy, whose name was actually Biddy Maxwell, who had served as the sole chair for years. But Diandra had worked her charm on the old woman and in the face of the girl's youthful exuberance, Biddy decided to take a back seat and stay home, nursing her hot water bottle. The old woman's absence created a perfect void for Diandra to leave her mark. The girl had pulled out all stops, including upping the ante of the silent auction so that not a single item cost less than $10,000. It was also her idea to invite celebrities living outside of Beddington Place who possessed some horsey cachet, and to hire live music, specifically a fife and drum corps. When the main guests of honor, a pair of grizzled codgers who in their youth had founded the Beddington Hills Hounds, were scheduled to take the stage, the drums were cued up for a dramatic roll. Ever the fashion plate, Diandra had tricked herself out for the evening in a Dolce & Gabbana short silver sequin evening dress and matching four-and-a-half-inch peep toe stiletto pumps.

Another interesting detail I'd picked up was that Diandra's production had ballooned monstrously over budget, spiraling at least three or four times the amount the hunt had spent before. This situation, I'd heard, was worrisome to the board, although Diandra remained confident the invitees would be so mesmerized by her efforts they would spend a fortune drinking, which in turn would lead to exuberant overbidding for the auction items.

From what I'd seen at other parties, including a Farmerettes barn tour, the Save The Beavers of Beaver Dam gala, and the Equine Foundation extravaganza, she had a point, because the more soused people got, the more exciting the auction. To encourage drinking, Diandra had ordered not one, but three wet bars to be installed around the room, and had scotched the idea of caterers in favor of providing only cheap, salty finger snacks, like chips and pretzels. Incredibly, she had argued for and successfully won a battle to turn a time honored hunt party tradition of an open bar on its ear, and make only the first drink of the evening included in the ticket. Following that initial cocktail, a signature drink Diandra concocted herself of grapefruit infused vodka topped off with a dash of cran, every other beverage consumed on the premises had to be paid for. Historic Hall never looked better, thanks to Diandra's keen eye for décor. The humble 200-year-old building, at one time a Methodist church, had been transformed into a sleek downtown venue. Diandra deployed a squadron of teenage barn girls to scrub, polish, Pledge and Windex every inch of the hall's banisters, door knobs, stair risers and wide planked wood floors. Every cob web had been brushed from the window sills. Instead of the usual cheesy plastic table covers, white linen cloths had been draped over long serving tables positioned on both sides of the room, and stacks of sparkling glassware, not plastic, stood at the ready.

"Have you tried that new med spa?" Janey asked Chessie, who was fussing with her hair. Both women were wearing little black dresses from the most recent Lilly Pulitzer collection. Tamsin was wearing a leopard print dress by Tibi. "I just had this incredible treatment, they call it pulsed light photorejuvenation. It's only $2,600 for the series and it gets rid of all your sun spots."

"Really," Chessie said. "Is it same thing as a chemical peel?"

"Please stop your chatter," Diandra said, yanking things from a bag. "And all that talk about sun spots and peels — stop it! It makes you sound so old! Look, here are the votive candles. Janey, place these on all the tables. And Tamsin, do something about the overhead lighting. It's so naff."

"Diandra, it says in the rental contract there absolutely can be no candle light," Tamsin said. "And you can't cover over the existing light fixtures. They're terribly afraid of fire, so sorry, but that's out."

"Do you think I care about a silly contract?" Diandra said. "Contracts were made to be broken. Please! This room has to be drop dead beautiful, so just do as I say! Now! Chop chop!"

While Janey set out the votives and Chessie stepped away to make a call, I watched from the sidelines as Diandra paced the room, tweaking and fiddling and fixing. Moments later Michael Swett arrived in a tux, a statuesque, raven-haired woman on his arm.

"We're early, sorry, but I didn't want to get caught in the crush," he said. It was good timing because there was no one on duty yet to collect ticket money. Rich as he was, I'd noticed Michael Swett was really cheap. He rarely paid for anything, and at every gala and party, he was a champion crasher. "Allow me to introduce Suzette. She's a friend." I shook her big hand. In four-inch heels, she towered over Michael, who was at least six-feet tall himself. Suzette's straight, coal black hair hung to her waist, and she had rimmed her dark eyes in kohl. She had high, sharply planed cheekbones like a Comanche Indian; in fact her whole aura was distinctly Native American.

"Hello," she said in a friendly way, her voice deep and raspy. "Pleased to meet you. Thank you so much for inviting me to your party."

"Oh, it's not my party," I said quickly, after Swett lavishly kissed me on both cheeks. His continental savoir faire was annoying. We hadn't seen or spoken to each other in a week, ever since the Shangri La incident, but here he was acting like nothing had happened. I decided to play along and behave the same.

"Paige is a reporter," Michael said. Suzette raised one eyebrow. "She's been staying in Beddington Place on assignment from Hello! magazine, scribbling amusing things about the gentry. Although haven't you expanded your horizons since you've arrived, my dear? Haven't I seen you quoted on Page Six?"

"Wasn't me," I said, lying. "Pleased to meet you, Suzette. I am working tonight, so do you mind telling me what you do, and your full, name and profession?"

"I'm a therapist," Suzette said. "I specialize in couples therapy and role play."

"That's interesting," I lied. "Could you describe your practice?"

"It's a very private practice, "Michael said. "And she's not a doctor, at least not in the traditional sense."

More people were piling in. An aging platinum blond I'd never laid eyes on flung herself on Michael like they were long lost lovers. "Darling! How are you!" she cooed, grabbing him by the lapels and pressing her filler enhanced lips against his. "It's been ages! Do catch me up on everything! This is my new husband, we met on St. Bart's! Where do you get more drinks, I've already drained this one."

"Binky!" Swett exclaimed. "You look wonderful! Did you have your face lifted?" Binky and her new husband moved away and Michael greeted more people and I tried to catch the introductions. The room continued filling and I recognized more people I'd met, people who had been to the same string of events and parties I'd attended. There were people from the Historic Society and the Old Homestead crowd and the garden clubbers and some eco-environmental groups. The hunt people were out in full force, their leaders ostentatiously dressed to show off their red jackets and specially laced and braided leather belts. Otherwise, the majority of the men at the party were clad in old money Beddington Place drag, plaid, or pink, trousers embroidered with tiny whales; their women favoring Lily Pulitzer cocktail dresses in silk twills and metallic jacquards. Tamsin and Janey, I saw, had done a hasty bathroom change, swapping out their original outfits for new ones, Janey all fluffy now in Marc Jacobs organza, with Tamsin bucking the dress-only code to wear a slinky Only Hearts tulle camisole paired with a pair of butt-hugging Prada trousers. Tamsin, I noticed, rarely missed an opportunity to show off her rear end. "Tam, are those Jimmy Choos?" Janey squealed when she got an eye load of her friend's footwear. "I saw them last week in Neiman's and almost got them for myself."

"I did get them first," Tamsin said smugly. "But you can borrow."

I decided to take a look at the auction items. It was the usual offerings of on-trend jewelry; flying lessons, horseback riding lessons, a private cooking lesson with an area top chef, a week of doggy day care, a case of wine, a spa day, French lessons, a ski vacation. The prize auction item of the evening was an elaborate oil painting, an enormous five-by-seven-foot canvas of a fox carrying off a rabbit. It was a beautiful painting, if unsettling, and I couldn't stop staring at it.

"Does that painting make you horny?" the man standing next to me asked. In this particular crowd, he didn't exactly blend in. Unlike the preppy guys with their aquiline noses and English Episcopal school boy good looks, this guy's hair was a little too long, his nose too broad, and his jacket, while nicely cut, was black leather. A quick look at his shoes, (expensive, classic, Italian) inferred he had good taste, but since they were unpolished and run down at the heels, I wondered if he was a poser or a just formerly rich Beddington Place guy who had run through all his money.

"Horny? Not quite," I said, looking down my nose. I had a good inch and a half on him, thanks to a borrowed pair of Tamsin's high heels.

"Aw, come on, it's erotic to see a predator with its prey," the guy said, teasingly. "Tracking and stalking and killing is part of the life force. It's primitive. It's visceral. It's earthy. Plus it's a gorgeous painting. Look at that color. Look at those brush strokes. Look at that attention to detail. Look at the way the light falls on the floor of the forest."

"You must be the artist," I said, extending my hand. "I'm Paige Turner, the journalist."

His eyebrow lifted. "Hey, pleasure to meet you but I should tell you I never read. I don't watch TV either and I rarely use the Internet. I'm too busy painting and I don't have time for that shit."

"Bully for you," I told him.

"So, um, you dig this crazy scene?" the painter said. "Breathing in the molecules of all these Beddington maniacs? Thank God I haven't spent my whole life in this crazy place. I'll never be one of them."

"Really? Why is that?" I asked. "And by the way, what's your name?"

"Roy, Roy Ralston. Yeah, as in the dog food company, but I'm no, dog. Well, I am a horn dog, but that goes without saying."

"I wouldn't know," I said. "So, um are you a local?"

"Well, yes and no. My family is from here. I went to Rip before they sent me off to boarding school. I went to Putney, actually, in Vermont. You've heard of it? After graduation, I split for the west coast to attend the San Francisco Institute of Art. Didn't finish. Stayed in California for awhile, hanging around Monterey, Santa Cruz and Big Sur for a couple of years. Lived on a commune in Soquel, painting the Pacific. Eventually the images bored me. I split for Mexico where I got caught up in the Mexican art scene. I followed in the footsteps of Diego Rivera and the Chicano tattoo artists for awhile – have you seen the work of Ricardo Ortega? Amazing. After that I spent some time in Austin, Texas, where I got into painting portraits of all the top country western stars. That was pretty crazy. After a portrait I did of Willie Nelson made me famous for 15 minutes, I traveled along the Mississippi where I turned my attention towards natural realism, painting birds and snakes and just about every weird kind of rodent you've ever dreamed of. You ever see a Mississippi river rat? No shit, they are as big as cats."

"Ick, I don't like rats," I said.

"No shit, who does?" Roy said. "Then I got the call that one of my babies was being born. See, ahem, I'm always getting notified by some woman telling me she's knocked up and having my child, but this time the, woman said she was having it here, in Beddington Place. She was somebody I'd been in and out of a relationship with for years and I guess I must have impregnated her on a booty call. So that's what's brought me home and now I'm painting the local wildlife. I'm selling canvasses as fast as I can paint 'em. Two people have already come up to me inquiring about that fox."

"It's a pretty awesome fox," I admitted. "So confident, so rapacious, so vulturine. I wonder how many people identify with the predator. Great job you did with the rabbit, too, but its expression is so depressing. Look, it's not even dead. Its eye is still open."

"It's not dead but it's given up," Roy said. "The person regarding the art will subconsciously choose which animal they identify with. Are they the prey or the predator? That's life in a nutshell in Beddington Place. Eat, or be eaten."

Just then Chessie meandered over with a cocktail in her hand. "I think this was a bad idea, the cash bar," she murmured. "Don't look now, but it looks like there's about to be a mutiny at the drinks tables."

I turned to see Diandra striding purposefully to the bar. "I need everyone's attention!" she said, shouting in to a microphone. "Please listen up!" Just as the horses she trained, so did the party-goers respond immediately to her commanding tone.

"I understand some of you are upset about this change in protocol," she said, adjusting the microphone's volume. Then she gave one of her stunning smiles and flung herself into rally mode. "Just remember how every dollar you spend tonight is going to a good cause. We're here to help the retired fox hunters, a noble and brave pair. Bless their hearts! These men are elderly. They require our consideration and our care, and who is better able to care for them besides us? So don't be shy. Drink up! Now, as I'm sure you've all noticed, it's a beautiful evening, but very warm. I know you must all be parched! And while I hope you've enjoyed the special cocktail of the evening, which by the way, is my very own recipe, please keep in mind we also have masses of wine and beer to get rid of, as well as every kind of spirits! So think of our poor retired huntsmen. Think of what your generosity will do for them. Now is not the time to stay sober! Bottoms up, everyone! Cheers!"

With that she took an enormous swig of vodka, straight from the bottle, which set off a boisterous shout.

"Hear, hear!" one old goat shouted. "Look at that girl drink! That's the spirit! Bottoms up!"

"That Diandra," Chessie said, admiringly. "She sure knows how to win the crowd."

"Pretty annoying if you ask me," a familiar male voice said behind me. "Especially when you consider the price of the ticket, which was 150 smackers." I turned around to see Alex's friend Lucas, his girlfriend Penny barnacled to his side. "Well, hello, Paige, darling," Lucas said. "So good to see you. You're working, right?"

"Hmm, I see it's the usual hoi polloi," Penny sniffed, looking around. "Is Darby here? She said she might join us for dinner."

"Who's Darby?" Roy Ralston said, ogling Penny's chest.

"Paige, I think we're going to take a spin around the room to see who's who is here," Lucas said. "Will we be seeing you later? Alex claims he's dropping by. He's a fox hunter, you know. But he never did get his jacket."

"That's because he alienated the hunt master," Penny said, acidly. "Had a little affair with his wife."

"That guy," Michael said, his eyes on Lucas, as the pair moved off into the social swirl. "He makes me sick."

"Why do you say that?" I said, curious.

"Because he pretends to be straight when he's gay, that's why," Swett spat.

"How do you know he's gay?" Chessie demanded. "He was with a woman."

"That's nothing," Swett said. "Anybody can be with a woman, including another woman. Half the married women in the horse world are gay for each other, haven't you realized? Anyway, I know about that guy. He's a Dartmouth man and he was gay with his freshman roommate the entire first semester. I know this because my half brother was there at the same time. But when he went home on break, he came back engaged and, was married before he even graduated. Talk about not trusting himself to be single!"

"So then what happened," Roy Ralsten said. "Is that woman he's with now his wife?"

"No. He divorced. He was only married for a short while. No kids. That should tell you something. This one he's with now? She's a vixen, a gold digger his friend Alex introduced him to. She pretends to be from money, but I know she has to work. He's been with her for about a year. I predict it will be over when she realizes what a cheap skate he is and that the only ring he's going to put on her finger will be cubic zirconia."

Chessie made a tsking sound. "Well, who could blame her? A woman needs commitment. What's she supposed to do? Wait around until her ovaries shrivel up?"

"Please," Roy said, clutching his stomach. "No talk about ovaries. I'm squeamish."

"Yeah, if it's not a fox murdering a rabbit, you don't want to know," I said.

"OMG, he sounds exactly like Diandra," Chessie tittered.

"So what makes you say the guy is gay now?" I said to Michael. "You know, young people, even college students, experiment. That doesn't mean he's gay."

"Oh, he's gay," Swett said with authority. "Personally I think he's in love with Alex. Someone told me they were caught sunbathing on a horse blanket with a bottle of baby oil between them? Chessie, I think it was you."

"That's disgusting," Chessie said. "I never said any such thing. Besides, Alex is a stud."

"He's a stud alright," Swett said, smirking. "Boys, girls, cows, pigs, I've heard that man will shag anything."

"Hey, knock it off," Roy said. "I told you I'm squeamish."

"I think I'm going to get another drink," Chessie said. "Would anybody like anything?"

"I'll take a Beefeaters," Swett said. "On the rocks, lemon twist." As soon as Chessie walked away, he dropped his voice to a low whisper. "I heard her husband's in big trouble," he said. "I heard the feds are on to him."

"I heard he was running girls, he's the money guy behind a massive escort service," Roy said. "I also heard he's running guns."

"Where did you hear that?" I said to the painter. "I was under the impression you just hole up in your studio and concentrate on your art."

"There's only so many watering holes around here," Roy said, shrugging. "You hear things."

"Oh, look," I said. "The retired fox hunters have arrived."

The codgers came in to much fanfare. The fife-and-drum band, stepped it up. "Welcome Monty McCallum and Edmund Darrow," Diandra proclaimed in a stentorian voice from a podium set in front of the stage.

"Uh, oh, I better get to work," I said, dashing off. I pulled out my little camcorder and began filming. One of the red coats, Gary Goldfinger, one of the Masters of the Hunt, relieved Diandra of her mini mic and clamped it on his lapel. Along with the jacket, he was wearing breeches and highly polished knee high field boots. A royal blue cravat was tied around his neck, and he was wearing white gloves and a top hat. "Hear ye, hear ye," Goldfinger called out. "The Royal Order of the Fifteenth Division of the Anachronists of the Westchester Mounted Brigade, legionnaires of the territories known as Artemisia, Gleann Abhann, Merides, Ansteorra and Trimaris, has called ye to order! We are here to anoint with balm and money our beloved elder brethren, noblemen who have ridden to hounds for generations. Ladies and gentlemen, I give you Monty McCallum and Edmund Darrow, true gentlemen, amazing riders, and heroic huntsmen, true leaders of our pack!"

The crowd clapped wildly as the two old men clambered up on the stage. "Thank you for your generosity," the first of the old men said. "I am Monty McCallum and I've lived my whole life in Beddington Place. I'm 95 years old. Edmund here is 87. At one time, I used to think of Edmund as an obnoxious little whipper snapper. Can you believe that?" The crowd roared with laughter.

"Edmund here says he has a couple of things to say, but while I've got your attention, I'm going to speak first. The first thing I want to say is this is a terrific event and I'm so glad you're all here. But I'd be remiss looking around the room, not to see that the hunt and its brethren have changed. In my day we didn't have any Jews, and that's not what we called them, Goldberg, or Goldblum, or whatever your name is. Although you seem like an okay fellow, that is if you buy me another drink!" There was more laughter from the crowd.

"In my day we didn't have any Eye-talians, either," the other old guy said. "But it looks like we've got plenty of 'em now! Linguine! Spaghetti!

Spumoni! Tortoni!"

"Thank you, gentlemen," Goldfinger said, grabbing for the microphone. With Diandra's help, he hustled the men off the stage. "Now, ladies and gentlemen, Biddy Maxwell, our party co-chairperson is here to tell me it's time to party down! Band, strut your stuff! Everybody, remember 'The Battle Hymn of the Republic'? Let's hear it! And thanks for coming, everyone!"

While a bunch of white Anglo-Saxons began doing their own rendition of the watusi, flip cam in hand, I went over to the retired fox hunters. "Would you mind telling me a little more about what you just said?" I asked. "I'm a journalist and I'm filming a news story."

"Sure thing, little lady," McCallum said, preening. "Whaddaya want, to know?"

"Maybe you could tell me a little more about the actual hunting back in your day," I said. "What was it like then in the field? How would you compare it to the hunt now?"

"Well, for starters, we weren't pussies," Darrow said. "We rarely let the fox run to ground. We always got it. And if it did run to ground, we sicced the dogs on it — and we had twice as many dogs then — and they would get it out. Those dogs were fearless. They'd grab that fox and tear the bastard apart. Blood everywhere. It was marvelous."

"And the riders were much bolder," McCallum said. "There was no such thing as a hilltopper. Everyone rode as hard as fast as they could. And if a horse stumbled or got s injured, there was no crying or molly coddling or any silly business about loading it on to a trailer and hauling it to the vet. We just shot them in the field. There was always a backhoe at the ready to dig a pit. Actually, Mr. Sutter, who owns most of the hunt land, he adheres to the old principles and I admire that. A horse busts something and Sutter just hauls out his rifle and shoots it. Keeps sacks of quick lime around to cure the pit. They still fox hunt twice a week on Mr. Sutter's property, you know. Crack of dawn, every Wednesday and Saturday."

"Would you say that some of the level of barbarism associated with fox hunting could be considered a cult activity?" I said.

"Barbarism? We call it good fun."

"Isn't it true that the hunt master anoints the forehead of the newest member with the fresh blood of the fox?" I asked.

"Why not? What's wrong with that?" Monty asked.

"Ahhh, Paige, I've been looking all over for you," Michael Swett said, barging in. Was he trying to stop me from gathering more strange and damaging information? "I see you've discovered our guests of honor and they're treating you to a wealth of history. Did you know these two practically invented fox hunting in Westchester?"

Monty took out his teeth and massaged his gums. I thought this might be a good time to turn off the mini cam.

Briefly turning away to give the man some privacy, I saw the mood of the room had changed. People were definitely getting loaded, but instead of getting happier, they were getting surly. The lack of food and the cash bar was working on peoples' nerves, although it didn't slow down the drinking. Not to mention, the drums were deafening and the fifes sounded like a pack of coyotes closing in on a Shih Tzu.

"Hey, where are you going with that money?" Gary Goldfinger called out as Diandra swept past him with a sack.

"It's safer with me than sitting in that cash box where anyone could steal it," Diandra said indignantly. "Besides, I'm using it to pay the bartenders."

Penny walked over to where I was standing, holding a drink.

"Ewww, they called this apple cider but it's sour. I can't drink it. It was the only nonalcoholic drink they had. Can you believe they don't even have bottled water?"

"Did you find your friend?" I said.

"Darby? "

"Yeah" I said. "That woman you were talking to at The Big Kahuna who was standing at the bar. I thought you knew her. When you said you were going to the ladies room, I saw you talking to her."

"She's just a woman I happen to know is Alex's girlfriend," Penny said coolly. "Have you seen Lucas? I don't think Alex is coming and I'd really like to leave."

"It does seem like a good time to bail," I agreed. "Although I'm going to stick around to see if The Real Housewives of Toronto show up. They're the reason I'm here, actually."

"Well, just because they're expected, there's no guarantee," Penny said. "I have to leave because I see that dominatrix, and I don't want to be associated with her. Calls herself a therapist. She's got some nerve."

"That woman is a dominatrix?" I said, incredulous. It was too good to be true. I could just see my headline now. "An interview with the Beddington Place 'Domme.'" How do you know her? Please, give me the scoop."

"She used to walk my dog," Penny said. "Before she got the idea, to be a dominatrix, she was a dog walker, for crying out loud."

A fresh commotion started up near the door as not one, not two, but three of the Real Housewives of Toronto arrived in tandem. Lucky Lagerfeld elbowed her way in first, dressed in haute equestrian. She had on a silky shirt unbuttoned halfway down her chest which she wore with hunting boots, and white Tailored Sportsman side zip breeches so tight and form fitting it showed off her camel toe. Bringing up the rear and jostling for position were Toby Fish, ludicrously overdressed in silver sequins, and Greer Horagin, who wasn't even expected to come, wrapped in Armani silk. Over the din or their arrival, I thought I heard Janey and Tamsin and Chessie jabbering about their outfits. Within moments, the two old codgers, McCallum and Darrow, made a rush towards the Housewives who they mistook for hookers hired for their entertainment.

"Greer Horagin?" Penny exclaimed. "What is she doing here? I just read that she's bankrupt!"

"I'm sure they've accepted a healthy fee for their appearance," I said, drily.

A few minutes later, the fife and drum corps were replaced by a guitar duo playing a baroque cantata.

"Oh, don't you just love this music?" Janey said, enraptured. She and Tamsin were swaying to the sounds, Tamsin's eyes closed, as if she were dreaming. "I'm thinking I should book these guys for my next party," Janey said. "I'm planning a huge event, Paige. It's to benefit the Brazilian rain forest, which you know is being ruined to make it possible for more women to get Brazilians. That controversial hair treatment, I mean, not the bikini wax. That's where they get the keratin, you know. It's the stuff that makes your hair straight. They strip it from the rain forest. That's what my hairdresser said."

"Your hairdresser is an idiot," Chessie said.

Chessie's hairy midget husband Phil walked over, a pretzel in his hand. I didn't remember seeing him come in. "Is this all they're giving us to eat? Chessie, I need food," he said. "This is a shitty fucking pretzel."

Suddenly a fast and furious voice cut through the buzz and chatter. "You fucking bitch, you look like a fucking car ran over you four times, and then a lawnmower, and then like you got shot."

"Yeah, well you look like a fucking pregnant mermaid bitch who got attacked by a shark," a different female voice responded.

"Holy crap, the Toronto Housewives are going at it," I said, delighted to finally have something to blog about. "Excuse me, but I've got to get a video." I pulled out the camcorder and made a running pass through the throng. By the time I reached the Housewives, the fight had turned physical as Lucky and Toby kicked and clawed each other, Lucky trying to bite Toby, who was pulling cruelly on her hair. Toby let out an extra loud screech as Lucky sank her teeth into her arm. Meanwhile, Greer, was sobbing. "Stop it, stop it," she cried.

Gary Goldfinger stepped up to the plate to break it up. Manfully he hauled Lucky off Toby, no easy feat. Lucky was so worked up, she took a swing at him. "Hey!" Gary Goldfinger cried out, ducking to avoid her pummeling fists. A couple of plaid pants jumped in to restrain Lucky, whose teeth were still bared. "Hey, watch those nails," Gary admonished Toby, who was still working her varnished claws. "Scratch me and you'll be sorry, " Gary warned. "And I don't care if you are a celebrity."

"Wonderful, wonderful show," Michael Swett said, clapping, before calling out to the crowd. "Drinks on the house for everyone! Show's over, the girls are going to kiss and make up, let's everyone get back to the bar and having fun!"

There was a rush for the booze and Diandra walked over, scowling. "What are you up to?" she hissed. "They were all going to drink again anyway and you know they would have paid."

"Good public relations, darling," Swett smoothly said. "You'll see, my little pumpkin, this spurt of generosity will pay off in the end. Besides, I think you've embezzled enough loot for the evening."

Greer Horagin walked over to me. Her mascara was running. "Aren't you Paige Turner, the celebrity columnist?" she said worriedly. "I do hope you're not planning on writing about this. I don't think I can, handle much more negative publicity. These last few weeks have been very hard for me."

"Oh, no worries," I lied. "I'm just here to write about the fox hunters."

Janey gave a little scream of delight and held her arms open. "Billy, darling, you've arrived," she said to a curious looking, owl-like man wearing a Brooks Brothers suit and tortoise-shell glasses. A beautiful if ludicrous green suede tricorn hat, complete with an ostrich feather, perched on the top of his head. He was also carrying a briefcase.

"This is my husband, Billy," Janey said to me. "Billy, this is Paige. Darling, you're so late. Did you just get off the train?"

"Yes, the king has just left his counting house where he's been counting all his money," Swett rudely said. "How are you, Bill? Rich enough yet?"

"Some of us enjoy working for a living, Mike," Janey's husband said, his tone mild and unassuming. "How are you, precious?" he said to his wife. "Are you having a wonderful evening?"

"This man is one of the richest men in the world," Swett said to me. "But he has to work for it. How boring!"

"Hey," I said. "Some of us like to work."

"Not me. Say, Bill, what's up with the hat? Who are you impersonating? Robin Hood?" Swett guffawed.

"Janey got it for me," Billy said, shrugging. "She found it on some website."

"I found it on Headgear for the Upwardly Noble," Janey said proudly. "I love that site. Everything is so authentic and well crafted. And screw you, Michael. This is the first I've heard you've got something against feathers. What about that marabou fan you just bought? Don't tell me it's just a decoration."

Roy Ralston was staring across the room.

"Omigod, I think I'm in love," he said, staring with eyes of lust at Darby. Greer Horagin, who clearly had her eye on him, looked aggrieved.

"Just go for it," I told Ralston. "Get over there and sweep her off her feet, or at least tickle her with your paintbrush."

"Do you know her? Maybe you could introduce."

"You don't need me. I think she's pretty artsy. In fact I know she grooves on guys who make jewelry. She's probably a pigeon for painters. Go on, horn dog. Go for it."

"I think I will, thanks," Ralston said. "But I need a tip on what to say. I'm not really that verbal. I'm more visual, if you get my drift."

"Why don't you engage her in a conversation about your painting?" I suggested. "Try that bit you gave me about the fox and the rabbit. Talk to her about predator and prey. Or just tell her that even from across the room, you were attracted to her aura." I watched him dart across the room, making a beeline for Darby.

"That girl is taken," Penny said, watching.

"Can't blame a guy for trying," Swett said, buggering in. He'd disappeared from our crowd for a moment. Who knows where he'd gone off? "I don't believe we've met. My name is Michael Swett. And you are?"

"Lucas's fiancé," Penny said. "We got engaged this very evening."

"Oooh, I love engagements," Janey squealed. "Show us the ring."

"Um, we don't have a ring yet," Lucas said, vaguely. "Penny doesn't trust me to get a ring on my own. Says she wants to pick it out herself."

"Cartier only, Chessie advised. "Or Van Cleef and Arpels."

"Bulgari!" Tamsin cried. "Harry Winston!"

Lucas gulped. Penny smiled.

There was a roar from behind. It was coming from the stage. I couldn't believe my eyes: Toby, now wearing a pair of sparkly silver spurs, was riding Lucky. Lucky was on her hands and knees, laughing up a storm, while Toby straddled her, slapping Lucky's butt and cackling wildly.

"Pony play!" one of the old codgers cried out.

"You go, girl! I love you, Toby" Janey shouted.

"Whoa! What's that I'm seeing?" said Billy. "Is that a game?"

"Ride 'em, cowgirl!" Biddy Maxwell bellowed.

"Ladies, what are you doing?" Gary Goldfinger cried out. "Could we have some decorum here? This is an important fundraiser!"

"I want some of that!" Darrow said, gripping McCallum around the shoulders. "These are the best whores I've ever seen!" he howled. "Find out how much they need to raise to bring those lassies to ground. They did bring them here for us, didn't they, Monty?"

"Absolutely the best party I've been to all season," Michael Swett said to me. "I hope you haven't stopped recording."

Swett's date Suzette suddenly took the stage. "Allow me, ladies," she said, smiling. She pulled out her own lariat whip and brandished it at Lucky. It was a darling thing, a bat really, with a neat braid and a silver tip and a tassel. "Allow me to demonstrate how to use it," she said, smartly smacking Lucky's ass.

Lucky let out a convincingly loud yelp and the company hollered and stamped their feet in huzzahs.

"Jolly good show!" yelled a man with a British accent. "All that's missing is the hounds!" With that, a brace of dogs were unleashed on the aisle who sped slavering towards the stage.

"Tally-ho!" Toby Fish shouted with glee, giving Lucky a good dig with her spurs. At the shock of the pain, Lucky bolted on her hands and knees a few feet across the stage, her great mane of hair thrown back, squealing like a mare. Toby spurred her on with another heel jab and Lucky reared, pawing the air wildly. She let out a great snort and screamed, just like a horse. The crowd made whinnying sounds, cheering.

"Brilliant!" Diandra called out. "Last call! Last call!"

There was a stampede towards the bars.

"Well done, Diandra," Swett said. The girl stood breathlessly before us, her eyes glittering.

"We've taken in more money tonight than in hunt history," she declared. "And I made it happen. Wasn't that an amazing performance? That was my idea, to put spurs on Toby. Then I directed them to be horse and rider. They're such exhibitionists, they both loved it! Of course Lucky wanted to be the one wearing the spurs and riding Toby, but there just was no way. Can you believe the height on Lucky? She's an Amazon! But who was that woman who appeared out of nowhere with that whip?"

"That was the dominatrix," I said. I looked at Michael Swett who looked away.

"Suzette's not a dominatrix," he said softly. "She's a role play therapist."

"Dominatrix? A real dominatrix?" Diandra demanded, pulling a face. "That's vile. I don't want to hear another word! Let's talk some more about me. Didn't I pull off the most amazing party? Please tell me some more how I'm amazing."

"Diandra, you're our goddess," Janey declared.

"Yes, adorable one, you're perfect," Chessie said. "You are adorable, you know. We all think you're just precious."

"Thank you," Diandra preened. "But you can't say I didn't work hard on this. For weeks I've thought of nothing else. I deserve all the credit, really."

"I have to go," I said, wondering who'd been taking care of Diandra's horses while she'd been party planning. Meanwhile I had to rush back to the cottage to edit and organize my post. Suddenly I was in love with my pocket-sized HD camcorder. I had a sudden clarity of what Ric meant when he said it was so important. "Thanks everyone for a wonderful evening," I said. "Tally-ho!"

The rest of the evening passed in a blur. After a juicy edit and the addition of extra audio voice over sound bytes by yours truly, me, within hours of hitting YouTube and TMZ, my video went viral and I was gold. Elated, I called Ric to tell him the news.

Somebody else answered.

"Baskins and Robbins," a saucy young voice said.

"Oh! I must have the wrong number," I said, taken aback.

"You want Ric?"

"Uh, yes.

"He's right here. He just finished his solo."

Ric came to the phone.

"Who was that and where are you?" I demanded.

"Hey, honey, I'm at the Coco Bon Bon. On La Cienega. That was, Tickled Pink. Isn't she nice?"

"Listen I've got some great news," I blurted. "I Twittered a video tonight and it went viral. I've gotten…."

"That's great, that's great," he interrupted.

"Ric, I got 200,000 retweets in 15 minutes."

"That's great. That's great," he said.

I heard a woman giggle.

"I gotta go," Ric said. "We have to play the head."

"What?"

"Yeah. The bass player is soloing and I have to get back on the bandstand and play the head."

"Oh okay," I said, feeling bugged I had no idea what the hell he was talking about. "It sounds like your band is taking off. Good for you, but don't forget you're a screenwriter! I love you."

But he'd already clicked off.

You Can Still Have Your Milk Delivered

I can't believe I paid $350 for this ticket and there's not a single thing to eat, not even a sliver of cheese," growled a pretty woman in stilettos standing behind us in the line. The line was very long and there was only one bar, and the natives were getting restless. It was Monday night at Roganoff's and, once again, party time. Tonight I was in the company of Tamsin and Michael Swett; the occasion a cocktail reception acknowledging Martin Rogonoff's restoration of one of Beddington Place's historic landmarks, an old Revolutionary-era sporting house. It was a pricey ticket, this event, but firmly rooted in charity: all proceeds from the evening were earmarked for a fund devoted to historic restoration across the county.

"Just as long as there's enough to drink," grumbled her companion, another portly middle aged man who may or may not have been her husband. "Damn these summer formal events," he said, tugging at his collar. "It's too blasted hot for a coat and tie. I heard Roganoff spent millions renovating this dump. So what gives with the air conditioning? Why don't they turn it up?"

Elbowing a pair of slow moving septugenarians out of the way, Swett butted ahead to wangle three glasses of Sancerre from the brawny bartender. Leaving him and Tamsin temporarily to their own devices, I, picked my way across the crowded dining area into an adjacent, heavily windowed conservatory for a little eavesdropping and eyeballing. The crowd assembled this evening was nothing special at first glance; they were a generic group I surmised must be the "Profiles in Preservation" bunch, mixed in with a gaggle of garden clubbers. Also in attendance were the wetlands zealots, real estate agents, and horse people. Although re- enactment, not renovation, was more the horsey people's scene, the riders who had forked out for this evening's event were the cream of the crop of the WRA. They were the landed gentry hoping to find out one way or another whether or not Romanoff would be realizing his long-planned dream of uniting monks with horses to create a unique kind of sanctuary. Ever since purchasing the landmark plot, the former reality star had talked of little else.

I strolled over to a woman I'd attempted to interview a few weeks before. She was one of my first refusals and I never did get her story. "L" worked for Marla Tudor, the town's numero uno celebrity, and, alas, took her boss's gag order against talking to the press seriously . I liked "L" anyway, since she seemed like a real person, plus she was the only woman in the room besides me wearing boots. At my approach, "L" offered a thin smile and directed my attention to the woman standing beside her, a lady I'd been introduced to at another gathering; a sprightly, birdlike woman of an advancing age. From the stick- on tag affixed to her suit shoulder, I squinted to read her name. I recognized it as one of the family names carved into a slew of crumbling tombstones strewn about the old local graveyards. For one of my video blogs, I'd taken a tour of Beddington Place's oldest and most venerated cemeteries, populated with the remains of Biddles, Rockefellers, Lows, Lounsberrys, and other New York City and railroad-affiliated glitterati. Now this lady was saying that she and her husband of 45 years were bailing Beddington to relocate to Maine, because of the increase in taxes.

"Forty thousand dollars a year!" the old lady exclaimed. "And what do we get in return? Nothing! Nothing! Not even garbage pick up!"

"Beddington Place just won't be the same without you," "L" said soothingly.

"I know you," the woman said, looking at me beadily. "You're that reporter I see everywhere. Why don't you write something about how the old guard are leaving? All our good friends have left. When my husband and I moved to Beddington Place, it was so nice. Of course everyone was wealthy, but we were never snobbish. Everyone was so sweet and dear. Why, I was on a first name basis with the butcher and the milkman, and in those days, they both delivered!"

"You can still have your milk delivered," I said with assurance as one of the new local dairies had been the topic of one of my recent Live From Beddington Place video blogs. "As for the meat, why not go straight to the source? I just interviewed a farmer who hand-raises his own pigs. He sells the meat to a cute farm-to-table grocery store right in the Hills. Have you been?"

"I remember when that place was a nice family-owned business," the old woman said disdainfully. "It was marvelous. Such service. Your maid called in your order in the morning, first thing, and by noon, a nice young man delivered it in a box to the house. On a bicycle! All for a 15 cent tip! He'd put it right in your icebox, he would, and he was always somebody you knew and trusted. My family had a charge there for years. Now the place has changed hands and they call it something else. There's no delivery and I can't bear to go in. It's filled with yuppies and guppies and run by people who never lived here. Everything handmade and local, they say. Fiddlesticks! A simple loaf of bread is six dollars!"

"So you feel like your people are being ousted by people you consider your inferiors?" I said. "Sort of like a class war?"

"Yes, I do, but don't quote me. It's one of the reasons we're leaving."

I was perishing for another glass of Sancerre, but the line was too long at the bar. Silver Surfer, the nickname I'd given to that hunky older-guy realtor was standing alone, so I said goodbye to the not-so-rich anymore old girl and "L," and went over to talk to him. We'd met at the re-enactment when he was with Pudding. His real name was one of the ones I'd seen on, the village tombstones, but I called him Silver Surfer because of his hair, which he wore on the long side, which gave him a cool, aging Beach Boy, surfer-dude look. He'd retained the teen habit of flicking his hair from his eyes, just as I imagined he must have done in boarding school. Unlike the rest of the local realtors I'd tried to interview about celebrity buying habits, he loved talking about the Beddington boldfaced names and their eccentric buying habits. His very best info, however, he shared with me only under one condition: that as a source, he remain anonymous.

"Hey," I said. "Good turnout, don't you think?"

"Everyone wants a chance to shake the hand of Martin Rogonoff," Silver Surfer said. "And, of course, his beautiful wife, Michelle."

"So what's new?" I said, knowing he was always up for talking shop. The man never tired of discussing real estate, which he deemed a sexy subject.

"You've heard how two huge rival agencies are opening up new offices," he said.

"No, I haven't," I lied, because of course I had heard. I'd been marooned in Beddington Place for over a month, and by now I had the inside track on whatever passed for breaking news.

"It's going to be bloody," Silver Surfer said with relish. I knew he loved nothing more than a battle. "It's going to be brutal. They'll go after each other tooth and nail. It'll be a blood bath as they fight for dominion."

"How so?" I said, feigning ignorance of real estate wars. It was certain there would be a raid for the best agents, but I wondered what else was in store, and, more importantly, if it was something I could blog about and make money from.

"It'll start with the agents, raids and an elaborate game of spy vs. spy," Silver Surfer purred. He was like a big cat, salivating over a choice piece of meat. "Next will be a series of brutal assaults via email, and escalating braggadocio press releases, and possibly a shake up in managements. It will get low down and dirty. Heads will roll. The war will be advanced through competing advertising campaigns, and influence through the media. You'll see. You may even be a part of it since you're blogging about everything now."

"How rough do you think it's going to get?" I said. "Are you saying people might lose their jobs?"

"Worse," Silver Surfer said.

There was a general flurry and rustling when Martin Rogonoff made his entrance. He came into the room, preceded by his wife, who stepped to one side as Martin approached the podium.

"Excuse me, show time, I've got to get closer," I said, pulling out my notebook.

"When my wife and I bought this place, it was practically crumbling," Romanoff began.

He talked about how the first time he saw the building, and how it was love at first sight. "Beddington is one of the most enchanting places in the world," he said. He joked how his wife warned him buying the old wreck was grounds for divorce, and how her being so dead set against it only made him want it more. "But every beautiful thing you see here is Michelle's design," he exclaimed, proving himself a man very much in love with his wife. "These are her colors, her decorating themes, she chose every fabric, every stick of furniture, the plates, the glass ware, it's all Michelle." While he was talking, my eyes flicked over to his wife, who with her youthful complexion and gamine haircut looked decades younger than her husband. I thought about a situation Martin had been in his reality show where he and a woman whose name I couldn't recall had to jump out of a plane into the Indian ocean into waters known to be swarming with sharks. The guy might make his living now chanting yogic ohms, but he was a mean, tough, mutha and everyone knew it.

Martin wrapped up with a slide show depicting images of his tavern. "To expand the footprint, we took down an adjacent old poultry rendering building slated for demolition," he said. "It was a pitiful thing, covered in aluminum siding. Lo and behold, under two tons of rubble, we discovered an amazing cache of chestnut flooring and chestnut beams. Gorgeous timber! We reclaimed every bit of it!" The room broke into a round of applause while I furiously scribbled notes.

"Excuse me," said a woman at my elbow. "You're Paige Turner, the reporter, aren't you? I'm sorry but there's no writing allowed."

"What do you mean?" I said. "This is a public event."

"No media was invited, I have no idea how you got in," she huffed. Although the woman had great cheekbones and could have been quite attractive, instead she'd chosen to adopt a sucking lemons expression and dress herself like a frump.

"Isn't that the girl with TMZ?" I heard someone say.

"Let me have that notebook right now," my persecutor demanded.

"I will not," I said. "This is a free country."

"Martin Rogonoff owns this property and everything in it," the woman said, making a grab. "You need permission from his publicist to write anything, and anything you write for publication will have to be approved by him first."

"Bullshit," I said, grabbing back. We tussled over the notebook for a few seconds. I was panting.

"Wait a minute," I said. "This is ridiculous. Let me make a phone call. I need to straighten this out."

The bitch let go of my pad.

"All right," she said, straightening her clothes and patting her hair. "One minute."

I pulled out my phone to quickly dial Pat. Luckily she picked up.

"Pat, help me," I croaked. "I'm at Martin Rogonoff's and they want to take my notebook."

Pat began squawking. "That's crazy," she said. "Put whoever is hassling you on the phone right now."

I passed my phone to the woman. It was gratifying to see her smug face melt down and go slack when Pat gave her what for.

"You listen to me, sweetheart," I could hear Pat yelling, yelling being her specialty. "I am Paige Turner's editor — '

"She must go, right now," the woman said stolidly.

" — and I'm telling you she's not."

"Oh?"

"I'm telling you right now I have no hesitation spreading that old story on every international news site if you don't let Paige do her work."

"What story?" the woman said haughtily.

"Don't play coy with me. Romanoff. The rumor."

"The rumor?" The woman stopped in her tracks.

"Martin Rogonoff. The rumor," Pat repeated. "The rodent rumor. You know what I'm talking about."

The woman turned linen white. She was trembling.

"You think that story is dead?" Pat cackled. "Ha. Think again. Rodent rumor. Rodent rumor. Google it. Now shut up and get away from my reporter." In a trice, the woman handed me back my phone, her face ashen.

"Write whatever you want about tonight," she croaked. She looked close to passing out. "Just don't write anything about you-know-what."

"What?" I said. "You don't want me to write about the chestnut beams?"

The woman slunk away. Michael Swett sidled up, laughing. "To think she had the nerve to bring up that old rodent story. I forget now. Was it supposed to be a gerbil or a hamster? Pat is the only human being in the world who could handle that scene," he added. "You were right to call her."

"Well, it's not like you were going to help," I told him. "We both know your track record."

"Ouch," Swett said. "Let's go do some shots."

"I thought they were only serving wine at this thing," I said.

"Please. You doubt me?"

At the bar, Swett ordered two Jameson's.

"Bottoms up," he said, swigging his.

"You can have mine," I told him. "I'm not that into whiskey."

"If you insist," Swett said, drinking up.

"I think I have to go back and listen to what the town historian is saying," I said, after a moment. "He's at the podium now, I better get over there."

"I can't listen to that old bore," Swett said, signaling the bartender, for another. "If I have to hear another word of his blather, I'll kill myself. This bar is awfully nice, though, isn't it? I think we should come for lunch. Speaking of, I'm starving. How do they get away with this? Three hundred and fifty dollars a ticket and all they offered me was a dinky peanut butter cookie."

"You paid?" I said. "I thought Tamsin got us all in on her freebie realtor tickets."

"Never mind," Swett said. "I say we quit this joint and get some dinner. I know a swell place you haven't been to yet."

"What about Tamsin? I said.

"She'll find her way," Swett said airily. "Why don't you run along and powder your nose and I'll meet you out front in a minute? Bartender!"

Outside, when the valet brought up the car, Swett asked if I had a couple dollars. "Sorry, darling, I don't carry small bills," he said after I tipped the kid. "In fact, I think I left my wallet at home. Can you put dinner on your expense account?" I grimaced.

Two minutes down the road, Swett did a U-ey.

"Whee," he said as the car spun around, me gripping the upholstery.

"What the hell?" I said as he fumbled with the clutch.

"Changed my mind, darling," he said when he got the car back under control and moving in a fresh direction. "First, we must stop at the barn. I want to check on my horsey."

"What horse is that?" I said. "Would that be Cassius?"

Swett shot me a suspicious look.

"How do you know his name?" he asked.

"Because I've been helping take care of him," I said. "After I ride with Alex."

"You're riding with Alex?" Swett said, surprised. "I didn't know that. Are you screwing him? Every woman who rides with him does, eventually."

"No, I am not screwing him," I said with asperity. "I have a boy-friend."

"So I've heard, but he's back in El Lay and you're here now, flirting with Mr. Hunky. Besides, I heard your boyfriend is in the film business and you know how those people work. That's why the ones who want to stay married move their asses here. It's so boring in terms of new people they meet to have sex with, they just give up and have sex with each other. But the husbands still fuck guys. I dare say I could fuck any married man in Beddington." He laughed.

I chose to keep my mouth shut.

"Watch out," Swett said, swerving to avoid a raccoon crossing the road. The night was dark and foggy. Every headlight on the road — and, there weren't many — hurt my eyes.

"Could you drive a little slower?" I said.

"I am driving slow, for me. You should see me when I drive fast," Swett said. "Besides, I'm a really good driver."

"Okay," I said, gripping the arm rest.

"You know I put my horse with Alex because of Miranda van Ooonk," he said conversationally, his eyes back on the road. "Light me a cigarette, will you? I hate that bitch. Some nerve she's got, calling herself a trainer. She couldn't train a dog! She talked me into buying this horse, said he was 'made,' jumps everything, but he's green, totally unschooled. She really took me to the cleaners! I wonder how much she really paid for him! The final straw was her handing me a bill for shoeing when the fucking horse is barefoot! That's another reason I bought him. He's an Irish Thoroughbred. Never ate a thing but grass until they brought him here. Totally natural foot. Miranda completely forgets that I know this and bills me for fucking shoes. Is that the limit? I expect to get ripped off by trainers. Every one of them is a thief. But Miranda is over the top. Screw that whore."

I digested this information. It was just more grist for the mill.

His foot seemed heavier on the accelerator and he kept looking at me between puffs. I was beginning to perspire with severe passenger anxiety.

"I'd sure love to give Alex a blow-job," Swett went on, knowing it annoyed me when he was lewd. "I bet he has a big cock. Even bigger than mine."

"I'd sure love it if you'd concentrate on your driving," I said. "Are you sure you wouldn't like me to take the wheel? I can drive, you know. I have my license."

"Don't be silly, darling," Swett said. "I'm great. Look, no hands."

Suddenly a million things were happening all at once. Swett sped around a sharp curve, and standing stock still in the middle of the road was a beautiful doe, it's liquid chocolate brown eyes huge in the headlights. Swett cursed and spun the wheel to avoid hitting it, at the same time jamming the brakes hard. I braced for the thud of impact, there was none; instead, a horrible screeching of tires and someone screaming. I realized it was me. Swett's car leaped like a gazelle off the asphalt and launched itself into space.

We were flying. When the tires touched down, we careened off the road; there was a loud thunk and a terrible grinding of metal as the nose of the car scraped over rocks and gravel, gaining momentum after it left the road's shoulder. Then there was a deadly silence. I blacked out.

When I came to, I realized the car was in a ditch. I had the taste of mud on my lips.

The airbags had gone off. I desperately clawed mine away from my face to avoid suffocation.

"Are you all right?" I said minutes later as we gingerly extricated ourselves from the wreckage. I was unhurt, but the BMW looked done for. The doe, unscathed, must have run away.

"How's that for stunt driving?" Swett said, swiping at icky air bag residue clinging to his face. "Oh, bloody hell. I think my arm might be broken. Don't worry, everything's under control."

Wheels Are Not in the Contract

I woke up the next morning, every inch of my body bruised and aching as though I'd been in a fight. Shivering under Tamsin's eiderdown — she kept the air conditioning set at frigid — I thanked my lucky stars I was alive and hadn't been seriously injured. After the tow truck arrived to take Michael's car away, Janey showed up in her Rover to drive him to the hospital, while Diandra drove me back to Tamsin's. The first thing I did when I let myself in the guest cottage was ease into Tamsin's soaking tub, heedlessly using up gallons of her hot water and two full containers of her expensive soaking salts. Next I double dosed myself with Excedrin PM and fell into a heavy, dreamless sleep. Now it was nearly 11 a.m. and I resisted opening my eyes, never mind getting out of bed.

Squinting against the morning light peeping in under the drawn shades, I groped around the night table, searching for my Alleve. Tossing back two pills with a chaser of Evian, I reached for my phone.

The first person I dialed was Michael, but he didn't pick up.

The next person I called was Ric, but he didn't pick up either.

The third person I called was Pat.

"Where's my stuff?" she demanded. It was only 8 a.m. in Los Angeles, but Pat was already at work. An early riser, she worked like a fiend, until noon.; after that she could only be reached via voicemail from either her gym/spa or her salon. Pat was pushing 50, but she looked sensational in her leopard-print catsuit. She worked an amazing Jane Fonda as Barbarella look, but it was a look that required effort; a team of personal trainers and aestheticians and dermatologists worked with her every day, not to mention her annual trip at Christmas-time to Brazil for surgical reconstructions. So far she'd rebuilt her ass, her face, her boobs, and even her vagina. Pat liked younger guys; her current main squeeze was half her age. Sex with near minors invigorated her; all I knew was she was a terror in the morning and I dreaded what she might say.

"Okay," I began. "There's been a little problem."

"You're the problem," Pat growled. "I'm waiting for copy. Weren't you supposed to file that story about the lust crazed yoga nut flinging herself on Martin Rogonoff at a toney garden party? I'm already seeing competitors posting on it, but like the Reader's Digest version. So, where's the dirt? What gives?"

"Um, I never connected," I said, dismally. "My source for the back story disappeared before we could talk."

"And what about George Further? Don't you have something for me on him?"

"Well, he was supposed to be at the dog park the other day, but then he wasn't," I said, lamely.

"Track him down," Pat barked. "Find out what his plans are to play more women after his Oscar-nominated performance."

"I'm working on it," I said. "But first let me tell you about this car accident."

"Who was in a car accident?" Pat said quickly. I could practically hear her ears pricking. "Please tell me it was somebody big like Marla Tudor. Please tell me it was a DUI. Please tell me you got the dish. Was she alone in the car? Is there a police report?"

"Will you forget about Marla Tudor and these fucking celebrities?" I said, practically crying. "I was in a car accident. The car was totaled." I found myself suddenly sniveling. "The driver was hurt, but I'm okay."

"Good, because you need to get to work," Pat said briskly. "I'm waiting on three stories you promised. Also, enough with these milquetoast stories about dog adoptions and runs for cancer and goat cheese farmers. Seriously? Who gives a crap? And if you're going to cover these galas, make sure to get good snaps of any wardrobe malfunctions. Close up! Use that zoom lens! That's what it's there for. Upskirts, downblouse, I want nipple!"

I winced. "Listen, Pat, about this accident. I really need my own car. This hitching rides with other people is insane. There's no cab service here to speak of, and I know you're not going to spring for a hired car. But how about letting me work out some kind of publicity mini-lease arrangement with one of these dealerships? There's a half dozen of them, on the strip who would I think would jump at it."

"No, no way," Pat said. "Wheels are not in the contract. Besides, I thought you were getting around."

"I was. Until this accident. The driver was intoxicated and speeding. Pat, I've got to have my own car. This is dangerous."

Pat sighed. "Let's see what you can deliver. How about a story on that dominatrix you told me about? Who are her customers? Anybody famous? And what about swingers? Didn't you say there's a whole tribe of them?"

I hung up.

There was a thumping at the door and a young female British voice sang out, "Anybody home?" and then Diandra was sashaying through the door. "Well, aren't you the lazybones?" she said, swanning into the sleeping alcove and casting her eyes about. "I've called in first to see how you are, and then to make you an offer."

"How's Michael?" I said, reaching for my robe. I pushed back the covers and gingerly crept out of bed. Diandra flicked her grey green eyes over me in an appraising manner.

"Busted his arm, stupid boy," she said, languidly taking a stroll around the room, her quick, nimble fingers reaching out to fondle things. Pausing in front of a gilt mirror, she adjusted a lock of her hair. "Poor thing won't be able to ride for six weeks, that's what the doctor said."

"Hmmm," I said, noncommittally. "So what's up?

"I've come to make you an offer. I'd like to give you my car."

"Were you eavesdropping on my conversation?" I demanded.

"Of course not!" she laughed. "Don't be absurd."

"Well — "

"Please don't say no," she said, waving her arm in protest at my surprised expression. "I've got three, including the truck, and mostly I'm driving Janey's car anyway. Please, take my sports car, the CR-Z. I don't need it right now and if I can do you a favor, why wouldn't I?" She smiled winsomely.

"I couldn't," I said, already thinking that I could. She was right; she didn't need it and I did. The car would free me from relying on Swett and Alex and Tamsin and even occasionally Chessie for rides. I could be independent.

"You could. You can. You will," Diandra said, charmingly. "Here's the keys. Now if you would be so kind as to drive me to Java Joe's, Janey is waiting for me. Why don't you stay and have coffee with us? Hang out a while. Don't take this wrong, but you look like hell! Poor thing, wrung through the mill last night, weren't you? Were you very hurt?"

"I feel lucky I wasn't killed," I exclaimed, opening an armoire. "Michael shouldn't have been driving. That was my mistake. I should have never let him take the wheel. Just give me a minute, would you, while I pull on some clothes." I rooted around in Tamsin's antique cabinet, Diandra's eyes boring in to my back as I searched for my fave shirt and jeans. As I was fastening my bra, I heard the clump of her boots crossing the wood floor. She stepped into the bath for a quick snoop.

"Fabulous tile," she shouted from the loo. "Tamsin has marvelous taste." She stayed in the bathroom, looting through Tamsin's things. I shoved my feet into a pair of espadrilles and dug around my purse, hunting for lip gloss. When Diandra emerged a moment later, I was ready to roll.

"Would you like to drive?" she said as we approached the car. I stopped dead in my tracks, heart sinking. In the late morning sun, the thing glittered. It was a ridiculously glitzy automobile, a brilliant metallic blue, tricked out with enormous mag wheels and oversized headlights. In other words, a car for a teenager.

"Beautiful, isn't it?" Diandra said proudly, mistaking my reserve. "I bought it with my first big paycheck."

"I had no idea being a horse trainer was so lucrative," I said, stalling.

"Trainer and barn manager," she corrected.

I didn't care for the car at all, but it was wheels.

"You do drive a stick, don't you? I just assumed."

That settled it. I was a sucker for a stick. Rationalizing that the CR-Z was just a temporary thing — what I really had in mind was a sweet, Audi A5 convertible I'd seen on a dealer's lot —I accepted Diandra's offer of the keys and opened the door. A choking wave of Armani cologne came pouring out.

"Sorrrrr-eeeee," Diandra giggled at my coughing fit. "My favorite scent."

Minutes later, trying to find a parking spot in front of Java Joe's, I saw the joint was jumping. Every outdoor seat was taken, as well as every one inside. Positioned in the best place to catch the thin stream of air conditioning, Janey claimed the prize booth, valiantly fighting to hold on to it by the veneer of her teeth. This was not easy, given the brigade of stroller moms jostling and elbowing and fighting each other for every square inch of turf. These mothers of young children were really annoying, but as subject matter, imminently saleable. Two weeks before, I'd done a 3-minute video blog I'd titled, "Stroller Moms, pick up your toddler crumbs." On YouTube this video got thousands of hits, which won me a spot on Good Morning America, which for a week earned me angry glares from all the coffee shop regulars who accused me of exploiting the locals. Then one of the kids featured in the video caught the attention of a casting scout, who signed the kid up with an agent, who got the kid a spot in a cereal commercial, which instantly turned every grievance against me into gold. Overnight, I went from villain to hero. Suddenly a whole lot of people were clamoring to get into my "Live From Beddington Place" video blogs.

"Hey Paige, howzit going?" said one of the regulars, Stuart, an aging preppy dude who whiled away his afternoons drinking coffee and hanging out. He was part of a group of rich, smart, older men who didn't work, but who spent their afternoons at Java Joe's, razzing and verbally abusing each other. Besides their shared interest in German motorbikes — they all drove them — the common interest of the group was books, which they loved discussing. Old books. Classic books. I found this endearing. One day Stuart reached out to let me know that while he was a fan of my blogs, he and his gang had no interest in starring in any of them. That enabled us to become friends, sort of.

"Hey Stuart, how goes it?" I said, watching Diandra bully her way to the front of the coffee line. "Full fat, cappuccino, please, and I'll take the whipped cream," she told the barista. She was still young enough to not care about calories. "Paige, what will you have? Shall we share some lemon cake?"

"I heard you were in an accident last night," Stuart said to me, sotto voce. "Everything okay?"

"Thanks, I'm fine," I said to him and making a beeline towards Diandra. "I'll take a tall coffee, with room for milk," I said to her. "Also, do you realize there were three people in front of you who are very upset right now?"

Diandra's eyebrows shot up in surprise.

"Tell them I've very sorry," she said sweetly. "I didn't realize."

I went over to where Janey was sitting and talking on her phone. To save the chairs, she had her voluminous Chloe bag on one of them and a trendy hat thing known as The Fascinator on another. "Sit, sit," she said to me. "I won't be a minute."

I looked around the room to give her some privacy. I saw Alex coming in. He was with a new woman, a tall, willowy dark complexioned babe with meticulously flat ironed hair, the top half of her face obscured by enormous dark glasses. She was wearing riding pants and tall boots with a crisp white short sleeved tee shirt so clean it could never have been worn. Looking at the pants and the boots, I decided they hadn't been worn either. By contrast, Alex was in extreme rumple mode, dressed in a pair of old, loose fitting jeans, battered work boots, and a cotton shirt so thin and worn, dark, curling, chest hairs poked through it. His black hair was damp and matted. A visual immediately sprang to mind of his head clamped for hours between some woman's legs. But which woman?

My evil attention to this matter was abruptly turned away by a change in the tone of Janey's voice.

"Please don't," she said, her voice pleading. Once again, I looked away, but there was no escaping her anguish. "I wish you wouldn't," she said into the phone. "That's so hurtful. Listen, I can't discuss this right now. I've got to go. I have someone here with me." I thought I saw her eyes tearing, up briefly as she put away the phone.

"Hey," she said, shaking out her long, loose, flowing hair. Janey was one of those women who relied on extensions. I saw it all the time in Los Angeles; it was a way of clinging to youthful looks, but the long hair also was great camouflage for chin tucks and eyebrow lifts and other facial work.

Diandra plunked herself down with our drinks. "I don't know if you care for sugar," she said, dropping on the table multiple packets of cane sugar, refined brown sugar, and Nutrasweet and Equal. She dumped a combination of them into her whipped cream coffee and took a sip.

"Yum," she said, smiling and wiping her lip. A dark cloud crossed her face when she saw Alex hovering. "Oh no, it's Pig Pen," she said to Janey. "And who is that he's with?"

"'Lo," Alex said to me, taking the closest seat. A rich, rank, plummy smell of horse and fresh sweat rose off him. As a summer intern at one of the women's service magazines, I'd written a lot about pheramones, a natural aphrodisiac, whose influence I understood to be extremely subjective. The bottom line was you either loved someone's stink or you didn't. Alex's pungent aroma certainly didn't seem to be hurting his chances with this new woman, whom he introduced as Locket. With only a pair of iced skim lattes between them, Locket was leaning so far across the table as to practically be in his lap. I noticed that under the table she and Alex were, playing kneesies, and that above the table, the more Locket leaned forward, the further away he leaned back. It was riveting to watch him at play like this; it was like watching a snake charmer.

"Hey, Paige, Locket's an actress," Alex said. "She just did a film with Aniket Chatterjee, the Indian director. She's Indian."

"I am Bengali," Locket pronounced with pride.

"There's a smokin' scene in the film where she makes out with another woman," Alex said. "Another Indian actress named Dona. What's the name of the movie again, Locket? Paige is a journalist. She'll probably blog about it."

"The film, it is called Cha-E-Chuti," Locket said to me. "And Dona, she is also Bengali."

"They're not allowed to kiss in Indian movies, or they stone them to death," Alex said. "Now what do you think of that?"

"Oh, now it's not quite that bad," Locket tittered.

"I'll have to check it out," I said, pulling out my notebook. Anything with a lesbian scene, Pat ate up.

Meanwhile Janey and Diandra were bickering.

"Why did you have to sit next to him?" Diandra griped, casting a withering look in Alex's direction. Alex was oblivious; he was too busy playing Locket. I watched in fascination as he dropped his voice lower and lower so she had to slide closer and closer to hear anything he said. In, return, she kept emoting great sighs and licking her lips.

"I was here first," Janey squeaked. "He just arrived."

"Whatever," Diandra said, sniffing. "We'll just ignore him and that Indian tart. So what's on for today? I've already ridden two horses. I'm done. Where shall we go to lunch? Shall we go to the club? We haven't been all week."

"Hey, Diandra, don't you have a barn to run?" Alex said, tearing himself away from Locket to taunt his young rival. "You rode two horses and you're done? I've got six to ride. My day is just getting started."

"Fffffpht," Diandra huffed, unable to resist tangling with him. "I don't exactly see you slaving. And you're foul. Why don't you go home and have a wash?"

Alex colored. Diandra saw it and it spurred her on.

"While we're at it," she said, going for the jugular. "Where did you learn to sit a horse? I saw you last week at the Hunter Trials. It was embarrassing."

Locket looked alarmed.

A long moment passed and then Alex smiled. When he smiled, his eyes were dazzling.

"Diandra, I have to hand it to you" he said. "You flatter me with your barbs. But we both know the truth, you little minx. We both know why you were staring at me at the Hunter Trials. You can't keep your eyes off me, can you?"

Diandra went white, furious. "Hardly," she sniffed.

To break it up, Janey broke in.

"I think lunch at the club would be nice," she said to Diandra coaxingly. "They have that smoked salmon club panini you love so much. And Bloody Mary's."

"Then let's go," Diandra said, standing up. "I'm starving. Paige, are you in?"

"Hey, Paige, I'm just about to give Locket a riding lesson. She tells me she's never been on a horse. Bring your camcorder. You should film me giving her some pointers. Plug her new movie while you're at it. That'd make a good blog for your sites. Hey, Diandra, you come, too. I'll be happy to give you a lesson."

Diandra's expression was daggers. Janey didn't know where to look.

"Hey, you two, knock it off," I said. "What I'm going to do is check in on Michael. Has anybody heard how he's doing? Is he at home or the hospital?"

"He's home," Janey said grimly. "I brought him there late last evening. He was in agony. They gave him a ton of painkillers. Big old selfish meanie, he wouldn't share."

"Well, I'm going to pay him a visit," I said. "I'd like to bring him, flowers. Is there a florist you would recommend? Or should I just pick something up at the Koreans?"

"Best bring a bottle," Diandra said. "The liquor store is just down the street."

I walked out of Java Joe's. Alex and Locket were right behind.

"Sure you don't want to change your mind?" Alex said. "I can hold your camera and film you giving Locket a demonstration. You could warm up Butterscotch." He guffawed and squeezed Locket tightly around the waist. Locket simpered.

"Poor Butterscotch," I said. "But thanks, think I'll pass." I walked towards Diandra's car. Suddenly I was looking forward to driving the CR-Z.

"Hey, isn't that Diandra's ride?" Alex said, surprised, when I flicked the remote opener.

"Indeed it is," I responded, sliding behind the wheel. I adjusted the leather seat and fiddled with the rear view mirror before donning one of Diandra's multiple pairs of shades. A half dozen designer sunglasses were strewn across the passenger seat, Chanel, Gucci, and vintage Oakley. "She very kindly has loaned me her car. Seeing how my regular chauffeur destroyed his vehicle last night in a messy accident."

"I heard about that," Alex said somberly. "Swett shouldn't drink and drive. Or drink and ride, either."

"He does that, too, does he?" I said. "Well, can't say I'm surprised." I turned the key in the ignition. The engine responded with a low, satisfying thrum. "Do you have any message you'd like to pass along? Like how his horse is doing? That's where we were headed last night when he lost control of his car. We were on our way to your barn. He wanted to check on Cassius."

"Cassius is fine," Alex said gruffly. "Never better."

"Okay, I'll tell him," I said. "Have fun, you two. And Locket, better wear a helmet."

AWOL from AA

"*T*hese posies are very nice, darling, but I would have much preferred bourbon," Swett said, waggling his eyebrows. He was amusing but it was hard not to frown. It wasn't even noon and he was already on his third julep.

"Your medicine," I asked, drily.

"It is," Swett said. "Along with Zoloft, Ambien, and cannibis."

"Have you informed your physician about this?" I said, rifling through his cabinets. I was looking for a vase, but instead were great stashes of hootch, along with a selection of fine porcelain. Swett had an intriguing collection of barware, including every sort of cocktail and high-ball glass. As for eats, there was no food to speak of, unless you counted an open jar of pearl onions.

This was the first time I'd been in Swett's house. Although we'd driven up to it a number of times, he'd taken some pains to keep me out. Once I'd pleaded to use the loo, but he put me off, claiming the plumbing was "uncertain" and that "the maid hadn't been around." Now that I was inside, I didn't understand the resistance. While clearly not on the grandiose scale of Tamsin's castle, Swett's place was perfectly nice. Small, but well proportioned, the décor was a delicious mimicry of old school, English gentleman's quarters, cluttered with books and battered leather. The architecture itself was a folly; it was a 1940's stone cottage designed to replicate a medieval dovecote, such as the Scottish one at Eglinton Mains farm in Ayrshire. The attention to detail was so minute that even the double ornamental Roman crucifixes flanking the front door had been excellently rendered. Swett once had commented to me that his Beddington Place home was "merely a temporary crash pad to tarry until Mummy passed," and he inherited the family's Newport mansion.

"I'm rich now," Swett once said to me. "But when Mummy goes, I'll be wealthy."

I'd noticed, but so far had refrained from commenting on Swett's heavily bandaged arm, resting in a paisley sling devised from a Hermes scarf.

Arranging peonies in a silver martini shaker, I watched as Swett painfully arranged himself on a velvet settee. Using only one hand, he still managed to roll himself a cig. His first inhalation was accompanied by a cough and a sputter.

"Are you sure you should be doing that?" I said, handing him a glass of water. "You sound awfully tubercular."

"Dad smoked til his dying day," Swett said. "I intend to match his record."

There was a knock at the door and Swett called out, "You may enter," and two women, one rather corpulent, the other scrawny, advanced, into the room. Both of them wore suspicious expressions plastered across their faces. Between the two of them, they didn't look like they owned one decent outfit.

"You're Michael?" the chunky one said.

"Yes, I am, and I am pleased to make your acquaintance," Michael said, not getting up, but sticking out his hand. "And this is my dear friend, Paige."

"She's a drunk too?" the scrawny one said.

"Um, no," I said. "Although I do have a drink now and again. Michael, who are these people? What am I interrupting?"

"Just an AA meeting," Michael said, sighing. "Court ordered, I must say. It's such a bore, but I've appeared before the judge and this is part of my atonement."

"What happened?" I said.

"Such overkill. Alas, this isn't the first time there's been an incident. While I've been under the influence, you understand. It appears I've been relieved of my license and must attend some therapeutic sessions and 90 days of sobriety."

I looked at the two ladies, who looked back at me rather coldly. "But who are these women and what are they doing here?" I said.

"Don't be tiresome, darling. They're from the meeting. If I can't get to AA, AA comes to me."

"What?"

"I've asked them to come here, sweetheart, don't be dense. This is so much better than sitting in some dreary old basement drinking watery coffee. I have never understood why they must always hold these meetings in basements. Seated on a folding chair rife with other people's germs. Ugh. Not my thing."

"Michael, we can't have a meeting with all this liquor around," Scrawny said. I looked around and she was right; there was an open bottle of wine on a dresser and along the window sills, soldierly rows of whiskey bottles. "This house is full-a booze. I'd say that's a problem."

"We can fix that!" Swett said. "Paige, be a dear and grab all the bottles and empty them down the sink. I'll help! Race you to the kitchen!"

We both snatched up the evil bottles, two in each hand. Swett followed me into the kitchen, slightly breathless.

"Just pretend to pour them out," he whispered hoarsely in my ear. "Quick! Run the water so it makes that glug glug sound! That's a girl! Hurry! Then let's get this meeting over with and get those gals out."

"How did you convince them to come here instead of going to a meeting?" I said, mystified.

"Darling, you are so naïve. Money, honey. I made an enormous donation to the Bill W. club in Beddington Hills. They're practically eating out of my hand." Who knew that's all it took? I ran the water harder and Swett began to shout. "Yes, pour that alcohol right down the drain! Devil, be gone, I defy you!"

"It's AA, not a revival meeting," I cautioned, worried his behavior would draw the women into the kitchen.

"Don't worry about that," he said, grabbing one of the whiskey bottles and taking a swig. "Have you ever been to one of these meetings? You'll see. Here, pass me one of those mints from the cupboard and lets get back in there."

In the living room, the ladies were waiting.

"You got rid of that awful fast," the heavy one said suspiciously.

125

"Really? I thought we were taking forever," Swett said. He settled himself on the sofa and directed the women to a matching pair of upholstered chairs. "Paige, would you be so kind as to sit down. You know, you've been drinking quite a lot these past weeks. And weren't you just in a nasty automobile accident where alcohol was involved?"

"But you were driving!" I exclaimed.

"Denial is the first sign of a problem," Swett said piously.

'Hear, hear," Chunky said.

"I think I'll be leaving," I said, getting up.

"No!" Swett said, his expression pleading. "Darling, I swear, we won't be but a moment. This a going to be a very abbreviated meeting.

Besides, I want to take you to lunch. There's someone I want you to meet."

I looked at my watch. It's not like I had to be anywhere.

"All right," I said. "But no more than half an hour."

"Now, Michael, you begin," Skinny said. "You remember what you're supposed to say, don't you? Say, 'My name is Michael and I'm an alcoholic.'"

"My name is Michael and I'm an alcoholic," Michael repeated, looking appropriately shamefaced.

"Michael, would you like to share the story of how you came to this sorry state?" Chunky said.

"Actually, I'd rather not," Swett said. "Can't we just jump to the part where you read me the 12 Steps? What's the first one again? Isn't that the one where I admit I am powerless over my addiction and that my life has become a sham? I can do that."

My phone made that notification sound when someone has sent me a text. Excusing myself, I returned to the kitchen. The message was from Pat. It said, "Where the fuck is my story?"

I called her right back.

"Hey," I said. "Guess who I'm with? I'm with your friend Michael Swett."

"Tell him to take you right now to the Yacht Club," Pat said. "I just got a hot tip a former First Lady is going to be there. And Michael Bolton."

"The First Lady is dining with Michael Bolton?" I said, incredulous.

"Not the current one and not with," Pat said. "And I'm still waiting for that story on Glenn Close. Paige, you're disappointing me."

"I'm on it, I'm on it," I lied. "Besides, I think that's where we were going anyway. Swett said he was taking me to lunch and that's his club."

"Great. I'm counting on you," Pat said. "At the yacht club, I want you to follow the former First Lady into the rest room if you see her go in. Ditto Bolton. And bring your cam. Images, baby, I need images."

"I'm not following anyone into any bathroom," I said. "And even if I did, I certainly won't be taking pictures."

"Listen, if Lindsay Lohan happens to be there, you'll get right in the stall with her," Pat ordered. "And since when did you become so delicate?"

From the living room, I heard a hymn being sung and then there was a loud moan followed by violent sobbing. It sounded like a calf was being slaughtered.

"Hey, Pat, something's going on here. I've got to run. I'll have something for you tonight, I promise." I clicked off and ran back into the living room where Swett was crumpled on the rug in a fetal position.

"Lars!" he cried. "My wonderful Norwegian Elkhound. I ran him over when I was drunk! My favorite dog!"

"I think it's time to go now," I said to the women from AA .

"I think he's made good progress," said Scrawny.

"One day at a time," Chunky said.

I had barely hustled them out the door when Swett struggled to his feet, his balance hampered by his broken arm.

"Well, that got them out quick enough," he said with satisfaction. "Nothing more disturbing than a broken down man, crying for his dog. Although you would suppose they must get used to it, being in AA. A lot of drunks are big criers, you know. The ones who aren't mean drunks."

"Would you rather be a mean drunk or a crybaby?" I asked.

Swett didn't answer. Instead he said, "Let me have a quick shot and we'll be off. I've made a reservation."

We stepped outside to glaring sun. A car was in Swett's driveway, a white Lincoln Continental convertible, circa 1963.

"Do you mind?" he said. " I could tell the driver to put the top up, but I love the wind in my hair."

"Whose car is this?" I said. "Yours was totaled in the accident and you said you lost your license."

"It's mine," Swett said airily. "Part of my inheritance from Dad. An SS-100-X. Everything on it is original. Dad bought it from the dealer straight off the assembly line and it's been tenderly garaged and serviced ever since. It's the same model Kennedy got shot in."

A large, very dark complexioned man emerged from behind of, the house, zipping up his pants. Another person who obviously had been refused admittance to the bathroom. He was a handsome man, quite muscular, with smooth, otherwise clean shaven facial features, accented by a soul patch. He wore a plain but well-cut powder blue suit with a matching peaked cap, the brim set low to shade his eyes and forehead.

"This is my driver, Mr. T.," Swett said. "Actually his real name is George but I prefer to call him Mr. T. It was either that or Mandingo," he added, laughing wickedly. I looked worriedly at George to see if Swett had annoyed him but the man's expression was a blank. "I'd love him to answer to 'Mandingo' just because he is so very black. You've read those 'Mandingo' books, haven't you? George is so big and strapping. He's simply oozing ferocity. He looks like he could just grab a man by the throat and..."

"Okay, I get it," I said. "Can we leave? I guess I'll follow you in my car, er, I mean Diandra's car. Unless you'd like me to drive you."

"Ugh," Swett said. "I wouldn't drive to a whorehouse in that car. It's so trashy. I wondered what that hideous machine was doing here. So you're driving it now. Very cute. She'll soon have you under her thumb, too, I see."

"I don't know what you're talking about," I said.

"Listen, leave your car," Swett said. "Come in mine. There's plenty of room. I have to be back here soon anyway. I've got another appointment.

A delicious, delightful, not-quite-divorced man I met in Salem, is meeting me for a play date. I just love these so-called straight men," he chortled. "Show me an unhappily married man and I'll show you a queen!"

As we drove to the mansion-lined gold coast of Greenwich by the Long Island Sound, palace after palace unfolding before us, each one more dazzling than the last, Swett began laying out his proposition.

"The girls got a little excited over those Real Housewives of Toronto that night at Historic Hall," he confided. "Tamsin especially was wetting her pants. She dreams of being Lucky Lagerfeld, although why anyone would want to be Lucky when she's so crazy is anyone's guess. I suppose Tamsin is reacting purely to the height and the glam and the overall gorgeousness. Not to mention Lucky looks so good near a horse. Anyway, she and Janey and I have cooked up an idea. Diandra has had a lot of input, of course, and I think with a little cajoling, Chessie can be persuaded to come in."

"What's the idea?" I asked.

"A television show, our own program," Swett said. "We're thinking of calling it 'The Real Horsewives of Westchester County.' Has a nice ring to it, don't you think?"

"I think they call it 'Housewives,' not 'Horsewives,'" I said.

"Don't you see? That's the charm. That's what makes it different. Our show will be very horsey. Our world — the Beddington Place horse world and the North Country hunt — will play a big part. Of course it will, be very glam and very dangerous and very sexy, just like us."

"So you'd show cast members tumbling off their horses and breaking their limbs and horses getting injured and foxes getting shot," I said. "Well, that would be something different."

Swett made a tsssking sound. "Paige, don't be a pain. The show will focus on homes and clothes and shopping and charity balls and galas and of course what makes our world turn, i.e. the petty jealousies, the back stabbing, the pledges of loyalty, the whole BFF thing. That's what will make it so fascinating. And as I believe you've observed, we have plenty of material to work with."

"So will you be part of the cast?" I said. "You would make a great character."

"No, no, my role is behind the scenes," Swett said airily. "I prefer to be the puppeteer, not a puppet. My role is executive producer."

"I see," I said. "And why are you telling me this?"

"Because we need a writer, darling," Swett said a bit pleadingly. "Someone to give the thing shape. Of course the stars — and that would be Diandra, Tamsin, Janey and Chessie — and we have a few others in mind, some people you've already met, and I was thinking we would ask Princess TaTas if she moves in. Of course most of the show would be improvisational, the stars' dialogue being whatever comes out of their blessed mouths, but we need situations, darling. Set ups. That's where you, come in. Not to mention the pitch. Of course you won't be collecting a salary until we sell the pilot, but I'm sure you don't mind working on spec. Understand it's a brilliant project. You'll be getting in on the ground floor. It's a marvelous opportunity I'm offering. Most writers would jump at it."

This was a lot to absorb.

At the yacht club, Swett rejected several tables not to his liking, demanding one on the terrace overlooking the boats so we might catch a breeze.

"Can you imagine they wanted to seat me inside on a day like today?" he complained. "They would have never done that to Dad."

The maitre d' came over with a pair of menus. "We'll need one more," Swett said. "I'm expecting another guest." The maitre d' looked askance at my outfit, which was my usual boots and jeans. With them I was wearing a nice tank top with a bit of ruffle at the hem.

"What is it?" I said as the maitre d' was frowning.

"No denim allowed at the club, miss," he said.

"Oh bother," Swett said, his nose wrinkling. "Darling, don't you have something in your bag, a little skirt? I'm sure there's no rule about the boots, although I must say your choice of footwear in this weather is rather baffling."

"I was planning on riding later this afternoon," I said. "Alex invited me to go with him down to the river."

"Swimming with the horses in Muskrat Dam," Swett said. "Hmm. Sounds pretty sexy. I'm jealous. I bet Cassius can swim. Plus you get to see Alex all wet and dripping."

Meanwhile, the maitre d' was waiting.

"Sir," he said. "You are responsible for your guest."

"All right. I can take care of this. Here's 50 dollars, now go away," he said, pressing bills into the man's meaty hand. So much for club rules. A server arrived to take our drink orders, Diet Coke for me, gin and tonic for Swett. I sat back and took a long look around, alert for anything to satisfy Pat's need for celebrity sensation. The main dining room and the patio were nearly full with white men wearing white pants and boat shoes and blonde women in flowered frocks. There were a few family groups of young parents lunching with their progeny. One stunning athletic cougar-type dining with an attractive young male caught my eye. Unlike the other yacht club diners, this pairing actually looked like they had just come off a boat, being a little mussed and slightly ruddier than the others.

"You see that woman over there," Swett said, looking exactly where my eyes had just been. "The lady lunching with her kid? By God, I haven't seen her in years. I should go over and say hello. We went to Hotchkiss together; she was in the class behind mine. I can't believe she's a mom. How old do you think that kid is? Fourteen? Fifteen?"

"I don't know. He must be 21. He's drinking a beer, isn't he?"

"Oh, that," Swett said dismissively. "They don't mind about the legal drinking age here. If she orders it, he can drink it."

"But it's illegal to serve minors," I pointed out.

"Don't be tedious. This is a private club," Swett said. "Excuse me for a minute while I pop over and say hello. When the waiter comes, put in our order. I'll have the Eggs Chesapeake. I suggest you do the same."

While Swett table hopped, I made a phone call.

"Ric," I said when he picked up.

"Hey, babe, howzit going?" Ric said. "Sorry I haven't called you back but it's been really crazy. Have you been keeping up with what's happening? Fires are breaking out all over L.A. The hills are burning. I'm just waiting to see if I'll have to evacuate."

I immediately felt suffused with guilt. Ric could have been hurt and I was out of the loop. I didn't know a thing about the fires. Ever since I'd arrived in Beddington Place everything else had become a news black out.

"Are you okay? What are you doing with the cat?"

"The cat's fine. I gave it to my sister in Marina del Rey a couple of weeks back. I just haven't been home enough to feed it."

Now I felt annoyed. It was my cat.

"Really?" I said. "Where've you been?"

"I've been jamming nonstop with my new band," Ric said. "We're practicing. I told you, we've had a couple of gigs. Tickled Pink's been a big, help. She's…"

Someone was tapping at my shoulder. It was the club maitre d'.

"Miss," he said. "There are no portable devices allowed."

"Ric, I've got to go," I said. "I'll have to call you back." I hung up.

Swett returned to the table with a new man in tow. "This is Orestes Milikides," he said. "Say hi."

"Hi," I said. "I'm Paige."

"Orestes is a money man," Swett said. "He was the money behind 'Co-ed Fever,' and a number of other art house films. He's hot to jump on board with a new franchise, which is why I'm bringing him in."

"You will be one of the Horsewives?" Milikides said to me. "You are very beautiful. You have wonderful breasts."

Before I could respond to this comment, there was a flurry of activity at the entrance of the patio.

"Oh there you are," Diandra exclaimed, striding towards us. With her were Janey and Chessie.

"I thought you might be here," Diandra said, lavishly kissing me on both cheeks. "Enjoying a nice lunch."

"How'd you know we were having a meeting?" Swett said, annoyed.

Clearly, he had not been expecting Team Diandra's presence. "This is Orestes Milikides," he said, forced to make introductions. "He's our new investor. Don't you love his name? Me-lick-i-deez," he pronounced. "With the emphasis on 'lick.'"

"Gross," Janey said.

Chessie pursed her thin lips.

"A little bird told me you were meeting," Diandra said. "Mind if we join in? After all, Janey and Chessie are also investors."

"I haven't committed yet," Chessie parried. "I still have to talk to Phil about it."

"He's a businessman," Swett said. "Tell him it's an offer he can't refuse."

"Billy's in," Janey said jealously. "He thinks the idea is simply marvelous."

"Billy just wants to keep you busy and out of his hair, darling," Swett said. "His goal is to fill your day."

At that slight, Janey decided to throw a tantrum. "You think my husband is investing hundreds of thousands of dollars into this project just to keep me busy? That he doesn't give a rat's ass whether or not we can create a marketable product that viewers will lap up? A product that will create incredible advertising revenue and generate merchandising opportunities that will make us all a lot of money? You think he has no respect for my business savvy and that he doesn't believe in me? Wow," she said. "That's kind of demeaning, isn't it?"

"If the shoe fits," Diandra muttered. In a louder, brighter tone, she said, "So, shall we get a bigger table? Now we are six."

What followed was a virtual replication of every lunch meeting I'd ever been to or heard about in L.A. whenever one of Ric's projects went into pre-production. Which is not to say that every project he'd been attached to got made. Over plates of chicken salad and eggs Chesapeake, Swett, Janey and Diandra bandied back and forth possible story strands, the action jockeying principally between Diandra repeatedly performing heroic feats a la

Wonder Woman on horseback, while Janey and Tamsin indulged in beauty treatments. Chessie, once she convinced Phil to play along, would provide domestic footage by allowing the cameras entrée into her and Phil's bathroom at home where she would demonstrate her wifely duty of shaving and waxing him. Orestes principal contribution to the conversation was to say he thought Phil's personal grooming habits would be a great hook because, as he said, "Americans are obsessed with body hair removal." At that, Diandra began to choke.

"What about the kids?" Janey said. "Aren't we going to include the children?"

"Please, not your children," Diandra rudely said.

Janey pouted.

It was the first I'd heard she had kids.

Half an hour later Swett looked at his watch. "Sorry to break up, the party, folks. Terrific first meeting. Let's do it again next week — Janey? Your club next time? I'd love to stick around but I've got an important rendezvous."

"With that guy you chatted up last night at Café Allegra?" Diandra asked slyly.

"How do you know about that?" Swett said, bristling.

"My eyes and ears are everywhere," the girl replied, batting her eyelashes.

When I stood up from the table, Orestes stood up, too.

"Please do not leave," he said. "We are still talking. We have not yet discussed your role in this venture. Please stay. I will drive you."

"That's okay," I said. "My car's at Michael's anyway." As I brushed past Orestes, he reached out and pinched my butt.

"You would make a great Horsewife," he whispered. "Don't say no so fast."

I pulled away and picked up my handbag. By the time I caught up to him, Swett was already outside the club, denouncing his driver.

"Where is that son of a bitch anyway?" he growled. "All he has to do is bring the car around. I hate relying on a hirelings. ”

"Your car was totaled," I reminded him. "Besides, this arrangement lets you off the hook."

"How so?" Swett said, curious.

"This way if there's ever a problem, you can always blame someone else."

"Good thinking," Swett said with satisfaction. "I knew there was a good reason for keeping you around. You're a smart cookie, Paige. No doubt about it."

"Hey," I said as we stood there waiting. "Do you think I have time to hit the loo?" I really had to go. Before he could answer, I dashed back inside the club to ask the first person I saw where I might find the restroom. A Guatemalan busboy pointed the way, and moments later I was closed into a stall, my pants pushed past my knees, luxuriously relieving my bladder.

I was making a grab for the toilet paper when my heart froze at the sound of a familiar voice standing just a few feet away. It was the former First Lady. I recognized her voice from a Barbara Walters special.

"Damn it," the former First Lady said. She must have been talking on her cell as no one else was there. "Goddammit, this is the only place on the planet they won't let you speak on a cell phone. Sorry, but I'm in the bathroom and the signal is so lousy I keep getting cut off."

I had to make a decision. Dare I fling open the door, camcorder in hand, and surprise record the former First Lady without her permission? Or should I exit the stall and introduce myself as a journalist and ask her if she had a few words for the camera? Dare I ask her if she would comment, on the banning of the use of cell phones at the Yacht Club? I thought that might be a good question. Before I could make up my mind what to do, there was a knock on the door. It was the former First Lady.

"Yoo hoo," she said, her voice musical and friendly. "Do you think you're going to be very long in there? I've got to go real bad and the other toilet is out of order."

I zipped and flushed.

If You Choose Not to Jump, There are Go-Arounds

"Listen up, everyone, this is a big ride," Diandra said. "I ask that you follow my rules. My rules are very simple. Rule one is that I lead. I will assign your positions. No one may pass without permission. If you choose not to jump, there are go-arounds. We're going to be doing a lot of cantering, but if at any point you feel you're not up to it, please stay at the rear of the ride."

It was a stellar Saturday morning and there were six of us going out, not including Diandra, our fearless leader. For weeks, she been urging me to join her Saturday ride, a weekly outing she assured me I'd enjoy. "Such stimulating company," Diandra said, describing the participants as athletic riders who were, "an important interior decorator, a world famous skin doctor, a Broadway costume designer, and the drop dead gorgeous daughter in law of a famous old British actor."

There was one more rider, she added, a local woman who rode every other week. A personal detail Diandra noted about this last rider was that she was, "Actually very talented in the saddle, but very timid. She was in a dreadful accident where she had to be air lifted from a field after she'd fallen off her horse. She was riding with a man friend."

I'd been told to get to the barn at 8 a.m. and that my horse would be tacked up and ready. Instead, at 8:35, Diandra's barn was morning-chores chaotic. Water buckets were being emptied, stalls being mucked, and horses led out two and three at a time to distant paddocks for their daily turn out. All these chores were being handled by a lone Mexican man who kept his head down, avoiding eye contact.

Outside the barn, a half dozen horses were tied to the fence, flicking their tails against flies. They all looked rather thin and dusty and forlorn; none had been groomed, let alone saddled. Sighing, I rummaged around in some cabinets until I found a curry comb and a hoof pick, and set to work on Space Cadet, the little Thoroughbred mare I'd been assigned.

"Why are you doing that?" a tall, cool blonde in Tailored Sportsman breeches said shrilly. She and another woman dressed as her twin stood in the shade under the barn's overhang, drinking iced lattes.

"Esteban will take care of it," the twin said. "That's what he's paid for."

"Is that his name? Esteban?" I said. "You say he's a groom? And here I thought he was a mucker."

Holding a pick in one hand, I tapped Space Cadet's fetlock to see if she'd lift her foot. She immediately complied in a perfect manner. "Good girl," I said encouragingly. Space Cadet was a sweet-natured mare, and I thought we would get on. "Good girl, Spacey," I said again when she anticipated me by lifting her next foot for me to pick. I patted her on the neck and whispered sweet nothings in her ear. She responded by whickering softly.

"It's not the mucker's job to tack up," I said to the two women, who were regarding me in a manner I didn't consider friendly. I wondered which of Diandra's clients they were. Neither one of them looked like an interior decorator, or a dermatologist, either. "That's a job for the groom, isn't it?"

"There's no specific groom here," the first blonde said a little sullenly. "Esteban functions as both. You're right, it's not his job to get the horses ready, but Gwen and I throw him a little extra to take care of us."

"I'm not brushing the dirt off any horse," the other blonde declared. "All that hair and dirt would get on my clothes and ruin them."

Two more blondes I didn't recognize showed up, and then Penny.

"What are you doing here?" I said in surprise. I hadn't seen her since that night at Historic Hall when the Real Housewives had staged their performance. "I mean, it's great to see you, but I didn't know you ride."

"There are a lot of things you don't know about me, Paige," Penny said. "I'm just full of surprises."

The four blondes appeared to know each other well through their regular Saturday outing. It seemed they all also took private jumping lessons, with Diandra, and chattered about their progress.

"Can you believe she asked me to take a 3 1/2-foot-jump right after I was out with that injury for a month?" the one in plaid Pikeur said. "And I did it — I wouldn't dare to cross her! — and it was great!"

"She's so inspiring," said Ariat breeches. That was the only way I could tell them apart — by their riding outfits. Like clones, they all wore their blonde hair in identical Brazilian Blow Outs, and they were all tall and thin. One had a perfect complexion — she must be the skin doc, I guessed; and one was just a little bit taller and prettier than the others. She could be the daughter in law of the famous actor. One was a little reserved — it turned out she was the costume designer, and the one with the raunchiest, filthiest mouth was the decorator, whose every utterance was a cuss.

"Fuckin' A!" she crowed when the costume designer passed around her phone to share her latest work images.

"How well do you know these women?" I half-whispered to Penny. Like me, she had gone to fetch grooming supplies and was vigorously brushing a ribby Welsh cob called Rascal.

"I ride with them sometimes," Penny said. "But our acquaintance is hardly intimate."

Between filling water buckets and ferrying wheelbarrows of soiled bedding and manure to the dumpster, Esteban managed to get the other horses tied to the fence brushed and saddled and bridled. There was a, minor skirmish as to whether or not the costume designer's mount took a standing or a running martingale. Just as everyone was preparing to get on, Diandra emerged into brilliant sunshine from the dark interior of the barn, clasping the reins of an enormous liver chestnut Percheron-Thoroughbred gelding she gaily informed us had been a stallion the week before. Its body still churning and burning with residual testosterone from just having its balls cut off, the animal was already sweating, its eyes showing white and rolling to the back of its head. Before she got on, Diandra showed it her crop.

"That's for nothing, imagine what you get for something," she said, giving its neck a whack. The animal half-reared and pawed the air, nostrils flaring. Diandra snapped her stick at it again, this time striking it on the flank. "Don't you dare," she said, warningly.

One by one we approached the mounting block, save for the decorator, who pitched herself into her saddle straight from the ground. As soon was she was astride, she pulled a flask from her vest pocket. "Swig of Grand Marnier, anyone?"

"Sally, isn't it a little early to be drinking?" the especially good looking one said.

"Not if you count it as drinks from the night before," the decorator chortled. At least now I knew her name was Sally. "Consider this an eye opener. It's like orange juice."

"Sally, you get behind me, and then Gwen," Diandra directed, ignoring the flask. Gwen, I deduced, was the skin doc. "Kimberley, you're behind Gwen." The one called Licia, who I deduced, judging from her boots, which were fashion, not function, must be the costume designer, was told to get behind Kim. "Paige, you're next, and Penny will be right behind you. Penny, are you jumping today? I thought you could bring up the rear."

"I might jump, I might not," Penny said. "I'll decide once we're out there."

Diandra placed her foot in the stirrup and nimbly pulled herself up. "Easy, Frisco," she said to the horse, who immediately reared and spun. "Let's go, ladies, we're headed to Muskrat Dam. This is a two-hour ride. I'm going to set a quick pace to get there, then we'll have about an hour to have some fun. After that, it should take about 40 minutes to get back to the barn. By then it will be rather hot, so we'll walk most of the way on the return."

"I hate walking," Sally pouted. "Can't we at least trot?"

"The horses will be spent by then, we have to give them a rest," Diandra chided. "Besides, Paige and Licia's and Penny's horses will be working in lessons this afternoon and it's already hot."

"Our horses are going to be on a two hour ride in 90-degree heat and they'll have kids on them this afternoon?" I said to Penny, who lagged behind, fiddling with her stirrups. "That seems cruel and unfair.""They're school ponies, they have to earn their keep," Penny said. "How much are you paying for this ride anyway? A trail ride is $90 for the first hour, and ten more for each hour after that. Or that's what Diandra told me. Maybe she gave you a discount. The friend rate."

I didn't answer. Diandra had offered me the ride for free.

We walked off the property and hit the road, Diandra's idea of leading being to break straight into a canter. My little mare was a dream, eager, forward, and ready to run. I could see she was going to be a handful to keep properly behind, and wondered why Diandra, hadn't put me closer to the front. As it was, I was making constant adjustments to keep her collected. She was determined to pass Licia's horse. Licia, despite her fancy outfit, wasn't much of a rider; she held her reins tight and short, and her posture, while straight and regal, was also unbalanced as she'd never learned the knack of keeping her heels down. When I momentarily eased up and let Space Cadet get too close, Licia's mount, Roman, a buckskin gelding whose shoulder had been crudely marked by an iron brand, pinned its ears in annoyance. At this, Licia turned around and gave me a dirty look. "Keep that mare behind," she said grimly.

When she inveighed me to join her Saturday ride, Diandra told me it was aggressive. "We set a good pace and go fast," she said. She also described the Saturday riders as "my best," and pooh-poohed my concerns. And I was concerned, as my rides this summer were mellow twice weekly, outings with Alex; walking the horses to Muskrat Dam and entering the river on horseback for a pleasant wade around. The horses adored standing ankle deep in the river; Butterscotch, the Haflinger pony, particularly loved plunging his whole head in. On the way back, Alex chose trails that encouraged meandering, pausing for a few minutes in grassy meadows where the horses might graze, or walking through a farmer's fallow field were the grass was tall and lush, the swathe of the bridle path just wide enough to permit two riders to ride side by side. The Beddington Place scenery was so fabulous, it made me catch my breath. There were hills and dales and valleys and woods, and the river, which we crisscrossed many times. It was magical. It was cinematic. It was exhilarating. It was poetic.

This ride, on the other hand, would be a test of my mettle. On the ground, Alex was an immature, insufferable prick; on a horse, he was Mr. Safety. Not for a single moment when I was with him on a horse was I concerned I might get hurt. I didn't know what to expect from this crowd. I knew it was very different to go out with two horses for a late afternoon summer walk, than a hard, fast, rollicking ride with six horses in the morning when the horses were full of it and fresh. Big ride outs were fun, but they could also be scary. The bigger the ride, the less control you could exert over your horse. By nature, horses are herd animals, and prefer to stick in a pack; when the lead horse takes off, they all start running. Also, out on trail rides, the horses maintained their own, often violent, tempestuous, relationships with each other, relationships they brought straight from the paddock if they were turned out in bunches. Turned out for the day and left to their own devices, horses, just like people, developed their own loves, hates and passions.

We trotted out to the road and passed through a short path leading us through a scrappy wood, and then it was back to the road again to walk under the I-684 overpass. This was scary. I had never ridden a horse like this, beneath a thundering overhead highway. Above us, the loud rumble of trucks and cars and streaming traffic made me anxious, and without thinking, I tensed up on Space Cadet and clutched her reins too tightly.

The mare's reaction to my anxiety was to trot on faster. The good part about riding her was that we'd quickly bonded; the bad part was that she was now responding to my fear. All my training as a rider told me the best thing to do was relax and let her go, and after she got past her own burst of anxiety, gently check her and half halt her and post slowly until she relaxed and collected. Instead, I wrongly seized up even harder on the reins and pulled on her mouth; her response to this was to grab the bit between her teeth and move faster. I was definitely starting to freak out.

Penny rode up alongside.

"Listen," she said, "I can see from your shoulders that you're really stressed. I know you're scared. I get scared on these rides, too, sometimes. But everything is fine. Space Cadet is not going to run off with you. She'll, never pass Diandra because she knows Diandra would kill her and eat her. Don't think about the horse. Think about you. Take some deep breaths. Let it in and let it out. Inhale, exhale, do that a few times. Come on, I'm doing it with you. Let's breathe together."

Miraculously Penny's advice worked, and within moments, I was able to let go my death hold on the reins. The pressure off her mouth, Space Cadet smoothly shifted into a athletic, bouncy trot. She really was a dear little thing. I could easily fall in love with her.

"Now smile," Penny said. "Did you know smiling releases endorphins? As soon as you smile, you'll feel better."

I tried it and she was right. "How do you know so much about this stuff?" I said. We were still very much part of the ride, but I had allowed more space to grow between me and Licia. Just in case Space Cadet was in season, I figured it was safer to not be near the boys. For some reason, the mare's estrogen level seemed to have no effect on Rascal, who quietly trotted behind.

"Didn't anybody tell you I'm a therapist? I work with people with eating disorders."

"But don't you have an eating disorder yourself?" I said. "That time we were at The Big Kahuna, you said you order but never eat."

"That's true," Penny said. "That's why I'm so effective as a therapist. Because it takes one to know one." I could hardly argue with that logic.

"So who are these girls on this ride?" I said after we'd trotted on for a few more minutes. Up ahead, the rest of the gang were trotting faster. If anybody knew the dish on these girls, Penny would. Plus she had been riding with them for months; with her professional training and powers of observation, I was interested in her thoughts.

"The decorator and the dermatologist have been friends since boarding school," she said obligingly. "They're both married and they own those horses and they ride together every weekend. Tomorrow they'll go out alone on some long, crazy ride. They're crazy. They go fast. They run down hills, they don't care about anyone behind them. I try to stay far away."

I digested that. "Okay," I said. "Which one is the daughter in law of a famous British movie star?"

"Kimberley is supposed to be related through marriage to Alan Bates … or that's what Diandra says. Who knows? She could be married to Joe Schmoe. Everybody in Beddington lies about everything. She's probably just another gorgeous young married, obsessed with horses. Around here, those women are a dime a dozen."

"Does she own her horse?" I said. It was an important question. Owning a horse in Beddington Place was an automatic wealth signifier, since boarding and showing were so expensive.

"No, she's leasing. That's Rolex she's on. Diandra got him at her favorite place to get horses, the kill broker."

"The kill broker?" I said, horrified. After I'd been cued in about "Alpo Camp," I did a story about equine rescue, interviewing an Beddington Place based investment banker who spent all his free time horse rescuing. He screened for me an underground documentary film about the abuses at a kill broker in New Jersey that was seriously stomach turning.

"Yeah, that's where she gets her horses," Penny said. "It's not such a bad idea. She buys them for their weight in meat — you know their price is based on the pound -- and brings them to Beddington Place to be re-trained as hunter jumpers. That's where the money is, in dressage and hunter jumpers. The ones that don't cut the mustard, she sells or uses as hacks for day riders. Sometimes they wind up in her lesson program. You know Diandra has a huge lesson program."

"So she's a popular and competent trainer," I said, musing. So far Diandra had struck me mostly as a brat, and a social climber. And it was true that people in Beddington Place were suckers for a British accent. It was good to know there were positive things about her.

"Did I say 'competent?'" Penny said sweetly. "I don't remember saying that."

We joined up with Diandra and the rest of the crowd, and rode on together through some low brush. Unlike the rest of the trails I'd been on, this terrain was dirty, litter-filled, and degraded. Several large, ugly structures could be seen at a short distance; it took me awhile to realize we were passing by the prison. A narrow trail just about the width of one horse had been cut through a ragged, partially blacktopped area, cordoned off to one side by chain link and razor wire.

"Is this the back of the prison?" I said, excited. "Where they keep the murderers?"

"This is the sister prison," Kimberley said. "Medium security. This is where they keep the lady bank robbers and arsonists and forgers and drug dealers. Across the street is where they keep the killers."

"Ugh, both of those places gives me the creeps," Diandra said, shuddering.

"Why? Afraid one day you'll be locked up with them?" Sally teased.

"How do you know so much about it?" I asked Kimberley.

"I'm a volunteer," she said. "I work with the literacy program."

We rode on, and the woods once again became thick and healthy. I let some space grow between me and Licia's horse, Penny and I riding about a quarter of a mile behind. It was a beautiful ride. Finally relaxing on Space Cadet, I was able to admire the graceful canopy of trees, and the musical chatter of the birds, and the thrilling sight of a red tailed hawk making lazy figure-eights overhead.

With no warning, the ride in front came to a halt.

"What's going on up there?" Penny said. I strained my eyes to see what was happening. Diandra and the rest had come out of the woods and were now standing on the asphalt.

"It looks like they're talking to some riders," I said. "They're on the road, right at that place where we cross the highway to Viney Wood." Diandra and Sally and Gwen and Kimberley had come to a stop and were talking with two people on horseback. On the blacktop just beside them, cars whizzed by at 45 miles an hour which made Licia's horse prance and fret. In a few minutes, Penny and I caught up.

"Roman! Quit that immediately!" Diandra admonished the animal when Licia failed to make him mind. "Sit deep in your seat, Licia," Diandra advised, "and stop jiggling your reins. Roman, you behave yourself or I'll give you what for," she threatened. "Now what were you about to say, Tom?"

"Just wanted to warn you about a muddy patch up ahead," the man said. Tom was a good-looking guy on an awesome Hanoverian bay in side reins. It was standing still now, but if he was using those reins out on the trail, it probably was a monster. "Once you get into Viney and head towards Muskrat Dam, you'll see most of the footing is good and you can have a canter. Just watch out for that area right past Wonderland Farm. There's a ton of mud and it's slippery. The drainage is bad, they need to lay down some Item Four. We were going too fast and it got pretty hairy. For a, moment I thought we were going to wipe out."

"I'd definitely take it slow at that part," the woman said. I couldn't tear my eyes off her ride, a pretty black and white Tobiano.

"Fuck, and I was so looking forward to having a gallop," Sally sulked. "Geoffrey didn't screw me properly this morning and I've still got rocks to get off. Diandra, can't we just jump over the mud? Blackstone despises mud, but he can fly right over it."

"There's too much mud to jump it," Tom said. "Believe me, if I coulda, I woulda. But it's too dangerous. I'm telling you, we were moving right along and then suddenly we hit that bad patch. It was bad. Gaye and Cowboy nearly went down. Cowboy coulda broke a leg or something. Be careful out there, Diandra. It's treacherous."

"Thanks for the alert, Tom," Diandra said cheerfully. "By the way, have you met the newest addition to my Saturday ride? Bring Space Cadet up here, Paige, and meet the neighbors."

"Hi," I said. Space Cadet stood as still a statue but every muscle in her body was tensed. Her ears were perked forward and her tail was slightly raised. "Take it easy, girl," I said to her in a voice I hoped was soothing.

"Paige is a famous writer," Diandra said smugly. "She's going to be writing a TV show, starring me. Isn't that outrageous?"

Sally, Gwen, Kimberley and Licia looked at me with new interest. Gaye and Tom smiled and looked expectant.

Suddenly Penny's ride, Rascal, let out a wild whinny, bucked, and tore off. He bolted across the highway, dodging trucks and SUV's. He made straight for an opening in the woods by the road where riders could pick up the trail. He knew exactly where he was going and he went for it. The last thing I heard was Penny screaming.

"After her!" Diandra shouted and we all shot off, Space Cadet at the rear. True to her Thoroughbred breeding, the little mare easily slipped gears into racehorse mode and was soon passing all the others. Within moments, she passed Licia and then Kimberley. It only took a few more strides for her to bear down on Gwen, and then we were behind Sally. Sally's horse, Blackstone, was a fast Thoroughbred, and full of venom for the mare, he pinned his ears and kicked out. Dodging his hooves, Space Cadet pushed herself on harder. We were moving so fast I was dizzy. I was elated and petrified. My heart was pounding and Space Cadet was moving effortlessly. The sensation was in its own way, exhilarating. The sensible part of me reckoned it would be safer to slow down, but at the same time I knew the worst thing I could do would be to try to pull her up. Bred and trained to win, I feared the mare would be so galled if I tried to stop her, she'd toss me off.

Instead I wrapped my left hand in her mane and caught the reins up in my right. I pushed my heels down and sat deeper in my seat and let nature take its course. Forcing myself not to look at the trees whizzing by, or the ground beneath, I focused instead on the figure of Diandra who was galloping ahead. She was lengths in front of everyone else and closing in on Penny and Rascal. I could hear Penny shrilly calling for help. I caught my breath as a series of jumps loomed ahead, but Rascal easily took them. Miraculously, Penny took them, too, muscle memory positioning her into hunt seat; at the moment of take off, she rose in her stirrups to take the weight off Rascal's back, her position a perfect two-point.

"Keep back from Frisco; he kicks," Diandra harshly warned. My eyes were riveted to Diandra's back as she expertly steadied the powerful animal with her well-placed hands and seat; pointing him at the jumps, he effortlessly carried himself over. Space Cadet was also exuberant, taking all the jumps. Her form was perfect, she was excellent. Lacking any real form of my own, all she required of me was to stay on.

Bursting with energy, his body still surging with testosterone, the only recently gelded Frisco accelerated on Rascal in record time. It was electrifying how fast he covered ground. With the drumming of Frisco's hooves thundering up behind, Rascal intensified his efforts. I was impressed how fast the little cob could run; although he had been galloping hard for ten minutes, he still had energy to spare. He was running hell for leather. Penny was off her head.

"Stop him, stop him, please help me!" she screamed.

Led on by Sally, the rest of the rescue posse was coming up behind.

I glanced back to see Sally practically standing in her stirrups, an equestrian Valkyrie, her long hair flowing out behind her beneath her severe Charles Owens helmet. Gwen was riding hunched over her saddle, jockey style, while Kimberley, who had no form, marshaled her horse, reins held too high, her legs flapping. Licia had managed to overtake Kimberley, Rolex, her horse being slow and unmotivated, despite all the crazy energy.

Just as suddenly as he had bolted off, Rascal now came to a dead halt, pitching Penny forward. The muddy stretch Tom had been talking about, 15 yards of dangerous slick was just ahead; to keep himself from sliding, the pony had come to a complete stop. In a flash, Diandra was off her horse and running over; seconds after Penny dismounted, Diandra grabbed Rascal by the reins and violently cropped him.

"You bad, bad animal!" she cried, beating him about the ears. "I could kill you and feed you to coyotes!"

"It's okay, Diandra," I said, hoping to restore order. Everyone was breathing hard from the exertion and the horses were heaving like bellows. Space Cadet was covered in a thick lather. "That was terrifying, but it looks like everyone is okay."

No one but Diandra had dismounted. That felt peculiar. Instead of anyone getting off to check Penny's vitals, let alone express empathy, they all frowned and consulted their watches.

"I'll be okay," Penny said, after a moment, her voice thin and reedy.

Her pale face was deathly white and her mascara had gone all drippy. She pulled off her helmet and sank to the ground, her back against a tree, her legs splayed out before her. Breathing heavily, she clasped a hand over her left breast. "I think I should go back to the barn, though, and not go on with the ride," she said. "But we are almost to Muskrat Dam, and I know the rest of you want to keep going. I don't know what to do. I don't want to spoil everyone's morning."

"I'll go back with you," I blurted.

"Good, because it's still early and I need to get in my run," Sally said bluntly. "And Diandra, don't think that what just happened I consider a proper gallop."

"That's because you were completely out of control and just running after whatever was running in front of you," Kimberley sputtered. "I don't think you're a very good leader, Sally. You pay no attention whatsoever to what is going on behind. I could have gotten killed. You have no business having us chase after Diandra like that. We should have stayed put and let Diandra do her job. It's her job to catch Rascal and save Penny, not ours."

"You're just upset because Rolex is so pokey and you barely know how to ride," Sally shot back. "Maybe you should lease a better horse or take more lessons."

"There's nothing wrong with my horse!" Kimberley squealed. "Don't you dare insult her!"

"Ladies, please," Penny said. "And Kim, that horse is a he, not a she."

"Huh?" Kimberley said, confused.

"Paige, are you really okay to go back with Penny?," Diandra said. "Penny? Are you all right to ride?"

"Just give me a few minutes, I can do it," Penny said.

"Here, I'll give you a leg up," Diandra offered. She was clearly itchy to get back on schedule. "Sally, bring up Blackstone and hold Frisco for me, will you?"

Penny stood at Rascal's left side and took up the reins. She lifted her left leg and Diandra grasped her foot and boosted her into the saddle. Then Diandra vaulted herself back on her mount, and Penny and I turned our horses away from the rest of them and headed back towards the stable. A few minutes later we heard a war whoop through the woods as Diandra and her Saturday ride set off on their big gallop.

"That was freaky," I said to Penny when we were safely on our way. "Why do you suppose Rascal took off like that? What on earth scared him?"

"Rascal isn't a bolter," Penny said calmly. "I made him run like that. I spurred him. I orchestrated the whole thing."

"But why?" I said, mystified.

"Because I wanted to be alone with you, and this was the only way."

And Why Was I Defending Tickled Pink?

"*W*here'd you learn to ride like that?" I demanded of Penny as we picked our way home along the trail. "That was some stunt. You're like a circus rider."

"I don't think it's a good idea for you to keep riding with Alex," Penny said primly, ignoring my questions.

"Really? Why is that? On the trail, he's very safe."

"He belongs to Darby, is why," Penny said as though stating an uncontestable truth. "They're star-crossed lovers. They've been together in past lives. They're soul mates."

Oh, brother, I thought, really disliking this kind of talk. "Really," I said. "And what makes you say this?"

"Because it's true," Penny said. "Darby and I have read it in the cards. It's in the tea leaves. It's destiny. And if you think you can change that, forget it."

"Well, he doesn't act like anybody's star-crossed lover or soul mate," I said sarcastically as Space Cadet carried us over a small stream. I loved being on a horse on such a beautiful day, the pleasure of the woods, hearing all the woodland sounds, enjoying this moment of tranquility and Nature's majesty. I loved the way the mare looked straight down into the gurgling, water, carefully placing her hooves along the rocks and crevices. "In fact, I'd say he acts quite single."

"He does that to make her jealous," Penny said. "It's part of their erotic dynamic. He makes believe he's interested in other women to get her worked up. He needs her to be jealous to fire his libido. He's kind of slow and lizard-like by nature, in case you haven't noticed. What makes him hot is seeing how deeply she needs to possess him. So him acting like somebody else might possess him drives her wild, which in turn makes him wild. It's complicated."

"I'll say," I said. "Sounds cracked."

"Well, I can see how it might seem crazy, but the point is, it's their crazy. They feed off each other. Jealousy is their sexual dynamic. It's an erotic game going on between them for hundreds if not thousands of years. I know this."

"Yeah?" I said. "How?"

"Because Darby and I go to the same psychic. That's how we met. We've been to séances together, we've had dozens of psychic readings, we've both been past life regressed. It was through past life regression we discovered we're sisters. Darby was my sister in a past life. Once we made this discovery, we embarked on a journey. Our journey brought us to Alex. He's been to the psychic too. It is all pre-ordained."

"Whoa," I said. "I don't believe in that kind of stuff." At the, word, "whoa," Space Cadet pulled up. "Good girl, you know your voice commands, don't you?" I said to the horse. "How adorable." To Penny, I said, "So wait a minute. You're basing your entire story about Darby and Alex on something told to you by a palm reader? You do realize that sounds nuts."

"She's not a palm reader," Penny said huffily. "She's a licensed hypnotherapist. Most of the work she does is stop smoking. But she's also a bonafide past life regressionist and a gifted psychic, plus she's Wiccan."

"Shut the front door," I said as Space Cadet navigated us around a tree. "Please tell me what you're smoking because I want some of it."

"Paige, I'm serious. I'm warning you not to develop any romantic ideas about Alex because he can never be yours. He's Darby's."

Was he Darby's? I thought about that night at the lake when we'd been swimming and how it felt to have his eyes on me without my clothes. I knew at that moment I felt desire for Alex, even if he was a creep. I spent a lot of time at his barn, helping out with the horses, and riding Butterscotch, which meant spending time with Alex. Some of the things he said were really wacko. While we mucked stalls, or brushed down the horses' legs, or after we finished the chores, or just driving around in his battered wheels, John Prine or Townes Van Zandt in the CD player, Alex spouted on about his theories on women. He really was a sickening misogynist. But other things he said were sexy, like when he'd recite a line of verse written by,

Antonio Machada or Garcia Lorca, his favorite poets.

"He doesn't act like he's taken," I said definitively. "And in any case, I don't want him. But if you're asking, I'm pretty sure I could have him. He's highly takeable. And excuse me for saying this, but I think there have been lots of takers. From what I hear, everybody's had him."

Penny decided to switch gears. "Do you think he's attractive, do you think he'd make a good husband?" she said. "Aside from simple lust, what's your interest? You do recognize you're very drawn to him, as so many women are."

"He is attractive," I admitted. "In a low, dirty sort of way."

"Alex is undeniably attractive," Penny said. "I've been pierced with his aura myself. But luckily I've got Lucas and we're getting married. Don't you want to get married, Paige? I mean, how old are you, anyway? Clock's ticking."

"Of course I want to get married," I said, annoyed. "Just not right away. Besides, I have a boyfriend. He's in the film business back in L.A."

"Oh, really?" Penny said. "I heard he's dating a porn star. That's what I heard. Just sayin'."

"He's not dating a porn star," I said, defensively. "Ric's a screen-writer, but he's also a musician. He's in a band. For a goof, the band did something with that adult actress, Tickled Pink. She's not really a porn star. She was in that big vampire film, remember, and she had a starring, turn for an entire season on some HBO series." I felt myself getting mad. What the hell? And why was I defending Tickled Pink?

"Hmmm," Penny said. "I thought she was into gang bangs and anal. If he were my boyfriend, I'd keep closer tabs. When are you going back to L.A.?"

"When my editor tells me to go, I'll go," I said with irritation. "In the meantime, I'm working. Actually, I just got an interesting offer. I've been invited to write a script for a possible reality series to take place in Westchester."

While I had zero inclination of becoming Michael Swett's unpaid scribe, suddenly the idea of creating a reality series seemed pretty useful. At least it was a handy thing to say as a raison d'etre for my being in Bedding-ton, and if I could wrangle money or leverage out of it, why not talk it up? Certainly Penny was impressed.

"Well, then," she said. "That's quite an assignment."

We rode on in silence for a little while until Penny brought up Alex. Again.

"You know, you don't have to be afraid to talk to me about your feelings for Alex. All of us have felt that way."

"All of who?" I said.

"You know. Me. Darby. A girl named Annie Breen."

"Who's Annie Breen?" I said. "Have I met her?"

"She's a girl who had a baby with him. It happened about a year ago. And then she moved away."

Now I was the one who was astounded.

"There was a lovesick woman who had a baby with him?" I said. "That's heavy."

"It was," Penny said. "It was a terrible burden for Darby. She so badly wants to have his baby, but he refuses to give her his sperm. The only sex he'll have with her now is oral, because he said it's too dangerous for them to bring their progeny into the world. And that's caused unimaginable pain to Darcy, as you may well imagine."

This was definitely in the realm of too much information.

Luckily my phone was ringing.

It was Alex.

"Hey," he said. "Are you alone?"

"No, actually I'm with Penny," I said.

"Don't tell her it's me," Alex said. "Come over to my barn as soon as you can. I have to see you."

"I can be there in about an hour," I said, thinking that we were still about ten minutes from Diandra's and I wanted to bathe Space Cadet.

"No, sooner," Alex said. "I need you here right away."

"All right," I said, responding to the urgency. "I'll get there as soon as I can."

"Who was that?" Penny said.

"Nobody. Listen. Do you mind picking up the pace? Are you okay to trot? Something's come up and I've got to be somewhere."

"Was that your editor?" Penny said. "Or something about that script? That's so exciting, Paige. Who knows? It could make you rich."

"Someone once asked me if I'd rather be rich or famous," I said, giving Space Cadet the signal to move out. Eager to get back to the barn and her water and her hay, she immediately started trotting. "I think I gave the wrong answer."

After handing Space Cadet off to one of the horse-crazy teenagers who hung out at Diandra's barn, I jumped into Diandra's little car and sped off to Alex's. The first thing I saw when I arrived was George, Michael's driver, standing outside in the sun. We nodded to each other and I entered the barn where Michael Swett stood in the aisle, throwing a tantrum.

"What the hell is going on here," he chuffed. "Cassius is miserable. He's lost weight. He won't even look at me, wouldn't take an apple. I don't understand what's happened."

"He's been bad, he's being punished," Alex said.

"But when I got here a half hour ago his head was tied to his stall door," Swett sputtered. "And no one was here! What kind of disciplinary measure is that, Alex? He could have broken his bloody neck!"

"Doubtful," Alex said. "I was just teaching him a lesson. Isn't that, why you brought him to me? For training?"

"I meant training him to take any jump," Swett sputtered. "Not to have the spirit knocked out of him. Alex, I've ignored all the rumors circulating around, but it seems I've made a mistake. I'm taking Cassius out of here tomorrow. God knows what you've been doing to him. He's not the same horse. He's a wreck."

"You've spoiled him, Swett," Alex said dismissively. "You're soft. That's why he keeps refusing every jump. He has no respect for you. And

154

you know that, which is why you've hired me to fix it."

"Well, now you're un-hired. You're fired, Alex. I don't believe you fixed anything. I think you've made it worse. And Paige, what the hell are you doing here? You just show up?"

"He called me," I said.

"He calls and you come?" Swett said. "Omigod, you've joined his coven."

That was upsetting.

"You know what?" Swett said. "I'm going to leave you two love birds alone. Alex, expect the horse shipper in the morning. I'm taking Cassius out."

"I'm not a love bird," I said to Swett.

"Uh huh. That's what they all say. Listen, I'm done here. Paige, if you know what's good for you, you'll be done too. If you want to ride, ride, with Diandra. She'll always give you a horse."

Then he left.

Alex and I stood there, staring at each other.

"Why did you ask me to come here?" I said. "Did you think I could stop Swett from taking Cassius out of your barn? And that stuff he was saying? Is it true? Do you really abuse horses?"

"You know my training methods, Paige," Alex said somberly. "I'm tough but I'm not abusive. Tying a horse's head to the wall is not an unusual practice. Cassius has to learn. Look at Marcus Aurelius. Look at Galahad and Lord Kensington. Do they seem abused? What about Butterscotch? Do you think I spend my day beating him? That's just a lie my enemies like to spread around."

"No," I said slowly, although at times I did think he was unnecessarily rough. Particularly with Butterscotch, who was the smallest. A couple of times when I'd had trouble tightening his girth because he was blowing out, Alex kneed him in the gut. Another time when pony was uncooperative about taking his worming paste, Alex clocked him. His explanation was, "Haflingers are stubborn; you've got to show them who is boss."

I picked up a broom and began sweeping.

"I'd like to be your friend, but people have been talking about you to me," I said. "It makes me uncomfortable."

"People are always talking about me," Alex said. "Running me down, talking trash."

"Tamsin keeps warning me about you. And just now, Penny."

"Penny?" Alex scoffed. "She's just looking out for Darby's interests."

I picked up the hose and began filling water buckets. There were barn chores still to be done. I could hear Alex moving around up in the hayloft, pulling bales down. I glanced up through the chute where the hay bales would be dropped and caught a glimpse of Alex, stripped to the waist, his lean, muscular torso glistening in the afternoon heat. I thought about what I'd said to Penny, how if I wanted, I could have him. A montage of erotic scenarios rapidly ran through my mind: his hard thighs, the way he dropped his voice lower and lower until it seemed he was whispering in my ear, and how he looked early in the morning with his sexy, sleepy eyes and rumpled bed head. I imagined going up in the hayloft right now and stripping off, and what would happen afterwards when we laid down on the straw, a clean horse blanket beneath us. Briefly, I imagined blowing him but instantly changed my mind, not ever wanting to be on my knees before this man. I ran through a number of positions our lovemaking could take: standing up, lying down, him sordidly taking me from behind. Then I remembered a romantic image, the first time I had laid eyes on him when he rode up on that beautiful horse. I imagined us on a weekend, trip together, far away from the Peyton Place of Beddington, staying at a beautiful B&B, Alex riding up to me with a rose in his hand, just like that stupid show, "The Bachelor" to which I was horribly addicted.

"Hey," I called up to him, since he was still in the loft. "You ever thought about taking a little trip up to Vermont?"

"Vermont?" Alex said. "It's the wrong season. I would go in the winter, for snow shoeing and skiing."

"I was just thinking about taking a break from this place and doing a weekend at one of those adorable, country-style bed and breakfasts. You know, the kind of place where the beds are all canopied and they serve you waffles with real maple syrup."

"I hate that kind of bullshit place, it's so pretentious," Alex said. "I'd go to Vermont, but I'd go camping. I've got a bag and a tent."

My cell was ringing. I picked it up.

"Hi, a bunch of us are going out tonight to Salem," Diandra sang in my ear. "The plan is to get some dinner and then hit The Hide Out. Why don't you come? It'll be fun."

"Sounds good," I said and hung up.

"Who was that?" Alex asked, descending the ladder from the loft. "One of my numerous enemies and detractors?"

"Er, no," I lied. "Just my editor. Listen, I've got to get going. Sorry about Swett. But you'll get another client to fill that stall. All you have to do is turn on the charm to a new, unsuspecting woman."

"Do I detect a hint of jealousy?" Alex said. He was looking at me steadily and I didn't like it, not one bit.

"Absolutely not," I said, firmly, forcing myself to take a hard look at him. He was sweaty. He was dirty. His too long black hair hung in his eyes. He was a cave man. I put the rake back in the feed room next to the extra buckets. The feed room could do with a good cleaning. Loose grain was strewn everywhere which only attracted rats, and the dirt floor was littered with a jumble of farm implements and tools that should have been hung up. Items from the tack room where the saddles and bridles were kept had migrated into the feed room, including a some dusty old web and leather halters, their clasps gone to rust. A tangle of lead lines, lunge lines and other training equipment was another heap on the floor. I picked from the pile a long, highly flexible whip, a training tool I'd seen used by big cat act trainers in the circus. "What do you call this thing?" I said, playing with the wrist loop.

"That's called a driving whip," Alex said, his eyes penetrating. "You snap it from behind to drive the horse along, whether you're working in the ring or from a carriage.

"Why do you have such a thing?" I said. "Ring work, I've perceived, isn't exactly your forte. And who around here drives a horse and carriage?" We stood there in silence for a moment, Alex working hard to hold my gaze. I deflected his attention by petting his dog, Lupa who had sidled up beside me. I rubbed my hand over the top of her huge head and into the muscles of her thick, muscular neck. I kneaded my fingers into her loose skin and smiled when she moaned with pleasure. She was a sweet, comical thing. Suddenly she let out a pained yelp and moved away.

"What's the matter, girl?" I said, dropping to my knees to see what was the problem. After a moment, Lupa gingerly approached, allowing me once again to touch her. I parted the thick gray fur on the side of her neck and took a close look, drawing back, gasping. The dog had a deep, bloody wound on her throat. It was open, it was raw, and the flesh was torn.

"She hurt herself, is all," Alex said, turning away. "Got her neck caught in a trap or something, or bitten by a raccoon."

"If you think she might have been bitten by a raccoon, don't you think she should see a veterinarian?" I said. "Raccoons are carriers of rabies. Is Lupa up to date on her shots?"

"She's all right," Alex said gruffly. "Besides, I don't have money for the vet."

"I'll pay for it," I said, stroking the dog, who was now licking me. "Just tell me where you take her and I'll see she gets care."

"Don't interfere with my animals," Alex said, his voice hardening. "She's fine. The horses are fine. Swett's horse was fine, and if he'd have left, him with me, I would've made the knucklehead perfect. That animal has the potential to be an outstanding field horse. But no, he had to waltz over here with his big car and his chauffeur unannounced and interfere with my training methods. Goddamn pansy."

I stood up, giving Lupa one last pat.

"Let me at least clean the wound and put some ointment on it," I said. "We can talk about the vet later." I started going into the tack room where he kept the first-aid kit, but Alex grabbed my arm and stopped me.

"I think it's time for you to leave," he said, his voice low and even. "And mind your own business about Lupa. She's mine, I'll take care of her. I don't need your help, do you hear?"

"Sure," I said, unpinning his fingers from my bicep. "Watch it, will ya? You're kind of rough." I walked past him and out of the barn and headed to my car. Or Diandra's car. I was driving it enough it seemed like mine. As I opened the door, Lupa rushed past and tried to jump in. I stopped her just in the nick of time. Alex stood on the gravel, glaring.

"Sorry, but your dog wants to come with me," I said.

"Get over here," he snarled at Lupa, who cringed and whimpered and quivered. I hesitated. Maybe I should just take her with me. But she was his dog and she loved him and if sometimes she was afraid of him, it shouldn't be my problem.

"Get over here, Lupa," he repeated, this time in a monotone.

The dog sank to her belly and began crawling and whimpering, across the 25 or so feet between them. It was pathetic and terrible to watch. When she came close enough, he grabbed her by the scruff and hauled her to her two hind feet. Lifting her into the air until her face was even with his, he lunged his head at her quick as an adder, sinking his teeth into her neck. The dog let out a hideous yelp and he released his grip, dropping her drop to the ground. Then he kicked her in the ribs. "Get out of my sight, you bitch," he said as she crawled away, the contempt in his voice dripping. I stood stock still in horror. I could not believe what I'd just seen.

"You're sick, Alex," I said. "You need help."

"Get out of here," he said harshly. "Go play with your little friends."

Could It Be Pheramones?

A couple of hours later I was at The Hide Out. Diandra was feeling festive, frisky and holding court at three tables jammed together to make one long banquet. This evening's group included Kimberley, Gwen, and Sally from the loco Saturday ride, Tamsin, of course, and Janey and Chessie. Tamsin's brother Sal, and Janey's husband Billy and Chessie's Phil, were also crowded around. Looking around the tables, I recognized Gary Goldfinger, one of the hunt masters, and Miranda Van Oonk, the countess. At her end, Miranda was holding her own court, surrounded by a rich-looking older couple who like Miranda, were wearing riding clothes; a stocky prematurely balding man who might have been her date, and a celebrity, Kai Mason, a delicate redhead who had starred in a hot FX zombie-thriller series called "She-wolves & Muther-suckers," and who was engaged to Matt Flannery, a sexy male movie star.

"Hi, Paige, I'm Kai," she said, excitedly. "I think you remember me. As you probably already know, cuz you're so tuned in, my fiancé and I have just decided to move to Beddington. We're buying a house on Guardian Hill! Matt's already talking about joining the volunteer fire department. It'll be great experience if he ever plays a fireman! We've actually met before. You interviewed me for TMZ in L.A. when I first started on 'She-wolves.' Remember?" I did indeed. "Oh yes, yes, you were really great," I lied. "You said some remarkable things."

"Paige! You made it!" Diandra squealed, as excited as a teenager. "Look, I saved you a seat!" She patted the empty chair beside her and I sank into it with relief. Furtively checking around the room, I wondered if I'd underdressed. Diandra had chosen for her outfit for the evening a pair of skin tight snakeskin print side-zip trousers which she wore with a pair of Tod's loafers and a crisp white man's shirt. A beautiful vintage watch hung off her slender wrist, and at her throat was a chunky strand of huge, iridescent pearls. Her hair had recently been cropped even shorter; tonight she wore it swept back in a pompadour lacquered with brilliantine. Dark red lipstick burnished her pillowy lips. She must have just had a facial at the hands of the mysterious

Iranian woman known as Gimme who worked on all the Beddington Place bold-faced names; her often spotty complexion was glowing. For a change, she was laughing and happy.

"Hey," I said. "Is anybody eating? Or are you just drinking your dinners?"

"Darling, you know we don't really eat," Janey said, giggling. "If we're starving we might share an appetizer, but we never do entrees. Not worth the calories."

"Order something if you're hungry," Phil said genially. "It's my tab tonight. You wanna eat, eat.""The calamari is really good here," Tamsin said. "Oh no, that's not here. It's that other place where they do the great calamari. This is the place we get the crab meat cocktail." She took another gulp of her margarita before succumbed to a hiccupping fit.

Sal slapped ineffectually at her back.

"Take it easy, sis," he said. "Slow down with that stuff."

Diandra snapped her fingers and a server ran over. "My friend will have the peaky-toe crab and the salmon tartare," she ordered. "And a glass of that Meursault Les Chevalieres. You don't sell that by the glass? Then we'll take a bottle. Phil," she called down to his end. "It's alright if we get Paige her own bottle, isn't it?"

"Whatever she wants, Diandra," Phil said. "Or whatever you want." He laughed.

"Omigod, there's Rene," Diandra breathed.

I turned to look where she was looking and saw a sultry looking girl with Slavic features entering the dining room. Head up, hips tucked under, she carried herself like a contestant on America's Next Top Model. "And who's that she's with?"

"That must be her sugar daddy," Sal said. "Or if he isn't, he should be. Hey, I'd be that chick's pocketbook in a heartbeat."

"Sal!" Tamsin squealed, slapping him on the wrist. "You're with me tonight, remember?"

"Who's Rene?" I said to Diandra.

"Oh, she's just somebody I used to give lessons," she said. "She never became a great rider, but she has a natural seat."

"Who is she?" I said. "Anybody I ought to interview?"

"Possibly," Diandra said. "She's been dabbling in fashion. She has contacts. Her father is a clothing designer. Not super famous, but not a nobody."

"Yeah, Paige, you should branch out from celebrity gossip to fashion tips. Snippets, cuttings, seconds." Tamsin tittered.

"Tidbits," Janey said. She giggled. "Don't you just love the word 'tidbit'?"

"Was Rene important to you?" I asked Diandra, taking a risk.

"Important?" Diandra's eyebrows lifted. "Important how?"

"Well, like, were you lovers?" I suggested.

Diandra blanched.

"How dare you," she said. "I am not a lesbian. Who told you that?"

"The reason Diandra was so attached to Rene is because Rene is really rich," Chessie said. "And you know a rich client is a good client! Although I don't know how rich Rene is anymore. She's divorced now. She used to be married to a very wealthy man. They met when she was modeling."

"What kind of model?" I said. "She's a little short for a model, isn't, she?"

"She wasn't a fashion model," Chessie said, her voice dropping to a whisper. "She modeled for catalogues. She modeled underwear. And other things. Kinky things. There was a rumor she worked sometimes for the Beddington Dominatrix, remember you met her, the Domme, at Historic Hall? She was with Michael Swett that evening, God knows why."

"So this Rene was a kinky lingerie model and maybe a pro-domme?" I said, pulling out my notebook. This was getting interesting. "Then what happened?"

"Well, she married one of her wealthy clients, is the story I heard."

"So she retired from modeling but they didn't stay married and she got a fabulous settlement," I hypothesized. "Any kids?"

"Yes, a baby girl. And she's so young herself." Chessie's voice dropped. "Rene and Diandra were really close for a time," she said only for my ears. "Diandra would have done anything for that girl, but then something happened."

"What happened?" Sally loudly said. I'd nearly forgotten she was at the table. She was seated across the way. She must have been reading Chessie's lips. "Sorry for butting in, but I met Rene at my church's fundraiser. Tell me if she's a psycho before I get in too deep."

"Stop discussing Rene!" Diandra said agitatedly. "It's difficult enough to see her and not go over and speak.""But why wouldn't you speak?" Sally persisted. "I don't get it."

Down at her end of the table, Miranda Van Oonk was at the punch line of a joke. "And then she said, 'I'll treat you like milk, I'll do nothing but spoil you, har har har!'"

Everyone around her screamed with laughter.

"Hey Paige, I know someone I'd like you to meet," Kimberley said. "Someone to go on a date with. You are single?"

"No, um, I have a boyfriend," I said. My peaky-toe crab had arrived and having not eaten all day, I was dying to dive in. I picked up my fork and was about spear a nice sized chunk of crab when I heard Alex say my name.

"Paige," he said. "I'd like to have a word with you." He had bathed and changed and was looking quite presentable in cords and chambray. Gwen, Sally and Kimberley were staring at him like he was lamb chop on a plate. Janey frowned at the sight of him, and next to me, I felt Chessie stiffen. Diandra was rigid and her mouth had gone all white. Down at the far end of the table, Sal, Phil and Billy were engrossed discussing baseball. Finally Tamsin spoke.

"Hey, there Alex," she said cheerfully, working her southern twang. "What's shakin'? Care to join us for dinner? Oops, s'cuse me, we're not eatin'. And all the seats are taken. Shame."

Alex grunted. "I'm here to meet someone. Then I saw Paige with your bunch. I'd like to have a word with her. Alone, that is.""Is that okay with you, Paige?" Chessie said protectively. "Because if it isn't, I'll just mention it to Phil and he'll ask this man to leave."

"Chessie, and that is your name, isn't it? I don't think we've been introduced," Alex said. "Relax. There's no need to call in the goon squad. I'm not a mugger and I'm not armed. I just want to talk to Paige about a minor incident she witnessed so there's no misunderstanding. She is a reporter, as you know. It's important she gets the facts right."

"It's fine," I said to Chessie. I got up. Alex immediately began walking back towards the restrooms, down a poorly lit corridor. I followed. Along the way we passed two more dining rooms and a coat check. Around a corner, there was another bar. At it sat a familiar figure. It was the guy in the checked cap from Shangri La.

Alex stopped near the door to the men's room. He was scowling.

"What do you want?" I said. "You want to explain to me why you bit your own dog?"

"It's my training method," Alex said harshly. "Dogs do it to each other to exhibit dominance. Biting is a language they understand. Lupa must be reminded she is subservient. She gets ahead of herself sometimes, and I have to put her in her place. She needs to understand things."

"She's a dog," I said heatedly. "You talk about her like she's a woman! And a woman you don't have much respect for either, if you want to think of her that way."

"So now you're jealous of my dog?" Alex said, his voice low and cunning. "I see the way you watch me caress her. Would you like me to caress you, Paige? Or bite you, or beat you up? Would you like me to do that?"

"You're insane," I said. "Leave me alone. Go away."

I turned on my heel to leave, but he grabbed me by both shoulders and pressed me against the wall. His lips, just as I had imagined earlier in the barn, bore down against mine. His lips were open. The heat of his body was enveloping. At that moment I both feared and hated him, but my body was responding. He was kissing me. I was kissing him back. He pressed his entire torso against me and I moaned and began to press against him. We were kiss-

164

ing and grinding up against each other. I was hot. I was wet. Then I reached out and touched him between the legs.

That was a shock.

He was soft.

He wasn't hard, not at all.

At my touch, Alex jerked himself away.

"What just happened?" I said, confused.

"You fucking bitch," he said. "You had to ruin it."

He shot me a look of the deepest disgust and went into the men's room.

It wasn't like I was about to follow.

Instead I returned to the table where the party was still yakking and laughing up a storm.

"What took you so long?" Chessie said, worriedly. "What did that crazy creep want? I heard last year he got some married woman pregnant. Did you know he's the head of some cultish harem? I heard it's like a coven. They hold séances and orgies."

"Orgies?" I said. "That's rich." I picked up my glass and had long pull of the Meursalt. It was very good. Diandra had picked well. To get the taste of Alex out of my mouth, I took another swig and then another.

"Let's do shots," Diandra suggested, picking up the beat. "They have great tequila here. You can have Patron if you want, but they have much better stuff. Let's have the El Conde Azul Blanco. It's $150 a bottle, but so worth it."

I looked around the table and saw Miranda Van Oonk making out with her boyfriend. Tamsin was whispering in her brother's ear. Janey had pulled her chair closer to Gwen, Sally, and Kimberley; they were locked in a passionate discussion about hair dressers. Phil and Billy were consulting their iPhones.

"Sure, why not?" I said to Diandra who smiled like a Cheshire cat.

"Did he seduce you?" she said, softly. "Sooner or later, he seduces everyone."

"Hardly," I said. "More like the opposite."

"Well, if he wasn't seducing you, what did he want?"

"I don't know," I said. And it was true. I really didn't. The only thing I was sure of was that whatever happened just now with Alex wasn't something I planned to discuss. The fancy tequila arrived in front of us. A full bottle. The waiter poured out two shots. "Here's to moving forward," I said to Diandra, lifting my glass.

"Cheers," she said. "Bottoms up."

Leasing is So Tiresome

"*E*xcuse me, I did say well done," Kimberley said to our server who appeared both mad and bored. "Could you take this back to the kitchen and tell them to cook it some more?" We were lunching at a trendy Beddington Place village restaurant known as The Kettle, a tiny luncheonette and gelato emporium with extremely limited seating. Squeezed into a red leather booth under an enormous oil painting, me, Kimberley, and the artist Roy Ralsten, were having a meeting. So far Roy had said very little, preferring to concentrate on working his way through multiple glasses of Chianti, and doodling sketches on his paper napkin of hawks, kestrels, and other birds of prey. "I can't eat a thing before 8 p.m." he informed the server, who offered him a menu. "Actually, I rarely leave the house before 3 p.m. so this is a special occasion."

"Should we be honored?" I said. Roy didn't look so hot. His clothes were rumpled, and his skin was sallow. Violet, bruised looking bags had formed under his eyes. He was there to give support to Kimberley, who I planned to interview about her literacy volunteer work at the women's prison. At the same time, she was hoping to promote her new single, a country western song just released on CDBaby. Unfulfilled to merely be a Sports Illustrated swimsuit model and the D.I.L. of a famous old movie, star, Kimberley was inspired by Princess Tatas to launch a music career of her own.

"I want to sing a few bars of my song," Kimberley said, clearing her throat. "'You look after the baby/ You pay the bills/You make me feel special/ You cure all my ills.'" Everyone in the restaurant was staring. A dog tied up outside began to howl.

"Okay, Kimmy Poo, that's enough," Roy Ralsten said, putting down his doodle pen to cover her mouth with his palm. "Hey, sweetheart," he said, turning his attention to me, "Take a look that painting behind you. I painted it."

Acknowledging the gruesome image of a giant snake devouring a deer and who thought it was a good idea to hang such a thing in a restaurant, I looked at my endive and apple salad longingly. It was bad manners to eat before Kimmy Poo was served. "Tell me what inspired you to work at the prison," I said to her, mentally tuning out Roy and his boozy, dissolute face. "An unusual choice for someone who travels in your circles, I would think."

"It all came about through my relationship with a former felon," Kimberley said, her voice dropping at the word 'felon.' More loudly she said, "She's a poet."

"I know her," I said. "Leeza Luciano. I saw her at a reading. She was awesome. How did you two meet?" "We met at the prison," Kimberley said. "Leeza was an inmate. She's had quite the life. Did you know she was a bank robber?"

"I think I might have heard something about that," I said.

"She's an incredible poet," Kimberley said. "But enough about her. Let's talk about me. How are you framing this story? And what about wardrobe? Will the camera show my whole body? Boots or stillettos? "

"I think the camera will stay pretty much above your waist," I said. "You know I'll be shooting the segment myself with my cam, right? Relax and be yourself. My pieces are produced to look au natural and impromptu, not all scripted or polished."

"Oh, wow, that's a bummer," Kimberley said, crestfallen. " I've already booked a hair and make-up person and a stylist."

"Keep your crew," Roy said authoritatively. "Always look your best for the camera."

I looked outside The Kettle's plate glass windows fronting the main street. It was raining cats and dogs. The morning had been a deluge. Navigating the unpaved roads leaving Tamsin's cottage, I was forced to plow Diandra's little car through huge pot holes and puddles.

"Oh, look, Roy, there's that woman," Kimberley said, excited as a Chihuahua. I looked where she was looking and saw Darby at the counter. "It's that woman you're so infatuated with."

"Go get her, tiger," I said to Roy.

"I texted her a couple of weeks ago, but she never texted back," Roy grumbled. He polished off what was left of his wine and signaled the server.

"I heard she's hung up on some horse guy and there's no point pursuing her."

"Hmmm," I said when Ralsten received his next drink. "So how are you two connected? I didn't know you were friends."

"Roy's doing a series of portraits of my fur family," Kimberley said. "He's painting my King Charles Cavalier spaniel, my husband's boxer, my son's Dalmatian, and my daughter's pet lamb. Plus he'll be painting the three horses we'll be putting in our barn, that is when we get our permits. We're still uncertain who we want as our architect. We're thinking about a guy who worked on the design for the new World Trade Centers, or the architect we used for our house in Malibu."

"But before that, we're going to do a painting of your new horse," Roy said encouragingly. "The one you just purchased."

"You bought a horse?" I said. "What happened to your lease on Rolex?"

"Oh, you know, leasing is so tiresome," Kimberley said, twirling her hair. Her well done burger arrived and she surveyed it at length. Using her fork and knife as a makeshift spatula, she carefully removed the meat from the bun, and then stacked the bread to the left side of her plate. Next she removed the lettuce and the tomato and all the French fries. Then she cut, the patty in half and surgically removed a one-inch square portion of meat from the center. This piece she cut in half, then quarters. Finally, she put that bit on her fork and lifted it to her mouth.

"Yum," she said, after prodigious chewing and swallowing. She put her silverware down in a decisive gesture, took a sip of water, and patted her lips. "That was so worth waiting for. That was simply delicious."

"So you've dropped your lease?" I pressed, feeling worried. I'd been riding regularly at Diandra's ever since Alex had flipped his lid, growing more familiar with how Diandra ran her business. While she was out merrily shopping and lunching with her friends, no one kept eyes on the farm. The horses got themselves into trouble, which frequently got them hurt. Large and powerful as they are, horses are also insanely fragile. From the blog interview I'd done with that horse-rescuing CEO, I'd learned no respected barn manager left the animals alone for hours, which Diandra did all the time. At her place, I'd noticed horses whose owners showed up regularly received better care, were given more hay, were groomed more often, received things like dental care. By contrast, Diandra's own string of school ponies and hack horses were treated shabbily. In her opinion, these horses were lucky to be alive. I knew that without Kimberley's leasing him, Rolex's future was uncertain.

For a moment Kimberley looked pained. "I know," she said, a shadow crossing her pretty face. "I feel bad about him, I really do. He's been great for me, he's really my speed. Which, as you know, is kinda slow. I know I'm not the world's greatest rider. I don't need a lot of horse. But when I offered to buy Rolex from Diandra, she turned me down flat."

"You're kidding," I said, remembering how many times in the past weeks Diandra had called the horse a piece of shit. Diandra had no love for Rolex at all. The only horses that interested her belonged to her A-list hunt clients, expensive, registered Dutch and German Warmbloods and Irish draughts she'd been commissioned to train. The motley crew of paints and cobs and Quarterhorses kept in her stable, even Space Cadet, the little mare, had no safe berth with her. I understood the moment Rolex became sick, or needed special shoeing, or created any extra expense at all, off he would go straight to Alpo camp, a k a the kill broker.

"Why wouldn't she sell him to you?" I said, confused. "I'm sure you offered a fair price."

"I did, but she refused it," Kimberley exclaimed. "She said it was because I would be taking him out of the barn. To keep with my other horses. Diandra said she would not want him out of her care, that he was too important to her."

I did not know what to say. It was hardly my place to tell one of Diandra's favored clients that just about anyplace she might move Rolex would be an improvement for him. I decided this might be a good time to change the topic. "So, um, what kind of horse did you get, and how did you, find it?" I asked.

"I got the most amazing horse," Kimberley gushed. "A mare. She's a Westphalian, which is closely related to a Hanoverian, the most desirable breed of sport horse. Nobody else in Beddington Place has one. I will be the first! Really, I'm so excited." She waved her hand dismissively at Roy, who rolled his eyes. "He hates it when I run on like this," she said. "But I am interested in bloodlines."

"Now tell Paige how you're making a trip to Germany to obtain this magnificent beast that you've already paid a fortune for, sight unseen," Roy said. He kept glancing at Darby, who exquisitely ignored him.

"You're going all the way to Europe just to collect your horse?" I said. "Wow. Why don't you have her shipped? There's horse transport specialists. In fact, I just talked to a guy about it a couple of weeks ago up at The Hide Out. Really great guy. I have his card. Maybe you should call him."

"Thanks," Kimberley said. "But I'm already booked. Diandra is going with me. In fact, she brokered the whole trip."

"Kid's a genius, isn't she?" Roy said. "Kid's so smart she wangled an all expenses paid trip to Germany, courtesy of Kimberley."

"Oh, shush," Kimberley chided. "You're just jealous."

"With wangle being the operative word," Roy threw back.

Kimberley blushed. "Well, it is fun spending time with her," she, said defensively. "She's so lively. Plus she enjoys going dancing, doing fun things. You know, my husband is so busy. He's traveling for work all the time. It's so dreary staying home night after night. So when Diandra rings me up and says let's go out, I can't resist."

"Mehinks Kimberley is a bit smitten with Diandra," Roy said to me. "In a lovely, girlfriends sort of way."

"Oh shush," Kimberley said again. "You're just jealous."

"Okay, so let's move on to your work at the prison," I said, pushing away my plate. I longed to order dessert but the only person in Beddington Place who ate dessert was Diandra. "What exactly do you teach?"

"Excuse me, I'll be right back," Roy said, getting up from the table.

"Well, let's see," Kimberley began. "It is a literacy program, but the first thing I do with my students is teach them yoga breathing."

But before we could get serious about the interview, Kimberly took a call from her nanny, which removed her from me and into an extended, child-oriented conversation. I pulled out my old Blackberry and started dialing. I dialed Ric, who I hadn't talked to in days. Every time he called, it was a bad time to pick up, and whenever I called him back, he was too busy.

"Hey," he said, picking up. My heart lifted a little. I did miss him. I especially missed our Venice mornings when we'd go to Gold's Gym before heading to the Rose Café for oatmeal and skim lattes. Sometimes we'd stroll the canals, or shop on Abbott Kinney.

"Hey yourself," I said. "How's it going? Any news?"

"Everything's great, babe," Ric said. "Everything's way cool. And I do have news and you'll love it. Turns out I am working on a screenplay."

"That's fantastic," I exclaimed. I was so happy to hear Ric was doing what he was supposed to be doing. Every time he talked about spending more time on his music, my heart sank. "What's the job, honey? Is it one of your original ideas, or is it a work for hire?"

"Kinda both," Ric said. "I pitched a rough script to a producer I met at The Whiskey and it kind of took off from there. He had some ideas I thought were great, so we're going in on this together. We're rewriting the script, and we'll develop it. I'm not just going to be a screenwriter on this project. I'll be getting producer credit. It might even be more than that. Hell, I might even direct."

This didn't sound good, not one bit. Ric was a lot of things, but he sure as hell was no director.

"Wait," I said. "Does that producer credit mean you're putting in your own money?" A lot of producer deals were like that.

"Nah, nah, not at all," Ric said, but I didn't believe him. Something in his voice had changed. "Don't worry about it, babe. It's all good. So far, all that's happened anyway is I'm writing it. And I'm being paid."

That mollified me, slightly.

"I'm glad you've got money coming in," I said. "Do you need me, to send some dough to cover the rent? For the moment, cos of all this work

I've been doing, I'm loaded."

"No, that's okay. But thanks for offering. Actually, I've got somebody living here temporarily while you're back east, and she's paying rent. Don't worry, it's just temporary and she'll be outta here before you return. When are you coming back, anyway?"

"Somebody's living in our house?" I said, the hair rising on the back of my neck. Kimberley had terminated her conversation and it was time for me to get off the phone. Also she was looking at me very curiously, no doubt listening in on my words.

"It's just temporary," Ric repeated. "And I told you she's paying rent."

"Who is it?" I said, my voice becoming shrill.

"It's Tickled Pink. They're refinishing her floors and stuff, you know, tiling the bathroom, at her new place in Coldwater Canyon. She needed a place to stay while they're doing the reno. I told her she could crash here. It's only for a couple of weeks, Paige. No reason for you to get excited."

I felt burned.

"Listen, Ric, this isn't okay," I said. "I wish you had talked to me about this before telling that girl she could move in."

Before he could respond, there was a call waiting. It was from Pat.

"Ric, hold on, I'm getting another call." I clicked and got Pat. "Hey," I said, mustering a cheerful, upbeat tone. "What's cooking?"

"I'm upset, Paige," Pat said. "I'm very upset."

"What's the matter?" I said quickly. I couldn't imagine what she could be upset about. Work was going swimmingly.

"It's Stanley Pucci," Pat said. "He's very unhappy."

"What's Stanley Pucci got to be unhappy about?" I exclaimed. "I haven't even written anything about him."

"Well, that's the point. Are you deliberately ignoring him?"

"Well, then, I'll interview him," I said. "Contact his people and set something up."

"That's not going to happen," Pat said.

"Okay, well then why are you calling me to tell me this?" I said, exasperated. Kimberley was tapping her fingers on the table and looking around the room. In a moment she was going to get up and leave, I just knew it.

"You can't alienate people like Stanley Pucci, Paige. He knows everyone in Hollywood and Beddington Place and you don't want to alienate him."

I still had Ric waiting. "Look, Pat, I'm in a meeting. Can we discuss this a little later? I'll call you back. Promise."

"You bettah," Pat said and hung up.

Kimberley had gotten up and walked over to the bar, where she was now chatting with Roy and Darby. I got Ric back on the line.

"Thank God you're still there," I said. "I apologize, but that was Pat."

"Yeah, Pat," Ric said. "Of course you'd rather talk to her than me."

"That's not true," I said, not sure if I meant it. "But you and I have always agreed, work comes first, so you know I have to take her call, whenever."

"Sure," Ric said, his tone impassive.

"So, um, where exactly is Tickled Pink sleeping? I'm sorry if that question annoys you, but I have to ask."

Before he could answer, I got another call waiting. It was Pat again.

"Paige, I'm just telling you, you can't afford to alienate these big shots," she said. "Especially after what you did to Martin Rogonoff."

"Martin?" I said. "What did I do to him?"

"It was that 'rumor' reference," Pat said. "That bit about the rodent. You really upset that publicist. That's the sort of thing that gets around, you know. And it's very alienating. To say the least."

"But you're the one who brought up it up!" I exclaimed, a bit too loudly. Everyone in the restaurant was staring. "Hold on a minute. I want to clear this up with you, but I've got someone on the other line."

I clicked back to Ric. He was still there.

"Paige, I just want you to know I think that your life out there has become pretty sordid," Ric said. "I don't think you have any right to ask me unpleasant questions about Tickled Pink, or our relationship. I read all your stuff on TMZ and I read about that sex club you went to, and meeting that dominatrix. I don't think you have any business telling me how to live."

"Sex club?" I squealed. Now everyone in the restaurant was openly staring. "What are you talking about? I never went to any sex club."

"Oh, yes, you did," Ric said. "That place you said was like a speakeasy. I read your blog. That woman performing illicit acts in the bathroom? Please. I know what a sex club is. I wasn't born yesterday."

"It wasn't a sex club!" I hissed. "And I only mentioned that dominatrix because it gets the site more hits."

"See what I mean," Ric said, his tone bitter. "I don't even know you anymore, Paige Turner. And that's the truth of it."

"I've got to go," I said. "Pat's still on the other line." I clicked off Ric and went to look for Pat, but she had hung up, too.

I put my phone back in my bag and pretended to look for something buried in it. I felt my eyes welling up with tears. My life was in shambles. My editor was angry with me, and my boyfriend had moved in a porn star.

Roy Ralsten had returned to the table. Darby had disappeared. Where was Kimberley? "Something wrong at home?" Roy said.

"I don't want to talk about it," I said, sniveling. "It's unprofessional."

"Hey, you don't have to be professional with me," Roy said. "I thought we were friends. So tell me what's happening. I promise not to divulge your secrets."

Just then I saw someone staring in from outside the restaurant, someone wet and dripping and oblivious to the rain, which was fogging up his glasses. The person was staring at me through the window. It was Alex.

"Is he actually stalking me?" I said, amazed.

"Who?" Roy said. "Who is stalking you?"

"Him," I said, pointing at the window, but Alex was gone. There was no one there.

"Forget it," I said, feeling flustered. Roy was looking at me strangely. "Where's Kimberley? We should get on with this thing."

"Kimberley?" Roy said. "She had to book. She had another appointment. She said to tell you she'd touch base. She just told me she may not be available to do the interview after all. She might have a work conflict."

"Swell," I said, feeling defeated. "And she's left me with this tab, too. She must think I'm on expense account."

"Aren't you?" Roy said, surprised. "We just assumed."

My phone was ringing. This time it was Michael Swett, calling to say his horse had been murdered.

A Grisly Sight

*I*t was a grisly sight: Cassius on the ground, flat out, a lightweight turnout sheet, once red, now faded to geranium, draped over him. While his head had been mercifully covered to spare his eyes from being plucked out by crows, his elegantly turned, white-socked legs were on full display, as were his muscular hindquarters. His left front leg was splayed at a curious angle; a deep gash cut across his cannon bone. His ruby red blood had pooled in the dirt underneath him. The horse was dead. There was no doubt about it.

I knelt down to pull back the sheet for a last, lingering look at his patrician face, a face I had brushed and stroked with a soft brush a dozen times. In the short time he'd boarded with Alex, Cassius and I had become friends. He was a lively creature; but very social and affectionate, and one of those rare horses who came right up to you in the paddock, eagerly thrusting his muzzle into your hand. Cassius had an open heart and was a horse of good faith; extremely trusting, he thought everyone was his buddy. Under the sheet, his soft, intelligent, dark brown eyes were wide open, but they held no spark or light. A blue-bottle fly alighted on his cheek, and my hand instinctively flew out to banish it.

"Oh God, I can't look," Michael Swett said. He was standing at the, gate, seemingly frozen, despite the heat and humidity. There was no shade, and it was sweltering in the sun; after only a few minutes, rivulets of sweat streamed down my sides. I drew up the cover and carefully rearranged it over Cassius's head. Then I stood up and took a deep breath, but the rank odor of sun-baked manure in the field where Cassius lay was overpowering.

"Then don't look," I said, turning away. It was unbearable to see the horse like this, knowing only a short time ago he'd been cavorting. Or maybe not, I considered, taking a longer look around. It had been awhile since I'd been up to Diandra's paddocks. Following their blowout, Michael transferred Cassius from Alex's barn to Diandra's stable, a move that had caused a quite the stir in the Beddington Place horse community. The move was widely considered to be yet another black mark against Alex, as Swett went around telling anyone who would listen that his horse had been abused.

"Did you realize there was no grass up here at all?" I said conversationally to Michael, looking around. "It's practically a sand paddock." I wanted like crazy to ask him what had happened, but he didn't seem ready to answer. Instead, like any decently trained reporter, I focused on the murder scene, if it was indeed there had been a murder. As a crime scene, it didn't quite square up, although the atmosphere was hardly bucolic. I already knew Diandra's paddocks were barren and rocky, but I didn't realize to what extent. Instead of the rolling fields I heard her describing to, potential clients, in reality it was just a couple of fenced in acres of hard- packed dirt. Dirt that turned to mud when it rained; when it wasn't raining, it was a dust bowl. The ground itself had been churned and heaved up by so many horses for such a long time, it was nothing but rocks and dirt, strewn with bits of old baling twine and the manure of multiple horses. At midday, there wasn't a wisp of hay in sight, and the two large plastic water tubs tethered to the fence, a lank piece of hose draped across them, were dead empty. I wondered how long this had been the case, since horses require constant water.

"I've never been up here," Swett said huffily. "For the safety of the boarders, Diandra told me it was off limits. Besides, this is a full service facility. That's part of what I'm paying for: service. The groom always brings Cassius to me, and brushed and tacked up."

The better to hide what really goes on here, I thought.

"So do you know what happened?" I said, finally cutting to the chase. I didn't want to be here, but Swett had demanded my presence, and I had to admit, the possibility of a blog headlined "Horse Murder in Beddington Place" written by me was gripping. While Swett fumbled for an answer, I took a good look at the horses living in this dreary state. There were about eighteen of them, a mix of mares, geldings, ponies, even a couple of minis, all mixed together in one unsegregated paddock, just as they would have stood at a kill broker's feedlot. Some were standing, stock still in the heat, while others milled around listlessly, searching for something to eat. There was no grass or anything to divert them, which had turned some of them into nervous cribbers who tugged and bit the fence. Until this moment, I had no idea Diandra's herd was so large. Their dispirited demeanor could easily be attributed to the hot weather, but I also wondered if they might be thinking about the dead horse in their presence. I knew some of them had come into Diandra's hands off the kill broker's lot. That's how she got them on the cheap. They were horses who had seen neglect and slaughter. Cassius had never lived in such a place. He hadn't been at Diandra's very long, certainly not long enough to have made any horse friends. I wondered at the wisdom of Diandra having turned him out at all into what surely had to be a hostile environment, packing him into an already overcrowded paddock where the pecking order was well established, and in the minds of the alpha horses, territory to defend.

"Diandra said he was kicked," Swett said. He was crying a little and I felt sorry for him, although not half as sorry as I was for Cassius. "Diandra said he was making a nuisance of himself, pestering the other horses, and so he got kicked. They were just teaching him a lesson. She said it happens all the time. She didn't seem to think much of it."

"Did she say who she thought might have kicked him?" I asked.

"She thought maybe a horse named Frisco," Swett said. "Which one is that?"

"He's the Percheron-cross over there," I said, pointing. Frisco was standing glumly in a corner, fruitlessly seeking shade. At the moment, he looked too hot and tired to kick or kill anything. "He was only gelded recently," I said, remembering. "In terms of testosterone, he's still like a stallion."

"All the more reason why Cassius shouldn't have been turned out with him," Swett said darkly. "I had no idea. I was told Cass got a grass paddock to himself, his own groom, that he was being treated like royalty. This was an utterly irresponsible thing to do, turning him out with these monsters."

"They're not monsters, they're horses," I said quietly. "But you're right, it probably wasn't very smart to turn him out with a gang, especially when he's new to the herd."

"You know what this horse means to me?" Swett lamented. "He was like a brother, or a son."

"Where is Diandra anyway?" I said, uncomfortably. How long was this poor dead animal going to lay here? I didn't know the procedure for removing a dead horse, but I had a feeling it wasn't going to be easy — or pretty.

"She's at lunch," Swett said bitterly. "She's with Janey and Tamsin."

A few minutes later a police officer showed up.

"What the hell?" I said.

"I called the police," Swett said. "I'm not convinced this was an accident."

"Whew," the officer said, breathing heavily. "That's some hike to get up here." He pulled out a notebook and flipped it open and carefully wrote down the date and time. "So whatta we got here, besides a ton and a half of dead horse? Are you the guy who called the station house? Are you saying this is a result of foul play?"

"Yes, I think my horse was murdered," Swett said dramatically. "I believe my former barn manager came over here and killed him."

"Whoa," the officer said. "What makes you say that?"

"It's very simple. I'm giving you the motive. He's angry. I removed the horse from his care. I paid him a lot of money as a client, and now he's lost that income. He also has a vendetta. You see, he's held a grudge against the horse because he couldn't make it jump. He's a complete control freak and a lunatic. Ask any woman who goes out with him. In fact, ask this one. Paige, you dated him."

"I did not date him," I protested. "We hung out."

"Sir, do you think he actually killed your horse?" the officer said. "And is the animal insured and will you be making a claim on it?"

"Take a look at that leg. It's obviously been broken," Swett said. "This man drives around with a baseball bat in his car. He says it's for some softball game he plays in, but I don't believe it. He keeps it under his seat.

He must have come over when he knew no one was around and

cracked my horse's leg."

"Why would a horse hold still when a person was approaching it with a baseball bat?" the officer said. "Wouldn't it run away when it saw someone coming at it with a weapon?"

"Cassius was very trusting," Swett replied. "Also he knew Alex, and for some time Alex was feeding him. I doubt he would have run away. In fact, I think he probably stood there stock still while Alex took a whack."

The officer walked over to the horse and took a look at the broken leg.

"I don't know," the officer said. "All I know is, you can't just leave this thing to rot out here."

There was a commotion as the gate opened and the horses scattered to get out of the way. Diandra was walking briskly towards us, her beautiful features compressed into a scowl, her blue eyes flashing.

"What's going on here?" she said in a high handed tone of voice. "Who called the police? And where is the removal person?"

"She called the police," Swett lied, nodding toward me. "She believes there's been foul play and she wants to get to the bottom of it."

"Wait a minute," I started to say. "I didn't — "

Diandra turned to the officer and opened up her mouth.

"You can go," she told him imperiously. "There's absolutely no reason for you to be here. One horse kicked another. It happens in herds all the time. It can happen between any two horses who are turned out together. Even horses who love each other will kick out if one of them becomes annoyed. It's unfortunate what happened to this man's horse, but he is insured, he will grieve, and then he will purchase another."

"No, I won't!" Swett burst out. "Cassius was irreplaceable. He was one of a kind."

"Don't pay any attention, he's talking nonsense because he's upset," Diandra said to the police officer. "Now if you can just wrap it up here and be on your way, I'll handle this matter privately."

The officer had closed his notebook and put away his pen, but he didn't look like he was leaving, at least not right away.

"Go, go," Diandra said, waving her hand at the police officer.

"This man made a very serious accusation that someone hurt his horse," the officer said. "Are you sure you wouldn't like to call a vet, someone who can examine the animal and see if it is in fact a horse kick, or trauma from brute force? If it was a bat, there could be splinters which could be used as evidence. And has a veterinarian seen this animal? I'm assuming it didn't die right away from a broken leg. Someone had to have come to put it down, isn't that correct?"

"I gave it the euthanizing shot myself," Diandra said, impatiently. "It was suffering."

"It! It! Why do you keep referring to Cassius as an 'it?'" Swett cried out, enraged. "Have you no respect for him and what a marvelous spirited being he was? And how valuable he was to me?"

"It was insured for half a million dollars," Diandra said to the police officer. "That's its value. This is just a lot of drama and completely unnecessary. Actually, I think your presence is fanning the flames, making the owner more excited. There was no foul play. No crime was committed. There won't be a report on this, will there? I should hate for it to be in the police blotter. The people who own the property would be so distressed."

"Well, we do give it to the newspaper to publish when a rabid animal has to be destroyed," the officer said, uncertainly. "The horse wasn't rabid, was it?"

"Of course not," Diandra said impatiently. "It was absolutely up to date on all its shots."

The officer took off his hat and wiped his forehead. "Boy, it sure is hot up here. Hey, I just took a look coming in and those water buckets? Those horses look kind of thirsty."

"What do you know," Diandra began, before reversing direction and remembering it wasn't one of her clerks she was talking to, but actual police. "Of course," she said instead, briskly. "They must have drunk all the water; it evaporates so quickly in this heat." She pulled out her cell and began dialing. "Estaban!" she barked. "Agua para las caballos!" Next, she decided to switch tactics and turned her full bore charm on the officer, batting her eyes at him coquettishly, and exaggerating her British accent.

"Will that be all, sir?" she said, lowering her lids and looking up at him from beneath a thick fringe. She'd recently chopped her hair even shorter at the back and the sides, leaving only a curtain of heavy bangs she wore swept at an angle across her forehead. "Is there anything more I can do for you before you go?"

The copper coughed. "Boy, it sure is dusty up here," he said. "And full of rocks. I don't claim to know a lot about horse care, but aren't paddocks usually less crowded and nicer?"

"Not really," Diandra said, not missing a beat. "You should see how they keep them in Florida. Crammed in together head to tail on sand with only string fencing. They're very much herd animals. They'd rather be together in hell than in heaven alone."

"I see," the officer said. He had put his hat back on his head and seemed ready to walk back down the hill to his car and his air conditioning, and probably a thermos with a cold drink. "Can you tell me who owns this place? I gather you're the barn manager and pay rent here? But who is the land owner? If you can just tell me their name, I'd like to have a word."

"They're in the south of France," Diandra said quickly. "Besides, they're not involved with anything that goes on here. Nothing with the, barn, I mean. They just do it for the farm credit, a deduction, you know. It's a tax write-off ."

"I see," the officer said again. He took off his sunglasses and took a long look at me. So far I'd said as little as possible, not wanting to be involved in this melee. Not only did I have nothing I wanted to contribute, but I felt I was learning a lot more about this Beddington Place universe. I was also curious to find out who Diandra's land owners were. I'd heard a rumor the wife was a retired old movie star, and Pat's invective to scare up more stories was pressing. The heat was really on now to come up with new material. Maybe this was just what I needed.

"And who are you and what is your reason for being here?" the officer said to me. "Do you own one of these horses? Did your horse kick his horse?"

"No," I said, taken aback. "I don't own a horse. I'm a friend of his — and hers," I said, not really liking this turn of events. How did I become under inquiry? "I'm a media journalist and I was at work, I was interviewing someone when Mr. Swett called and asked me to meet him here."

At the words "media journalist," the officer once again pulled out his notebook.

Diandra looked furious.

"And who do you work for, miss?" the officer said, pen in hand. "Name and professional affiliation please? And you do know you're are not allowed to report on or otherwise interfere in an active investigation."

"I'm not working now," I protested, wondering if he was posturing and trying to intimidate me. As far as I knew, I could report on whatever I pleased. "I'm just here because I know these people. I'm not writing about this, I'm not reporting on it, I'm not here in any sort of professional capacity."

"You say that now," Swett said bitterly. "But if you think it's juicy enough, you'll file a story. I can see the whole thing now. 'Blue-blood millionaire's beloved pet horse dies in mysterious incident on a movie star's property in Beddington Place, while said movie star is away.'" He let his own words sink in for a moment and then smiled wickedly. "Come to think of it, that would make a really good story. Hand me your cam, Paige, I'm going to start recording."

Swett was right, it was a good idea. I pulled out the camcorder.

"Give me that thing," Diandra squealed, making a grab for it. There was a scuffle as Swett held the device high in the air, and Diandra jumped up and down to get a hold of it. Swett, much taller, laughed and nimbly danced away. Diandra stood still for a minute, and bit her lip. Then she squared her shoulders and took a flying leap, pouncing on Swett, knocking him to the ground, and then pummeling him.

"Oh sweet Jesus, knock it off," the officer said, pulling Diandra off

Swett. "Cut it out or I'll have to arrest the both of you." Diandra pushed, her disheveled hair off her face with two hands and glared at Michael in disgust. Michael got unsteadily to his feet and straightened his collar.

"Hit a man when he's down, why don't you?" he shot out at Diandra. "If not for this bum arm, I could have taken you."

"Big baby," Diandra shot back.

The officer ignored them and turned his attention back to me. He frowned. "I don't like it one bit that you're a reporter. And are you the one who called the police? I'd like to some identification, please."

"Don't you know who she is?" Diandra said to the officer, incredulous. "What's the matter with you, man? Do you live under a rock? She's Paige Turner, the TMZ blogger, and a reporter for Hello! magazine. Ever since she set foot in Beddington Place she's been doing nothing but nosing around in everyone's business, making trouble, producing evil, rancid programming and content for e-online and Extra and the BBC."

My eyes widened at this information. The BBC? Really? That sure was news to me. Were they picking up my stories and running them? Was I being remunerated?

"She's everywhere as a reporter," Diandra continued blabbing. "Everyone in Beddington Place is complaining how snoopy she is, poking her nose around in people's closets, and depriving the celebrities of even a shred of privacy. "

"That's not true at all!" I exclaimed. "Half of them seek me out!"

"She's just feathering her own nest, making a name for herself," Diandra rattled on.

"Hmmm, is that true?" the officer asked, tapping his pencil against his pad.

"Not at all," I responded indignantly. "I'm not an investigative reporter, I just write about fluffy stuff."

"Now that I think about it, I think there was some kind of complaint involving you, something that happened at Martin Rogonoff's," the officer said, slowly. "Didn't you get in a fight with someone? Wasn't there some sort of altercation?"

"This is ridiculous," I said. "What is going on here?"

"And weren't you involved in a car accident where alcohol was involved?" he asked.

"I wasn't driving!" I practically screamed. "HE was driving and drove us into a ditch," I said, pointing a finger at Michael Swett, who was looking at me quite hostilely.

"You were as loaded as I was," he said. "I distinctly remember you matched me drink for drink. You're the one who urged me to get behind the wheel."

"That's not true!" I said again.

Diandra, Swett and the police officer were all staring. I was hot. I was sweating. And the rank smell of dead, sun-cooked horseflesh was rising, up all. It was awful. It was terrible. I felt like I might pass out. "I need a cold drink," I said.

"It better not be a frozen margarita," Swett said smartly. "I know Tamsin's got you hooked."

A new person stepped into the paddock holding a rope and a winch. It was a short, squatty, late middle-aged woman wearing work boots, a denim shirt and denim jeans. She had the shoulders of a linebacker. Needless to say, she didn't look like one of Diandra's pals. "Hey, who's the responsible party here?" she said. "I got a call to pick up a dead horse."

"Please will everyone stop referring to Cassius as 'a dead horse,'" Swett said, once again teary. It was impossible to keep up with his mood swings. "I can't help myself. I'm so emo," he declared. The strain of the day was definitely showing. His normally sun-kissed golden tan skin looked as haggard and dry as a lizard, and in the past hour, the man had aged ten years. For the first time I noticed the deep lines around his mouth and that the skin of his neck looked loose and wobbly. All this time I had imagined he was just a few years older, but now I saw that he was older, much older, and that seemed a pity.

"This man is the horse's owner and I'm the barn manager," Diandra said, completely poised and professional. "I'm the one who called; please speak to me only because this man is too distraught."

"Okay, but who's payin' the removal fee?" the woman said. "I get, paid in advance, up front, before the horse gets on the truck."

"You said on the phone it's four hundred dollars," Diandra said. "Cash." She pulled a wad of bills from the pocket of her breeches, peeled two off, and thrust them into the woman's hand. "How long will this take? Can you be quick about it?"

"Hey, I'm not interested in making a day of this," the woman said. "I've got two more horses to pick up."

She walked over to where Cassius lay. Working quickly, she bound his hind legs together and looped the rope around both legs. "Is there a way I can bring the truck up here? There's no way I can drag this back down the hill and all the way back down that path," she said. Diandra walked over to the far side of the paddock where a high blockade fence screened the paddock from the road. She opened a latch and pushed on a panel and the fence swung open, creating a road access.

"Think you can squeeze your vehicle through this space?" she asked the woman.

"Nope, but I can bring the truck around and park right by that door," she said. "It's big enough to get the body through okay. All right, I'm going to get the truck now and bring it around." She turned to Swett, me, and the police officer. "It's kind of crude how I have to do it. If I were you, I'd leave."

"I want to watch," Swett said to Diandra stoically. "I loved him. Oh, God, how I loved him."

"All righty, I see my work is just about finished here," the officer said. "Mr. Swett, I must advise you that once the body leaves the premises, there's nothing further I can do. I strongly recommend you don't allow it to be taken away until you have a veterinarian examine it and take X-rays. It has to be a vet who is familiar with making a legal forensic determination. You have no case whatsoever if you don't do this, and it's possible without that report, you could jeopardize your insurance. You should contact your insurance agent immediately, and tell him or her what has happened. In any case, it's also my responsibility to inform you that it's probably not a great idea to go around making accusations against your former barn manager unless you can back up your claims."

"I don't know what to do," Swett said, clutching his head. "I can't watch, I can't watch — Diandra, tell me what to do," he pleaded.

"Get a grip, fella," said the officer.

"Yes, by all means, get a grip," Diandra muttered.

"Help me," Swett babbled, clutching my arm.

"The only help you need is calling your driver take you away from here," Diandra said, sternly. "Trust me, Michael, it was an accident. Now let the removal person do her business and let's be done with this, for God's sake."

"What do you think I should do?" Swett asked me, his eyes, pleading. "I'm sorry for what I said to you just now. I didn't mean it. Paige, tell me what to do. I loved that horse so much." He started sobbing.

"I don't know," I said, feeling at a loss. Could Alex have snuck up to Diandra's paddock in broad daylight to break a horse's leg?

I was distracted by the sound of the removal woman's truck idling outside the blockade fence. There was a roar of passing traffic. In a nanosecond it came to me how someone could have parked on the road and climbed over some rocks to vault himself over the lowest point of the fence. For someone agile and athletic, it wouldn't take any time at all, and only minimal effort.

"Don't let them take Cassius away," I blurted. "At the very least, get that X-ray."

"Too late," Diandra said.

The police officer had left and now it was just Swett, me, and Diandra. While Michael clutched my hand, Diandra assisted the removal woman with the hitch and the winch. The woman walked back to her truck and flipped a switch, and the rope started moving, dragging Cassius. Swett let out a little scream as the big horse's body first lurched across the hard dirt. He was big and he was heavy and the engine that propelled the winch gave out a harsh, high pitched whine.

"She really should oil that thing," Diandra said, wincing at the horrible sound. "That sound is hideous."

"Don't look," I said to Swett, hoping he'd turn away, but we were both riveted. Cassius's body progressed inexorably inch by inch closer to the stockade gate. The scarlet rug pulled away, revealing his poor, sad face.

"Hey, that's still a good outdoor sheet, if you want to go over and grab it," the removal woman said as she continued to guide the winch. "No sense throwing it out with the body, unless you don't think you'll ever want to use it."

"What do you mean, 'throw it out,'" Swett said, bewildered. "Isn't Cassius going to have a proper burial? Diandra, what does she mean?"

"Hey, buddy, I'm taking this guy to a landfill in Long Island," the removal woman chortled. "He's going to get tossed on the pile, what do you expect?"

"That's not right!" Swett screamed. "Diandra, stop her! Please!"

"It's for the best, Michael," Diandra said, soothingly, patting Michael's back. "This is easy, it's expedient, and the price is right, okay? You don't want to go spending thousands of dollars on cremation and burial now, do you? Especially when you're just renting that cottage and don't have any property."

"I could have him laid to rest on Mummy and Da-Da's property," Swett gabbled. "I could have a headstone carved. 'Beloved horse,' or something."

"Michael, stop being such a drama queen," Diandra said, becoming, impatient. "These histrionics are giving me a migraine. Are we almost done here?" she said to the removal person. Cassius was at the back of the truck now. The woman lowered the tailgate.

"Alley oop," she said, and the winch moved again and in one horrifying jerk of the rope, Cassius was flung on to the flatbed. "Sure you don't want that sheet?" she called out to Michael. "Last chance."

The Dark Side of the Horse World

By Paige Turner

Beautiful Beddington Place has a dark side that rears its head a little bit more than the wealthy equestrians care to admit. In recent years, there have been horse barns burned for insurance, Beddington- based Olympic riders accused of doping their horses, or using illegal spurs on them so the animals perform in intense pain. The most recent horse related scandal just occurred today, a situation described by one person as a case of cold blooded horse murder. An 8-year-old Thoroughbred was found in its paddock with a mysteriously broken leg. According to an insider source, the horse's death came about as a result of a blood feud between two high powered trainers. Without going into the stomach turning details, suffice to say the horse is now buried in a landfill. Was he executed Jimmy Hoffa style? Whispers of what really happened have tongues wagging all over this tony town. The New York Post as well as The Daily News both saw fit to send investigative reporters to cover the story. The local police have announced a gag order, and no one is talking. A rumor is circulating that the horse's death is part of a complex psychosexual drama associated with an S&M cult and a swinger's club.

This is Paige Turner, live for TMZ. Stay tuned.

Eviction

I woke up the next morning with a dog licking my face. It was Twinkie, Tamsin's long haired doxie, slobbering over me with a focused, industrious vigor, relentlessly rousing me from a deep, but restless sleep.

"Quit it, hotdog," I said to Twinkie, who gazed at me with love. I gave her a good natured rub on the head and pushed her back down on the covers. "How'd you get up here anyway, you little scamp," I said as the bed was high and Twinkie's legs very short. I listened carefully for signs of movement in the house, filled with a sudden anxiety that someone was lurking. But the only sound was the angry buzzing of a trapped wasp, futilely flinging its body against a window.

Pulling a dressing gown around me, I stepped into the front room to liberate the wasp. There was no point opening the window; it would only get trapped against the screen. Opening the front door with the intention of somehow herding and then shoo-ing the thing out, I was startled to see Tamsin standing there in ice blue jods, a riding crop gripped her hand.

"Did I wake you? I'm so sorry," she said insincerely.

"What's up, Tamsin?" I said tiredly. "If you're looking for Twinkie, she's right here. As a matter of fact, when I woke up, she was lying on my bed."

"Oh! Well, I'm not here to accuse you of stealing my dog," she said. "Although I did hear a rumor you were about to make a move on my brother."

"What are you talking about?" I said. "I have no interest, romantic or otherwise, in Sal."

"Maybe not. Or so you say. Honestly, Ah don't know what to believe. Janey fills my head with such nonsense."

"Janey said what?" I said. "That's ridiculous. Why would she?"

"I don't know," Tamsin said, shrugging. "It was just a thing she said. Don't pay it any attention. It doesn't mean anything. I for one don't believe for a moment you'd try to make a move on Sal, although he was looking at you all googly eyed at The Hide Out last night. When that disgusting Alex showed up. What were you doing with that man, anyway? Sal said when you came back to the table you looked like you'd just been boned. Oh, don't be embarrassed if you screwed Alex in the tinkle room. Everybody's done it."

"Including you?"

Tamsin ignored this and stepped around to examine her landscaping.

"I must get Manuel to trim these more carefully," she said. "He just goes at my bushes like a savage."

"Listen, did you drop by to check up on your gardener, or is there something you want to say," I said. "You look like you're on a mission."

"Well, I am actually," Tamsin said. "It's kind of awkward."

"You're here to tell me that TaTas is never coming back here to look at houses and that my whole excuse for being here all this time has been for naught?" I said. "You know, my editor is still waiting for the follow up on that story."

"What a memory you have, Paige," Tamsin said. "And you're so funny. TaTas. I don't know. I haven't heard back from her people yet. But as far as I know, it's still a go. Anything is possible. But I did come over with the intention of telling you some bad news. It seems my mother is coming for a visit. Can't bear the heat in Birmingham, poor dear. Trouble is, even though to you my house might seem very spacious, it's not really suited to long-term guests. Which is why I'm evicting you. How fast can you get out?"

"Wow," I said. "Thanks for giving me so much notice."

"Well, it doesn't have to be today," Tamsin said, relieved I wasn't going to put up a fuss. "She's flying to Maine first to visit our baby brother, but she doesn't get along too great with his wife. Or should I say, his second wife. She didn't get along with the first wife either. Anyway, she'll be here soon enough. I'd like to have the place empty for a day or two to give it a good airing. So, chop, chop, you need to book."

"Let me think," I said, thinking. Thanks to the popularity of, my recent blogs, I was pulling in enough dough to stay in a B&B, except Beddington Place had none. There was, however, the Holiday Inn.

"All righty then," Tamsin said, happy to end our conversation. "Would you mind very much sending Twinkie out? I'd come in and fetch her myself but I don't want to surprise anybody in their underwear." Wink wink.

"Tamsin, there's no one hiding in the closet," I said, annoyed.

"Whatever you say," Tamsin said airily. "Michael says that producer friend of his he introduced you to, what was his name? Miliki-what?"

"Milikides."

"Right. What a peculiar name that is. It sounds so, um, dirty. Michael says he's very keen on you. Can't keep his hands to himself. I thought you two might have something going. Not saying I wouldn't if I was in your shoes. Though I am glad I'm not. Aren't you working on that script? I thought Milikides might have stayed over so you two could have a work session. Isn't that what writers do?"

I closed my eyes, silently counted to ten, and took a deep breath.

"Tamsin, come and get your dog, please. And I'll be out of your hair asap." I stepped back inside the cottage and made a beeline for the Keurig. I needed caffeine.

"Oh, come on, Paige, don't be a sorehead," Tamsin said cajolingly, still standing in the doorway. "It's not personal." I had to remind myself that she wasn't the enemy, and in fact had been my friend.

"It's just that you're so attractive and unattached and Miliki-dese, Miliki-dose — and isn't that a ridiculous name? I feel smarmy just pronouncing it," Tamsin said. "Anyway, he could be your meal ticket out of this jaded, sordid, low-class profession you've become immersed in. "

"You mean journalist?" I said. "And you think that's worse than being a realtor?" I laughed bitterly. The coffee was ready. I filled a cup. "Want one? It's your coffee, anyhow."

"Thanks, but no thanks," she said. "Janey and I are doing a cleanse.

For the next three days it's strictly juice and veggie drinks for me, and absolutely no caffeine. Maybe an itsy bitsy glass of champagne, because I can't do without my mimosas, which we're having tonight by the pool. Why don't you join me and Sal, unless you've got something better cooking? I envy your social life. I really do. But you'll probably be busy at your new place, won't you?"

The wasp found its way out.

"Omigod, this place is filled with bugs," Tamsin shrieked as the wasp blew past. "The minute you leave, I'm calling the exterminator."

As soon as she and Twinkie were gone, the dog having to be dragged away, I pulled on some clothes and jumped in Diandra's little car. Overhead, the sky was rapidly darkening. I turned on the radio to 107.1 The Peak to hear the news and learned a major thunderstorm was brewing. I drove straight to Java Joe's where Stuart, one of the regulars, was still sitting at an outdoor table. "Get something fast before the sky opens up," he said by way of greeting. "Tropical storm blah-blah."

"I heard the weather report," I said. "Need anything?"

"I'm good," he said, lifting his mug. "I'll save you a seat."

After ordering a coffee and a lightly toasted croissant with cream cheese, I came back outside to sit down next to Stuart. He immediately set down his newspaper.

"So what's this I'm hearing about an investigation?" he asked, his eyes invisible behind dark glasses. "The scuttle is some rich dude is going around accusing another dude of killing his horse?"

I shook my head sadly. "It's not out of the realm of possibility, unfortunately. Is there really an investigation? And how'd you hear about it?"

He held up The Daily News. "Plus, I got a pal in the police department," Stuart said. "Doesn't sound like anything will come of the investigation, though. My source said there's no evidence."

"Well, there was a dead horse," I said. "I saw it."

Stuart's eyebrows lifted.

My phone was ringing, "Sorry," I said. "I've got to get this.""Pat," I said into the phone. "Wassup."

"You tell me 'wassup,'" Pat firebreathed in my ear. "What the hell is going on there, Paige? I just got a call from some woman who said she's throwing you out of a rental cottage because not only have you been bringing in men, but you've also contaminated the property with fleas and bedbugs. She hinted this was hot info for TMZ, the downfall of the celebrity reporter turned call girl, um, that would be you, plus she claims she knows another celeb gossip reporter who is dying to report it."

"Tamsin called you?" I said, furious.

"Tamsin, Shmamsin, what the hell kind of name is that? You know her? She claims to be your landlord. She said you stole her clothes. She also said you're late with your rent. She claims to be a personal friend of Ronald Strump. So how come you haven't given me anything on The Ronald? You've been there for weeks and so far not one word about The Ronald? What gives?"

"Well, I — "

"And what about the rent?" Pat said. "Did you really stiff her?"

"I don't pay rent," I said through gritted teeth. "She invited me to stay in her guest cottage as her guest. And she gave me those outfits."

"Well, I guess the honeymoon is over," Pat sniggered. "So what'd you do to piss her off? Is it true you've been having sleepovers, and what's this business about the bugs? Beddington has bedbugs? That's good dish. Bedbugs in Beddington Place. I like that. Even if they're your bedbugs. Who'd you sleep with to get them?" she chortled.

"Did she tell you the name of this so-called celebrity reporter?" I said. "I'd like to know the name of my alleged competition."

"Someone called Kimberley. She's also a country western singer."

I groaned.

"Everybody wants to horn in on my gig," I said bitterly. "Figures."

"You know this Kimberley?" Pat said. "She any good? Does she have good camera presence? I need her number — oh wait, I've got it here."

She ended the call before I could.

I threw the Blackberry in my purse. Stuart looked at me pityingly. "Trouble at work?" he asked.

It was starting to rain. Stuart picked up his newspaper and his coffee cup.

"Come on inside and complain to Daddy," he said. "I'm all ears."

"Thanks, but I can't," I said, wondering if Stuart was indeed old enough to be my father. I thought not. "I've got an appointment with a celebrity rolfer. Some dude named Ralph. He works on all the bold-faced names in town. He's giving me a free session so I can experience what he does as part of the piece on him. Have you ever been rolfed?"

"Can't say I have," Stuart said, standing up. "I heard that it hurts."

"It can't hurt any worse than that Vajazzling thing I did," I said, ruefully. "Just because Jennifer Love Hewitt did it, I had to try it, too. I had to try it for Hello! so I could write about it."

"Vajazzling?" Stuart said. "What's that?"

"First they give you a Brazilian bikini wax and then they glue Swarovski crystals to your pudendum," I said. "It's a cooter thing."

"God, your job is awful," Stuart said. "What was it like?"

"It was awful," I agreed. "But my boyfriend loved it. That was a couple of months back, when I was still in L.A. God, that seems like a long time ago, doesn't it?"

"I've grown so accustomed to your face," he sang. "This coffee wouldn't be so sweet without you."

I squeezed his hand. "Thanks, Stuart."

The rain was coming down harder and I was starting to get wet. Stuart held the door to the café open. "Coming?"

"No, thanks," I said again. I crumbled up my paper cup and handed him the croissant plate. "Take this in for me, will ya? I'll see you later."

"Peace, baby," Stuart said, flashing the two-fingered sign.

You Could Call It 'Rape'

*F*ifteen minutes later I was in Beddington Hills, stretched out on a massage table in a tiny back room above a tattoo parlor, stripped to my skivvies.

The rolfer, whose name was Ralph, spent like five minutes washing up. He stood at the sink with his back to me, humming. Turning towards me with a towel in his hands, he drilled his eyes into my body so intently it felt invasive. His vision was like an X-ray exposing every bit of bone and cartilage, not to mention veins and cellulite. Slipping his dried hands into a pair of light blue rubber gloves, he approached me. My stomach quivered.

"Ouch!" I said as he dug both thumbs into my flesh. A clap of thunder outside drowned out my next shriek. Ralph began working on my right knee, which I'd said was stiff and creaky, no doubt as a result from all the running I'd been doing across wet lawns and down dirt roads, chasing down Beddington Place celebrities.

I saw stars when Ralph the Rolfer dug two thumbs and both forefingers under my kneecap, probing and pushing against resistant flesh. I felt like I was dying. This was torturous. I'd read up on rolfing and knew it was a far cry from even the firmest of Swedish massages, or the most vigorous chiropractic adjustment. I expected it to hurt, but this touch was, in a word, punitive. "Holy shit, are you sure this is supposed to hurt this much?" I gasped.

"Inhale and exhale," Ralph said, calmly. He circled around the table and gripped my naked thighs. Grasping my right hamstring in his meaty hands, he began squeezing and pummeling.

"Ouch, ouch, ouch," I shrieked.

"You know, a lot of what we perceive as pain is really resistance," Ralph said in a robotic monotone. "This is about recognizing where there is conflict within the structure and then fixing it."

"Is there a name for this particular form of torture you're inflicting on me," I grunted between gritted teeth as he left off tearing at my leg to take apart my hip. Amputation, I was certain, couldn't have felt worse. Ralph wiggled and then waggled my hipbone with one hand like he was separating bone matter from cartilage. Then he methodically worked one index finger under the bone and began digging.

"They call it visceral manipulation," he said, above my screams. This agony went on for several minutes. I broke out in a cold sweat. I felt close to blacking out. A few minutes later I got a breather while he stopped to don a fresh pair of gloves.

"Lay back down please and open your mouth," he instructed as I struggled to get up.

I obliged, not entirely willing. Soon two of his exceptionally large, and strong fingers entered my oral cavity. At first it was just exploring, his fingertips tracing a line along my gums. Next came some pressing and a test probing of my molars. After that came a bit more pressure at the gum line, followed by stronger pressure, and then actual gripping of the tissue that makes up the gum.

"Wider please," Ralph said.

I opened my mouth a little more with growing apprehension. Ralph began a vigorous exploratory tapping of my mouth's interior connective tissue, that rubbery band of muscle and cartilage and the soft, wet pink tissue that makes up the inner cheeks. Then he used his thumb to bear down and press and probe whatever it is that connects the upper and lower jaws. This hurt. First my entire body went rigid and then my eyes began tearing up.

"Ow, ow, ow," I gurgled, struggling again to get up.

"Relax, it's just pressure," Ralph said, pushing me back down. His fingers were in so deeply, half his hand was in my mouth. Breathing became difficult, which made me feel panicky. Slowly and inexorably, he increased the pressure and began to vigorously knead. His fingers delved in deeper to manipulate the interior of my entire mouth, pressing first on the roof, and then back towards my larynx. His hand was inside me up to the knuckles and it hurt. It hurt a lot. Waves of pain and indignation and salty tears washed over me like the sea.

"Well, I don't think you have TMJ," Ralph said in a calm, detached voice as I fought passing out. "And I'm not detecting any osteonecrosis of either the mandible or maxilla, which is a good thing. But what I do perceive is a considerable lack of elasticity, especially at the back of your throat. You have an extraordinarily low gag reflex. Do you have trouble giving oral sex? It's almost like you've developed a wicked case of lock jaw."

"Hurts," I grunted around his hand. "Hurts lots."

"Now, now, let's not be silly," Ralph said. "On a scale of one to ten, how would you rate the pain?"

"Eleben," I choked out.

"Oh come now, you're exaggerating," Ralph said, his prying, pressing fingers roaming around my hard and soft palate. "Still have your tonsils, I see," he said, giving one a tweak.

"Arrrgh, arrgh," I grunted.

"Yes, it hurts, but I'm helping you. We're almost done here," he said. His digits intrusively dug deeper and there was a sudden, sharp searing pain. A gush of hot tears drenched my cheeks.

"Stob, stob," I garbled, making a grab for his hand. He batted it away.

"Almost done," Ralph said, giving me a final jab. The pain was excruciating. I saw stars. The moment it stopped, my body went limp. I drank in big gulps of air once he extricated his fingers. Ralph pulled off, plastic gloves and dropped them in a can. Then he went over to a small sink in one corner of the room, flipped on the faucet and began vigorously washing his hands.

"You know, you're in very bad shape," he said, his back to me. "I gave you this sampling session as a courtesy, but I strongly recommend you sign up for the entire series. That's ten sessions 350 each, for a total of $3,500, but I would be happy to give you the friends and family discount. Let's say three grand. We could start tomorrow, or if you prefer, I'm sure I can schedule your first appointment for early next week."

"Are you crazy?" I sputtered, sitting up an grabbing my clothes which sat heaped on a chair. pulled my tee shirt over my head and began thrusting my legs in my pants. "You think I'd pay somebody to hurt me like that? I can't believe any celebrities pay you do to this."

"I don't share private details about my clients," Ralph said coldly. "I'm just giving you my professional assessment." He was frowning, but then he suddenly smiled. "You know, people who in pain often find rolfing a release. I hope once you've calmed down you'll discover something positive about your experience. May I remind you, I gave you this session free of charge because I anticipated you'd blog about it, but considering your response to my talents, I do want to say that you're planning on writing or saying anything that isn't completely positive, I'll have to charge you today's session. That will be $300."

"No worries, I'll think of something great to say about you and your practice," I lied.

"Good. And I'll want to see the piece before it goes out."

"Actually, I'll tell you right now what I'm gonna write," I said, finishing up getting dressed. "I'm going to say that I went for therapy and what I got was raped. You fisted me! Isn't that how would describe what just happened?"

"I think you have a lot of anger, " Ralph said sympathetically. "And for the record, in rolfing, the orifices are manipulated. A very important session towards the end of the series engages both vagina and the rectum."

That's all I needed to hear.

"Someone from Hello! will be in touch with you shortly," I lied.

"Have a great day," Ralph said. "And if you write what you said, you'll be hearing from my lawyer."

The rain was pelting down harder by the time I reached the car. It was only early afternoon but the sky had gone dark. Black thunderclouds scudded overhead, buffeted by an increasingly chill wind blowing in from the north. The streets of Beddington Hills were deserted. Debris swirled by the curb; the red and white striped awning over the windows of the coffee shop were flapping wildly, making an awful racket. I unlocked the car door and flung myself in just as a gust of wind and rain slapped me across the face. Suddenly feeling freezing cold, I started the car and turned on the seat warmer.

I felt a wild and crazy urge to flee town, if only for a short while. Without thinking where I was going, I drove south on Beddington Center Road to where it joined up with Route 119. I drove past the volunteer ambulance corps and the A&P. I passed a bank and gas station and a yarn shop, and then a funky local watering hole with a dozen pickup trucks parked out front. I drove past two dead-end, residential streets where I glimpsed a row of small, pretty, clapboard houses where I supposed the regular folks lived. Then I spotted the entry sign for the Parkway and I turned on to it, my foot on the accelerator.

There weren't many cars on the highway at that time of day, so I let the speedometer creep up. It was the first time I'd felt free to explore the possibilities of Diandra's wheels, to take advantage of it being a sports car. The few vehicles in front of me turned off at the next two exits, and the road opened up. The Parkway was deliciously curvy. Despite the rain, I was having fun. I adjusted the rear view mirror and the position of my hands on the wheel. I stepped on the gas. Trees flew by, then the image of two deer grazing in the long grass along the shoulder. The intensity of the rain picked up and I ramped up the speed of the wipers. I turned on the radio and once again got The Peak. An old tune by Janis Joplin was playing, "Me and Bobby McGee." I began to sing along. Exit after exit hurtled past.

A huge thunderclap broke overhead; the rain was now coming down in buckets. The sky was drenched and saturated to the point that it was blacked out. Visibility was down to zero. Then the windshield started fogging and the car hydroplaned. Trying to activate the dehumidifier, I reached over to the dashboard and began punching buttons and spinning dials.

The Thornbush exit was approaching. I had to get off the Parkway. Lightly tapping the brakes, I decelerated, squinting through the fogged up window, trying to determine the right lane. Without warning, Diandra's little car slid on the wet pavement. There was a sound of rushing water, and everything came to a halt. The engine cut out and within moments, water began seeping in.

Frantically starting the car again, I punched in a change of station, searching for weather news. "That was Richard Marx, and 'I Love a Lonely Night,' that 1980's classic," an announcer said. "And if you're outdoors, it's time to come in. We just got word to expect heavy rain, thunderstorms, and flooding on the Parkway. Coming up, Helen Reddy — "

I turned off the radio.

More water came in and I put the car in reverse. I was able to back up a foot or two before the engine once again sputtered out. The water was coming in faster now, drenching my shoes. I deliberated what to do for a moment before deciding it was time to bail.

Grabbing my handbag, I gingerly opened the car door. A wave flowed in; the water gently lapping against the car upholstery. I leaped out and slogged through murky green-gray water that reached to my calves. There were no other cars around. Besides the pouring rain, it was deadly silent.

I pulled out my cell phone. I knew I had to call someone, but I couldn't think who. I wondered if Diandra's car was ruined. I wondered who might pick me up. I began to feel alone and helpless. I began sobbing.

Lunch at Roganoff's

Come on, come on, I pleaded with the ignition, but it was hopeless. I hoped it was just a dead battery and nothing worse. Superstitiously holding my breath and counting backwards from ten, I turned the key in the starter for the fifth and last time. Alas, nothing happened.

My phone squawked out the ring tone, alerting me to a new text. It was from Janey and even her typing was impatient. "Drop everything and get over here at once," she commanded. I quickly typed something back.

"Stuck in Diandra's car on the Parkway hit a flood plane," I texted. "Car won't start."

"No worries," she rapidly typed back. " Sending tow now. Come to Roganoff's."

Not five minutes later a tow truck rolled up. "Yo, you Paige?" a burly guy in rubber waders and a zip-front jumpsuit asked. I admired his assurance and economy of motion as he attached an iron chain to the undercarriage of Diandra's car and flicked a switch. Within moments, the car was out of the water and back on dry asphalt. In another minute it had been hauled up and tethered to the flatbed. I pulled out my wallet, prepared for the worst. The burly guy waved me away. "It's already been taken care, of," he said. "Need a lift?"

A few minutes later he deposited me on the highway just outside the restaurant.

"Hope you don't mind me dropping you off like this on the side of the road," the tow guy apologized. "But it's a bitch turning this thing around in that parking lot."

I thanked him for the ride and stood there for a moment as he pulled away. Foraging in my handbag for lipstick and a mirror, I hastily applied fresh gloss to my mouth, and then picked my way across the wet graveled lot, clogged with Escalades, Lexus's and Range Rovers.

A pretty young woman dressed all in white immediately intercepted me.

"You have a reservation?" she said.

I pointed at the farmhouse table crowded with people at the rear of the dining room.

"I'm with them," I said, eyes pinned on Diandra, costumed in an outlandish get up where she apparently was channeling Thomas Gainsbrough's "Blue Boy." Her lanky frame was draped in a closely tailored, classic pale blue velvet cut-away jacket worn with matching knee pants. Under the jacket was a bow-tied flowing blouse. Her shapely albeit mannish calves were encased in oyster-hued opaque hose, and delicately beaded velvet slippers adorned her feet.

"Excuse me, but I'm late," I said to the hostess, barging past. Janey, Tamsin, Chessie and Diandra were seated with two guys I didn't know.

"Well, here you are at last," Janey said to me while directing a supplicating smile towards the hostess, who was frowning. "I've asked everyone here for a work meeting. We're well on our way developing a project I'm calling 'The Real Horsewives of Westchester County.'"

"Thank goodness you got here, Paige, because we need you to mediate," Janey continued. Her assertiveness was surprising. I'd never seen her so take charge. "Please tell our darling friend Tamsin she desperately needs a hair re-think. That bun has got to go. I don't want anyone to get the idea that just because we're not New York City gals, we're a bunch of Republican hayseeds."

"There's nothing the least bit hayseed about me," Tamsin chuffed, patting her hair like it was a pet. "And for your information, this is not a bun, it's a chignon."

For a moment Janey looked daggers.

"Oh come on, Tamsin, darling, even Chessie thinks you need to cut your hair," she said a moment later, cajolingly. "Look at how soignée and chic Chessie looks. And don't you dare challenge me on my French. Look how Chessie is working that that sang-froid preppy thing. You wouldn't even know she's not a Wasp! Tamsin, you need to cultivate a particular image. Paige, tell her. She'll listen to you. She hangs on your every word."

I raised an eyebrow at Tamsin, but she wasn't having any. It didn't seem the time to start grilling her about her call to Pat.

"I think Tamsin's hair is great," I said instead, causing Janey's filler-enhanced lower lip to quiver. "That said, I think your hair is perfect, too, Janey. Everybody doesn't have to have the same hair. Everybody should have a signature look. You don't want to look too cookie cutter. For example, for weeks when they first started, I could barely tell those Beverly Hills girls apart."

"You know, a lot of those Bravo Housewives do look the same," Tamsin said. "Thank you, Paige. I'm sticking with my image. And I am a Republican, like it or lump it, Janey darling."

Once again, Janey looked daggers.

"Hey," I said to the two men I'd never met. "I'm Paige. I'm a writer. And you guys are — ?"

"I'm Ben," said the one with short dark hair and a close cropped beard, thrusting out his hand. "And this is Brad. We're the video team. Janey said we'd be filming today, but we've been slow getting started. Everybody was waiting for you, I guess."

"Hi, I'm Brad," said the other guy, who looked very much like Ben except his hair was longer. In response to my staring, he said, "And yes, we're brothers, we're twins. Fraternal, not identical, plus I'm four minutes older."

"So you're ready to start rolling film?" I said to Janey, who really was in charge, at least according to Ben and Brad. "So, um, what's the set up? We're filming this scene in this restaurant?"

"Well, that was the plan," Janey said. "But then we found out from the hostess, and she is quite the stickler for details, that we were supposed to ask for and get permissions, not just from Martin, but from the town. Apparently there's some silly rule about shooting permits."

"I don't think that's quite right," Tamsin chimed in. "I believe the rule is you can shoot anything you like, but not for more than three days. That three-day rule went into effect back in the day, when everybody got so riled up when they were shooting Fatal Attraction."

"Omigod, what a bore," Diandra said, annoyed. "And what year was that? Ancient history. What's a rule anyway? I've never met a rule that couldn't be broken. Janey, tell that crew to turn on their cameras. Let's start filming! I've got people to see, horses to ride."

"You're going to ride in that outfit?" Brad said, incredulously.

"Don't be an idiot, of course not," Diandra said. "I'm wearing this for the lunch scene. And speaking of lunch, are we getting any? And why haven't we been served?"

"There's some confusion about that, too," Chessie said to me quietly. "Janey said the meal was on the house. Martin was giving it to us for the publicity. She said that's how all the reality shows work free stuff, but, there was some misunderstanding, and now we aren't getting lunch."

Janey was tapping her butter knife against her plate. I gave her my full attention.

"So what do you need from me?" I said to her. "And thanks for getting that tow truck."

"Well, you can start by telling Tamsin to take her hair out of that bun," Janey said shrilly, not willing to give it up. "And after that you can craft a set up, a scene, introduce some topic to get us going. Also I need you to come up a reason for me to walk across the room. I can't just sit here. Nobody would be able to see my shoes."

"Oh, right, your shoes," Tamsin sneered. "Of course everyone must see your new shoes. Listen, Janey, I'm sick of you putting on airs and acting like a bigshot. Just because you're footing the bill for the crew doesn't mean you get to be boss."

"Yes, it does," Janey said pettishly. "Billy said so, and Billy is the underwriter. All he asks is that he gets full producer credit, which is something I'll have to discuss with Michael later."

"Where is Michael anyway?" I said. "I thought he was a principal of this project. Executive producer. And what happened to his friend, the other money guy, Milikides?"

"I thought you knew everything about that guy," Tamsin said, slyly. "Weren't you holed up with him in my guest cottage? And here I thought, you were working on the script."

Ben and Brad were fiddling with their cameras. One of them bumped into a diner, who grumbled. The staff clearly looked put out. If the restaurant didn't allow cell phones in their dining room, I didn't see how they could be happy about a film crew.

"Michael's out, Milikides is out," Janey said. "I didn't care for their ideas. I told Billy about the plan to produce a fresh riff on the 'Real Housewives' series and he said, 'If it makes you happy, go ahead.' It's a good idea. It could be a real money-maker and a boost for Beddington Place that would really put the town on the map. Tamsin's in for the exposure it will give her real estate business, and Chessie, you like it, too, don't you? Although we haven't really figured out yet what your character represents."

"I've never seen Janey act so bossy and high-handed," Chessie whispered in my ear. "Scary, isn't it?"

"For your information, I'm just coming into my own, Chessie," Janey loudly said. "And don't think I can't hear what you're saying to Paige, because I can hear every word." She coughed and cleared her throat and then banged on the table with her knife. "All right, everyone. Listen up. We've got ten minutes to come up with a concept for this scene, and 15 minutes more to shoot it. We're on a tight deadline in terms of time and budget, so let's get to work. Now, what is this scene about?"

"How about it's what a passive aggressive bitch you've become, pretending to be all palsy-walsy with Tamsin, when deep down you hate her guts," Michael Swett said. He'd just arrived at the table, the hostess in hot pursuit.

"Sir, sir!" the hostess said.

Two women stood behind the hostess. One was really old and one was a lot younger. The old one looked prematurely embalmed. There was something familiar about her.

"I don't understand how this could happen," the younger woman was saying to the hostess. "This is the table where my grandmother always sits. It's our table. It's reserved."

"Yes, I know, I know," said the hostess, wringing her hands. Obviously whoever the old broad was, she was a good customer. "I'm very sorry. I tried to tell them the table was taken. But none of them wouldn't listen, and they all barged right past. And, um, the table was available. And your grandmother wasn't here."

The old woman and the younger woman began arguing with the hostess whether or not the table could be considered "permanently reserved." While they were going at it, it dawned on me where I had seen the old lady. She was Biddy Maxwell, fundraising chairwoman for the Beddington Hills Hounds. I'd had a lot of fun skewering that wild and wacky night when Toby Fish and Lucky Lagerfeld and that Horagin woman created such a scene. My video and voiceover detailing the ordeal Pat had quickly sold to TMZ, and then the piece had picked up steam, was reposted on dozens of secondary sites, and then, joy of joy, somebody had even made a bootleg video of it that got thousands of hits on YouTube. The idiotic thing had gone viral. In Beddington Place, people associated with the hounds had died from shame. Tamsin told me that Biddy blamed and held me solely responsible for the scandal.

Right now I was hoping that Biddy wouldn't recognize me.

But she did.

"YOU again!!!" she cried, peering at me and pointing a witchy, crooked finger. "You should be ashamed. Not only are you sitting at MY table, where I eat lunch with my granddaughter every day, but look at your companions, these dreadful people you're associating with! Men brandishing film cameras! Women dressed up like tarts! And what is this costume you are wearing, young man?" she said to Diandra, not recognizing her. "You look like a pouf. You're ridiculous."

"That's enough, Granny," the young woman said. "We can sit at another table."

"I expect so!" Biddy said.

Just then Ben or Brad bumped into Biddy with his sound equipment, nearly braining her.

"Juliet!" Biddy groaned to her granddaughter. "Help me! Get me, away from these people!"

As the hostess hustled them away, Swett settled into the banquette. Sidling up beside me, he stage whispered, "Some friend you are not telling me about this meeting." He signaled for a waiter. "Young man, please bring me a glass of that excellent Chauvigne Domaine Richou I had here last night. The bartender may still have the open bottle. I don't believe I quite finished it. I had to leave quite suddenly, as there was a minor emergency with Mumsey."

"Michael, I did so tell you about this meeting," Janey broke in. "Did you not get my message?"

"I wouldn't know," Swett said. "My phone fell into the commode this morning quite by accident. Not having a phone is terribly inconvenient. But I did find out about this meeting," he said, casting a reproving eye towards Diandra, "and I would like to discuss with you, Janey, the part where your husband is taking over my role of executive producer, and underhandedly attempting to oust me from my own project."

"Billy did no such thing!" Janey squealed. "He's decided to take charge of the bankrolling. Money is his specialty. After all, he's made buckets of it! You must admit, Michael, although we all love you dearly, you're excellent at spending money, but not taking care of it."

"Ouch," Swett said without rancor. "You're striking below the belt." He took a swig of his Richou. "Not to mention I've never taken you for a penny-pincher, missy. I've seen you drop two grand on a pair of shoes. Didn't you buy seven pairs of Louboutins last week in Neiman's?"

"I hope Brad and Ben are getting this," I said to Chessie. "It's actually good material."

"It's tame, it's tiresome, it's timid," Diandra said, peeved no one was paying her attention. Batting her eyelashes at the camera, she licked her lips.

"Please do start filming," she said to Ben or Brad. "You can start with me."

"Hold your horses, will you?" Tamsin said, taking a break from her nonstop texting. "Before anybody starts shooting anything, I just have to make one more call."

"Uh, since you've asked me to help you script this scene, allow me to bring up an important point," I said. "To wit, does this scene have a point? I'm liking the squabbling, but where is it going? These shows are only as good as their rival characters. We should be using this scene as an opportunity to set that up."

"We're not rivals!" Janey and Swett both exclaimed at the same time.

"We love each other," Michael said, reaching out to squeeze Janey's hand. "Even if she is Jewish, she's my bestie, my dearest."

"He's like my sister," Janey said, giggling, and squeezing back. "Oh, I'm sorry, Michael. We haven't discussed whether or not you're straight or gay or bisexual and how it's a thread in the show. And now I've let the cat out of the bag while the camera is rolling, haven't I? My bad."

"I insist you edit that bit out," Swett ordered Ben or Brad. I was hopelessly mixed up myself which twin was which.

"Oh, Michael, leave it in, it's so juicy," Tamsin said. "I know you're upset, but think of it as 'taking one for the team.'"

"Somebody get me a fresh drink and I'll reconsider," Swett said.

"Here's a direction," I said. "Let's talk about the dead horse. Everyone is talking about it, so why not us?"

"Us?" Tamsin said, indignantly. "Since when did you become an 'us'? Janey, you never said Paige was a cast member."

"We haven't fixed on the cast yet," Janey said evasively. "But all the other Housewives series have at least five women. Ben, Brad, turn off the camera. We're not ready to film. We're still discussing."

"So who is the cast?" Tamsin demanded.

"Well, there's you, me, Chessie and of course, Diandra," Janey said. "But we definitely need more people."

"Well, I don't want Paige," Tamsin huffed. "I'm adamant about that.

Besides, she doesn't even live in Beddington Place. She lives in L.A. She's just here as a reporter, camped out in my guest cottage."

"And not for very long, either," I added, giving her a withering look.

"What about Mother?" Tamsin suggested to Janey. "Everyone, loves her. And while she's staying with me, she'll need something to keep her busy."

"What about the dead horse?" I tried again. "What does everybody think? Was it an accident or was it a murder? In any case, it's a juicy subject you could all sink your fangs into."

"Did she just say 'fangs'?" Tamsin said to Janey. "What is this? The Westchester version of True Blood?"

"I veto that topic," Diandra said swiftly. "There was no horse murder. I said it before and I'll say it again. One horse kicked another. Any explanation otherwise is nothing but speculation and, in my opinion, libel," she said, glaring at me.

"Then why didn't you have an autopsy like the officer suggested?" I pushed, hoping the twins were getting this on film.

"And by the way, they call it a necropsy," Swett said. "If we're going to talk about it, let's get it right."

"I hope you're getting all this," I said again to Ben or Brad.

"We are," Ben or Brad said. "Billy, er, Mr. Epstein, was right. His wife's friends really are obnoxious."

"Epstein? Is that Janey's last name?" I asked.

The twins looked amazed.

"You don't know who her husband is?" Ben or Brad said incredulously, as though I must be the stupidest girl on the block. "Mr.

Epstein is one of the wealthiest men in the free world. He's listed in Forbes. Made all his money in broadband. Practically invented it. He's underwritten foundations, funded African orphanages. He's got his own game farm. As far as rich people go, the guy's a titan."

"I must have heard somebody say her last name once, but I never put two and two together," I said.

"Well duhhh," the other twin replied, out of Janey's earshot. "Please don't mention this, but Mr. Epstein said to let her think we're working for her and not him. He's already thinking ahead. If it turns out his wife can't sell the pilot, it doesn't matter, because it's worth it to him to document her every movement. What we're doing is sort of private detective work. It's a way for him to keep tabs on her, find out what she's up to, what she's spending."

"Very clever," I said. "But I guess he didn't get to the top of the heap by being stupid."

"I think we should discuss who else we're going to have in the cast," Diandra interjected shrilly. Unused to playing second fiddle, she was jockeying for top position. "I say we go for the biggest celebrity Beddington Place has. With someone really famous involved, everyone will want to watch us. Who do we know we can get? Tamsin, what celebrities have you recently sold houses to? You must have some names."

"Most of them don't spend that much time here," Tamsin said.

"They're always jetting off to L.A., or the Hamptons."

"This is a waste of precious time," Janey fretted. "Nobody's concentrating. I only booked Ben and Brad for two hours, and our time is nearly up. I say let's meet tomorrow, right after my hair appointment. Let's do an entire segment on how we choose our friends, which will also further the plot."

"Janey, just to let you know, we got some good material just now," one of the twins said. "Worry less about what you say, than where you are saying it."

"Oh! Right! Location is everything, isn't it?" Janey said, suddenly pleased. "Speaking of, did you get enough footage on the restaurant? I hope we see Martin! He's often here, you know, just hanging out! I know we didn't get anything to eat, so you couldn't work in any advertorial food shots, but do you think you captured the ambiance, and got enough beautiful people for the background?"

"We'll need to get releases from everyone in the room," Ben or Brad said. "Maybe your pal the hostess can help out with that."

"We got a little of everything except for Chessie," the other twin said. "She didn't say much."

"Oh, dear," Janey said, frowning. "That's not good. Chessie, talk to Ben. Or is it Brad? You boys have me so confused! Chessie, don't be such a poker face. And open your mouth! Tell these men where you live, what your husband does for a living, where you buy your jewelry. Ben, just so you know, Chessie is a jewelry fiend. Diamonds and gold really are her best friends! But she never says where she gets it. Maybe for the pilot, we'll get her to divulge her secrets."

"Oh no, no, I don't want to be filmed right now," Chessie protested.

"Oh come on, Chessie," Janey coaxed. "You know those little bits they always have on the reality shows where one person talks directly to the camera? Usually to say something real mean, or to tattle? You're always so closemouthed, Chessie, but I know you can be a viper. Come on, be a good sport, and tell us something revealing, like how you got all your money."

"What are you talking about, Janey," Chessie protested. "My Philly's just a humble landscaper."

"Oh come now," Swett said. "We all know about that string of polo ponies your family owns. And you hardly ever mention your son, but isn't he a well known player?"

"Leave my son out of this!" Chessie cried out. When she had regained her composure, she gave a little speech. "Really, guys, I am telling you, I'm not going for this. I only came along today because Diandra begged me, and you know how I hate to disappoint her."

Diandra smirked.

"So you're just appeasing Diandra," Janey said, sighing. "I get it. And here I thought we were such good friends. "

"We are! We are friends!" Chessie said.

"So I mean nothing to you? Tamsin means nothing?" Janey pressed.

"That's not true," Chessie said, her voice choking up.

Swett slithered around to whisper in my ear.

"This is good stuff, I like it, we finally have some emotional conflict." He gestured to the twins to keep the camera rolling. "Chessie, tell us what you're feeling at this moment."

Chessie took a deep breath and drew herself up. "Janey, it's just, it's just that you do things that make me really uncomfortable. Philly and me don't come from a lot of money. Growing up, I had to scrape for every nickel. When you were in high school getting your nose done and taking tennis lessons, I had to work in a cafeteria."

She wiped her eyes with her napkin.

"Chessie, I seriously do not think that you are in any way, shape, or form, different than me," Janey said stiffly. "Than moi. Sorry, but I need to practice my French. I didn't know how you felt, Chessie, and I'm sorry. We're all almost equals here. Ben, Brad, keep the camera rolling."

"Stop with the camera," Chessie said, covering her face. "I can't do this, I won't do this!"

"You may be needed after all," Diandra said to me. "Chessie, is clearly bailing." She sighed. "I suppose we could pretend you live in Beddington."

"All righty, then," Janey said to Chessie after a long moment. "Have it your way. But I just want you to know I think you're a big poop and I'm not inviting you to my party."

"A party?" Diandra said, perking up. "You're having a party? Well, I certainly hope I'm invited."

"Of course you're invited, Diandra," Janey said. "Don't be silly. Who would dream of having a party without you? Anyway, I just decided about five minutes ago. A big party would be perfect for our pilot. I think I'll have it on the night after the pace. I'll give it a name and send out engraved invitations. What do you think about calling it, 'A Midsummer Night's Dream,' in honor of the Shakespeare musical?"

"It would be great for the pilot for our show," Tamsin agreed. "Everyone adores a big party scene."

"Yes, and it will be a great way to showcase my new house," Janey said, warming to the subject. "I've just spent a fortune having it landscaped and decorated. If we use it in the show, I can write it all off."

"It was Phil's company who landscaped your property," Chessie sniffed. "Be sure to mention that."

"Well, Chessie, if you think after the way you've just treated me that I would give Phil's company a plug, you've got another think coming," Janey said. "Right now I'm feeling insulted."

Chessie looked crestfallen.

I took Chessie to the ladies' room for a little pep talk.

"Don't worry," I said to her when she went into a stall and I stood by the sink applying lipstick. "In a couple of days you and Janey will be back to being friends. Janey's not the type to stay mad at her friends very long. I think she's just very excited about doing this show, and she wants everything to be perfect."

"Janey's crazy," Chessie said through the stall door. I heard the sound of flushing. "You don't know her like I do. In fact, you barely know her at all. You just know her through Tamsin and Diandra."

"Well, that's true enough," I said. "But I think that your friendship is important to her, and she really does want you to be part of the show."

"I don't care about the show," Chessie said, coming out, her eyes filled with tears. "I just want everybody to get along and for nothing to change. I don't want my dirty laundry aired on television. Everything is changing so quickly right now. I'm sorry, I'm crying, please forgive me."

I didn't know what to say to this, so I patted her hand.

"I don't know what the problem is, but I'm sure it will all work out for the best," I said, gamely. "Just give it time. You and Janey will work it out."

"She doesn't know the meaning of friendship!" Chessie declared.

"In her mind, it's all about shopping and lunch! You've been very kind, Paige. I really appreciate all you've done. I feel very close to you right now. I feel like you're my sister."

"What have I done?" I said, baffled. I had no clue where all this emo was coming from.

"You haven't poked into my business. You haven't asked a lot of questions. You take me as I am. You haven't blogged about my husband."

"Chessie, I really have no idea what you're talking about," I said, confused.

"Here, I want to give you something," Chessie said, fiddling at her wrist. She undid the clasp of a gorgeous platinum and gold bracelet studded with pave diamonds. "It's genuine David Hurman," she said. "It's worth thousands. I want you to have it. You know Hurman lives in Beddington Place, don't you? I'm surprised you haven't interviewed him."

"I can't take this," I said, taken aback.

"No, no, I want you to have it. Wear it. It'll look great on your wrist. I might ask you to give it back to me at some point, but for now, I want you to keep it." She pressed the bracelet into my hand and kissed me on the cheek.

We went back to the dining room just as Martin Roganoff was entering.

"There he is!" Janey squawked. "Ben, Brad! Train your cameras on me! You've got to get this shot! Yoo hoo, Martin! Over here! Martin! Martin!" she hooted.

"Oh, no you don't," Tamsin said, raising her voice and butting in. "Martin, over here!"

Both women leaped up from the table and ran headlong toward Martin Roganoff. Both began pawing him.

Diandra narrowed her eyes. "That behavior is so vulgar," she pronounced. "Those two should be ashamed of themselves. I can't believe they're so common!"

"Did you get that?" Tamsin asked the videographers, after Martin shook her off. Janey, a starstruck expression plastered on her face, continued to cling to his forearm.

"I wonder what he's like in bed," Michael mused. "I've always fancied him."

Meanwhile, Diandra slid over to give me a poke. "I just got a text from Janey's mechanic," she said. "He said when you drove my car into all that water, it flooded the air intake valve. Basically you wrecked the engine. He says it's going to be very expensive. How would you like to handle this? I'll need the money right away. Cash."

"The engine's wrecked?" I said incredulously. "I thought it was just the battery."

"Apparently not," Diandra said. Her normally placid brow, furrowed. I could almost see her brain at work as she hatched a plan. "Is there someone you should call?" she suggested. "Like your boss?"

"My boss isn't going to pay for this," I said to set her straight. I was getting a little tired of everyone acting like I had a multimillion-dollar contract, or a bottomless expense account. "Tell you what. Give me the number of the garage and I'll talk to the guy myself."

"Oh no," she said, rearing back. "Not so fast. This mechanic is a friend of a friend. He's doing the work off the books so I won't have to run it through my insurance. There's a cash machine I can take you to right now in Beddington Village. It's right next to the pastry shop."

Before I could respond to this bare-faced hold up, I had to answer my Blackberry, which was ringing.

"Hey, Pat," I said, not unhappy about the interruption.

"Paige, I just got a hot tip that Mariela Ellen-Stern is running buck naked down a dirt road and the police are trying to catch her!" Pat brayed into the phone. "Evidently she's gone totally bonkers, she's batshit nuts! This is great stuff!"

"Sorry, gotta go," I said to Diandra. "It's work." I ran over to the hostess who was still smoldering at her station. Most of the luncheon crowd had departed. "How do I get a taxi?" I asked, slipping a twenty in the hostess's hand. "Is there a cab service?"

"Um, not really," she said unhelpfully. "There's a cab in Catoonah, by the train station, and another in Beddington Hills, but they run on the commuter schedule and there's no dispatcher." This was not good news.

"Need a lift?" a familiar male voice said at my shoulder. I spun around and saw it was Ralsten, the painter. "Hey, I saw you with your friends, but I didn't want to bug you. You seemed kind of busy."

"I was, but now I've got to get somewhere and fast," I said. "Do you have a car? Can you take me?"

"My pleasure," he said, raising an eyebrow. "Consider me at your service."

A Naked Jog Down A Dirt Road
By Paige Turner

"A few minutes ago, the residents of Poser Pass, one of the most prestigious addresses in Beddington Place, were treated to the unusual sight of what appeared to be a naked jogger running down the dirt road! But this was no ordinary jogger. The individual running was none other than the soap opera star Mariela Ellen-Stern, wife of the internationally famous philanthropist Jacques Ellen-Stern. With me now is Rudolph Rancher, a retired film producer, staying with friends near the famous clock tower. Mr. Rancher caught more than a glimpse of the actress as she was trotting down the street. Mr. Rancher, would you please say what you saw?

"I was working in the garden when Bitsy, my Pekingese, started barking her fool head off," Mr. Rancher said. "I couldn't believe my eyes. I thought I was hallucinating. It's not every day that you see a buck naked beautiful woman on the road. Well, she wasn't entirely naked. She was wearing Nikes, but that's it."

Mr. Rancher says he only saw Ms. Ellen-Stern from the backside. "It was a beautiful butt," Mr. Rancher said. "The lady has a good haunch on her. Very shapely."

According to this witness, the police put Ms. Ellen-Stern in their vehicle. It's been learned that the actress has been taken to a facility. The Hollywood word on the street is that the 29-year-old actress has suffered a breakdown after her show was cancelled. In beautiful Beddington Place, it's just another amazing day in the neighborhood.

Stay tuned for more celebrity news and hot happenings.
This is Paige Turner for TMZ."

The Real Horsewives of Westchester County

A couple of hours later I was headed back to Tamsin's cottage, preparing to pack up, when a very strange thing happened. I walked in the door and confronted a woman I'd never seen before and she had her clothes off.

"Who are you?" cried the woman who was hastily draping herself in a humongous bath towel. At the sight of her, I yelped. From the look of things, I had clearly interrupted her bath. Decency dictated I apologize for barging in, and back right out the door, but for some reason I just stood there, stupefied. The last thing I could have anticipated when Ralsten dropped me off at Tamsin's cottage was finding a woman old enough to be my mother, half naked on the tiles.

"Um, I'm Paige, I live here," I said, carefully, recognition of who this must be slowly dawning. "You must be Tamsin's mother. Aren't you a bit early?"

"Early for what?" the woman said tartly. "Oh, I know I said I'd be here next week, but the plan changed. I have no control over anything anyway. I just do what I'm told. Tamsin, my daughter, she said the guest house was vacant, but I must say, it didn't look vacant to me. Quite the opposite. Some slob has been living here, seems to me." I blushed. Living alone these past weeks hadn't done much to improve my housekeeping skills, which were, at best, minimal. In L.A. Ric grumbled I wasn't exactly Nancy Neat-nick. I wondered what kind of roommate his pal Tickled Pink was; were her panties and makeup all over the floor, or was she some kind of clean freak?

"Sorry about the mess, but I wasn't expecting anyone to come in," I said. "Except Tamsin and Tamsin's cleaner. And she only leaves fresh towels and changes the linen. She also changes the flowers," I added, blushing again, feeling guilty about the largesse.

"Flowers! Oh, how that girl can spend money," the older woman barked. "She's even more reckless with money than her father, and that's saying something. Oh, dear." The towel slid a little down her scrawny torso and I averted my eyes in case she lost it.

"Hey, you know what? I'm going to leave you to your bath now," I said, glancing longingly towards the large, claw-foot porcelain tub. I wished I could tear off my clothes and climb right in, but obviously that wasn't happening. "What do you say I come back in an hour, which will give you time to get dressed, and then we can mosey over to the house to talk to Tamsin. This place is way too small for both of us, and she did tell me I had a few days to find a new place. Possibly you can move into the main house for a little while? Just until I get my, er, shit together. Sorry, I apologize. I didn't mean to swear."

"Swear away, honey, for my money you can swear like a goddamn sailor," the old lady said. "But don't think for a single minute I'm going to stay at her place. It's a monstrosity, that house. Why she built it, I have no idea. All for ego, to impress the neighbors. Besides, my son doesn't like having me underfoot. He says I get on his nerves. Fuck that," she said, shockingly. I wasn't used to old women swearing. "Fuck that," she repeated, more vociferously.

"Oh, she's not so bad," I said, defending Tamsin. Even if she was a bitch, for months, she'd been my benefactress. "She can be very generous, you have to give her that. And she has excellent taste. Personally, I think this place is gorgeous."

The old lady harrumphed. "She doesn't have an original idea in her head. Just tears pages out of magazines and then bullies some poor decorator into copying it."

I shrugged. "Works for me."

"What do you mean by that?" the old lady said. "You work for Tamsin? Are you her newest decorator? You won't last, you know. She gets a new one every year."

"Ouch," I said. "Not hardly. I'm a reporter actually. I work for Hello! TMZ, eonline, a bunch of websites. I'm a celebrity reporter, er, I report on celebrities."

"That's a career?" the old lady said incredulously. "Who knew." I didn't what to say to that.

"OK, well, you know what? I'm going to leave you to your bath," I said again. "But we will have to work out who's living here for the next day or two because there's only one bed."

"Then curl up on the loveseat, " the old lady said smartly. "There's plenty of cushions. By the way, my name is Alice and I don't mind if we share. I've been so lonely since my husband died. He was a helluva guy, my Albert."

I left Alice to her bath and walked over to Tamsin's house. The back door was open. A few minutes later, I was standing in her den, in front of her huge flat screen TV. No one was home, not even a maid, but by now I was on good terms with all the pets, especially Twinkie, who greeted me like a long lost friend. I picked the remote off the coffee table and sank down into one of the pair of matching George Smith chairs. Twinkie immediately jumped up to join me, followed by the Chesapeake Bay retriever, Ollie, and the basset hound, Hush. I turned on the TV.

The first thing that came on was the Bravo network, which was airing a segment of "Tip Top Chef," starring Clive Connors, recently voted one of the World's Sexiest Men. Clive was blathering on about food porn in his cheeky Welsh accent. I'd heard a rumor he'd been under consideration to take over the kitchen at Roganoff's before he got scooped up to star on, his own show.

Clive was discussing rack of lamb. "Yum, yum, yum," he said, pressing a rather large one into a hot pan. "Love that sizzle. This is a terrific special occasion dish, if you've got a birthday or an anniversary coming up. But I've deliberately made it quite simple to prepare, because when you've got guests, you don't want to be all flustered."

I sat back and scratched the dogs' heads. "Bet you'd like some of that meat, wouldn't you," I said. I loved how they stared at me with total adoration and thought how great it would be to have Ric look at me like that. I immediately flashed on the image of him canoodling on our sofa with Tickled Pink, and a hideously jealous fantasy visual of them spending time alone together made my heart ache. I wondered if they were cooking meals together in our tiny Ikea kitchen, or sharing Indian take-out, seated at the glass topped rattan table we'd picked up at Pier One. I thought about the delicious chicken tikka masala from Agra Indian Kitchen on Lincoln Boulevard, which I liked to sop up with the restaurant's homemade naan. I felt a little teary. Hell. It was true. I was jealous and homesick, too.

A commercial came on, and then another, and then another. That was one of the annoying things about Bravo; so many commercials.

Suddenly, in the midst of commercial wasteland, time came to a standstill.

What I saw next stopped my breath. An image popped up on, the screen of Diandra in full hunt regalia flying by on a horse, instantly followed by a saucy rollicking montage of Tamsin and Janey modeling hats in a millinery store. In another bit Chessie was tearing strips of hot wax off Phil's hairy back, while Michael Swett, wearing a tuxedo, berated his driver, that enormous black man he called Mr. T. threatening him with a riding crop. "Coming this fall," Andy Cohen's familiar voice chimed in. "Watch what happens."

I was flabbergasted. Gobsmacked. How had they pulled this off so fast? I was aware Janey and her crew had been filming snips and bits all week, but how had they managed to pull together enough footage to sell the package to the network and so fast? My heart was pounding. What in the world was happening?

The sound of footsteps in the hall set the dogs off into a frenzy of barking.

"Oh, it's you," Tamsin said, standing in the family room doorway. "How'd you get in?"

"D-did you see that?" I stammered.

"How'd you get in?" Tamsin repeated, her voice not very friendly.

"You left the back door open," I said, my eyes still on the TV. "Your mother needed some privacy. You didn't tell me she was arriving today. It was a bit awkward. She was about to have a bath.

"Oh, bother. I forgot to say. Well, now you've met her. Alice. Isn't she a pip?"

"Well, she handled our meeting well, considering she was in a towel," I said, finally tearing my eyes away from the TV. The commercial was over. Maybe it was all a bad dream. I turned my attention back to Tamsin and the problem brewing in the cottage. "So, what's this bunkhouse arrangement? You don't really expect me to live with her? Do you?"

"Oh, only for a night or two," Tamsin said, vaguely. She lifted Twinkie into her arms and dramatically collapsed on the other sofa. "Just deal, okay? I have to."

"And what's this I just saw on the TV?" I said challengingly. "A promo for the Real Horsewives? Tell me the truth. Did you know how fast this was all happening?"

"Yes and no," Tamsin said, yawning. "Janey is amazing. I always thought that girl was a lightweight, but she proved me wrong, she did. I think once her husband got involved, he made a bunch of calls. I guess he knows the producers personally, or maybe he's is a shareholder in the network? It's really a mystery, but in any case, it's happening. It is. We just have to come up with more footage and fast, because Janey's got some big creative type on retainer who's pulling it all together, bam, bam, bam. I'm going to be a reality star. It's exciting."

"You don't seem that excited," I said, aware Tamsin seemed less than her normally effervescent self.

"Rough day at the office is all," she said. "I could use a martini. What about you? How about it?" She shifted Twinkie off her lap and pulled herself up off the sofa. "I might have to make mine a double. You might want to do the same. I have some important information to share, and some of it isn't pretty."

"What do you mean?" I said, following her over to the bar area. From my random sorties into Tamsin abode, I'd noticed there was a bar in every room. "Can it be any worse than you saying I have to find a place to live in, uh, six hours? This really is a bummer about your mother. Did I forget to mention she deliberately let her towel slip in front of me? Oh, and by the way, she doesn't like you very much."

"Really? What did she say?" Tamsin said, pulling out a large shaker and filling it with ice. She poured in a lot of Beefeaters, and then a dribble of vermouth. "Now where the hell are the olives?" She gave the whole thing a grand shake and then poured out our drinks. "Mother is pretty funny, actually, if you forget about the part where she killed her husband."

"Killed her husband?" I said, handing her the olive jar. "You mean your father?"

With a tiny, perfectly proportioned silver plated three pronged fork, Tamsin skewered out a few olives. Plopping two each glass, she handed me my drink. "To friends," she said. "Salud. Paige, I just want you to know that no matter what happens, I still like you."

"Go back to the part where you called your mother a murderer," I, said, clinking glasses. "She mentioned your father to me. She called him her darling Albert."

"Well, he wasn't my father, he was my stepfather," she said. "She put a bullet through his heart. Killed him in cold blood. He was Sal's father. Sal's my stepbrother. My real dad died when he was very young. I was still a child, really."

"No shit," I said, returning to the sofa and sitting down. I wanted to get comfy to hear about this. Twinkie snuffled over to try to climb into my lap. "Keep talking."

"Well, she got off pretty easy, all things considered," Tamsin said. "I hired a really high powered attorney to represent her, good daughter that I am." She sat down and patted the leather beside her and Twinkie leaped up. The dog circled around twice and began furiously burrowing into the half dozen kilim and tapestry pillows. "Stop it, Twinkie!" Tamsin cried, giving the dog's behind a little smack. "You're devastating my decor, sweetie. Mommy doesn't like that."

"Tamsin!" I said, trying to get her back on topic, never an easy task. "Tell me more about your mother."

"Well, under the advice of her attorney, she pleaded self defense.

She said for years he'd abused her, tried to kill her, even though there was never evidence. Well, there wouldn't have been anyway, given his family background. Sal's family is, was, er, you know, connected." She pushed, one finger against her the cartilage of her nose and pressed it sideways. "So maybe he was pushing her around. Or maybe he wasn't. Who knows? Anyway, she pleaded not guilty by reason of self defense, but the jury wasn't buying, it and the judge sentenced her to seven years. Manslaughter, they called it. The lawyer did a great job; that was the lightest sentence. She served three years at the prison for women, which I think you know about because Diandra rides through there. Didn't you go on a trail ride with her and that wild bunch? Diandra told me something happened, and you rode back to the barn alone with whatsername, Penny. That one who says she knows me, but doesn't."

"She never said she knew you," I said. "Only that she knows of you. There is a difference."

"Whatever," Tamsin said, yawning. "Boy, am I tired. I really need a nap. Are you almost finished your drink? Don't leave, though, before I tell you this thing that's so very important."

"So your mother was incarcerated basically around the corner from this house?" I said. "How convenient."

"Yes, that's the main reason I moved to Beddington Place. For the convenience of having her close."

Suddenly Tamsin looked haggard and seriously exhausted.

"Don't get too hung up on this, Paige," she said. "I've talked way too much. I should shut my big mouth. It must be the liquor talking. Just, go now. Pack your bags and scram. Mother is staying in the guest house and that's that. Oh, and here's the thing I was going to tell you when I first came in. You're off the show. You're not a member of the Real Horsewives crew or cast. Janey really wanted you to be a part of it, but even with Billy bankrolling the production, the rest of us still have some say. Just so you know, Chessie didn't care one way or the other if you were going to be in the show or not. She just does whatever Diandra tells her. But Michael and I voted against you. We blackballed you, if you want to know the truth. It has nothing to do with our friendship or admiration for you, but you being a celebrity reporter, we just didn't think it was fair. You're already on TV and in the tabloids. You got your 15 minutes. Now it's our turn."

"Is that why you cut all the stuff Janey taped that included me?" I said, feeling hurt. I was unnerved by this turn of events. In fact, I was still digesting how close I had come to being roomies with an indicted murderess.

"Of course, darling. We had to," Tamsin said, more sweetly. "Although you did look adorable in the early rushes. You're very photogenic. But I suppose you hear that all the time. I must say, I am envious."

"Did Diandra want me in or out?" I blurted.

"You know, I don't rightly recall," Tamsin said. "Isn't that funny? I can't remember a thing!" She picked up her glass and then mine.

"Run along, Paige," she said as if I were one of her dogs. "Start working your contacts. I'm sure you'll find a place to rest your head tonight, probably within the hour."

Now If You Would Just Sign This Piece of Paper

"So tell me again what happened," Chessie said half an hour later when she swung by the cottage to pick me up. "Tamsin's mother is moving in with her? Poor Tamsin."

"Yeah, but not forever, it's more like an extended visit," I said, clinging to the grab bar on the passenger seat of the Benz R Class Mercedes SUV Chessie was driving. An anxious driver, she gripped the wheel. Without turning her head away from the traffic, she said, "I'm kind of famished. Are you up for a little nosh?"

It was late in the afternoon and I was hungry, having barely eaten all day.

"Sure," I said, "Let's do it."

Chessie guided the big Mercedes into the parking lot of Beddington Place's Italian deli and immediately began loading up a cart. From the refrigerated section, she tossed in three different packages of imported cheese, sliced salami, and smoked salmon. From another case, she took a jar of herring, packed in sour cream. From the baked goods department she chose a dozen bagels: egg, sesame, poppy seed and cinnamon raisin. In the produce department, she palmed a Jersey tomato and a Bermuda onion. At the checkout, she peeled off a wad of cash. Her, eyes lit on a pile of individually wrapped mint chocolate chip brownies.

"Oh, I'm so glad I saw these," she said, adding them to her order. "These are Phil's favorites."

Back in the car, Chessie drew a pack of cigs from her Hermes bag. "Want one?" she said, but I declined. "I know it's a disgusting habit, but I just can't quit," she said, lighting up. She inhaled deeply, filling her lungs, and then, surprisingly, blew out her open window a perfectly formed smoke ring. "I never forgot how to do that," she said with pride. "When Phil and I were dating, he said my blowing smoke rings was one of the things that most attracted him."

"Oh yeah," I said. "What else did you do to attract him?" I said. I realized I didn't know much about Chessie other than she was quieter and more reserved than her friends. She also seemed more of a homebody, very married, and closely involved with her husband. She often mentioned the homey meals she made for him, comfort food like lasagne and chicken pot pie. And although they had live-in help, Chessie personally attended to things like Phil's laundry. Just like Janey and Tamsin, Chessie wallpapered herself in pricey accessories — the three of them were known for their big diamonds and expensive bags — but unlike the others, Chessie had a weakness for cheap, amusing things she picked up at Target and Forever 21; like fabric covered headbands and rubber flipflops and gold-plated lucky charms. "I'm not snobby," Chessie said after I admired a pair of sunglasses she said she got at T.J. Maxx. "Everything I own doesn't have to have a designer's name plastered on it."

After the deli, we left the black top, and turned down a rutted, un-paved portion of Muskrat Dam Road. A couple of hairpin turns Chessie negotiated only by violently jerking the steering wheel. We carried on along a stretch of dirt road I'd never seen, close to the reservoir. Chessie slowed the big car down to a crawl and the Mercedes jounced and bounced along a particularly rutted portion of road, pock-marked by treacherous holes that would have torn a lesser vehicle's axle straight off.

"Sorry," she said, struggling with the wheel, the Mercedes at one point threatening to slide off the road. "It is a little rough over here, but it keeps down the traffic. The town keeps making noises they're going to come in one day and pave it, but we hope that never happens. Phil and I prefer the road being so bad. Keeps out the riff raff."

"Must be hell on the shocks," I said. "It's bad enough in this SUV. I can't imagine doing this in a sports car."

"Now that you mention it, Diandra never came out here in that cute little car of hers," Chessie commented. "Is that why you've never been to my house?"

"Um, no," I said. "I've never been to your house because you've never invited me."

"Oh!" Chessie said, startled. "I guess you're right. Well, I'm glad, you called me about a place to stay. Phil loves company. Ever since our son grew up and left the house, it's been so quiet."

"Are you sure you have room?" I said. "I don't need much, but I do need my own bed and bath."

"Absolutely," Chessie said. "I'm going to put you in the spare bedroom, which by the way, has its own bath. There's no tub, but it's a very nice shower. It's also Cuddles room, but don't let that worry you. Cuddles is so sweet. He's really adorable. I know you're going to love sharing a room with him."

She stopped the car in front of a pair of large, wrought iron gates, flanked on either side by a 16-foot-high electric stockade fence, the kind of fencing I'd seen at zoos. The fence was shrouded by a mass of vines and shrubs, the dense foliage masking it to be virtually invisible. Chessie punched some digits into a security panel. Iron gates rolled open, and Chessie drove inside.

"Oh dear, Phil's men are still here," she said, looking ahead at several trucks and vehicles and a scurrying cadre of workmen. We drove down a snow-white gravel path. A house loomed ahead. It was a low-slung, bunker-like affair, painted a dusky, fern green that perfectly camouflaged it to blend seamlessly into the forest. From the vantage of the driveway, it appeared to be windowless. I didn't have much time to reflect on this, as there was an agitated flurry of activity going on in the driveway that, commandeered my attention.

"Don't pay this any mind," Chessie said. She put the car in park and got out. I did the same. We each lifted a bag of her deli purchases from the backseat and I followed her down a graveled passageway shielded by boxwood on both sides. Behind us, on the driveway apron, two workers were stacking boxes into a white van. Another man was loading a vintage Lamborghini Espada on to a flatbed trailer. "Wow," I said, glancing at the car. "Those are some wheels. Is it an Espada?"

"You know it?" Chessie said, surprised.

"Yeah, it's only the best Lamborghini."

"Phil loves it," Chessie frothed.

"Where's that one going?" I queried as Chessie put her key in a side door.

"Oh, probably out for servicing," Chessie said evasively. We entered the mudroom, a long, narrow, Mexican-pavered vestibule tricked out in Pottery Barn basics, including masses of baskets and cubbies and multiple coat hooks. An enormous dog water bowl, more like a tub than a bowl, sat on the tiled floor. What kind of dog, I wondered, needed a bowl that large?

"Listen," Chessie said, trundling on ahead. "Phil's working in his study and Cuddles is resting upstairs. I'll take you up in a moment to meet him, but let's get these groceries stowed away first. Then I'll give you the, grand tour."

We passed through an arched hallway leading to the main rooms downstairs. A hive of activity was going on.

"That's Nalda, our maid," Chessie said as we continued on to the kitchen. "And that's her brother, Alvaro, who's helping us out." These two were also busy packing boxes. Nalda was giving orders in Spanish. "Cuidadoso con esos rectángulos malditos," she said. "Usted hará a la señora enojada."

Boxes were everywhere, as well as tape, twine, and scissors. Alvaro moved along with a grim efficiency, following his sister's commands.

"No, no, no," she scolded him, followed by a flurry of Spanish as he unfurled a roll of bubble wrap in front of a cabinet. "La cajuela está llena de trastos."

"What's going on?" I said to Chessie, who steadily kept moving forward. In the kitchen, the size and scope of what you'd expect in a restaurant, she greeted two young Hispanic girls. They were packing more things, removing stacks of bowls and serving dishes and plastic storage containers, wrapping anything breakable in white paper sheets.

Chessie put the salmon and cheese and salami in the refrigerator and the baked goods on the granite counter. Using a can opener to pry the lid off the herring, she stuck in two fingers.

"Sorry, I can't resist," she said, popping a chunk of fish in her, mouth. "Want some?"

I had to fight off the urge to gag.

"What's going on?" I said when I recovered. "Are you moving?"

"We're just making a little change. We have another place in North Carolina and Phil wants to spend more time there. I know some people don't like the Carolinas in the summer, but we think it's the best time of year. But don't worry, the house isn't for sale or anything. If we do decide to sell, of course Tamsin will want the listing. Meanwhile, we told her we might consider a tenant. Listen, I want to give you something."

"What's this?" I said when she handed me the Mercedes' key.

"I don't want you to feel like you're a prisoner while you're staying here," she said. "As you see, it's a remote location. There's no way you can walk into town, or the train, or get anywhere without a vehicle. So, please, take it. I won't be around to drive you. You'll need it."

"But I've never driven anything that big," I protested. "What if I hit something?"

"Don't worry, it's got all these alarms that go off if you get too close to another object," Chessie said. "It's easy-peasy." She hesitated for a hairsbreath. "Now if you would just sign this piece of paper, we're all set."

I squinted at an embossed document with a New York State seal on it.

"What is this?" I said.

"It's the title to the car," Chessie said. "Just put your John Hancock right here by that X. Don't forget to date it. We've already signed it."

"Chessie," I said. " I can't do this."

"Sure you can," she said. "It's easy-peasy. If you like, give me a dollar."

"Chessie, I can't do this," I repeated.

"Sign it, Paige," Chessie said firmly. "If you want the room, sign the paper. What's the problem? You're getting a beautiful car to drive and besides, I promise, we'll take it back. I just need to put it in your name for a little while, okay? Come on, don't be a putz."

I signed.

"Great," Chessie said with relief. "Now let's go upstairs and I'll show you the room."

We left the kitchen to climb a flight of stairs. The walls were covered with framed photographs of a person I assumed was Chessie's son. He was on a horse in every picture and there were dozens.

"Did you see that preview for the 'Horsewives'?" I asked, feeling some need to talk. The scene at Chessie's house made me anxious, and when I'm anxious, I like to talk. "I can't believe Janey pulled it all together so quickly. It's already on the program roster! How'd she do that, do you know? I'm a little shocked, actually."

"Hmmm, I didn't see it," Chessie said noncommittally. "For some, reason, our cable has been out for a week. No TV. No Internet."

"No Internet?" I said, freaking. Without it, how could I do my work? "You still have cell service, right?"

"The land line works fine," Chessie said. "Our cell service has always been sketchy. There's so many trees out here, you see, and then the reservoir…" Her voice trailed off.

"I didn't realize the reservoir could cause a problem with cell service," I chattered. "I never heard of that."

"I don't really understand it myself," Chessie said. "I'm not interested in things like that. I'm more into pinochle."

Before I could respond I was stopped dead in my tracks by a frightening sound coming from one of the bedrooms. The sound was coming from behind a door. It was a low, rumbling, growling, terrible sound; it was feral, it was ferocious.

"Chessie, is that your dog?" I said.

"That's our Cuddles," she replied. "He's saying he can't wait to eat you. Ha ha, I mean meet you. Don't be put off by his vocalizing. He's very emotional and sensitive. He's not a dog, by the way. He's a pig. A pot-bellied pig and a big one. He's all love. Phil rescued him from a farm sanctuary when he was just six weeks old. He's an important member of our family.

"Let me give you a few instructions before we go in," she continued. "Don't look the pig in the eye. Don't make any sudden moves.

Don't stand too close. Cuddles is very protective. Don't stick your hand out for him to sniff — he might bite it! Also keep your voice low; he doesn't care for loud or sharp sounds. The most important thing to remember is that Cuddles is extremely territorial and possessive, so whatever you do, don't touch or move his things. Okay, are you ready?"

She turned the knob and flung the door open. An enormous black beast crouched on the rug, grunting.

"Omigod, what is that?" I screamed as the creature hurled itself towards me with bared tusks. Chessie immediately seized it by the collar.

"Cuddles, Cuddles, this is Paige, darling," she cooed to it soothingly. "There's nothing to be afraid of, baby," she said as the pig grunted and continued to make unfriendly sounds. "Sweetheart, Paige is our friend. Paige, it's okay now. You can pet him."

"Maybe later," I hedged. While Chessie stroked the animal's enormous head and shoulders, I cautiously took a peek around the room. Clearly the son's imprint was all over the place; the color scheme was cream and navy; the motif was a weird combo of equestrian and nautical. There were dozens of horseback riding ribbons, and framed photographs of boating scenes. An antique red and white doughnut life preserver had been rakishly hung over a door. The bedspread was rather juvenile, printed with pictures of sailboats. The room was filled with dark mahogany furniture; a king size, four poster bed, an armoire, and a tall bureau with lots of, drawers. A night table with a reading lamp stood to one side of the bed. On it was a candy dish filled with M&M's and a framed, signed photo of the wrestler, Brie Bella. The floor was covered by a wheat-colored coir carpet; in one corner was an enormous red, white, and blue dog, er, pig bed.

"There's a flat screen TV in the armoire," Chessie said, still stroking Cuddles who had committed himself to a low growling. "Although with the cable out, I don't suppose you can use it. We do have some DVDs you could watch. Will you be needing a desk for your work? Phil has an extra in his office. Nalda's brother could bring it up."

"No, no, don't go to any special trouble," I said, still not daring to look at Cuddles. "Are you sure this is going to be okay? I don't think your pig wants a roommate."

"Of course Piggy-Wiggy does," Chessie cooed again in a babyish voice. "Cuddles, I'm going to release you now. Go over to Paige and give her a nice, big, sloppy, kiss." In a normal, neutral tone, she said to me, "Now just hold perfectly still and he won't hurt you." I stood rigid as a mannequin while Cuddles did his thing. Only after he stuck his nose in my crotch did I seem to pass muster.

An hour later after we'd devoured everything Chessie had bought at the deli, Phil emerging briefly from his den to join us, I pleaded exhaustion and a desire to go to sleep. Cuddles followed me up the stairs and beat me to the bed, even though I'd just plied him with herring snacks. By the, time I'd shucked my clothes, he was already ensconced on the four-poster, snoring. Crossing to the armoire, I unpacked my small bag, figuring I'd return to Tamsin's in the morning to retrieve the rest of my stuff. I'd accumulated a surprising amount over the past several weeks; riding clothes, cocktail dresses, and a slew of personal grooming products, things Tamsin had grown tired of, or had thrown my way.

"So what's it going to be?" I said to Cuddles who opened one eye warily. He was curled up on top of the covers, dead center. I pointed at his dog, er, pig nest. "Come on, be a sport and get on your bed," I said, encouragingly. One of the pig's ears twitched. I went over and patted his bed. He growled menacingly. I immediately removed my hand.

"Cuddles, off the bed," I said in the same firm tone I'd heard used by Mark Stover, the celebrity dog trainer. To summon up my courage, I tried imitating Stover's tone of voice. "Cuddles!" I barked. "Get off the bed, now!"

Cuddles pinned his ears and raised his lip and growled.

Hours later, I was curled up on the coir carpet wrapped in an old quilt foraged from the armoire, dreaming I was in Honolulu being devoured by flying gnats. The carpet was itchy, the coir fibers penetrating the fabric of the blanket. All night I'd been scratching my arms and legs. Suddenly Cuddles' angry snorting pierced my dream state. His grunt was like thunder through a loudspeaker. He leapt off the bed and rushed to the door, which, was shut. Now he was grunting and snarling furiously, no doubt waking the whole house.

I hadn't bothered to draw the bedroom blinds and saw that it was still night. Outside in the courtyard, I heard the sound of sirens. Lights were flashing and an alarm went off. There was a furious pounding at the back door where Chessie had brought me in.

"This is the FBI," I heard a man's voice shout. "Open up."

There was a fearsome sound of fire axes chopping through wood, and twisting metal hinges, and bolts popping away from walls. Moments later, there was the sound of heavy boots clomping through the house.

"Hush, Cuddles" I said futilely as the pig increased his growling. "Let's be quiet for a minute." There was a timid knock on the bedroom door and Chessie poked her head in.

"Go back to sleep, there's nothing to worry about, it's all under control downstairs," she said, idiotically.

"What do you mean 'under control?'" I said. "What's happening?"

"Nothing, nothing, it's just some men here to have a conversation with Phil," she said. "Can you keep Cuddles with you? He'll be safer here."

"Cuddles safer?" I said, feeling quite alarmed. "What's going on?"

Phil suddenly appeared behind Chessie, his hairy, roly-poly belly spilling out from under his pajama top.

"Go back to sleep, young lady," Phil said. "There's nothing going, on here concerning you. Get back into bed. Invite Cuddles to join you. He's a great snuggler. Sometimes when I can't sleep, we wrestle."

"Cuddles wouldn't even let me on the bed," I said indignantly. "And he wouldn't let me use his nest either. I've been sleeping on the floor!"

"Well, it takes time for him to bond with new people," Phil said. He gave the pig a kiss on the snout.

"Hey, guys, is this really necessary?" I heard Phil saying to the FBI agents as he made his way down the stairs. "Bustin' down the door like that? C'mon, you coulda just rang the bell."

In front of me, Chessie began crying.

"They can't take him away again," she said between sniffles.

"Where are they taking him?" I said. "What'd he do?"

"He's innocent, my Phil is innocent," Chessie sobbed. "He's been framed."

"What are these guys here for, Chessie?" I said, realizing I had no idea what was her last name.

"Just go back to sleep, Paige," Chessie said grimly, pulling herself together, that frozen mask expression she often wore sliding back into place. She pulled the door shut and Cuddles grunted after her retreating footsteps.

"Shhhh, boy," I said, and this time the pig listened. He turned his head towards me and cocked one ear. I risked reaching out to rub his head, and he whimpered a little in pleasure. It seemed after all that we might become friends.

I pressed my ear against the door, trying to hear what was happening downstairs. Men were talking. One of the voices was Phil's. Then a different man's voice could be heard and then another and another. I cracked open the door to hear better. The moment that happened, Cuddles pushed through the opening with his nose.

"Cuddles, get back," I said, struggling to tug him back inside the room.

"Okay, start cataloging all this stuff," I heard one man say. "And somebody, grab the computers. Cellphones, Smartphones, Blackberries, iPads, Crackberries. Get it all. Phil, I'm taking you into custody, but first I am going to read you your rights. You have the right to remain silent. Anything you say or do can and will be held against you in the court of law. You have the right to speak to an attorney. If you cannot afford an attorney, one will be appointed for you. Do you understand these rights as they have been read to you?"

"No, no," I heard Chessie cry out. "You can't take him! He didn't do anything wrong! He's the victim of a set up!" At the sound of her agitated voice, Cuddles went ballistic. Strong as cannon fire and speedier than a bullet, he maneuvered himself past my legs and shot out the bedroom door. Flying down the corridor and careening down the stairs, the pig made a beeline for the intruders. I heard a female voice screaming and then a flurry of Spanish and the next thing I heard was Phil shouting, "Don't kill him! Cuddles, down!"

I heard a shot, and then I heard the pig whimper.

I was scared. I didn't know what to do. Soon enough the FBI might start searching the house and they'd find me and ask me who I was and what I was doing there. In the bathroom, a robe hung on a hook. Wrapping it around me, I crept down the stairs. Just as I reached the landing, an officer was cuffing Phil.

"Don't worry, honey," Phil said. Chessie was standing in a corner, crying. Nalda's arm was around her shoulders. Alonzo was holding Cuddles, who I was relieved to see was still alive. The pig had a blurry, bewildered expression. One of the FBI officers must have shot him with a stun gun. "I'll be out in a couple of hours and back home as soon as I can. Just call my attorney, will you? His number's in my phone."

"Sorry, but you can't give your wife your phone," one of the FBI guys said. "We're including it as part of the evidence. Don't expect it back anytime soon."

Flanked by two officers, Phil was led from the house in cuffs.

"Gather up all these boxes," said the agent who seemed to be leading the raid. There were a lot of agents. Some were carrying clipboards, while others were organizing and loading Phil and Chessie's personal belongings into waiting vans. "Don't forget to check the bathrooms and the vanities and cabinets. Also check the freezer and all the drawers of the refrigerator. Don't forget to look under the carpets. There's probably a safe somewhere. You never know where these guys are going to hide stuff, so leave no stone unturned." For the first time he seemed to notice me. "And who are you?"

he said.

"Well, uh, I'm a houseguest," I began, wondering how ridiculous my cover story would sound.

"Is that so?" the FBI guy said. "How well do you know your host?"

"Hey, that's Paige Turner, the celebrity journalist," one of the agents said. "I just saw her on TV a coupla nights ago. Some gossip show. She was reporting on that soap opera star seen running naked down a street." He glared at me and said, "How despicable and low is that to report on a poor woman who was clearly disturbed."

"Oh, so that's what you're doing here," the first man said. "Trying to scoop the authorities on a big crime story, huh? Pretty sneaky."

"No!" I said. "Nothing like that! I didn't even know Phil was in any trouble. I'm just a houseguest."

"Yeah, yeah, that's what they all say," the guy said, jeering. "You know what? I'm thinking I should slap a subpoena on you right now, and drag your ass down to court. You could be withholding evidence. Hand over all your notes on the Joneses, right here and right now."

"I don't have any notes on the Joneses," I said. "Until this very moment, I didn't even know their last name."

"Yeah, yeah, a likely story," the guy sneered again. He turned to one of his agents. "Go through her things."

"Don't you hurt my friend!" Chessie shouted. "You bullies, you treat her right — she doesn't have anything to do with this."

As they rifled through my things, my cell phone serenaded me with my ring tone for Pat.

The FBI agent nodded, go ahead, answer it.

Pat was all worked up.

"Paige!" she crowed into the phone. "I just got a hot tip! This is wild! It seems the FBI has arrested this guy who happens to be a big time something or other with connections in Miami and Dubai and that he's worth maybe billions, he's right in Beddington Place apparently, with money so well hidden nobody will ever get to it! Nobody even knows his real name! Supposedly he's connected to a major New York crime family, races cars, horses, boats, this guys is like the power behind the power. What dish! I don't care how you get the story, but this is breaking big. I want you to get the inside scoop and get the story to me no later than twelve noon. I have 15 media outlets already screaming for details and the phone won't stop ringing!"

"I think I know the case," I said slowly.

"Well that's a start," Pat said. "Well, can you do it? I want pics, I want video, and I especially want an interview with the wife who says she doesn't know anything."

"Pat you are not going to believe this," I said. "I'm right here in the house. The FBI is here. The guy's just been arrested. The family pig just tried to attack a police officer who shot him, but with a stun gun."

"In the house?! Omigod!" Pat shouted. "Did you say 'family pig'? Omigod. Paige, you are amazing! That's terrific! I'm so proud of you! I love how you get right in there! All right, listen. Be careful and don't get hurt. I hear this guy has his own army of goons. I heard he has guns in the house. I heard something about Oliver North and the Contras. Now how fast can you turn this around? Everyone is clamoring for information. When you reveal who the guy is, we're going to get so many hits! This is a jackpot, baby, holy fuck, I might have to give you a raise."

"I can't do it," I said. "Pat, this woman is my friend."

"What? What woman?"

"The wife. Her name is Chessie. She's married to the guy who just got arrested."

"Chessie?" Pat was incredulous on the other line.

"Yes, we've sort of bonded. She's been very kind to me."

"'Kind???'" Pat screamed. "Are you crazy? You're a journalist. Journalists don't have friends. Don't start your whining now, Paige, crying to, me about your scruples. You get right in there and nail that story. I'll need it by noon at the latest. No, wait, ten a.m. And if you don't deliver, I'm calling whatsername, Kimberley, the country western singer."

"Pat, I'm sorry but I can't talk about this right now," I said. "There's someone here trying to talk to me. I'll call you back."

"Don't you dare," Pat threatened, but I had already clicked off.

Chessie and Cuddles and the head FBI guy were standing in the doorway. The FBI guy's expression was severe.

"Is this car yours, miss?" he said, dangling the keys to the Mercedes.

I hesitated. Chessie looked at me coolly, any pain or misery she might be feeling at that moment disguised. Her lips were firmly set in a straight line. She seemed resolved, older, more dignified. Cuddles was quietly standing at attention next to her. The 5-carat diamond on her finger caught the light, sparkling, as she rested her hand on his huge head.

"Yes, it's my car," I said to the FBI guy who seemed surprised. "I can show you the title if you doubt me, but yes, that's my car, it is."

"They wanted to take it, impound it, or seize it as drug money property," Chessie said. "I told them it was yours. They didn't believe me."

The FBI guy looked exhausted. "Okay, forget the car," he said.

"All right," Chessie said to the agent. "That's settled. Get back to your packing. How long are you going to be here? I can ask Nalda to make, your men a pot of coffee. Would that help move things along, you think?"

"That would be really nice, Mrs. Jones, or whatever your name is," the FBI guy said. "That's very gracious of you, very human."

"We're not animals," Chessie said. "And my husband is innocent."

Let's Give 'em Something to Talk About,
A Little Mystery to Figure Out

*T*here was nothing for me to do at that point but leave. I asked Chessie what she would do without wheels, but she said not to worry; she still had Nalda and Nalda's car. "At least they didn't take that," Chessie said grimly, of the dented Civic, as we hugged in her driveway. "Although I guess soon enough they'll figure out Phil paid for it. We've always taken good care of our help. Nalda's been with us for so long, she's practically family."

"Try not to worry," I said, gamely, feeling more than ever I was talking out of my ass. I was slack-jawed, shell-shocked, I had no idea what was going on. Was Phil a dangerous criminal? Or, as Chessie had suggested, had someone set him up? And what information was the FBI going on when they staged this bust? After turning the house upside down, none of the agents had found a single illegal thing, not so much as a hash pipe. "I'm sure Phil will make bail in a matter of hours," I said to Chessie in a tone I hoped was comforting. "You've got a good lawyer. He'll take care of it."

"Yeah, he's very good, as long as you pay him," Chessie said drily. "Listen, let's talk after you get settled. Try and get some sleep."

"OK," I agreed, still trying to figure out what to do about Phil's arrest. I really didn't want to report on it out of deference to Chessie, but, I knew that if I didn't come through with something, Pat would have me axed. Ten minutes later I was still deliberating how to handle the situation as I steered Chessie's Mercedes down "Holiday Inn Way." I cautiously parked in a "Guests Only" designated spot. Rolling my battered Samsonite across the lot and up over the curb, I slipped through the electronic sliding doors and into the lobby, hit reception and got my card key. Checking myself into room 363, I hung out the "Do Not Disturb" sign. I threw myself on the bed, falling instantly into deep sleep.

I woke up hours later, startled by the sound of a maid's vacuum. The din was coming from out in the hall. I was groggy-eyed and dry-mouthed. I looked at my phone and saw it was nearly six p.m. Somehow I'd managed to sleep the entire day. The first thing I did was call Pat — to apologize, to explain, to try to keep my job — but she wasn't answering.

Next, I tried calling Ric, but he wasn't picking up either. I started to leave him a long pathetic message, telling him how much I missed him, but 30 seconds into it, his machine cut me off. That made me feel so sad and so bad that I did something I hadn't done in a long time. I felt the urge to write something for myself. I opened the minibar, grabbed a bottle of Sutter Home red, and pulled out a pen and a notebook. "It's not easy being a journalist," I wrote. "It's so much more complicated than the simple act of reporting. The first thing to remember is that nothing is what it seems. And even though a picture may be worth a thousand words, images can be distorting. In every situation, there are choices to be made, and it is up to the journalist to choose whether to be cruel or sympathetic to the subject matter. There is no such thing as unbiased journalism. There always is a slant. Modern journalism dictates that it's almost never your job to tell both sides of the story, and there will be times when you see there are more than two sides."

I sipped the sweet red.

"As a journalist I am forced to constantly remind myself that whatever I'm writing about, I must be sensitive to the subject's willingness to share. In every interview situation, the most I can hope for is to give a thumbnail portrayal of the whole person: their highs, their lows, what's good about them, what they're striving for, and yes, their faults and flaws. The things that make them human. Sometimes during the course of an interview, weird or bad things will happen, and then I have to distance myself to keep from becoming mad or upset, or vindictive."

The vacuuming in the hall stopped.

"There have been times in my career when I've fantasized getting even with a person — or their publicist," I scribbled. As a leftie, the side of my hand was smeared with ink. "Especially when they turn around and tell their story to another reporter after they've promised me an exclusive. That really sucks. There's also the issue of what to do when you stumble on a really big story that could make or break your career, but it's highly sensitive in nature, and what's more, it's a story that involves a friend, or someone you're beginning to care about, and the last thing you want to do is humiliate or hurt them."

My hand was cramping from using such primitive instruments. I was so used to tapping away on my laptop, writing with a pen was actually painful. I stopped to read what I wrote. It was ridiculous, it was self-pitying, it was blithering, it was the work of an idiot. I tore it up.

Through the flimsy motel walls, I could hear the steady thump, thump, thump of a bass. Somewhere a baby was crying. I wasn't going to get any work done, not with these distractions. I took a quick shower, and got dressed, pulling on clean pair of cream colored jeans and a pink shirt. Figuring it couldn't hurt to primp a little, I applied mascara to my lashes and drew on eyeliner. To my cheeks, I applied a bit of blush. After painting my mouth with a baby pink shade of lipstick that just happened to exactly match my shirt, I gave my hair a good brushing and stepped into my favorite pair of boots, hand tooled vintage RocketBusters I'd picked up in Santa Monica on the Third Street promenade. They were magnificent boots, with jet black toes and heels, the shaft a bright yellow leather decorated with the images of shimmying hula girls. Five minutes later, I was in the hotel elevator, headed to the main floor to hit the bar.

Stepping off the elevator, the thump was getting louder. The hallway was vibrating; there was an actual throb. I could hear music;, "Satisfaction," by the Rolling Stones, coming from Teddy's Lounge. I walked a little taller in my boots towards it. A woman in cheap spike heels and a satiny green cocktail dress passed me in the corridor, weaving slightly, headed, I hoped, for the ladies' room. In front of the double-glass doors to the lounge, I paused.

A squat, sullen man with a face pockmarked with pimple scars guarded the entrance to the bar. "Membership card?" he asked.

"Wha'?" I said.

"The singles mingle?" he repeated as if I were daft. "This is the Getaway Club's Singles Mingle. It's $35 without the card. You can join tonight for $20. You can apply that amount to your entrance. So that would be an additional $15."

I looked at him blankly.

"Card and fee, ma'am," he said. "This is a private party."

"Oh," I said, stomach sinking.

"Most of them charge a lot more," Pimple-scar said belligerently. "And you're helping a good cause. 10 percent goes to earthquake victims."

"I'll pay for her and for me," a tall, well-built man with a handle bar mustache offered behind me, flashing his Getaway card.

"It's not the money," I said to Pimple-scar, hesitating. I snuck a better look at my benefactor. His clothes and that 'stache were pretty awful, but otherwise he seemed okay. He had a nice body and pleasant eyes. They were brown, like a dog's, and friendly.

"I didn't realize a singles' party was going on," I said. "I'm just a guest at the hotel. I'm not sure I'm up for a singles' Meet 'n' Greet. Is it possible I could just sit quietly at the bar and get a drink? I promise I won't talk or mingle with anyone. Scout's honor."

The doorman looked at me skeptically. He looked me up and down, his expression suspicious. Then he stuck out his hand and took the guy's money. "Just wait while I stamp your hands."

'Stache and I entered Teddy's Lounge.

"Was that line about you being a hotel guest just a way to cheat the singles mingle out of their entrance fee?" 'Stache queried. "Although you don't strike me as the cheating type."

"Really?" I said. "And in your opinion, what does the cheating type look like?"

"Wearing a ton of makeup and mousse in your hair," the guy said, smiling. "Not that I have any idea of what mousse is, anyway. I'm not even sure how to spell it."

I decided to smile, too. "Well, it's a styling product. Although a kind of been-there, done done-that. To tell you the truth, I haven't heard of anybody using it in years."

"I think women were using it the last time I was dating," the guy, said. "Which was, um, 2008."

"So you are here for the singles night," I said.

"That I am, ma'am," he said, gravely. "Or is it 'Ms.'?"

"It's 'Ms.'" I said, suddenly feeling embarrassed. Was I actually flirting with a man I didn't know at the Holiday Inn? A man I'd let pay my way? "You're right. I'm not married. I'm not even engaged. I'm single and that's legit. So we're good to go in here. Let's get a drink."

"Name's Doug," 'Stache said after we'd bellied up to the bar. The room was crowded, although not overly. The vibe was weird; despite nearly everyone in the room looking to be at least 30, and the obvious presence of liquor, it seemed more like a dance at a suburban middle school. The guys were all lined up along one side of the bar while the ladies were all lined up on the other. Everyone but me was wearing Getaway Club nametags. I wondered if the guy at the door had deliberately forgotten to give me one. Everyone in the room took notice that Doug and I came in and sat together.

"Well, hey, Doug, I'm Paige," I said, shaking his hand and looking around for the bartender.

"What'll it be," the bartender said, dropping a bowl of popcorn in front of us. The bartender was swarthy and black-haired. He had trained his prodigious sideburns to creep down the sides of his face to join up with his short beard. He was friendly enough, but clearly all-business, which made, me think he was used to getting stiffed on tips.

"What do you have that's white?" I said. "Besides Chardonnay."

"Well, I've got a nice Sauvignon Blanc from California, but tonight I'm pushing the Ramona Pinot Grigio," the bartender said. "You know. From the New York City Real Housewives."

"How is it?" I asked.

"Pretty good. It's tasty. Citrusy with hints of mineral on the nose. It's from the Veneto region of Italy, home of Juliet and Romeo."

"Well, you've sold me," I said. "Any wine from the home of star-crossed lovers is the obvious choice at a singles scene."

"But Romeo and Juliet died at the end of the play," Doug said.

"That's kind of depressing."

"Depends on your outlook," I said, tossing back half a glass. "Die young and leave an attractive corpse. Bartender, hit me again," I said.

"Take it easy," Doug cautioned. "The night's young."

"It's been a rough day," I said, taking another gulp. "Cheers."

A giant dressed all in green, his long, thinning hair slicked back into a greasy pony tail, lurched over, standing just to the left of my elbow.

"'Scuse me," the green giant said. "I'd like to buy the lady a drink."

"Um, that's very nice of you, but I'm good," I said, mentally willing him away.

"Well, okay, how about a dance?" the green giant said. Damn, the, dude was persistent.

"Um, I didn't exactly wear my dancing slippers," I said, extending a cowboy boot-shod foot as evidence. "But thanks. Why don't you ask one of these other ladies to dance? See, I'm not really part of this single's mingle. I'm just a guest at the hotel who happens to be at the bar."

"Then why'd you come out if you're not looking to meet someone?" the green giant said, belligerently.

"Isn't this the Getaway Club? Maybe you should 'get away,'" I said lightly, smiling at my own wit. I hoped he wasn't too boozed up to take the hint.

"I know your type," the green giant sneered. "You're just one of those goddamn cockteasers."

"Hey, buddy, watch your mouth," Doug said mildly. "Move along and let the lady enjoy her beverage."

"Who are you?" the green giant said pugnaciously.

"Just a guy telling you to butt out," Doug responded.

"Eh, screw you," the green giant said. "There's plenty of fish in the sea," he said to me. "And they're a helluva lot prettier than you are."

"Thanks, I guess," I said to Doug when the giant had shoved off. "I don't know understand how anyone deals with these singles meet and greets, although any time you're a woman alone at a bar, it can be awful."

"It's rough," Doug agreed. "Whether you're a man or a woman. I, can hardly bear to do it. I really have to force myself. Of course I'm out of practice, since I was married for awhile."

"You're recently divorced?" I said. "I'm sorry. What happened?"

"Oh, just the love of my life decided she wanted to be with another person," Doug said lightly. "Actually, she decided she wanted to be with a woman. Turns out she's gay. Don't really get that she didn't know that before we got married, but I guess we were both sort of naïve."

"I'll say," I said. "Whew. That must have hurt."

"Oh, not near as much as it would have if she'd left me for an-other man," Doug said, smiling. "But you can't argue with sexual orientation. You're not gay are you? My radar for that kind of thing is kind of off."

"No, I'm not a lesbian," I said. "I like guys."

"Well, good," Doug said. "I qualify."

I looked around Teddy's Lounge. It was pretty grim. "Copacabana" by Barry Manilow came on and I decided it wasn't where I wanted to be, at least not at the moment.

"Say," I said to Doug. "I've got an idea. Want to go some place else? That is unless there's someone here you're interested in."

"Uh, not really," he said. "I only came because my ex-sister-in-law told me I need to get out. She worries about me. She likes me. She wants me to get a life. She's the one who signed me up for the Getaway Club in the first place. Plus she's kind of pissed at her sister for getting married to, me and acting like she didn't know she was a stone lesbian."

"So anything happening with the sis?" I said, teasingly. "Maybe there's some growth potential. "

"Nah, she's married with three kids," Doug said. "Plus her husband's a cop. Homicide detective."

We both smiled.

"So, I know a place that's a lot more fun than this joint," I said.

The bartender, still in earshot, shot me a dirty look.

"No offense." I put a tenner on the bar, and Doug matched it.

The bartender softened. "You guys should go check out The Big Kahuna," he bartender offered. "That's where it's happening."

"Exactly the place I had in mind," I said. "Come on, Doug. Let's roll."

We slid out of Teddy's Lounge, the green giant still glaring my way even as he attempted a hook up with a heavy hipped, 40-something, Botoxed-blonde.

"Want me to drive?" Doug asked.

"I'll drive," I said. "Get in," I said, hitting the wrong button on the electronic key to the SUV and starting the alarm up. There was a terrible racket. As I fumbled around pushing buttons, trying to disarm the thing, Doug gently took the key from my hand.

"Allow me," he said, stopping the alarm and popping the doors open.

I drove, not too well, but I drove.

"Did you just buy this car?" Doug said. "You don't seem too at ease with it."

"I haven't had it very long," I fudged, eyes straight ahead of me on the road.

The Big Kahuna was crazy-busy, the parking lot jammed. I was grateful the Mercedes had that nifty gadget where it parallel-parked itself. Inside, a big crowd was at the bar. There was not an empty seat. I left my name for a table with the hostess, who seemed to recognize me, and Doug and I plunged in to join the throng. Doug snagged us a couple of Sierra Nevada's while I found a place for us by the big picture window.

"Hope you like beer," he said, somewhat apologetically. "If you don't want it, I'll get you something else."

"Beer's good," I said, and it was. After a summer of margaritas and Cosmos — and the lousy wine at the Holiday Inn — beer suddenly tasted refreshing, crisp. I took another pull at the bottle and lightly smacked my lips. "A little hoppy but not to the point of excess," I said, showing off a little bit.

"You know beer," Doug said admiringly.

"Yeah, I've been around a microbrewery or two," I jibed.

"Have you tried Captain Lawrence?" Doug said. "They're a local outfit. Very popular label around here; everyone in Westchester is drinking it." I shook my head no.

"Let me get you a flight," he said, darting off.

I looked around the room and saw a few people I knew or recognized from town. I saw Miranda Van Ooonk yukking it up in a corner with the master of the hunt, Gary Goldfinger, and Locket, the sexy Indian film star who was with Alex that day at the coffee bar, was with them, engaged in what appeared to be a deep, engrossing conversation. And there was Rene, the model Janey said Diandra had a crush on. She was with a group of girls I didn't recognize at all, certainly not the bling-y friends that made up Diandra's horsey crowd. These girls' faces were fresh and seemingly devoid of make up; their lithe, slim yoga-trained bodies draped in loose silk and linen clothes, worn with discreet, tiny jewelry.

"Taste this," Doug said, back at my side. On the windowsill he deftly set up the flight tray which contained six small glasses. "This is the Pale Ale, the Liquid Gold, Sun Block, Brown Bird Brown Ale, the Captain's Reserve and the Smoked Porter," he said, pointing each beer out. "These are the brewery's year round offerings. They've also got a special flight of three seasonal brews, if you're up for trying them."

"Let's start with these, " I said, lifting a glass. "Maybe the brewery is something I can blog about."

"Oh, Captain Lawrence has been written and blogged about millions of times," Doug said. "The guy who founded the company is a, local hero who grew up in Beddington Place. Went to college out west and worked at Sierra Nevada. Anyway, he's been in business with his own company for a couple of years."

And then we were interrupted.

"Darling!" Tamsin cried, rushing up. "Whatever are you doing here?"

"Um, drinking?" I said, deadpan. I wasn't sure how I was feeling about Tamsin since she'd tossed me out on my rear.

"Paige!" Janey yelped right behind her. "I'm so glad you're here. You must join our little party. We've got about twenty people coming. They've given us the whole back room. They're setting up the table. We're just having one drink at the bar while they get us ready. Do come and join us. And, um, who's your cute friend?"

Was Doug cute, I wondered, considering him. He was tall enough and slim and his hair wasn't too bad if you ignored the mustache. Plus he had those really nice, soft, brown eyes. All this time I hadn't really looked at him, but I could see now that he was a good looking guy, even if his clothes — eek, and where exactly was that shirt from — were God-awful and unflattering.

"Hi, I'm Doug," Doug said, extending to Janey his right hand. "Paige and I just met at the singles mingle at Teddy's Lounge at the Holiday Inn."

Tamsin's eyes widened. "You work fast, don't you?"

"It's not what you think," I said.

"What do you think I think?" Tamsin snickered.

"Doug and I literally just met. After you threw me out and I went to the Holiday Inn, I didn't realize the hotel bar was having a singles scene, so I suggested we come here," I said, not entirely understanding why I felt the need to explain anything. "We're not, like, on a date. This is just a better place to drink."

"Hmm," Tamsin said skeptically. "And what were you doing at the Holiday Inn? I thought you were staying with Chessie."

"Well, if you two new lovebirds can tear yourselves away," Janey said, already looking over my shoulder. "Come over to our table. Everybody's coming. Michael's coming, and Sal and Billy — and Sally and Gwen and Kimberley and Licia — you remember those girls, don't you, Paige? Also that painter might drop by. What's his name again? Oh, I see Miranda Van Oonk right now with Gary Goldfinger. I'm going to invite them to join us, too. Paige, you know everyone. Who's that they're with?"

"That's the Bengali film star," I said. "Don't you remember we met her at Java Joe's?"

"Yes!" Janey said. "I thought I recognized her. She's got such a great look, don't you think? I could invite her to be one of the Horsewives, although Diandra would throw a stink!"

"Oh, and by the way, thanks for telling me that I'm off the show," I said sarcastically. "Not that I knew I was on in the first place."

"Oh! That!" Janey said, only the tiniest bit abashed. "The producers had a sit-down and they decided since you don't really live here, you were miscast. Rules are rules. The producers think there still might be some scripting, scene-setting work for you down the line, but right now it's not in the master budget."

"I thought you and your husband were the producers now," I said. "Or was I mistaken?"

"We are the producers! We are! But hush," Janey said. "That's not for publication. You know what? This conversation never happened. I'm going over now to introduce myself to that Indian film star. Please join us at the table, Paige. I'll save you a seat. I'm sure you'll be able to pick up some juicy detail to leak to TMZ. That would be good promo for my project."

"Yeah, Paige, that's a great idea," Tamsin said smarmily. "You know how we always feed you good gossip."

"Who were those women?" Doug said when they'd shoved off. "Are they your friends?"

"Yes, and no," I said. "Let's just say they're women I've been spending a lot of time with."

"But they're not like your BFF's," Doug said.

"Best friends, you mean? Er, no. I don't have BFF's really. I haven't had time, really, to cultivate any such thing. Those girls? You could say we have kind of a working relationship, plus I've been staying with one of them for a couple of months, well, staying in her cottage. See, I don't live here. I live in L.A." I said, omitting the part where I should have said, "With my boyfriend."

"Really?" Doug said, genuinely curious. "What do you do in L.A.?"

"I'm a celebrity journalist," I said.

He whistled.

"Don't be too impressed," I said. "It's a living. You might have seen me on TV," I added, not able to resist priming my own pump. "In some circles, you might even say I'm a little famous."

"I don't watch much TV," Doug admitted. "I gave the flat screen to my ex- after we broke up. It kind of went with the house and the furniture and the car and the dog, along with all the other good stuff."

"Gee," I said. "That's rough."

"Yeah, it is," Doug said, staring into his beer. "It wasn't anybody's fault. The sex was great anyway, while it lasted. I got the VCR and the old Trinitron. I just don't have cable."

We were quiet for a little while. It wasn't bad. It was strangely comfortable.

"So, if you don't mind me asking, why are you here?" he said after, a long conversational break. "I'm surprised a celebrity journalist can find anything to write about in Beddington."

"Oh, you're wrong there," I said, taking another slug of my Liquid Gold. "Hey, this is pretty good. I like it."

"There's more where that one came from," Doug said. "Now, as you were saying. Tell me all about your life, tailing VIPs."

"Well, Beddington Place is lousy with celebrities," I said. "The ones who are married with families like the quiet and a break from the craziness of L.A. They like how they can live normal lives, go to the grocery store, pump their own gas. They're attracted by Beddington's Norman Rockwell, picture-perfect, stage-set environment; down-home and countrified, but upscale countrified, like a Ralph Lauren ad. You know, glamorous and a little make-believe. Am I talking too much?"

"No," Doug said. "I never thought of this place the way you're describing it. But then, what do I know? I went to high school here. But my family weren't Hilltoppers. I'm from what they call the wrong side of the tracks."

"Beddington Place is a smart community," I said, warming to my own thoughts. "Because of the proximity to Wall Street, the best and brightest people in the universe choose to live here. Then there's the recent influx of bold faced name celebrities. The celebs like it because it's not just rich, it's sophisticated. It's not a backwater. Every amenity a celebrity is used, to in L.A. they can get in Beddington. There's yoga teachers and Pilates experts and personal trainers and cosmetic surgeons. There's an incredible golf club.. And even though those bold faced names are constantly being tapped to lend their name and their time to local charity events — and let's face it, any ball is a bigger draw when a movie star is calling the auction — the celebs don't mind because it's an ego boost and a rush when their neighbors shower them with adoration. You know, celebrities are human. Shit happens. Maybe things aren't going so well for them in Hollywood. Maybe their TV series got cancelled, or their agents aren't sending them the greatest scripts. They can take comfort knowing that even if their star fades in Hollywood, in Beddington Place, they'll always be golden." I was aware I was getting a little windy but Doug was hanging with it.

"Wow. That's deep. Very insightful. Impressive. I'm impressed," he said.

"Well, that's not what I write about," I said irritably, feeling I'd said too much. "That's just what I think. What I get paid to write is where they eat, who they hang out with, what parties they go to, what car they crashed. That's the information the gossip-driven heartland is interested in, not my cultural analysis."

"Hmmm, I dunno," Doug said. "Sounds like you should write a book."

Michael Swett appeared, looming over Doug's shoulder.

"Fancy seeing you here, darling," he said, bussing my cheek. "And who is your sexy, if ill-clad new friend? "

"Michael, this is Doug," I said. "Doug, this is Michael." Michael ran his eyes over Doug, scrutinizing him.

Michael fingered Doug's shirt. "Kohl's?"

Doug smarted, uncomfortable.

"Did I hear something about Paige writing a book?" Michael said archly. "Is that true, my dear? What would it be about?"

"I'm not writing a book," I said, annoyed. "The way things are going, soon I may not even be writing a blog. Something happened with Chessie's husband that's playing havoc with my job. I decided not to write about it, and Pat's pissed."

"Oh, that," Swett said dismissively. "Pat texted Kimberley and she got right on it. Good job, too. The story's already online. I guess you haven't had a chance to check out TMZ. Been rather busy, haven't you? I heard you blew out of Tamsin's in a huff and checked into the Holiday Inn where for the last 24 hours you've been on a bender. At least three people texted me to say they saw you in Teddy's Lounge drinking cheap wine by the barrel and dancing with some gutter-mouthed giant. Also the word is out that your boyfriend in L.A. has dumped you — for a porn star."

On every level, I felt enraged. "Where did you hear that?" I said, fuming. "That is so not true. And for your information, I was kicked out of, Tamsin's. She told me I had to get out because her mother was coming."

"Alice?" Swett said. "Love that woman. Such a sweetheart."

"You've met her?" I said, incredulously. "When and where?"

"Oh, before she went away," Swett said vaguely. "At some garden party."

I shook my head in disbelief.

"I don't understand you people," I said. "You don't care that Kimberley reported something awful about Chessie's husband? Have you no sense of loyalty? I thought Chessie was your friend."

"It'll all come out in the wash," Swett said dismissively. "We all have to deal with the glare at some point in time. That's what makes it fun. In the meantime Chessie's off the show, and now poor Janey has to find a replacement. And she better act fast. Otherwise she can't deliver on her contract. That would be disastrous. Kimberley will take your place, but we don't have anyone yet for Chessie. Can you think of anyone else who's a bit older and has a terrifically hairy husband?"

"Janey's replacing me with Kimberley?" I said, bitterly. "That's rich."

"Well, she's already horning in on your deal as a celebrity journalist," Swett said. "She's just a rookie, but Pat told me she's learning the ropes fast. She can't be more than 23. She gets carded everywhere."

"Hey, Paige, ready to bail?" Doug cut in, seeing how distressed I, was at these revelations. "This is getting old, isn't it?"

"Sure," I said. I was feeling sort of sick. "Michael, tell Janey I'm sorry we won't be joining her at her table. I'm just not in the mood to socialize."

"Whatever you say, darling," Swett said airily. "But before you go, can you confirm that rumor, the one about your boyfriend? Exactly who is the porn star he's fallen in love with? Kimberley is working on a lead she got this afternoon that he's ditched you for Tickled Pink."

"They're just friends," I said, grabbing my handbag.

"Sure, sure, that's what they all say," Swett said, laughing meanly. "And who could blame him? I've seen her films."

Ten minutes later we were in the Beddington Place diner and Doug was ordering me a grilled cheese.

"And she'll also have a chocolate milkshake," he told the waitress. "And I'll have a Diet Coke and a BLT."

"Diet Coke?" I said after the waitress had taken the order and gone away. "I didn't know guys drank Diet Coke. I thought that was a girl thing."

"Dunno," Doug said. "I've always loved the taste of aspartame. Go figure."

Our drinks came and I took a sip.

"We should switch," I said. "This is great but I don't need the calories."

"Aw, drink up," Doug said. "You're skin and bones anyway. I like a girl with a little meat on her. The women around here are all too skinny. They look like skeletons with bobble heads."

I laughed.

"It's because they all go to the same hairdresser. They all get the same blow out. You know, I wasn't always this skinny," I confided, sinking my teeth into the grilled cheese. It had been cooked on the griddle with loads of butter. It was delicious. "Well, I was never what you'd call fat, but I did grow up in a summer resort town and fudge and cotton candy and subs and pizza were just about all I ever ate."

"Really?" Doug said, picking up his BLT. "Oh good, they put on lots of mayo. Mayonnaise, by the way, is my second favorite condiment. The first is ketchup.'"

"Put them together and you've got Thousand Island dressing," I said.

"I love that too!" he said. "So what resort town was it? Now that we're alone, do I detect a slight south Jersey accent?"

"Yo," I said, wiping a smidgen of grease off my chin. "Good ears. Yeah, I'm originally from south Jersey. Atlantic City. How'd ya guess?"

"It was because you said 'sub,' not 'hoagie'," he replied. "I think they say 'hoagie' though, in Philly."

"Brilliant," I said. "Did you know that the word 'hoagie' is original, to the Philly area? And that every hoagie sandwich, including tuna, includes a slice of cheese?"

"I did know that," Doug said. "I spent a little time in Philly. But I don't want to talk about me. I'm bored with me. Let's talk about you."

"What else do you want to know?" I said, picking at my crust. "Full name, age, Match dot com handle?"

"You're not on Match," Doug said. "And I already know you have a boyfriend."

"Yeah, well, maybe, maybe not," I said, grimacing. "That guy wasn't entirely off base with that crack about Tickled Pink. We're kind of... apart at the moment."

"Well, I don't want to talk about your boyfriend," Doug said. "At least for the time being, let's forget about him. Back to you. What was it like growing up in Atlantic City?"

"It was strange and wonderful," I said. "But when I was a kid, I didn't understand how strange. For example, I thought it was normal to live right next to a casino. I thought everybody gambled. The junk food was great, though, and we had a boat, 'Old Faithful," a baby cabin cruiser that one of my stepfather's kept at the marina."

"Stepfathers?" Doug said. "Is that a plural?"

"Yeah, my mother was the marrying kind. Five times, exactly. One of her husbands was the commissioner of the Atlantic City Race, Course, which was my favorite place. He used to take me there to watch the thoroughbreds in their morning workouts. When I was a kid I dreamed of becoming a jockey, but my mother put the kibosh on it. She said there were no successful female jockeys. Her dream for me was I'd become a paralegal who would meet and marry a rich lawyer."

"Only marry a lawyer? Why didn't she want you to be a lawyer?" Doug asked.

"I dunno," I said. "She set the bar low for me. Or she just didn't want to have to pay for law school."

"Where's your mom now?" Doug said, finishing his sandwich. I'd already polished off my grilled cheese.

"She's dead," I said, briefly. "It's been five years. She had a heart attack a week after her 60th birthday. She was all dressed up to go out to lunch when her best friend found her."

"Sorry about that. What about your dad? Your real dad, not the steps."

"Don't know," I said, feeling sad. It'd been a long time since I'd even thought about him. "He died when I was a baby. She intimated he'd been involved somehow with the Atlantic City mob. You know, the present day version of that show, 'Boardwalk Empire,' kind of stuff. He must have been one of their lawyers. Represented them in their insurance cases when they burned their buildings down. Anyway, I don't have anything to remember him by at all. Not even a single picture."

"That's too bad," Doug said. "That must have been rough for you, growing up."

"No, not really," I said, thoughtfully. "Overall, it was pretty good. My mother wasn't a bad mother, but she was busy with her own life. I had very little supervision, but I liked that. She always gave me plenty of spending money; if I was hungry, I could go up on the boardwalk and buy a snack. I had friends whose houses I could go to after school, and their mothers always asked me to stay for dinner instead of going home to an empty house. The summers were glorious, I had freedom galore. I could do whatever I wanted, swim, surf, fish all day off the rocks. What I really liked about the summer was that I could go barefoot. I felt so lucky to not have anybody telling me I had to wear shoes."

Doug ducked his head under the table to take a look at my feet.

"Well, you look pretty damn good in those cowboy boots now," he said, smiling.

"You know, this is the first time in all the time I've been in Beddington Place that anyone has really asked me about myself," I said, wonderingly. "I hadn't realized that until just now. Thank you, Doug. Thanks for asking."

He seemed surprised and a bit embarrassed.

"Is that true?" he said. "It just seems like a normal thing to do, to, to, ask about the other person."

I let out a laugh that was more like a bark.

"Not in my experience," I said, wryly. "But then, again, I'm usually the one asking the questions."

"Well, let me ask you another one then," Doug said. "Are you in the mood to dance? They've got a pretty good dance floor at Teddy's. We could go back and have a nightcap. I think I've had almost enough to drink to take a shot at the Texas Two-Step. I forgot to mention this when we were still at the lounge, but there's always a theme to the Singles Mingle, and tonight just happens to be Country Western. That's why I thought you were part of that gathering. Your boots misled me."

Now it was my turn to be surprised and embarrassed.

"Omigod, that is funny/horrible," I said. "I had no idea. Also I always wear boots. They're kind of the only shoes I own."

"Why is that?" Doug said, sincerely interested.

"Because I never know when I'm going to have to wade through shit," I said. "Literally and figuratively. Some days you just step in it."

"I know what you mean," Doug said. "So, what about it? Wanna dance?"

A few minutes later I was steering the Mercedes into the Holiday Inn parking lot.

"Are you sure this is a good idea?" I said, navigating the big white monster into what seemed to be a very tight parking space. The sensors told me I was getting too close to another object and were beeping madly. "What if the green giant is still there and drunk enough to still want me to be his woman?"

"You're with me, little lady," Doug said gallantly. "If he tries to bother you, I'll just take him out back and smash his face."

"Please, don't," I said. "I'd prefer to avoid anything that might involve the police." I thought how upsetting and creepy it had been to wake up to those FBI agents at Chessie's. All evening I'd been trying to shrug it off, but the experience had been traumatizing.

"Okay, but I just want you to know that I'm here for you," Doug said. I couldn't understand how he could say such a thing since he hardly knew me. In the wake of everything that had happened, I felt very alone, and vulnerable. It wasn't a feeling I was used to, and I didn't like it.

Just as we entered the lounge, my phone beeped, telling me I had a new text message.

"Sorry, I've got to take this," I said to Doug. "Go on in and I'll catch up in a minute."

"Where the hell have you been?" Pat said when I called her back. Her text said she had an important lead on a story she wanted me to check out.

"I'm really sorry," I said. "I fell asleep."

"Sleep?" Pat said. "That's a crap excuse. Listen, I put that girl Kimberley on that breaking story about the Beddington Place kingpin, but she's too slow. If you're ready to come to your senses, I've got a fresh lead for you from an anonymous source. There's a housemaid who has a brother whose ready to spill the beans on the Jones family. He's pissed because he was ordered to work overtime and then they shafted him on payment. He claims his sister hasn't been paid in months. Find him and interview him and then do a video blog. The problem is, he doesn't speak English, and because he's an illegal, he refuses to appear in the video, but that's OK, because once you have the info, all you have to do is report it."

"I don't speak Spanish," I said. "And just who is your anonymous tipster?"

"Just mind your own beeswax, missy," Pat said. "It's an inside source. Your job is to find a translator and get me that story. It's almost ten now. I'll need it first thing in the A.M. Don't let me down, Paige."

"Was the source Michael Swett?" I blurted before she could hang up. "He's an old friend of yours and he knows Chessie and her husband."

"I don't know anyone named Michael Swett," Pat said. "Paige, you're hallucinating. Now get to work."

"But you do know him," I said, indignantly. "Don't you remember talking to him on the phone that first day I was in Beddington? That day I, was having lunch at the Roganoff's with Princess TaTas? He said you were old friends."

"Paige, I repeat, you're hallucinating," Pat said. "You're dreaming. Now be a good dog, er, girl and fetch me that story. Do a good job and I'll throw you a treat. I heard Gwyneth and her mom are going to Canyon Ranch this weekend. I'll send you there to check it out. You can even get a massage. On me. "

"Michael Swett leaked that information to you, I know it," I said, annoyed. "He speaks Spanish, plus he's spent lots of time at Chessie's. That maid's brother was just his type, not that Swett has a type. Boy, girl, cat, dog. That guy puts the move on anything," I babbled, not realizing Pat had clicked off.

I put my phone back into my pocket and re-entered the lounge. On the sound system, Carrie Underwood was wailing, "Undo It," as two couples swayed on the dance floor.

"Shall we?" Doug said, waiting for me at the bar. There was a fresh beer in front of him and another for me. I took a gulp and looked around. Aside from a couple on the dance floor showing off their smooth moves, most of the singles from the mingle had cleared out, and what was left were the dregs; the drunks, the freaks, the 40-year-old virgins, groups of gals who laughed too loud, and guys with bad toupes wearing sneakers and black socks. There were also the desperate people who dreaded going home, alone, and the predators, male and female, who would feast on them and suck their blood.

"I don't know, I'm kind of upset," I said. "That was my boss. She wants me to do an interview I'm not all comfortable with."

"What specifically is the problem?" Doug said. "I get the feeling when it comes to work, you're intrepid."

"I am," I said. "But I've never had to write about anything that affected me personally."

"She wants you to do a story on yourself?" Doug said. "Wow, that is kind of unusual."

"It's not about me, but about someone I know. I mean, I don't know them all that well, but I'm friends with the spouse. Exposing their dirty laundry now that the husband is in trouble seems, uh, like a violation."

"Isn't that what you do?" Doug said. "I've seen those celebrity gossip shows. Violating goes with the territory."

"It does," I wailed. "And right now I don't like it."

"Hey kiddo, for the moment, let's just don't think about it," Doug said. "Come on. Dance with me."

He pulled me on to the floor under the spinning disco lights. Drawing me close, he placed his left hand on the small of my back and took up my right with his left.

"Now just don't step on my feet with those clodhoppers," he said.

The music switched over to Mary Chapin Carpenter's "Shut Up and Kiss Me. " I couldn't fail to respond to its rollicking gait. Doug started moving and I did, too, awkwardly.

"Talk's cheap and time's expensive," Doug sang along out loud.

Was I creeped out or amused he knew the lyrics?

"There's something 'bout the silent type attracted me to you," he twanged. "All business, none of the hype."

"I can't believe you know all the words," I said, trying to keep up as he two-stepped me around and around. "Hey, you know I never did learn how to do this dance. I might be better suited to square dancing. Slow down, will ya? I'm getting dizzy."

"Lead and follow," Doug said, changing up his steps. "They call this the Traveling Cha Cha. Don't think so hard, okay? Just stay loose and let me do the leading." He clasped me to him and executed a fandango across the floor. I closed my eyes and decided to give myself to over to the rhythm. Within a few minutes I was really dancing.

"Hey, this is fun," I said, meaning it.

"Life's too short to be apprehensive, love's the symptom darlin,'" Doug crooned in my ear. "Hey, you're pretty good now, aren't you? You're sailing. And you said you never did much country dancing. You're a natural."

"Thanks," I said. "You're pretty good yourself." We pranced around the floor two more times and then the music changed. This time it was Joey and Rory singing "Cheater, Cheater."

"I love this song," Doug said excitedly. "Come on. You ever done the double shuffle?" He fastened both hands around my waist and lifted me in the air briefly before swinging into a fast paced heel/toe/backwards/ for-wards/two steps sideways movement that left me breathless.

"Whoa!" I said, laughing.

"Too aerobic?" Doug said. "Okay, how about a reel?" He grabbed my hand and bounded forward, twirling me along beside him.

"Enough! Enough!" I cried out.

"Not until you say 'uncle'" Doug said, pulling me closer. Through his shirt, I felt the beating of his heart and then his lips were on mine and we were kissing.

"Hey, get a room," I thought I heard someone snicker.

"Hey, you heifer-branded man," a mean voice said, interrupting. I broke the kiss to see it was my earlier suitor, the green giant. "What's a pansy like you doin' dancing with a girl," he said, his voice slurring. "Whyn't you take a piss in the pussy room, and leave this little lady to a real man?"

"You're drunk, buddy, go home," Doug said. I stopped dancing.

"You callin' me a drunk?" the giant said. "Take that back or let's take it outside. I can beat you."

For some reason, I felt no fear. I advanced on the green giant.

"What the fuck is your problem?" I said.

"Huh?" the green giant said.

"You're such a goddamn loudmouth. You can't mind your own fucking business. What's it to you? What am I to you? Go away or I'll smash your fucking face in the sidewalk."

"Lady, you're crazy," the giant said to me. To Doug he said, "Control your bitch, man."

"Let's get out of here," I said to Doug. "I told you I didn't want any scenes."

We bailed the dance floor and exited the lounge. In the lobby, Doug took my hand.

"I don't want to let you go," he said. "But I don't want to take advantage."

"Advantage?" I said, suddenly feeling the beers and the pinot. "I'm a grown up."

"Mm," he said, his lips grazing my neck. It felt good. Really good. "So am I."

"You know, I've got a room." I blurted. "It might be a good idea to lie down. Whaddaya think?"

"That's what I mean," Doug said, his lips still nuzzling. "I know you've got a room. That was just about the first thing you said when we were talking. I was confused. I thought you were a hooker." I pulled back from his embrace to shoot him a wry look.

"Paige, I really like you but I don't think it would be right if we went to your room just now," Doug said. "You're great, but you are wasted."

"Me? Wasted? Certainly not," I said. "I'm just in shock because all night I've been trashed. My boss is a selfish liar, and people are saying my boyfriend's taken up with a porn star, and I just found out today I'm not going to be on a TV show that I never wanted to be on in the first place. To top it off, I don't know what I'm doing here anymore and I have no place to live." To my own huge surprise, I started bawling.

"Aw, come on, it can't be that bad," Doug said, looking surprised but still able to be consoling. "You've had a lot to drink and you're exhausted. Listen to yourself. You're slurring your words. What you really need is sleep."

"You think?" I said. At the mere mention of the word 'sleep,' I instantly thought about the big, roomy, gorgeous bed in Tamsin's guest house, made up with exquisite, 600-count organic cotton sheets, and a hand-crafted white down comforter and a dozen plump hypoallergenic hand-stuffed pillows tucked into needlepoint linen shams. I almost started crying again about how hurt and angry and rejected I felt having been ejected from such a terrific space. Even Chessie's guest room would have been not so bad if only I'd had more time to make friends with Cuddles.

Suddenly I wanted to lie down very badly. But I also wanted to be kissed.

"We'll take this up again another time," Doug said gently. "For now, I'm taking you to your room."

We walked to the elevator and I pushed the call button. The doors immediately opened. We stepped inside the small space and I pushed another button and we rode up in silence. Exiting the elevator, we walked down a long hall. There were doors, lots of doors. All of them were closed and silent.

"Well, this is it," I said, pausing in front of a door so anonymous it could have been a door anywhere. It reminded me painfully of all the other nondescript doors I'd stood in front of, doors in hotels and motels in Las Vegas, Honolulu, San Francisco, New York City, Paris, Bangkok, London, Tokyo, Madrid; anywhere and everywhere else I'd followed celebrities frolicking or vacationing or getting themselves in jams. I was sick of hotel doors.

At that moment, I wished with all my heart I'd never have to see one again. I wished I was back in L.A. in my own adorable little rented house in Venice Beach, curled up in the Pottery Barn Seagrass Sleigh bed I'd fought so hard for when Ric and I furniture shopped for our first shared residence. Ric railed the bed was wildly impractical because the cat would scratch the seagrass, but I didn't care because it was so romantic. Except I wasn't sure who was sleeping in it now, and the thought of that made my heart ache.

"I'll call you in the morning," Doug said, but I knew it was a lie.

A white lie, a polite lie, but a lie nonetheless. Besides a shared interest in artisanal beers, what did we have going for us? Not much, was my guess.

"Sure thing," I said, allowing him to kiss me on the cheek. "Goodnight, Doug. You've been really sweet."

"Sweet? Are you giving me the dust off?" Doug said, sighing. "Whenever a girl tells me I'm sweet, I know it's going nowhere," he added mournfully.

I gave him my best lopsided grin.

"Okay," he said, cheering up. "I get it. But I'm still gonna call you tomorrow to see how you're doing."

"You do that," I said. "And by the way, you're a wonderful dancing teacher."

"Hey, you're a quick student," he said. "Don't forget to take off those cowboy boots before you hit the sheets."

When he'd gone, I hung out the Do Not Disturb sign and bolted the door. I shimmied out of my shirt and jeans and shucked my boots and socks. I went into the bathroom to take a pee. I was too tired to remove my eye make up or even brush my teeth.

Just as I was crawling in my underwear between the polyester sheets, having first made certain to remove the fake satin bedspread, the hairs on the back of my neck quivering a little in disgust thinking about all, the creepy strangers' bodies who probably rolled around on it, my phone rang. I hoped it wasn't Doug.

It wasn't. It was Ric.

"Hey, babe, what's up," he said. Glancing at the clock I saw it was only just past nine o'clock in L.A. "We haven't really talked in awhile."

"Guess not," I said carefully. "So, listen, I'm hearing a lot of stuff about you and Tickled Pink. Like you're together. Like you're a couple. You want to verify that?"

"Who's filling your ears with such crap?" Ric said. "Babe, there's nothing going on between me and Tickled Pink. I've enjoyed being with her and being part of her world. That's all."

"Really," I said, sourly. "To me it seems you're ready to ditch your screenwriting career to play second fiddle to Tickled Pink in a porno jazz band. You're up all hours, you're never available when I call, you moved her into our house, you lost our cat. She even answers your phone! Come on, Ric. You've been seriously distracted. Admit it."

"There was just the AVN gig and then a couple of nights at some clubs," Ric said defensively. "Jeez. You've got a memory like an elephant. You never let anything go, do you?"

"Were we fighting before I left?" I said after a long, uncomfortable silence. "I can't remember."

"No. Yes. Well, maybe sort of," Ric said in a more conciliatory, tone. "You've been traveling. I've been putting in long hours at the studio. I guess we haven't been connecting very well."

There was another pause. This one lasted even longer. The silence was kind of awful. It went on for so long I wondered who would be the first to break it. Finally, it was me.

"So," I said, coughing a little, my throat had so dried up. "You were saying that you miss me and you want me to come home?"

"Uh, did I say that?" Ric said, sounding bewildered. "Actually, now would not be a great time. I, uh, I'm still really busy. A lot of good things are happening for me right now. It's crazy."

"What things?" I said. "You sold a script?"

"Listen, I gotta go. Tickled Pink's in the car waiting for me. Let's talk in a couple of days and I'll fill you in. Meanwhile, take care of yourself, okay? And don't worry about the cat. Tickled Pink's fallen in love with her."

"Right," I said, but he'd already hung up.

Must Love Horses

I woke up before dawn to a solid downpour. There was thunder, and flashes of lightning. I huddled under the covers at the Holiday Inn, where I'd been holed up for two days; aside from the lousy bathtub, the place was actually starting to grow on me. A girl could get used to never making her bed, and there was room service and plenty of hot water. It was even good for work; the ice machine at the end of the hall was turning out to be quite the meeting spot. Two nights before, on a midnight run, I'd encountered the jazz legend Benny "Hot Licks" Bonjouria, performing that week in Catoonah at the jazz fest. We were both in our jammies, but Benny graciously let me pull out my camcorder for an impromptu interview, on the condition I didn't mention his fascination with Scientology.

My cell phone beeped, telling me I had a text message. It was from Chessie, calling to say what time her horse trailer would arrive at the Old Homestead. It was the day of the Riding Lanes Labor Day pace. Although I'd no plans to ride in the event, the day before, Chessie generously offered me the use of Congo, a coal black Thoroughbred she and Phil purchased before Phil's arrest. "He's bold and beautiful and he'll jump anything," Chessie said, not realizing Alex's little Haflinger pony, Butterscotch, and Diandra's mare Space Cadet were more in line with my equestrian abilities, which were decent but limited. "He's a magnificent animal — once you get used to him."

I texted her right back.

"Do you think they'll still hold the pace in this awful weather?" I typed, hoping against hope they wouldn't. My phone rang moments after Chessie received my message.

"They always hold the pace," she said. "Don't worry about that." Little did she know how worried I was. Immediately after learning of Chessie's offer, Tamsin texted me a warning that Congo had never been used on the trails, and what's more, was fresh off the race track.

"Okay," I said, wishing I had a cig or some Xanax, even a brandy flask. I definitely needed something to calm my nerves. I was also worried about my pace partners, who had been arranged by Diandra. She placed me on a four-person team made up of the crazy girl riders, Gwen and Sally, and Billy, Janey's husband.

Our assigned start time was 7:48 a.m. and I hoped by the time we set off, the worst of the storm would be over. Even so, I knew we would be slogging through mud, and mud scared me. The worst riding accident I'd been in had happened in mud. That was two years ago, but I still shivered at the memory. It happened at a dude ranch in Nevada I'd escaped to for a weekend of R&R after spending weeks on the road covering Eddie Vedder's tour of North America. While on a group trail ride, there'd been, a flash storm, and what was supposed to be an easy ride through Red Rock Canyon turned into a total nightmare. In the deluge of running mud, my horse slipped and fell, taking me down with him. I cracked my head pretty good on a rock. Although I protested I was able to ride back to the ranch, the guide thought otherwise, and I wound up being airlifted to a nearby hospital where they said I was concussed. A month later, I was still discombobulated. My only hope today was that Congo was sure-footed.

"I'll try to be there when you cross the finish line," Chessie said as I rooted through my handbag looking for the Valium that I saved for rough flights. No such luck; I was coming up empty. Instead I pulled out a stick of Nicorette and began chomping it furiously. "But don't be upset if I'm not. Phil and I might have, er, to go somewhere."

"Okay," I said, okay being the only word I could seem to utter. Protest of any sort at this point was beyond me. The last two days had been nothing short of hellish. Ric called to apologize, but when I asked him about Tickled Pink, his answers were evasive. He was equally unclear on the subject of what was going on with his screenwriting career, and kept repeating the phrase, "It's all good," which annoyed me. Meanwhile, although Pat was pleased with my bit on Bonjouria and another story I'd turned in about Jacques Ellen-Stern, I'd failed to do anything on the story about Chessie's maid's brother and his insights into Phil's lifestyle. And although Pat backed off from telling me on an hourly basis what an unprofessional piece of shit

I was for allowing friendship to get in the way of a story, I was beginning to wonder if she wasn't right. And I hadn't heard a peep out of Doug.

I dressed in the formal riding clothes Tamsin had loaned to me, struggling to zip up the tall boots that made me look like an accomplished equestrian. We both wore the same size shoe, only my calves were much larger. That was the difference between her years of private Pilates sessions in her home, versus mine at Gold's Gym in Venice Beach, seated at the calf machine across from Lou "The Hulk" Ferrigno.

It was raining lightly when I drove Chessie's Mercedes to the Old Homestead, parking in the designated "Riders Only" area. The first person I saw when I got out of the car was Alex Manos. He was with a woman I didn't recognize, a curvaceous brunette with big boobs and a sulky face who looked awfully familiar. Alex's dog, Lupa, tail wagging, trotted along beside them.

"Hey," I said, trying to exhibit some show of friendliness and giving Lupa a pat.

"Hey," he said back in a sexy tone, which made the brunette twitch. "You're riding? Who's your mount?"

"A loaner from a friend," I said. "I see you're riding, too," I added, noting that no matter what kind of freak Alex was, he always looked amazing in breeches. "Is this your pace partner? I'm Paige, by the way," I, said, sticking out my hand.

The brunette ignored it. "Alex," she said, in a whiny, nasal voice. "Let's go, we're going to be late. And you're going to have to give me a leg up."

Alex snickered. "I'll give you a leg up, all right," he said to her. "I'll give you a leg up all day long if I have to."

I walked on, passing trailer after trailer arriving for the pace. Even in the rain, which had dialed down to a damp drizzle, the fairgrounds were spectacular. A huge red- and-white striped awning tent had been set up in the sheep's meadow for the lunch, and positioned far up on the hill, the former Chief Justice's antique white farmhouse sparkled in the early morning misty light. Acres of emerald green loamy grass unfurled across the landscape like a lush natural carpet. All around, aristocratic horses were unloading from their trailers, their manes and tails formally tied off and braided, their impeccably groomed glossy coats brushed and slicked with Show Sheen. The more experienced horses stood calmly, waiting to be tacked up, while the novice horses pranced excitedly, ears flicked forward, eyes wide and alert. Every horse knew something was up, that they were at an event, and that perception got their adrenaline flowing.

Chessie's groom was waving at me from the far side of the field. I recognized him because he looked exactly like Alvaro, Nalda's brother. Upon closer examination I saw he actually was Nalda's brother.

"Hey, Alvaro, good to see you, my man," I said, grinning and giving him a high five.

"Shhh, my name, it is Manuel now," Alvaro said right back. "Call me Manny. Is better."

While I fiddled with my gloves and adjusted my helmet, Alvaro/ Manny opened the back of the trailer and dropped the gate. Seconds later the biggest, blackest, most bestial horse I'd ever seen was being led backwards down the ramp.

"Meet Congo," Manny said proudly, holding the horse by its lead. I looked at it and it looked at me. It was very alert and its nostrils were flaring.

"Um, how big is this guy?" I asked.

"He look to be over 17 hands," Manny said. "He enormous," he added proudly.

"What's his temperament?" I said. "Do you get the sense he's really big, but really gentle?"

"Oh, this horse very strong," Manny said. "Very forward."

My heart sank.

"Halloo, how are you doing, my dear?" I heard an familiar male voice say. It was Billy, beautifully attired as always by Janey in cream britches and a navy shirt. In one hand he held the reins of a nice, calm, Oldenburg. With him were Gwen and Sally, who were standing beside their mounts.

Esteban, Diandra's mucker, was with them, poised to give them all a leg up.

"Wow, that's some horse," Sally said admiringly, staring with naked lust at Congo. "I'd love to ride him. Want to switch?"

In truth I would have preferred her horse, Blackstone, who I knew to be a freight train, but at least I'd already seen him in action and knew what to expect.

"Sorry," I said apologetically. "But I can't. He's on loan to me for the day and I don't think his owner would like it."

"Pity," Sally said. "I'd love to try him. I didn't get laid this morning and I could really use the workout."

"You need to work on that husband of yours," Gwen tittered. "Or get a new husband."

"Yeah, right?" Sally said. Both women laughed.

"Ladies, we need to get moving if we're going to make our start," Billy said. "Paige, are you ready? Tally ho, and all that."

Estaban helped the three of them on and Manny helped me up. Boosting me into the saddle, he put his lips near my ear.

"Missus Chessie, she no gonna be here when you finish you ride," he whispered. "She say to tell you she sorry, but she must disappear."

"Disappear?" I said, a bit too loudly. "Like, uh, where?"

Manny shot me a look. "Out of the country," he said softly. "She and Mister Phil, dey book. The missus, she say to tell you keep the bracelet, and the Mercedes for now, but maybe she want them back later."

I blinked.

"You have good ride now," Manny said in a normal tone of voice. He slapped Congo on the butt and amazingly the horse did not spook or flinch. "Stick with your team, go fast, bring home ribbon."

"Hey, your English has really improved since we last saw each other," I said, wonderingly. "And here I thought you only spoke Spanish."

Once again Manny shot me a look.

"Win, win," he said, ignoring my comment. "Beat everyone. Win ribbon for Missus Chessie."

We received our instructions from a pace official: "Ride safely, do not pass anyone without permission, and stick with your team!" a thick waisted older woman in formal hunt attire shouted into a microphone as we clopped past the judging booth on the way to the start of the trail. The event began at the edge of a field, where the moment a steward waved the flag, we moved out as though shot from cannons. It had stopped raining, which was good, but I was still dismayed by the pace Sally set. There was no pretense of walking, or trotting, or any sort of warming up; instead we immediately went into a fast canter. It took some time for me to adjust to Congo's gait; he was so big, and his stride so large, to sit to it, I was constantly rebalancing. The horse, however, was responsive and well-trained. Gradually I began to relax and enjoy myself.

After the first meadow, we entered a narrow, rocky lane. It was dark and forbidding, overshadowed by towering ancient maple trees whose exposed roots were thick and gnarled; between the roots and the rocks, the already muddy footing was even more precarious. Fortunately Congo's enormous feet, each hoof the size of a frying pan, skipped over the deepest ruts; he was eager to cover ground and very forward, and unfazed by the sucking mud. Luckily he was also blasé about the madly dashing chipmunks and squawking birds. Thrashing through the forest, the horses only added to the cacophony.

In our team's formation, I took up the rear; directly in front of me was Gwen, Billy in front of her, and Sally leading. For the time being, Congo seemed satisfied to hold his position, which surprised me since I knew he'd been schooled as a race horse. Everything in a race horse's training teaches it to get to the front, but whenever Congo made even the slightest attempt to pass, he willingly acceded as soon as I checked him with a half halt.

From the dark passage, we emerged on to a dirt road. Sally cantered her horse along, her eyes peeled for yellow arrows. The riding lanes association had predetermined and mapped out the route; our job was keep our eyes open for signage and not take any shortcuts. I knew the pace had been set to cover an approximately 16-mile ride traversing rivers, and streams, two meadows, woods, riverbanks and dirt roads. Some of the terrain was terrifyingly steep. Along the route were two jumping fields, which I dreaded, as I had no plans to jump. I prayed Congo would be docile enough and tractable when I steered him towards the go-arounds.

The pace Sally set was grueling. We barreled along, rarely stopping to walk or even trot. Walking wasn't in Sally and Gwen's riding vocabulary; they were hunt people through and through, and fast and faster the only gears they knew. At this rate I figured we'd finish the pace in just under an hour, which even at the fastest winning time would be at least ten minutes too fast. We'd never get a ribbon unless we slowed down. Then I realized my team wasn't in it for the ribbons. They were in it to ride as fast an aggressively as possible.

Resigned to stick it out and just stay on, for safety's sake I locked down my heels and fixed my gaze on Gwen's horse's big behind, not daring to glance down at the ground. To calm my nerves and Congo's, too, I began to softly sing to him what I hoped was a soothing song.

The next thing I knew, we were bounding through an uncut meadow where the grass was slick with steaming dew. The rain had stopped completely, and the sun had come out; light streamed through the tops of the trees, creating a chiaroscuro effect. Up ahead I were the jumps; two cross rails and three fences, straight in a row. My stomach clutched.

"Tally ho!" Sally squealed, urging on her horse. Blackstone burst into a gallop, heading straight for the jumps, Billy and Gwen merrily barreling along in hot pursuit. Underneath me, I felt Congo gathering himself, charging ahead, powering to the forefront. There was nothing I could do to stop him, that was instantly clear. We were going over. There was nothing to do but grab mane.

"Well done!" Billy sang out as Congo and I cleared each fence with over a foot to spare. Incredibly my handful of jumping lessons over the years had paid off; at the crucial moment, I was able to get myself off the horse's back, give him his head, and balance myself in a perfect two point.

"Good boy, good boy," I crooned, when we completed the jumping course, rubbing encouraging circles on Congo's sweaty neck. But there was no time to linger on congratulations as Sally, still cantering, made a hard left turn. From there, she took up a stretch of the trail so steep it was little more than a ravine. One side was a wall of sheer rock, while the other dropped down a hundred feet to the churning, rain swollen river of Muskrat Dam.

"Carry on single file, it's narrow, watch your step," Sally called back to the rest of us.

"Easy, buddy," I said to Congo, who was tensing. Nothing in the horse's experience had prepared him for this work. I hoped he would take his cues how to handle himself from the more seasoned horses.

Even daredevil Sally had no choice but to walk this part. Walking annoyed her.

"As soon as we get out of here, we're going to make tracks," she griped. "The next part is an uphill climb and we'll take that at a gallop. We're losing time here, but in a minute we'll be through this section. And when that happens, get ready to haul ass."

"I don't mind the walking," Gwen whined. "I'm tired and so's my horse."

"Your horse isn't tired, Gwen," Sally bitched. "And even if he is, you're wearing spurs, aren't you?"

"How are you holding up?" Billy asked me, solicitously. "You were amazing at those jumps. Janey told me you barely know how to ride, so I'm impressed."

"Janey said I barely know how to ride?" I said, incensed. "How would she know? She's never seen me ride."

"Oh, well, Diandra mentioned something to Janey," he responded, vaguely. "She said she only put you on her old, half-dead nag babysitter horse so as not to worry about you. She's been concerned that you might get hurt."

"Space Cadet is not an old half-dead nag," I said indignantly on both the mare's and my own behalf. "She's a wonderful little horse and deserves a better life than she's got with Diandra."

"Speak of the devil, here's Diandra now," Billy said as a clatter of hooves thundered up. She was riding alone, on Frisco, the Percheron cross.

"Isn't it marvelous?" she said, breathlessly, oblivious to the mud. Her close-fitting pink silk shirt and clinging dress white breeches were as spattered as a Jackson Pollock canvas. Wisps of her fine blonde hair peeked from beneath the brim of her smart black velvet hat. She was exuberantly happy and in excellent spirits, as though plunging through field and stream on horseback in the wake of a storm was her favorite occupation.

"We're okay," Sally said as Diandra drew her horse abreast. "We've been taking it pretty slow, considering. I'm bummed because I was really looking forward to a rollicking ride and instead we've had to plod along because of this damned mud," she complained.

"She calls this plodding along?" I said to Billy. "Jesus."

"The WRA executive committee asked me personally to patrol the pace route to guarantee everyone's safety," Diandra said. "I'm supposed to be telling rogue riders they have to play by the rules, and not just run over people. But that doesn't mean we can't have a little rally. Sally, there's a wide straight stretch just ahead where we can gallop side by side. Billy, I'm counting on you to hold the fort. While Sally and I have our jaunt, you hold back the others. Whatever you do, don't let Gwen and Paige's horses charge ahead! That would set off a stampede," she laughed wickedly. "Totally dangerous and terrible. So, are we ready now? Let's go! Tally ho!"

With no further ado, Diandra dug her spurred heels into Frisco's heaving sides. The horse gave a terrific buck before surging into a gallop.

Sally let out a banshee war whoop; spurring Blackstone on, she took off in hot pursuit. Mud instantly churned up from the horses' pounding hooves, creating a blinding scrim of dirt and gravel.

"Fuck, I can't see a thing," I heard Billy curse, his voice half drowned out by Gwen, who was shrieking. "I've been blinded," she shouted, her horse, hysterical at being left behind, bolting. Unable to see where she was going, Gwen could barely keep a grip on the reins. Her horse seized the bit in its mouth and she flew past Billy as it raced to catch up to its buddies. From a distance I heard Diandra's commanding voice shouting, "Pull him up, halt him, Gwen, make him stop, you bloody idiot!"

Billy, meanwhile, was struggling to keep control of his mount. The Oldenburg, normally placid, was now rearing and spinning. Billy looked very frightened; he wasn't used to this sort of thing. The rides Janey and Diandra arranged for him were quiet, well organized rambles through the woods, rides where the sighting of a young buck with budding horns, or a hawk soaring overhead was plenty of stimulation.

Meanwhile, Congo was behaving.

"Stand," I said, firmly, heels down, sitting straight, and keeping my hands down and quiet. I turned him away from being able to look at Billy's horse, because copycat bad horse behavior was contagious. "Good boy," I praised Congo when he stood stock still, awaiting further orders. Once again, I patted his neck. "You are a very good boy," I intoned, inhaling, and exhaling deeply to cue him to match my breath. "Don't you pay any attention to that ruckus. Just because that horse is acting silly doesn't mean you have to."

Billy gave up trying to settle his horse and instead executed an emergency dismount. Landing with both feet flat on the ground, he held tight to the Oldenburg's hanging reins and gave them a vicious yank. The horse jerked its head away in pain from the pressure.

"Stupid, stupid horse," Billy bellowed in its frightened face. "What the hell were you trying to do? Kill me?

"Don't blame him, he's just a horse, he didn't want to be left behind," I shouted at Billy. "That was really dumb of Sally and Diandra, separating off like that! You know perfectly well horses instinctively will follow other horses. Besides, isn't that behavior against the pace rules? I thought — "

Before I could finish, Alex Manos was upon us, astride Lord Kensington. His pace team included the stuck-up brunette on little Butterscotch, and Michael Swett riding an energetic bay I'd never seen before that looked quite the handful.

"What have we here?" Alex said, looking down quizzically at Billy who was still off his horse.

"Stay out of it, Manos" Billy said, snarling. "As team leader here, I'm giving your team permission to pass. Proceed with your ride. Walk on. Get out."

"Team leader?" Alex sneered. "That's rich. I checked the board before we set off and it said Sally was your leader."

Billy looked daggers.

"What were you doing checking the board," he snapped. "What are you calling yourself now, a riding lanes official? You get away right now. Janey's told me all about you. She's through with you. She'll never take a riding lesson with you again, do you hear? And I will never suffer the humiliation again of having you refer to my wife as 'a spinner'!"

Whoa, I thought. Before Diandra, Janey had been a client of Alex? Was it possible that at one time she'd been a notch in Alex Manos's belt?

In contrast to Billy's red, puffed-up face, Alex was cool as a cucumber. Also unlike Billy and me, his team wasn't splattered in mud or even sweaty. Instead of cantering and galloping like my team, they must have walked safely through the mud with a minimum of trotting.

"Paige, darling, wherever did you find that horse?" Michael Swett said. "That's some animal. Surely you didn't buy it with your entertainment earnings? It must have cost the earth."

"It's Chessie," I said. "His name is Congo. She loaned him for the pace."

"Yes, I can see he's quite the African stud," Swett said smarmily. Nothing could keep the man down, not even his banged up arm from our, car accident, which he still wore in an Hermes sling. "Hmmm. I wonder if with Phil's troubles the horse is for sale. What's Chessie want for him? I'll pay cash, of course. That should cover Phil's bail."

"You'd have to discuss that with Chessie," I said. "And fyi, Phil's already out of jail. And who is that you're riding? Is it, er, your replacement?"

Swett grimaced. "I'm still not over that," he said, shortly. "Cassius was irreplaceable, he was one in a million. This horse is called Damascus. Alex is trying to sell him to me, naturally."

How the worm turns, I thought, remembering how only a few days ago, Michael had practically accused Alex of horse murder. "So, do you like him?" I said diplomatically. "He looks pretty energetic."

"Actually I think he's been doped," Swett confided. "Someone tipped me off he's usually twice this hot. Two potential buyers Alex had on the line who tried him dropped out because they said he was so temperamental."

The brunette shot Swett a dirty look. "Stop talking trash about Alex or his horses," she said impertinently. "I'm telling."

"Go fuck yourself, sweetheart," Swett retorted. "I've seen your cheap type come and go. I know who you are. I saw you on television. You were on "Survivor." You think you're hot stuff. Well, let me tell you this. You may be screwing Alex Manos now, but in two weeks he'll replace you. By then you'll be such a social pariah no decent man will touch you with a 10-foot pole, and you'll be sucking some plumber's cock, that is if you can find a plumber. I haven't been able to find a good plumber in years!" he chortled.

Horrified, the brunette backed Butterscotch straight off. I tried to catch the pony's eye, but he hung his head in humiliation.

"Ride along with us until we catch up with your team," Alex said to Billy. "You have to finish as a group anyway, or you'll be disqualified from the ribbons."

"Quite right," Billy said, resigning himself to the inevitable. "Paige, let's get on with it." He slung himself into his saddle and gathered up his reins. I picked mine up, too; Congo instantly collected.

"It's almost over now, bud," I said to the horse, like we were old friends. Maybe we were. We'd already weathered some major challenges. I clucked to him and we fell into line behind Billy, who was behind Swett, who was behind the brunette, who was behind Alex. Single file, we first walked, then trotted, then gently cantered through the woods. The mud churned beneath Congo's hooves and I held my breath we wouldn't slip.

We carried on this way until we came to a place that was all downhill. The sight of it made me sick to my stomach.

"Sit as far back as you can," Alex called back instructions. "You don't want to throw the horse off balance." Slowly, patiently, we negotiated a heart-stopping 500 feet of perilous footing. Congo, unfamiliar with such turf, was stiff as a board. At the front, Alex was the first to hit the flat, and the moment Lord Kensington took his first solid step, shot off in a canter. As the last in the line, I gasped as the rest of them surged forward; all my training had taught me to walk down hills, but Congo was out and out running. His genetically ingrained horse fear of being left behind was too rigidly embedded, and despite my demands on his mouth and his head, he was frantic to keep up. In a nanosecond I knew I was in deep shit, with no control whatsoever; within seconds he was bolting.

We swept past Billy and Swett and the brunette. Even Alex on Lord Kensington was no match. In his mind, Congo was competing in the Derby. All I could do was hang on. While I appreciated his speed, agility and poise, the reality of the situation was petrifying. Careening at 40 mph through the tangle of summer woods, Congo was fleet and determined. Above rocks, ruts and mud, the horse bounded, he leapt; he soared.

Not far ahead we came upon Gwen, on her ass, on the ground, her beautiful linen shirt torn and muddied.

"Fucking idiot tossed me," she shouted as we thundered past, her expression grim and determined. "When I catch that sonofabitch, I'm going to kill him." Congo barely acknowledged her or slowed down, and there was no chance for discussion. Moments later we flew past her horse, who stood at one side of the trail, quietly grazing.

Meanwhile, Congo kept going, his heart and his mind and his four long limbs all working in perfect equine synchronization. Miles back, I'd adjusted to his rhythm, and now was able to sit forward, heels down, elbows tucked, in touch with my gravitational center. Gradually I felt more balanced, confident. An incredible energetic thing happened. I traveled from a place of abject fear to a place of pure joy. I felt wonderfully free, unfettered.

"Yippee," I screamed into the wilderness. "Yippee!"

Up ahead Sally and Diandra were also having the time of their lives. Bounding through the another field, they were laughing like a pair of maniacs. At the sight of their horses, Congo snorted and ran towards them even faster, cannoning along like a freight train.

Diandra saw us first.

"Stop that bloody horse!" she bellowed. "Pull him up, I say!"

"Whoa, whoa," I said to Congo, putting on the brakes. Deciding now to behave, at the touch of my hand on the reins and a shift of my weight in the saddle, he immediately dropped back to a canter. We all loped along in peaceful harmony for a few minutes as the horses reconnected and the humans caught their breath.

"What happened to Billy?" Diandra asked me when we were close enough to converse. "And where's Gwen?"

"Gwen came off her horse when you took off like that," I said, reprovingly, wondering if it wasn't too late for Diandra to change her hoyden ways. "Billy's coming along, he should catch up any moment, although he probably did the right thing and stopped to help Gwen."

"Gwen came off?" Sally said maliciously. "She's such a lousy fucking rider."

"She's fine," I replied curtly. "I'm sure she's back on by now."

"Was anyone else on the trail?" Diandra asked worriedly, no doubt thinking how she would defend her behavior, given her role as a pace steward. "Did you encounter other riders?"

"Just Alex and his team," I said. "Actually, Alex kind of helped us."

"Helped you?" Diandra spat. "That's unlikely."

"He stopped, he didn't pass, he waited for Billy to get back on his horse," I said, reciting a litany of good horsemanship that wasn't in Diandra's playbook. "Then he led us down a really steep decline. He seems to be riding very safely," I said, pointedly. "They were walking through the mud, not running. Their horses weren't even sweating."

"It's a pace, you're supposed to race and run people down," Diandra said contemptuously. "Why else would we do it?"

"Don't tell me you were you scared, Paige," Sally said, her voice dripping with condescension. "I had no idea you were such an infant. Maybe you shouldn't have come with us. You know how we ride."

"Diandra put me on this team," I said defensively. "She knows my limits."

"I thought I was showing you a good time," Diandra said sharply.

"Anyway, it's good material for your blog, right? I can just see the headline now. 'Daredevil action along the Riding Lanes.'"

Just then Billy and Gwen rode up, both their horses in a lather.

"You would not believe what just happened back there," Gwen said, breathless. "Alex Manos got off his horse to shtup some woman he stood up against a tree! It was that dark-haired woman on his team! And the whole time they were screwing, that freak Michael Swett was recording it! He said he was going to sell it to Perez Hilton!"

"Swett probably paid him for the privilege," I heard Diandra mutter. "I wonder how much he paid."

"That's disgusting!" Sally gasped. "How come that woman gets all the luck! She's not even that pretty!"

"Weren't you two together?" Gwen said to me. "I heard something was going on. Rumors were floating all over town. I also heard you were arranging for him to have a screen test."

A screen test? Who on earth had set that story in motion? Suddenly I felt a little sick.

"Aren't we almost at the end of this ride?" I said, changing the subject. "How much further til the finish?"

"Three more miles, so let's go!" Sally said, refocusing. Her mind on the finish line, she pushed Blackstone back into a gallop. Struggling now to keep Congo in his team place, I buckled down to the task at hand and held, him steady. Head up, tail out, and utterly proud of himself, the horse broke into a joyous canter.

Together we headed into the home stretch, which carried us through a woodsy trail and along a short stretch of paved road that ran along Bridle Ridge, a tony residential neighborhood not far from the Old Homestead. The trail route had us trotting alongside people's front lawns; the people living in those houses were on their porches, waving. A wave of sentimentality washed over me; this display of community enthusiasm for the pace and the riders and these magnificent animals was so touching. For a moment I was overwhelmed with a sentimental gladness and humility for my chance to be part of all this. My eyes actually began to water.

Single file, we cantered through a meadow across the street from the Garvey field, and through a short stretch of wood along the highway. A police officer was directing traffic, stopping the cars to let the horses pass. Trotting over asphalt, we were soon back on the grass of the Homestead property, where the final jump, a low cross rail, loomed.

"Don't be a wuss; everyone has to jump it," Sally shouted. One by one, they took the jump, first Sally, then Billy, then Gwen. I looked at the jump and it looked easy. Nothing like those big jumps Congo had sailed over just a little while ago. I pointed him at it and got up into jumping position, pushing myself up on his neck and flattening my back and giving the big guy his head. A rush of adrenaline coursed through me as Congo, cleared the fence like a bird, I hung overhead, exhilarated, in perfect two- point, heels down, my back straight as a board. A moment later I was tumbling off him and rolling on the ground. Naturally, at the exact moment I came off, the pace photographer snapped my picture.

"Got it," she said with satisfaction before walking over to give me a hand getting up. "I guess you'd rather I deleted that, and not post it on the pace events website."

"Would you delete it?" I said, gratefully. "That would be terrific."

"Nah, it's too much fun," she guffawed as I dusted dirt off my butt, which thanks to all the flying mud had been my only clean part. "Everybody loves those embarrassing photos of people falling off. Naturally, the most humiliating photos are the most viewed."

"What happened?" Diandra said, storming up. Squinting into the glare of the sun, all I could see clearly were her tall black field boots, attached to a pair of muscular, slim legs. Having peeled off from the team to access a shortcut home, Diandra had sprinted ahead, making it back to the show grounds with minutes to spare before the rest of us.

"I don't know. My foot must have slipped out of the stirrup. I guess I lost my balance. Where's Congo?" I said.

"He's right over there," Diandra said disgustedly, pointing at the horse, who was mindlessly munching grass, his mission accomplished. "The idiot. All horses are idiots," she added, crossly. "I don't know why I bother."

"Well done, well done," Billy said heartily, coming around to shake my hand. "You were a super pace partner, Paige. Jolly good. I hope we can do it again."

"How did we do, what was our time?" I said to Billy when Diandra stormed off. The girl had places to go, people to see, new territory to plunder. "And where's Gwen and Sally?"

"They turned their horses over to Estaban and went home to freshen up," Billy said. "Gwen, especially, was filthy. Won't you join me at the drinks table for a refreshment? After that ride, I know we both could use it."

"What I'd really like is a tall, cold glass of water," I said. "It's not even ten o'clock."

"Well, I'm planning on having a G & T," Billy said, genially. "But I'm sure they have what you need."

"Okay, but first I have to take care of Congo," I said. "Where the heck's Alvaro, uh, I mean Manny?"

"Right here, miss," Chessie's groom/houseboy said, approaching with a leather halter and a lead line. I gave Congo a final pat and kissed him on his cheek.

"You're a real gentleman, Congo," I told him.

Billy and I strolled over to the big tent, where dozens of tables and chairs had been arranged. It was still too early for lunch, but the bar was, open. Looking around, I saw Miranda Van Oonk and Licia and Kimberley nearby, clutching wine spritzers.

"Did you ride?" I said to them, flashing the bartender my pace ticket which entitled me to free drinks. As a perk for forking out a hefty sum for the entry fee, you could pig out at the buffet table and visit the bar as often as you wished. Or maybe not. I recalled a recent conversation I'd overheard about the WRA setting a liquor limit.

"You've got to be kidding," Kimberley said, her nose wrinkling. "I couldn't bear getting up that early."

"I had a nail appointment," Licia said, freezing me out. "Kim, have you tried those new gel tips? The color won't chip or fade for weeks."

Billy drifted over to a small group I recognized from the hunt, including the old lady, Biddy Maxwell, and master of the hounds, Gary Goldfinger. After my unfortunate encounter with Biddy, she'd turned into my nemesis. To avoid her, I walked the perimeter of the fair grounds, a ice- cold Pepsi in my hand. I saw Tom and Gaye, that nice couple I'd met on the trail, and the realtors, Silver Surfer, and Pudding. Then I saw a woman I didn't recognize at first. On closer inspection, I saw it was Leeza Luciano, the poet/convict.

"Hey, fancy meeting you here," I said to Leeza, glad to see her and sticking out my hand.

"Hey, I remember you," she said, grinning. She was wearing a 10-gallon hat and cowboy boots and form fitting skinny jeans. A powder blue, Western-style shirt whose pearl buttons were undone exposed her generous chest. Leeza's hair was different; she'd had it professionally straightened and colored a deep, coppery red. "So what brings you here?" she said, genially. "And where's your sidekick?"

"Which sidekick is that?" I said, already guessing.

"That guy. That sexy guy, the guy you were with the night of my poetry reading," Leeza said. "You left before I could do my next set," she added, accusing. "I was disappointed you didn't stick around. I always save the best for last. Plus you missed the open mike. I do a lot of those events and that guy you were with always gets up and reads something, although to tell you the truth, one time when I was gettin' all choked up over something great he wrote, this girl sitting next to me burst my bubble, sayin' he didn't write it. Said he cribbed it from some Spanish poet."

"Hmmmm," I said. "Well, he's here now. He's around. He just rode in the pace."

"Awesome," Leeza said, looking around. "I shoulda realized he did horseback. So, uh, I see you're wearin' the threads. Did you ride too? Hey, am I out of line, buttin' in on your action? The dude isn't like, uh, your boy-friend?"

"I think of him more like a brother," I responded. "Like a brother from another planet." Leeza looked confused.

"Are you playin' with me?" she said, her brow beetling.

I was saved by Michael Swett who sidled up, brimming martinis gripped in both his hands.

"Darling," he said, slurping from each glass. "Why ever are you drinking soda? And who have we here? Please introduce me to your gorgeous friend." He waggled his eyebrows at Leeza who, disconcertingly, waggled hers back.

"Michael Swett, this is Leeza Luciano. Leeza is a poet and you are...?" I said, allowing my voice to conveniently trail off so he could fill in the blank.

"I'm a television producer," Swett told Leeza, looking deeply into her emerald eyes. I couldn't remember if they'd been green before. Was she wearing colored lenses? "I'm producing a series right now that might pique your interest. We're calling it The Real Horsewives. We're casting now. By any chance, do you ride?"

"Not really," Leeza said, coloring furiously. I couldn't believe she was falling so fast. "I only came today 'cos I've always loved horses. I was think-ing of taking lessons. I just don't know how I feel about the whole formal English thing. Does anybody here do Western? You ever watch the rodeo channel? I'd love to try barrel racing."

I saw Swett retract a flinch.

"Sweetheart," he said, taking Leeza by the arm and steering her away. "Trust me, you don't know what you are saying. Allow me to introduce you to a trainer. I know just the person to put you on a wonderful horse. In no time you'll be bounding after foxes and jumping stone walls, and you'll forget all about that silly barrel racing." As the words "barrel racing" came out of his mouth, he gave an involuntary shudder.

"Really?" Leeza said, eyes wide. "Tell me more."

I left this unlikely couple alone to patrol the grounds.

The sun was fully out now and it was getting hotter. Little rivulets of sweat were collecting in my pits. I longed to take off my hot boots, but had failed to bring other footwear. In any case, I wasn't the type to be caught dead in britches and flip flops.

"Hey you," a friendly male voice called out. It was Ralsten, the painter. For the luncheon Ralsten had tricked himself out entirely in white; flowing linen pants topped off with a linen jacket he'd left unbuttoned to reveal a 70's style patch of chest hair. On his head was a white Panama hat; his unsocked feet were clad in a pair of ivory Converse Chuck Taylor Vintage slip ons. He looked to be channeling poor dead George Harrison, circa the "My Sweet Lord" period.

"Nice kicks," I said, looking down. "I never realized you were such a fashionista."

"They're genuine John Varvatos," Ralsten said, fingering his boutonnière. "Ninety-five buckaroos on Zappo's."

"Nice," I said again, wondering where the conversation might go from here. When I first met Ralston I thought he had something to say, given the strange but captivating art work he'd exhibited at that old huntsmen fundraiser. The image of the stricken bunny limply dangling from the fox's jaws had stayed with me a long time, and I'd enjoyed our brief, but intense, dialogue about prey and predators. But every time I'd seen him since, we hadn't had anything like a real conversation. Maybe this didn't bother him, but it bothered me. It was, like so many other things that had happened in Beddington Place, disappointing. "So, what's with all the white? Are you trying to pull off a Tom Wolfe?" I said, teasingly, hoping at least for a fun banter.

"Who's Tom Wolfe?" Ralsten said, bewildered. "He a friend of yours in Hollywood?"

"No, silly, he's a famous author," I said, my annoyance level rising. How could this guy call himself a artist when he knew so little about the arts? "And he's also a famous dresser. Back in the 60's, he started wearing these beautifully tailored white suits, to set him apart from the pack. He even wore white in winter, just to piss people off. The white suit became his trademark."

"Hmmmmm," Ralsten said noncommittally, already bored, his eye roving around to see who else he could talk to. I persevered.

"He's best known for writing a novel called 'Bonfire of the Vanities,'" I said. "It's an amazingly crafted novel about ambition, racism, social class, and greed. You might have read it. It's a lot like what goes on around here."

"Hey, I remember that title. It was a movie, wasn't it?" Ralsten said, perking up.

"Right," I said, deflating. " You did say you never read."

"Only The Post," Ralsten chuckled. "And only on my iPhone." He took a sip of his beverage which I assumed was vodka straight up. "Actually, I've decided to take a page from Diandra's book and make an effort. She always looks so pulled together and people are impressed with that."

"That they are," I said, looking around to see who else I might talk to as this conversation was going nowhere.

"You know that girl Darby?" Ralsten said. I nodded yes. Out of the corner of my eye, I'd already noticed Darby walking past Alex like he didn't exist and how he looked right through her like she was a spirit creature. Those two were definitely embroiled in some elaborate game, but I for one would never get it. "She's here with her girlfriend," Ralsten said. "I think it's time to make my move. Wouldn't she be a sensational model? She could pose in my studio."

I looked at Darby who did resemble a model the way she draped and arranged her skinny limbs. Oh, she was posing, no doubt, but for, whom? Her long, wavy, coal black hair hung seductively over one heavily lined eyelid, the curls cascading down her bony spine like a waterfall. Like Ralsten, she was dressed entirely in white in an ankle-length, long sleeved, lace and cotton gown styled to look like a Victorian nightie. To complete the outfit she wore low-heeled, ivory, laced leather boots.

"I love her look," Ralston said dramatically. "I would paint her just like that."

I left Ralston to his infatuation and headed over to Tamsin's brother, Sal, who had commandeered a small table at the far end of the tent. He was with Lurch, that creepy host at Shangri La, the guy who admitted me to the club only to swiftly eject me. His dog, the Kuvasc, snoozed by his side.

"Hey, Sal, how's it going," I said, walking up.

"Hey, Sweet Cheeks," Sal said, leaving me to wonder was he referring to my face or my ass. "You remember… "

"Sure, we've met," I said, sticking out my hand. Neither man got up. Lurch shook it indifferently. If he remembered our initial meeting, he wasn't giving anything away.

"A pleasure," he said, not sounding like he meant it.

"Have you seen Tamsin?" I said to Sal. His forehead wrinkled, like I had just asked him a tough exam question.

"She said she had an appointment at the hairdresser's, or she could be showing a house," Sal said. "Labor Day, surprisingly, is a busy day for realtors."

"Who knew?" I said. "So what brings you, Lurch, I mean, uh, I'm sorry. What's your name again? What brings you to the lunch? You don't strike me as the horsey type, no offence."

"We're just talking a little business," Sal said. "Turns out, thanks to Tamsin's inside track on the market, we got a lead on a remarkable property. Bankruptcy situation. Short sale. An opportunity too good to pass up."

"Yes, we're working here, young lady," Lurch said brutally. "Get lost." His dog growled.

"Well, let me leave you to it," I said, taking the hint. "Have a productive afternoon, gentlemen."

The sun now beating somewhat unpleasantly on my head, I moved away from the tent to study the big bulletin board set up between the raffle ticket table and the table selling silk-screened tee shirts and monogrammed saddle pads. Displayed on the board were the names of all the competitors, along with their start times and their finishes. About 20 teams had registered to go out, and while most of the names were insignificant or unfamiliar, a few did stand out. One particular pairing caught my eye. It was a two person team made up of Janey and Tamsin. They'd both been in a state about the pace for weeks, talking for hours about the coordination of their outfits. It would have been far too simple or sensible to do one big, combined shop; instead they'd individually descended several times a week on the tack shop in the village, spending a fortune on riding clothes and new girths and bridles and saddles.

Janey sauntered up to stand beside me, gnawing a fingernail. With the pace still not over and late starts still coming in, it was impossible to speculate on the winning times, and who would be in the ribbons.

"Will you look at that," Janey harrumphed. I looked where she was pointing, her nails too clean and well manicured to have actually tacked up her own horse. "I can't believe Michael rode with Alex Manos," she sputtered. "And who the hell is their team partner?"

"Some reality show woman," I said. "I didn't recognize her at all. Somebody said she was on 'Survivor.' I just met her today, right before the pace. I talked to her! I didn't realize who she was since everyone looks the same under a riding helmet."

"That's so upsetting to me that you watch 'Survivor,'" Janey griped. "You really shouldn't be wasting time with that program. What you need to focus on is my Horsewives project. Which I need to talk to you about because I have a film crew here today. I asked them to film the luncheon and the wedding."

"Wedding?" I said, surprised. "And who is getting hitched?"

"Some people Diandra knows. She helped arrange it. I hope Reverend Willy from the Episcopal church is officiating. I love Reverend, Willy. It's supposed to be a wedding on horseback. I'm going to include it in my sizzle reel."

"Is Swett still producing?" I said. "I just heard him tell the prison poet Leeza Luciano he's a producer. Maybe he's the one who invited the Survivor girl to the pace to include in the sizzle reel," I speculated. "You heard, I assume, about that business in the woods."

"What business?" Janey said suspiciously. I smirked remembering what Gwen had said about Michael filming Alex and that girl for TMZ, and marveled at Swett's creativity to work multiple angles. I had to hand it to the guy. He always had something cooking.

"Nothing," I said to Janey. "It was nothing."

"And why is Michael wasting his time with that jailbird poet?" she fumed. "He has more important things to do, like replace Tamsin. That girl is such a bitch. You would not believe the fight we had."

"Why? What happened?" I said, all ears.

"Tamsin's impossible. Of course it's about the Horsewives project. She is sooo jealous. Here I am working my ass off to get Andy Cohen on board. You cannot believe the bribes and gifts I've offered! You know there's a rumor Bravo isn't going to do any new Housewives series. Those Miami chicks are the limit! But at the same time there's also a rumor some girls down in Scarsdale are working on their own Westchester pilot. They held a casting call in White Plains," she said, grimacing. "Scarsdale is so, not us, it's so down county. Besides, the Beddington Horsewives concept is so classy and so different, plus it brings on board a whole new elevated level of style and fashion. I just know it's a moneymaker. Just think of the merchandising."

"Hmm," I said. "So tell me what happened between you and Tamsin. Are you two not friends?"

"Well, I feel terrible saying this, but Tamsin is not a true friend! She spent our entire pace fighting. She wants the sizzle reel to focus on her stuff, you know, her real estate, because she says that's more compelling to a broader audience. She said if people want to see horses, they'll tune into Animal Planet! I totally disagree and then she called me a control freak. Did you know she tried to undermine my authority with the film crew, which, I may add, I hired out of my own pocket? She said the only reason my input is more significant is because Billy invested all the money. Duh! I didn't see her brother ponying up."

"Then what happened?" I said.

"Well, she did a mean thing. She smacked my horse Pardner with her crop and he freaked! Spooked! Took off! And she knows how petrified I am of a spooking horse! So of course I came off but luckily nothing was broken and Pardner just stood there looking at me on the ground like he couldn't figure out how I got there. And Tamsin laughing her head off, the evil bitch."

"Then what happened?" I said.

"Well, I told her she had to help me get back on, and she did, but when she was helping me, she said something nasty about my house, which you know I have worked so hard on. That made me mad, I pulled her hair and then she shoved me, and then I shoved her back, and then she kicked me. Kicked me right in the shin! She's Satanic! My leg still hurts. Look, let me show you the bruise mark."

"No thanks," I said, stifling a giggle.

"It's not funny, Paige," Janey said, petulantly. "I do wish you'd quit laughing."

"Sorry," I said, pulling myself together. "So were you able to finish the pace?"

"Of course," Janey said. "We're not idiots. The physical fight lasted only a minute, anyway. After she kicked me, I knew we couldn't go on hitting each other. She would win! Have you ever looked at Tamsin's hands? Her knuckles are huge. She's got fists! And that's a terrific act she does, by the way, coming off all refined and ladylike with that monstrous Italianate house of hers, all that gilt, well, it is beautiful, but I think she's very coarse. Plus I just found out something about her mother. That woman who kicked you out of the pool house? Well, that woman has a criminal record. How humiliating is that?"

"Did you discuss this with Tamsin?" I said. "A mother with a rap sheet is the sort of thing that could put off advertisers, although it could be great for ratings. So many people now have criminal records."

"Hmmm," Janey said, considering. "Well, on the way back, I told Tamsin I thought she should voluntarily withdraw from the cast. She blew a gasket. Was completely unreasonable. Went ballistic. Exploded, said a lot of things she'll regret, and while I'm sure she will apologize, meanwhile, I never forget. So we had two fights, one physical, one verbal. So we're done now.

Our friendship is finished."

"That's too bad," I said, meaning it. "I thought of you as two peas in a pod. Where's Tamsin now? How did you end it?"

"Well, we finished as a team. There were no further incidents. But as soon as we crossed the finish line, we separated. I don't care if I never see that girl again," Janey declared.

"Well, you'll probably see each other at lunch," I said. "The tent's not that big."

"Diandra better keep her away from me," Janey said darkly. "Next time, I'll scratch her eyes out."

Over the crackly P.A. system, a female voice announced lunch was being served. I made another pass at the drinks table to refresh my beverage.

"No wine for you? How about a mixed drink?" the bartender said. I realized he was the bartender from the Holiday Inn. It took me a moment, to recognize him out of context.

"Oh, hi," I said. "Thanks, but no thanks. Today, I've decided, is the first day I'm officially on the wagon."

"Good for you!" the bartender said. "Save you some money." He seemed a lot more chipper working outdoors than he was in that cave of the motel disco. "I'll let you in on a little secret. Now that lunch has started, they're switching over to a cash bar. But since we're friends and all, your soda's on the house."

"My lucky day," I said, lifting my plastic glass to salute him and wondering how we were now 'friends.' Was it because I was living in the Holiday Inn?

The tent was filling quickly as people queued up for food, an awesome steam table spread of fried chicken, barbecued chicken, lasagna, meat balls in tomato sauce, hot dogs, hamburgers, and sliced roasted loin of pork. Then there were the sides: mashed potatoes, corn on the cob, candied sweet potatoes, Caesar salad, fruit salad, string beans, baked beans, and marshmallows in Jello. An entire section was devoted to dessert. There were bowls of apples and bananas and oranges, and trays of brownies and cookies and layer cake, plus great slabs of sliced watermelon, glistening pinkly on chopped ice.

I forked up some Caesar salad and an Italian dinner roll and considered grabbing a chili dog, too, but decided against it. Virtuously avoiding the sweet table, I took a Clementine instead. Moving out of the line and searching for a place to sit, I saw most of the chairs were already taken as friends and pace partners saved each other seats. Even over the brief course of the lunch, I knew, allegiances would be made and broken. It was true what Alex had said that night on the lake, all that weird business about the Beddington Place horse world being populated with people who either feared or loathed each other, and those who just sucked up. It was a dog eat dog world as trainers and barn managers vied for the best clients, the wealthiest people, the celebrities, anyone with a name worth dropping.

"Is this seat taken?" I asked a man in street clothes who had planted himself at a table end. Beside him was one empty seat. The rest of the table was filled with teenage girls and their moms. They were a boisterous, bouncy, happy group, the kids stuffing their faces with mashed potatoes and fried chicken while the moms nibbled salad.

"Go right ahead, take the seat," the man said, shifting slightly. To make room for me at the table, he rearranged a pace program, a pair of salt and pepper shakers, and an ugly planter filled with hoof oil samples. "Is that all you're eating?" he said, eyeballing my plate. "You should get more food. Don't worry. I'll save your place."

"Thanks, but I'm on a diet," I said. "Although I have to say the meatballs look yummy."

"The WRA always puts on a good spread," the man chuckled. "When you factor in the booze, it's the best deal in town. I don't believe we've been introduced. You're Paige Turner, the celebrity reporter, aren't you? I'm a reporter too, well, an equestrian sports writer. Not exactly your league, but I cover the show circuit. Hunter jumper features are my beat."

"Really," I said, feigning interest. Show jumping, unless Madonna was taking the fences, bored me. "So what exactly does that mean? You travel to Wellington, Lake Placid, attend all the Grand Prix's?"

"You got it, that's my job, name's Bill Hendrix," the guy said. "I'm sure you've seen my byline."

"Sure," I said, lying. I never read horse magazines. "So you must be just back from the Hamptons. Did you cover the Classic? What celebrities were there?"

"Oh, you know," Hendrix said. "The usual suspects. Georgina Bloomberg, Candice King, McClain Ward," he said, naming people who were bold faced names only in the narrow stratosphere of high level show jumping. "The Hampton Classic is classic, and they got a heck of a turnout. The grounds were just lousy with A-Listers. Billy Joel! Steven Spielberg! Howard Stern! I see them every year!"

"Every year, huh?" I said, tucking into my salad. "It must be hard to come up with new things to say about them."

"Tell me about it," Hendrix said. "But in your line of work, it's the same thing. You must get tired of covering Princess TaTas."

I shrugged. "All in a day's work," I said.

"You know, we were both at Shangri La a few weeks ago," Hendrix said, dropping his voice. "I was at the bar. You walked right past me. Were you working that night?"

"So you were," I said, carefully. "You had your back turned to the crowd and you were wearing a checkered cap." I looked down and there it was, resting next to his lunch plate.

"Yeah, I was there. I was working. An undercover mission, you could say. A sort of reconnaissance. See, there's a rumor floating around about some bastard who hangs out at Shangri La. I heard he was going to be there that night. One of my sources tipped me off he's a big cheese in the Beddington horse world swirl. But he's also infamous on the down-low, buying and trading stolen horses, offing horses for insurance money, doping horses, involved in every kind of heinous horse scam. I'm trying to get a handle on who he is."

"Gee," I said. "Even if you figured it out, what would you do with the information? It's not likely 'Horse & Hound' would run a story about that, d'ya think? Aren't they more interested in training tales and who's in the ribbons? In any case, until he's charged and arrested, it would be libelous of you to write anything."

"I thought it would be an amazing scoop, if I could expose him, reveal him for who he is. But my source keeps giving me conflicting, information."

"Who's your source?" I said. "Is the person here today?"

"As a matter of fact, she is," Hendrix said. "You know her. I've seen you with her. Pretty young girl. She was with you that night at Shangri La."

"Would you excuse me for a moment," I said, rising from my seat.

I started walking towards Diandra who, as usual, was holding court.

"And you will be able to ride your horse to the Roganoff's for lunch," she declared to an admiring crowd. "Martin personally told me it was happening, and for a special fee, you'll be able to get one on one time with the monks."

"Did you have anything to do with making this possible, Diandra?" a woman I recognized from the re-enactment event gushed. It was Peg Dickler, the Republican booster babe, with Herbert, her hubby.

"It's always been Martin's idea," Diandra said, modestly. "Although I think it's fair to say I've encouraged him."

"Yay, Diandra," someone else cheered.

"Hey, Diandra, I'd like a word with you," I said, grabbing her and hauling her away. Behind a potted ficus, she dramatically pried my fingers off her arm.

"What are you doing, Paige?" she said haughtily. "Is there a problem?"

"Yes, there is," I said. "Did you tell that sad sack horse writer sitting over there about somebody you know who is hurting horses and making money off it?"

Diandra's eyes narrowed. "Oh, please," she said. "Don't be ridiculous. There is no such person. I was just having some fun. There's always been rumors about people burning down their barns for insurance money.

Are the rumors true?" she shrugged. "Maybe they are, and maybe they aren't. Listen, don't get your drawers in a twist. He was sniffing around. He wanted to hear this stuff so badly, I thought I'd give him a thrill. Besides, it's fun to screw with him. He's such a loser. I mean, seriously, who wears that cap?" She cruelly laughed.

Michael Swett came barging up.

"Kids, hurry, you've got to get over here," he said breathlessly. "The wedding is about to begin. Janey's got the film crew all ready. The bridal couple is arriving any minute and I need you on your marks."

"I'm not part of the cast anymore, remember?" I reminded him. "And from what Janey just said to me a few minutes ago, neither is Tamsin."

"Don't be ridiculous," Swett said. "We need you. You're one of the Horsewives' best friends."

"Can I catch the bouquet?" Diandra said eagerly. "I want do that. Pretty please!"

"Fabulous idea!" Swett cheered. "Diandra, you're brilliant!" Her hustled us over to a patch of lawn outside the tent where Janey and the film crew were waiting. Tamsin was nowhere to be seen. "Now, kids, when you see the bridal couple, I want you to be overcome with tears," Swett said. "Tears of joy, because you're so happy."

"But I don't want to cry," Janey protested. "It'll spoil my make-up!"

"You will cry!" Swett declared. "Everything is more poignant when someone cries! Film crew! Listen up! I want footage of the bride and groom, but don't forget the crowd. I need reaction shots! Focus on our crowd, not plebeians! And make sure to get lots of shots of all Diandra's client stars! And don't bother shooting anyone old or ugly! This show is all about beauty and Beddington Place style! Get celebrities! And don't forget the cute puppies!"

"Oh, look, here comes the bride now!" Janey squealed. "Isn't this romantic?" A beautiful Palomino was approaching, its shimmering white-blonde mane and tail lavishly braided with wild flowers. On its back, Penny was riding sidesaddle, her high-necked ivory satin wedding gown trailing on the ground. Beside her was Lucas on a big black Irish sport horse, Lucas looking especially dashing in canary breeches and a formal riding coat. A tiny girl in a pinafore, mounted on a Shetland pony, trotted on a lead line just behind them in the role of flower girl.

"Omigod, isn't that too precious. I wonder whose child that is," I heard a familiar female voice coo nearby. I turned to see who was speaking, and was surprised it was Sally, who didn't strike me as the cute-kid cooing type. Perhaps I had judged her too harshly, and despite her reckless riding and tactless remarks, maybe Sally was a decent, warm-hearted, human being after all. Until I saw her shove a fingernail of coke up her nose. So much for sentiment.

"Places, places, everyone," Gary Goldfinger directed. As Master of the Hunt, he was in charge of the wedding. A few minutes passed while the horses were arranged side by side. A look of concern crossed Penny's face as she struggled to keep the Palomino's hooves from trodding on her train. When everybody was ready, Goldfinger cleared his throat.

"Before we hand out the ribbons announcing today's pace winners, I invite you all to join us in celebration of a wondrous event. Today you will be witnesses to a grand event. This is the joining in holy matrimony of two of the most beloved members of our equestrian community," he said. "Lucas and Wendy."

"It's Penny, not Wendy," I heard Penny hiss.

"Beloved members?" Kimberley sniffed. "I've ridden with that girl a few times but nobody knows her. And I know for a fact she doesn't own a horse! As for the groom, yowza, yowza, where'd he come from? In this crowd, I never meet straight guys."

"Take it easy, girl, you're married, remember?" Ralston said.

"Who said he was straight?" Swett sniggered. "I've heard some things."

"To join this couple in holy matrimony we have a special guest, the right Reverend Leeza Luciano, who is not only a pastor, but an esteemed po-etess, and Reiki therapist," Goldfinger continued. "Leeza and I met through a mutual friend. She received her religious calling in a most unusual way, but her ardor for invoking the holy spirit is most remarkable, most remarkable, as I'm sure you will see today. As per the bride's request, the Reverend will be conducting the marriage ceremony incorporating both Wiccan and Native American traditions. We are asking everyone to bear with us for a brief interlude of prayerful worship for horses and universal love, at which time, we will all embrace and shake hands. Are you ready, Leeza? Let's begin."

"Tell me," Swett whispered in my ear. "Is this great material, or an awful embarrassment?"

"Thank you, Master Goldfinger," Leeza said, stepping up to a podium and shaking out her hair. I wondered how she and Gary met and who was their mutual friend? "Ladies and gentlemen, thank you all for coming. We're here to celebrate the marriage of Penny and Lucas, who met on the riding trails. What brought these two together was their shared love of equines, and to that end, they have chosen to be wedded on horseback. At the conclusion of this ceremony, after Lucas places the ring on Penny's finger, the couple will ride off together into the sunset."

"Sunset my ass," Swett said. "It's two in the afternoon. It's hours til sunset. How long is this going to take?" he fumed.

"Omigod, this is going to be the best footage," Janey whispered excitedly. "I heard she's getting a 5-carat canary diamond ring. None of the other Bravo shows has had a wedding on horseback. Guys," she said to the film crew. "Make sure you get a close up of that ring!"

Leeza closed her eyes and began to speak. "Before we begin the ceremony, I want to make an important announcement. Although we are gathered together to join two souls in matrimony, it must be recognized, each of these two people are on their own path. Each holds their own view of reality. Some will shelve their realities and face them on their death bed. Others will do so in time, to reap the benefits of change. Just as the leaves in the bottom of my cup told me this morning when I performed my daily tea rite, remember, not only are you not alone in the world, but every person you meet on your life journey is also you."

Leeza paused for a moment to let it all sink in. I thought it was very quiet. I couldn't get a gauge on how her speech was going over, if people were truly listening or were annoyed and tuning out.

"The important thing to remember as we stand here today is that everyone is a fellow traveler on the road," Leeza said. "When someone acts badly, hurts us, deceives us, destroys something that we love, we must accept that we don't know why they do it. We can only try to understand them from a place of love. My message is simple. It's a prescription for life. Stand on the truth, forgive yourself, allow yourself the space to satisfy your own needs as a person, and let fairness be the determining factor in the way you treat others. Thank you. God bless." She closed her eyes again and kissed the twig and leather crucifix hanging from her neck.

After a lengthy silence, Gary Goldfinger approached and whispered in her ear.

"All righty now!" Leeza said when he was finished. "Let's get these two married! Gary has just informed me it's time for the ribbons! Winning! That's what we're all here for! Penny and Luke, are you ready to take your vows?"

Still astride on their horses, Penny and Lucas grasped each other's hand. Penny stared at Lucas with sheep's eyes. Lucas was distracted. Instead of looking at Penny, his attention was riveted on Darby, who was creating a spectacle, weaving and whimpering around the lawn. At first I thought she was crying for happiness for Penny, her good friend, but then I saw Alex standing at the bar, one hip cocked, his arm snaked around the Survivor girl, who was giving Darby the finger.

"That sniveling is so wrenching," Roy Ralsten whispered rapturously in my ear. "It's giving me a hard-on. Do you think I should I go over and comfort her? I could be play knight in shining armor to her damsel in distress."

"For crying out loud," I said wearily.

Meanwhile, Janey's video crew was busy filming. Leeza's voice was booming, intoning the sacred words of the wedding covenant. Standing directly in front of the horses, she said, "Penny, do you promise to love this man? Do you take him to be your lawfully wedded husband, to love and cherish? In sickness and in health? For better or for worse? Until death do you part?"

"I do, I do," cried Penny fervently. "With all my heart!"

"And Lucas, do you promise to love this woman? Take her to be your lawfully wedded wife, to love and cherish her, in sickness and in health? For better or worse? Until death do you part?"

"Um," Lucas said, looking uneasy. "Could I take a minute? I need a little time."

"I said he'd never marry her," Michael Swett said loudly.

The crowd stood stock still in confusion until a low rumbling shook the air.

"Is that thunder?" Janey moaned. "Oh, shit, the cameras. It better not start raining."

But there was no thunder or crack of lightning, although the sky was turning black. A moment later there was another rumble and then a vibration and then the suddenly wind picked up. Agitated, Penny and Lucas's horses began to whinny, as did all the other horses standing in trailers parked around the Homestead grounds. The rumbling grew louder and more persistent and the sky grew even darker as big drops of rain began to fall. Unable to contain itself any longer, Penny's Palomino began to freak. Unfamiliar with the sidesaddle, Penny lost her balance and fell to the grass in a crumpled heap.

"Ouch! My ankle!" she cried out. "Lucas! Help!"

Just then an emergency siren began going off, piercing the air with a harsh wail.

"Shit, is that the warning alarm from Indian Point?" Janey cried out. "Ever since Fukishima, I've been terrified! Diandra! Tell us what to do! Should we evacuate?"

"Don't be an idiot, it can't be Indian Point," Michael Swett said authoritatively. "That's just Democrat bullshit talking. There's no danger there. Although I don't think I'll be sticking around for the ribbons," he added before taking off.

"Calm down, everyone!" Gary Goldfinger bellowed into a loud-speaker. No one was listening. They were scattering like autumn leaves. "Let's not lose control here! Ladies! Gentlemen!"

The wind and the rain picked up and a general pandemonium broke out. I felt strangely calm. All around me people were running and shouting, and Penny was still on the ground. Lucas, the reluctant bridegroom, had fled at the first opportunity. There was a frenzy of activity, as people ran for their cars or crowded under the billowing tent; horses were neighing and calling to each other while a band of Jack Russell terriers from the hunt foolishly barked their heads off.

"That siren is a tornado warning!" Diandra shouted near my ear. "On my iPhone, I just got an emergency weather alert! Janey! Michael! Paige! Grab our stuff! Hurry, hurry, hurry, collect yourselves, we've got to help Estaban collect the horses and get the hell out of here!" We all began trotting towards the exit gates.

"What about my film crew?" Janey was practically sobbing, stumbling in her party shoes. "I'm paying them by the hour, should they come with us?"

Just then Tamsin hurried up.

"Where have you guys been?" she demanded breathlessly, seemingly oblivious to the circumstances. "While you were all busy filming that silly wedding, and that guy never said 'I Do,' did he? Or gave that girl the ring! I've been chatting up the town's numero uno celebrity and she loves the 'Horse-wives' idea! She said she'd let us film her in her fabulous kitchen, making lemon squares! Isn't that fantastic?"

My phone was ringing.

It was Pat.

"Paige, do you have a minute? There's a few things I want to share."

"Pat," I said, "I'm kind of busy. There's a tornado coming. All kinds of hell are breaking loose."

"This won't take long. Stay with me. Listen, I know I've been giving you a lot of shit for not following through with that story, but it's only because I have so much respect for you and think you're such a great writer."

"What's going on, Pat," I said, panting a little from exertion. Who knew it was so hard to run in riding boots? "You don't need to butter me up."

"Okay," she said. "Here's the thing. All these stories you've been filing from Beddington Place have intrigued me. I'm totally down with it. I think it's the new Bev Hills. So, listen, I met this hot guy. He's totally into me. And he rides. And he knows people in Beddington. And by the way, I told him I'm an expert rider. That's rich. I've never been in the same room as a horse. Or barn, whatever. Here's the thing. I'm coming out. I'll be in Beddington Place tomorrow afternoon. You'll have to pick me up at the airport. JFK. 3 p.m."

A dozen thoughts rushed through my head. I could get in Chessie's car and drive away, catch the next flight back to L.A. duke it out with Ric, eject Tickled Pink from the house, claim my cat. Or I could stick around and see what developed with the Horsewives, see if that guy Doug was going to call. The rain was coming down in sheets and the wind was, growing stronger. I felt like anything could happen and matters were not quite in my hands. Since I didn't know what to do, I decided to toss a coin. I pulled a quarter from my pocket.

Heads, I'd bolt.

Tails, I'd stick around.

I flipped the coin in the air.

"Paige!" Diandra hollered. "Are you with us or not?"

CPSIA information can be obtained at www.ICGtesting.com
Printed in the USA
BVOW081550121212

308049BV00007B/199/P